PIECES
OF WOOD

KENNETH JAMES MOORE

During World War Two, the Nazis referred to their victims as "Vermin." At the same time on the other side of the world, the Imperial Japanese had a special name for their female victims, "Zaimoku", Pieces of Wood.

Dedication:

This novel is dedicated to the memory of Miss Minnie Vautrin, China's, "Oskar Shindler." In 1937, this fifty-one-year-old American school teacher saved thousands of women from rape, torture, and murder at the hands of the Imperial Japanese Army. At Nanking's "Safety Zone" - an area set aside by the Japanese invaders as a foreigner's haven - Chinese women fled in droves, seeking protection. At its entry gate fending off the pursuing Japanese, stood Minnie with arms outstretched holding an American flag. Known by the Chinese as the Goddess of Mercy, Minnie was beaten, cut, urinated and spat upon yet never once surrendered her post nor her flag. She died back home in her aptly named hometown of

Shepard, Michigan, in 1941.

Introduction:

Here lie five thou~~sand~~ ~~homeless~~ souls, belov~~ed~~
and daughters of whit~~e~~ ~~c~~lad folk~~s~~. The~~se~~ are of, o~~f~~
a homeless race suffered b~~y~~ ~~c~~ha~~i~~ns of ra~~th~~less Imp~~erial~~
Japanese army, by whom t~~he~~y were deprived of their r~~ights~~
and were taken to th~~e~~ ~~i~~s~~l~~ands here and there li~~ke~~
innocent sheep, and th~~ey~~ were fallen to t~~he~~ ~~ground~~
leaving behind them a~~n~~ ~~e~~ternal grudge.
Remember! A month of July 1944.

Prologue:

November, 2002.

"Who could have predicted the impact? We were each familiar with the atrocities of war. We were trained U.S. soldiers, after all.

Walk around the ovens. The pure evil of the design makes it hard to breathe as you stand there, inhaling the pain. Two doors at its front, one can remain locked keeping the writhing victim from thrashing out, while the other can be opened so the fire can be stoked.

Slide your hand over the course brick.

Feel the horror of 5,000 young girls' last moments... a daughter, a young mother, Chinese, Korean. What difference does nationality make? We are all humanity's children.

Did the mason take pride in his work? Two course of ornate red brick on the exterior, one course of fire-brick on the interior to survive the intense heat. His ovens still stand 60 years later. Was the mason a Korean slave, forced to work, knowing how his product would be used? Perhaps he was a native islander drawn from the huts and caves, an unwitting accomplice? Or, a Japanese soldier, using skills he acquired at an earlier time in his life, for him, an eternity ago? No, this was the work of a master craftsman, deliberate, precise; given ample time to apply his trade. Exported from mainland Japan, designed to withstand the fires of hell, the name indelibly etched on a signature brick.

Peer inside. Tempered steel bunks to hold the bodies. A vent at the back, smoke and screams pouring out. Passions cry out for revenge... but what end?

Let your heart race with adrenaline pouring into your veins. Is it the same feeling the Jap soldiers had? Or the Asian girls bound in barbed wire, waiting in line to enter the fire?

Step back, the light façade of the tree, peaceful, beautiful... good overtaking evil.

Take a breath. Try not to let the stark darkness of the ovens' doors get its hook into the back of your eyes. Swallow hard. Don't let the others see your tears.

-Jeff Gourley, US Air Force Para Rescue, Author's team member

CHAPTER ONE

1944: July 2nd; 10:47 a.m., on the island of Saipan in the Mariana Archipelago, as World War Two's, "War in the Pacific" wages on:

Running, stumbling, thrashing through the sweltering jungle nearly delirious, a U.S. Marine makes his way to the shoreline. Face blood-blotched, the remains of his uniform sweat-soaked, Captain Frank Clifford drops to his knees in the blistering sand, gags, then vomits. His mind is swirling as he mutters aloud,

"Ovens...*women*...burned...mutilated...thousands of them. Thousands of bodies."

On his knees in the water, Frank cups his hands. Struggling to recapture some semblance of the reality of the world around him, he splashes the cold ocean brine onto his face again, and again.

A nun in her early 30's, appears at his side. A warm smile bristling with life beams from her habit.

"Monsieur! Monsieur!"

Sister Maree Bertrand leans over, placing her hand on the shoulder of the young American officer. He stares up at her, slowly coming to grips with the fact that she is not a manifestation of the corpses of mutilated women from which he has just fled but rather, alive—very much alive.

"You're real."

"Oui! Bein sur. Merci beaucoup," she acknowledged and thanks him.

"Ovens, back there. *Women...thousands...burned.* Stacked like cordwood."

"Monsieur?"

"In the jungle, over there. Behind me. How...?"

At that very moment a shrill scream, the kind that emanates from deep within the soul, sounds to the right of the pair from a hundred yards down the beach. It is coming from Camp Susupe, a barbed-wire internment site on Saipan's shore. The screams are coming from a young boy, a native Chamorro sitting outside the internment camp's front gate. He's clinging with one hand to the razor-wired fence as blood drips from his clenched fist. With the other, he's pointing toward a native woman imprisoned inside. Upon hearing the scream, both Captain Clifford and Sister Maree sprint down the beach to the boy's side.

From inside the camp, a grizzled Army MP jogs to the gate. Through the coils of the camp's concertina wire, he sees the native boy, Sister Maree, and a clearly-tormented, young Marine Corps officer demanding, in no uncertain terms, to know exactly what the hell is going on.

15

CHAPTER TWO: PRESENT DAY

Sugar Shack Jack's, *Top of the World,* **Fine Seafood Eatery**; **Nags Head Township, The Outer Banks, North Carolina:**

"Oh my god, she's got a gun!"

A subtle breeze wrapped with a late afternoon ocean mist gently tousles the feathers of a large, yellow-beaked scavenger perched atop the guard rail surrounding the hilltop patio of the chic, upscale, ocean-side restaurant with the down-to-earth, street-savvy name. Next to the winged forager, a smartly attired, seventy-four-year-old woman calmly retakes her seat. Until moments ago - before being button-holed by two men and their female accomplice - she had been dining alone.

Shrieks ring out from a growing gaggle of eatery's patrons congregating nearby. Stepping away from their restaurant tables to deliberate amongst themselves what some saw or didn't see suddenly, one woman shouts, "Look. That's her! Oh my god! There she goes. She was hiding behind... Did you see that? She just beat that waiter over his head with her pistol! Hey, stop! Someone help. She's getting away."

Another voice from the crowd yells, "Call the police. Someone please, hurry!"

At her table, alone now once again, the restaurants only solo female patron leans forward putting forth the effort as a young waitress approaches, to read her name tag, wanting to address the restaurant employee by name rather than mere title. As she nears, the woman offers, "Oh, there must be some mistake, Nicole. That is your name, isn't it?"

"Yes, ma'am. It is."

"I didn't order that."

"Courtesy of the house, ma'am. Please, it's on us."

"Thank you, that's very kind, but no. There is much of the evening left for all these fine people to enjoy. Let's allow them to relax and return to their tables. It will be best if I wait in the lobby on the main floor for the police."

Wearing chestnut pleated slacks with a tailored, light wool jacket over a cream-colored turtleneck sweater crowned with a smartly-detailed, crimson-flowered scarf, the visiting pensioner confident and tall, pushes back from the table and begins to stand. Sensing that her hair had become somewhat disheveled while fending off her assailants, she removes the scarf from around her neck and fashions her tresses into a pony-tail. Past a certain age, it's a woman's attitude not looks alone that defines her beauty.

"If you'll please excuse me?"

Nicole, the eatery's waitress, was raised up the beach from Nags Head, in a backwater slice of Kill Devil Hills. Her mother, a Catholic, was a woman who preferred the company of vacationing strangers to that of her drunkard,

Protestant husband. For the past twenty years, Mrs. Constance Anderson refused a divorce, fearing God's wrath more than her husband's repeated backhand. Daughter Nicole had recognized early on, that words and how she presented both herself and them to others were critical tools for anyone in need of rescuing themselves from the downward spiral of the family into which they were born. Essentially raising herself, "Nicky" fought to be a straight "A" student. Since the age of ten she devoured every piece of printed material on which she could lay her eyes, repeating the "big words," in front of her bedroom mirror practicing both poise and diction for hours on end.

Selected to present the valedictory at her high school graduation ceremony, upon delivery Nicky knew her moment had arrived. Sucking up the full measure of her self-confidence – tossing aside both cap and gown - she marched down the beach to the posh restaurant on the hill with the funny sounding name, sought out its owner and asked for a job. Nicole was hired on the spot. Ultimately assigned the station that looks out across the far-reaching Atlantic, there she gained comfort and an increased sense of self-worth from the kindness of folks unlike her own. From "atop the world," she carried herself proudly, well beyond her age, waiting tables with an ever-present air of decorum, speaking eloquently in complete sentences, never once-imagining that she would one day bear witness—as she had just moments before—to two, thick-necked, beer-bellied men and their bleach-blonde female accomplice, getting the holy hell

18

beat out of them by a real-life, gray-haired, "Lara Croft"... right before her eyes.

Starstruck, now standing next to the elder's table, Nicole briefly reverted to an average, non-repentant nineteen-year-old, blurting out, "Oh my god lady, no, no. You can't leave. Sit down! Please! Don't go, not yet. Like, you're my hero and you're so beautiful and well, the food you ordered well, I'll get someone over here right away to clean it up. You can't leave without having something to eat. So please, sit down. Take this. It's free."

Poised and deliberate, Nicole's newfound friend nodded in agreement, smiled and retook her seat.

"See that man over there in the stained apron, the one with his mouth gaping open?" offered young Nicole, "That's our head chef. He and I well, I mean, the food you ordered is all over the floor ...next to the two ass-holes who tried to assault you."

In an apparent effort to keep additional expletives from spewing from her mouth, Nicole's hands moved quickly to cover her lips.

"Oh, god, I'm so sorry, ma'am. Please accept my apology. I don't normally talk this way."

"Please, Nicole. It's okay. I'm quite familiar with such terms. I've spoken them perhaps a bit too often through-out my career."

To the right of the table where Nicole now sat with her acclaimed heroine, lay two large males; both white, both adorned in monastic black robes, both unconscious.

Glancing back at the chef, Nicole noticed that he was now standing by the staircase gate holding a meat cleaver, blocking the only route the two fallen felons could take if they suddenly awakened and tried to escape. Knowing Bernard, she gave off a slight giggle, convinced that her rotund, Johnny-come-lately, fellow worker would more likely slice off one of his own appendages trying to wield that thing before inflicting harm on any would-be assailant.

"The third ... that girl," Nicole offered to the taunt-framed elder, "the one who stuck her gun in your face, don't worry. She won't get far. I saw her try to run down the stairs. She was limping badly. Wow, you really know how to kick ass, lady. Oh, gosh. There I go again. I'm an emotional wreck. I don't know what I'm saying. I just never thought I'd see anything like what just happened. I mean, you're amazing!"

Just then with siren's deadened, two of the Sheriff's department's SUV's arrived at the beach- level lobby entry to Sugar Shack Jack's in near unison with the dune buggies of the Nags Head Police Department's beach patrol. Bolting from their vehicles, each officer entered the scene, weapons drawn. Within minutes as dusk fell, a helicopter with searchlight lit was combing the beach looking for the fleeing female assailant.

Fat, thin, short and tall, the description of the two males accompanying a young blonde female in each of the nineteen previous cases, varied. The one constant was the eye-witness account of a woman in her mid-to-late twenties with a cross burnt into her right cheek, spear-heading each attack. Clad in innumerable guises invariably as a team of three, such trios had been targeting seniors and eluding authorities for sixteen months, escalating to "assault with a deadly weapon" ...and this wasn't the first time. But now, quite literally, there was a new sheriff in town. The baton had been passed just last week to a middle-aged, former Virginia State patrol lieutenant, an African-American named Trevor Aldridge.

A no-nonsense, Wyatt Earp-style lawman who is diametrically opposed to anyone in his community openly carry a weapon of any kind, Aldridge, having sprinted up the stairs to Sugar Shack Jack's *Top Of The World* restaurant's patio, was now on the scene at the upscale eatery in front of a crowd of its well-heeled patrons. Having ordered Bernard back inside his kitchen, the sheriff took the chef's place at the patio gate. As a tide of patrons passed in front of him, there he now stood well within earshot of Nicole and her new found friend, the one with captivating, dark brown eyes who no one in this area had ever seen before.

As Aldridge scanned the throngs lingering about the rooftop eatery, restaurateur Jack Worthington, a jovial sort who began his "Sugar Shack Jack" career serving cold beer and wine coolers from a bright yellow and orange, beach-side lean-to, was the first to approach the communities new - albeit considerably less than socially astute - law enforcement official.

"Glad to see you, Sheriff," said Jack. "Looks like the floor show got a little carried away this evening."

"I was called here on official police business, Mr. Worthington. I find nothing amusing about what happened here this evening."

These two men were soon joined by senior deputy, Malloy. Behind him, came Ferguson. Once having caught their breath, both deputies glanced towards the scene of the crime. At that scene, nonchalantly chatting, visibly enthralled by one another paying little heed to the two hapless offenders sprawled spread-eagle a few feet from them, sat the elder and the teen.

Receiving a quick nod from their boss, Deputies Ferguson and Malloy press through the crowd to the tableside where the evening's all-too-real 'floor show' had taken place minutes before.

"Ma'am, are you okay?"

"Yes, thank you."

"And you, young lady, how about you? Are you hurt? Did you see what happened?"

"Yes, I did. I saw the whole thing ...it was amazing! And yes, I'm fine ...heck, I'm great, thank you, officer, for asking."

Deputy Ferguson caught the eye of Nicole's patron. He noticed that she was even paced and skillful, a real pro of some kind of that he was certain, clearly aiming to reduce the anxiety level of her young associate and that of those all around. Opting to avoid disrupting the rising calm with further questions, Ferguson moved onto the two, male assailants.

Before checking their physical condition, Malloy stood to the side of both stilled lawbreakers weapon drawn as Deputy Ferguson, knelt by their shoulders. With trigger finger firmly in place, Sgt. Martin Malloy, a seventeen year veteran of the department, gently nudged the one bad guy nearest him with the tip of his boot. The recipient elicited a painful cry.

"Oh god!"

"Well, looky-looky. What do we have here," Malloy exclaimed to his partner as Ferguson rolled the first assailant onto his back. "...a monk with a giant swastika tattooed on his chest. He must be one of those motorcycle-riding shit heels who raided the Belmont Abbey up near Charlotte, last week. This one seems okay. His pulse is low. He's got one hell of a bruise on his forehead. It looks like he bounced off the railing. He's coming around." With that, Malloy handcuffed the first recipient of the elder female's, counter-offensive.

The news regarding the condition of the other offender was less affirming. Ferguson's outlaw was also draped in the traditional black garb of a Benedictine monk though this one's pilfered robes had been pulled up around his neck, allowing initial identification as he lay face down, to be limited to a hairy back, a butt crack and yellowed boxers.

Ferguson quickly reached to his shoulder, pressing his radio transmitter, "This is Deputy Ferguson, Badge number 227, requesting an ambulance at ..."

Preliminary evidence pointed out that this skinhead was also one of the six, chain wielding, neo-Nazi bikers who raided the Belmont Abbey in eastern North Carolina, stripping nine of its pacifistic prayer-offers naked, forcing "God's messengers" to lie prostrate on the hot pavement then dousing them with a barrel full of their sacrificial wine. That ultimately left one dead, his heart having given out. Though the citizens of the State were outraged and demanding justice, these extreme, right-wing, counter-culture, wingnuts had more to fear from the nearby chapter of the Hell's Angels motorcycle club than from law enforcement or the community at large. With guilt by association outcries plaguing the media, the Angels' rep had taken an undeserved and deeply serious trouncing.

Wars with rival gangs were one thing. What is not in the Angel's playbook was the wanton destruction of the lives and property of innocent civilians. Before such a biker war arose it was clear to Malloy and Ferguson, two deputies with nearly thirty years of service to the community between them, that they together with fellow officers of the Dare County Sheriff's Department and local law enforcement authorities had to put a stop to this near, year and a half long, mounting crime wave before the Hell's Angels did. With some citizens in the community down-deep in their souls wanting to sit back, put their feet up and let nature take its course - allowing the proverbial hawks to sweep down and end the rat's reign - such a lopsided blood bath occurring anywhere along the Outer Banks could conceivably disrupt the tourist trade for an indeterminate number of months, even years. No way could that be allowed to happen.

Deputy Ferguson, looking up at Malloy, offered his assessment of the second batch of damaged goods: "This one has a broken nose, his wrist is snapped near clean and both knee caps have been dislodged."

Ferguson feared that this piece of shit - someone he recognized from an earlier encounter – now breathing erratically - may soon lapse into cardiac arrest. Tony turned his head, staring up in awe at the seventy-four -year-old woman still-seated a few feet from him, offering a clearly audible sigh. To Nicole, as the deputy dropped his eyes refocusing once again on what remained of the pile of human garbage at his knee, it appeared to the young waitress that Ferguson had for the briefest of periods, lapsed into a state of utter bewilderment, expressing with his sigh a mixture of admiration, sympathy, and confusion with the words, "How the hell…" emblazoned across his eyes

Accurately assessing the forty-something officer's non-verbal communication, the nattily-attired stranger replied: "He had a knife. He wouldn't let go."

Seeing his chance to gain political mileage from the evening's events in front of a considerable number of the

25

local elite - those capable of picking up a two hundred dollar tab for two for the privilege of dining al fresco - came Eli Webber, the Mayor of Nags Head. An astonishingly resourceful opportunist, Webber had abruptly abandoned his wife now fuming, to quick-walk to join the sheriff and the area's famed restaurateur in their discussion, a discussion in which the head of the local government knew he had to be seen playing an active role.

The mayor's voice, deep and booming, was not difficult to distinguish. "Look," said Webber, sticking his finger in Aldridge's face, "I don't want any excuses. What happened tonight is the last straw. I want this god damn reign of terror to end right here, right now. 'Cut off the head of the snake and the rest will wither and die.' You savvy? You've heard that saying before, right? City council and I selected you to put a stop to this crazed young female and her antics before any number of tourists are found lying dead on the beach or worse, bleeding-out on the floor of one of our gift shops. Do your job god damnit, and do it now!"

At this point to know exactly what Sheriff Aldridge was thinking didn't require extensive probing by a clinical psychiatrist. The look on his face said it all. With one of the two sets of genes that distinguish man from ape missing from this hominid who inherited the township's head office, Mayor Webber allowed every thought that entered his head to escape without filter.

"Smooth, Eli, you raving imbecile," thought Aldridge. *The bodies of dead tourists on the beach...others bleed-*

ing out on trinket shop floors. That's the image you want to paint in the minds of this crowd?"

From the day he took office, Aldridge had hit the ground running. He had done his homework. He was trying to take this opportunity to prove it and he would if only the mayor would allow him to get a word in edgewise.

As Eli paused to draw a breath, Aldridge inserted; "From what I've been able to determine Mr. Mayor," looking straight in the eyes of the substitute head of the local municipality, "by studying the last sixteen months of reports regarding your Jane Doe, you and your guys have been barking up the wrong tree. This female ring leader - your Bonnie Parker wannabe - she's not a local. She fits the description of a now twenty-eight-year-old female drifter who goes by the name, "Tennessee." I looked outside of North Carolina and came across a series of decade-old rap sheets beginning in Texas that fit a woman of her description. One, in particular, identified her as Elizabeth Sue Woodrow, a minor who escaped from a Mormon compound outside St. Angelo, where she'd been dropped off at age twelve. According to these reports, she had been sexually abused for years before hightailing it out of there. Miss Woodrow is most likely our "Miss Tennessee"…some kind of rabid, anti-religion zealot."

Still standing by the sheriff's side, restaurateur Jack, acknowledging "Miss Tennessee's" plight, sarcastically uttered, "Gee, I wonder how she acquired such a negative outlook on life?"

"Piecing together observations by various police officials across half the southern States..." Aldridge inserts still standing in front of the over-stuffed mayor, "...the common thread is Aryan skinheads. This young woman possesses a real knack for seducing them into acting as her goons. I'll bet you a month's pay if you pull back the hoodies of those two pricks lying comatose over there, they'll be tattooed to the hilt with neo-Nazi symbols."

The "hoodies" to which Sheriff Aldridge was referring were the prayer covers worn by the Benedictine monks whose apparel had been seized by the elder woman's three assailants. Regarding the Nazi tats, Deputies Malloy and Ferguson had already established their presence.

Mayor Webber abruptly turns his attention to the well-poised, elderly woman across the walkway from him. "Look at her over there. Who the hell is she, anyway? Perhaps I should have hired her for sheriff...Sheriff?"

"I was heading over to take her statement when I noticed you rushing over here. She's clearly not in a hurry to leave so I thought I'd listen to what you had to say, first."

Over at the patio table, at the scene of the crime, Nicole was having a very hard time. She was not only trying to wrap her head around what took place minutes before but around this extraordinary example of mature womanhood who was still sitting inches away from her. Having never before encountered a sexagenarian-plus woman so fit and poised, then having watched as she vanquished two men nearly half a century her junior while crippling their female leader, Nicole wondered if this mysterious woman may have once been a G.I. Jane, or a cyborg, or something. Her thoughts running wild, or at the very least a former high fashion runway model who'd been raised in the Shaolin Temple by Kung Fu priests.

The woman in question was, of course, none of the above.

With a cool and steady ease, the out-of-towner carried on the conversation with Nicole, attempting to refocus the younger woman and address her concerns:

"No, I'm the one who must apologize. I didn't mean to disrupt everyone's evening. If I hadn't been lost in thought when those three young people approached, I may have handled the situation quite differently, perhaps finding a way to avoid such punitive measures."

The woman with mystifying eyes reached across to the center of the table for a glass of water, one that oddly enough hadn't tipped during the fray, and drank till the glass remained half full. She pursed her lips, rolling them into a circle, struggling to put aside the lingering memory of the man whose passing had brought her to this time and place. Removing a cloth table napkin from its metal ring, she dabbed either side of her mouth then reached down between the table's legs to collect her belongings. As she did, the memory of a time when as a teenager, she reached down in similar fashion to brush the leg of her high school's most prodigious jock, her way of determining the true nature of his character. The memory of that fate-filled moment years before in a high school cafeteria elicited a broad smile.

"You've always been there for me and you always will be, won't you?"

Upon her assailants attempt to snatch the seemingly helpless, woman's purse, make-up, perfume, keys, a flipped-open wallet prominently displaying her member-ship in the FBI's Retired Agency Society, along with photographs of her life-long friend for whom she had traveled to Nags Head to bury; all spilled out across the restaurant's patio floor.

"I love you with all my heart." She muttered aloud as she reached to collect her belongings, taking a moment to study a photograph of her and her now deceased friend holding a book that was dear to both." Oh, how I miss that self-righteous grin of yours. See, I told you I was right you atheistic prick but I guess you had to find out for yourself. See you soon, my darling." As she reached, blood dripped from a gash in her right forearm.

"Oh my god, you're bleeding!" shouted Nicole. Seated, she started to stand, wanting to fetch bandages. Jack- his eyes always on the swivel - held up his right hand, mo-tioning to Nicole to retake her seat. Turning to one of the teen's fellow waitresses standing nearby, he ordered the restaurant's first aid kit hurried to Nicole's table.

Tom Helgesen was sitting two tables down from the res-taurant's only unaccompanied, female patron when the attack occurred. Tom and his wife Cindy, were there cel-ebrating his retirement as head of the Dare County Sheriff's department, the law enforcement agency responsible for providing blanket coverage to each of the township police departments along North Carolina's Outer Banks.

Named after Virginia Dare, the first person of English ancestry born in what later became known as the United States of America, Dare County was now under the watchful eye of Sheriff Trevor Aldridge, still standing just a few feet away beside Jack and Mayor Webber at the top of the restaurant's patio stairs.

Sheriff Helgesen was a different breed of law and order professional than Trevor Aldridge. Tom felt a sense of pride and honor to knowingly be seen as a part of this "every-man's" beach-side, retreat. From the township of Duck to Kitty Hawk, Kill Devil Hills and Nags Head, the sands of these near-contiguous communities are the playground of all who live on the East Coast who can afford a three-day escape from its major cities.

Tom Helgesen a former Navy man entered its ranks through the ROTC program at Bremerton College. He had once been in charge of an explosive ordinance disposal team as a Lieutenant, Junior Grade. Discipline, decisive action and unseasonable bravery are traits deeply ingrained in this seemingly easy-going man. As Sheriff, Tom once shot a bank robber firing as he fled, a fully automatic machine pistol in Tom's direction. When the ambulance arrived, resuscitation wasn't required. The "suspect" had received a round from ten feet away, in the back of his head.

In the wake of the incident, unscathed and displaying no remorse, the local newspaper quoted Sheriff Helgesen, as saying; "He took not only the people's money but he also stole pieces of their dreams. The SOB got what he deserved."

But when it came to vacationers and kids from nearby universities including those from as far away as George Mason and Georgetown Universities who hit the beach doing all kinds of stupid, they too "got what they deserved." That generally meant if things got a little out of hand, one to three nights in the local pokey. With charges invariably dropped, kids were sent home accompanied by a kind note to their parents, a note that generally asked mom and dad not to be too hard on their knuckle-headed kid. "He/she was just blowing off steam. They'll be better adults for it."

Often reminding his deputies to follow a principle he dubbed 'compassionate protectionism,' it was his balanced sense of community, allowing for some excesses while keeping others in tow that after twenty-two years in office, elevated Tom to the most beloved and respected figure in the region. At the same time, of course, it made him the target of a small but vocal minority seeking change.

Rumor had it that Tom once had in custody this very same renegade female - the one who now and for the past year and a half - has been leading three-man hit teams in such brazen crimes throughout the community as burglary, vandalism, grand theft auto, and of late, armed robbery and assault. The rumor mill insisted that Tom had been suckered into buying this reportedly pretty young girl's fake ID and sob story, letting "Tennessee" off the hook following an arrest for allegedly acting as a go-between in the sale of a ten dollar bag of weed to one of the

Sheriff's beach-combing, undercover officers. The rumor, of course, was completely false. There was no evidence or corroborating testimony to support such an allegation. But the rumor persisted and that inevitably brought about Sheriff Tom Helgesen's early retirement. Enter Trevor Aldridge.

Trevor had never served in the military refusing as a young man, to join the Marines like his father and his father before him. Trevor got out of high school with a respectable "C+" average, finished two years at a community college, was briefly married, played some semi-pro ball then went directly into law enforcement. On the surface, Trevor is a descent-enough kind of a guy and a damn-near flawless *Letter of the Law,* police officer. Still, some from his past are quick to point out that something on Trevor's character development assembly line had failed to engage; the humanity spindle.

Like his hero Wyatt Earp, once a line in the sand is drawn, no room remains within Sheriff Aldridge or Marshall Earp for that matter, for compromise. Only one way forward remains …targeting the objective with extreme prejudice.

As the seventy-four-year-old mystery woman sat back up in her chair, she abruptly noticed a man a few years younger than her with short cropped, steely hair sitting to her right, chatting with Nicole.

"Oh, I'm sorry. Please excuse me," said the man with the Alice-in-Wonderland rascally grin of its Cheshire cat. "Hi, Tom Helgesen. I used to be sheriff around these parts. I just had to get over here and shake your hand before Sheriff Aldridge - that's him over there - came by to officially talk with you."

"Helgesen, is it?"

"Yes ma'am but please, call me Tom."

"So Tom it is. It's nice to meet you, Tom. I deeply regret what happened here."

"Coffee, ice tea or if you wish, I can ask the waitress from the bar to step over here to take your order," asked Nicole as she stood to leave. "Let me go and get things started for the two of you." In two-part harmony, the retirees insisted that the young teen stay. Tom, in particular, wanted someone on hand to collaborate the on-the-spot testimony he was about to give.

"I want you to know…" Tom began, facing the restaurant's enigmatic, lady patron "…that I have taught hand to hand combat at military bases and police departments up and down the east coast for over 25 years. I hold a Federal General Instructor's License with a series of specialized certifications in Subject Control, Arrest Techniques, and Defensive Tactics but I have never seen either a man or a woman handle themselves with such composure and effectiveness in a combat situation as you, ma'am. Thanks for the ring-side seat. I witnessed it start to finish. I doubt if it will but, if this whole thing ever winds up in front of a judge and jury, I'll gladly volunteer to testify on your behalf. It was clearly self-defense and a thing of great beauty I might add. You're damn good."

Attracting the attention of the others gathered for dinner at the haute cuisine restaurant, as both sat, Tom raised the fashionably attired woman's hand in triumph. All within eyeshot spontaneous broke into a rousing round of applause with a wolf-whistle or two adding color to the acknowledgment.

As hoots and cheers subsided, the woman asked the former sheriff; "What did you mean a moment ago Tom, when you said, *if?*"

To answer the question, the retired sheriff set forth his argument in retrospect as if both he and this lady he'd never seen before, were somehow, old friends: "I grew up in Bremerton, Washington, a beach community not unlike this one. When I was a kid, a gourmet meal to us was beans and hot dogs, mac and cheese, nothing at all like they serve here. We rode our bikes, everywhere. We didn't fear anything except, of course, our parents, our school principal and God, in that order."

"And when we were away from home, we watched our P's and Q's. I remember those days all too well," said the stately beauty picking up not only on the direction but also the intent of the thoughts being shared.

"If we stepped out of line," Tom continued, someone else's parents would set us straight. Disrespecting an adult for any reason, somehow always got back to our moms and dads and there would be hell to pay for it. Good manners like that displayed by Nicole here were constantly drilled into our heads."

"Oh yes, and testing one's metal by challenging others was an everyday occurrence."

"Yes, exactly. Who was going to be king of the hill, this week, right? I mean, a fight was just that, a fight."

"I wasn't necessary referring to physical altercations Tom, but.."

"Respect for yourself and more often, for your opponent, grew out of such face-offs. When I'd get into a street fight after school …"

"So, you were one of those kids?"

"I was but who better to tell you what I have to say?"

"I'm sorry, Tom. Go ahead."

"When I got into a fight as a kid it was always man-to-man, *mano a mano*, you know what I mean, right?"

"I understand the concept."

"If one of us guys reached for a rock, a bottle, or a knife, the crowd gathered around would scream, "pussy," "coward," "chicken." Good Christ, being called out for weakness or worse, cowardice is a stigma that can stick to a guy for a lifetime. One's social status depended upon who won sure, but how you conducted yourself carried far greater weight. You learned quickly how to rely on your physical strength but also..."

"That strength inside?"

"Yes."

"I'm quite familiar with that."

"Clearly you are as you demonstrated a few minutes ago." I've told young people many times over the years, when faced with an overwhelming challenge, never look outside yourself for help. Rather dig deep ...look inside. Win, lose or draw, once you tap into the resources you've been born with, all the strength you'll ever need not only in a street fight but no matter what you wind up having to face in life, will be there waiting for you, welcoming you back home each time you return."

"That's very sage advice. I respect you for that Tom, and I couldn't agree more." offered the mysterious elder.

"When it came to women, well hell," Tom offered as he continued his well-meaning rant, "No one had to stand up and tell us boys what to do. It was our job to protect women like you ...well not exactly like you."

For his progressive attitude and all his open-mindedness, Tom still demonstrated a lingering penchant for the traditional 1950s, male dominant role under which he was raised. He goes onto explain: "Now, the whole damn world is topsy-turvy."

"What do you mean, Tom?"

"The first thing anyone does these days is reach for a gun to settle a dispute."

"…or to get what they want?" offered the former sheriff's newly minted confidant.

"Yes, exactly. By the way, I didn't catch your name?"

"That was subtle. I didn't toss it."

"Forgive me."

"My friends call me, Mike. Please feel free to do so."

"Mike? You see, that's exactly what I mean. "You're an example of what wrong with this world."

Giving less weight to the man's words, 'Mike' responded to their tone. "How so?"

"You certainly do not fit the description of any "Mike" I've ever known."

"It's short for Michaelene."

"Now you see, that's far better and quite beautiful… a real girl's name."

"I believe you meant to say, "woman.""

Yes, of course…a real woman's name. It fits you well, as if your parents tailor-made it for you."

"You could say that my father did. My mother died giving birth to me."

"I'm so sorry to hear that."

"It's okay, Dad was an exceptional parent."

"What did he do for a living, may I ask?"

"He was an attorney and from the newspaper bio I read regarding your retirement, like you, my Dad at one point in his life, was also a Naval officer."

"A busy man, a single parent no less who made time for his kids, how rare is that these days? That's what the world today is missing, a sense of priorities."

"Kid, singular, I was the only one."

"Now, you've got young women today like this one they call Tennessee, running around armed to the teeth, seeking revenge for god knows what, waving a gun to get their fair share of what they believe they're entitled to. If you ask me," Tom continues, "it's like the whole damn world was turned inside-out then topsy-turvey and then upside-down."

"I noticed a deep scar on her face. She had been branded with what looked like a crucifix."

Having summed his immediate rant, Tom takes a deep breath, refocuses and asks, "So Michaelene, if it's okay with you, I prefer to call you that?"

"Yes, of course."

"What brings you to Nag's head? Why did you say you're here?"

"I didn't."

"Ma'am? Ah, Michaelene... if I can get some basic information regarding who you are and what you are doing here, I can pass that along to Sheriff Aldridge over there. My concern is for you.

The man's definition of tact no doubt varies greatly from yours and mine."

"I see."

"He can be less than subtle when it comes to getting the answers he wants from a perp."

"A perp? You said you saw what happened?"

"Yes, but he didn't."

"Point taken. Okay, I understand. My name is Michaelene Westgate. My friend passed away here ten days ago. I came to attend his funeral."

"So, where are you from?"

"I maintain permanent residence in Park Ridge, Illinois, a suburb of Chicago."

"You're currently retired, I take it?"

"Yes."

"You seem to have done well. What kind of work did you do?"

"Law enforcement."

"Wow. It must pay a heck of lot better in Illinois than down here in the Carolinas?"

"I'm also an attorney. And as I said, my father was an attorney. He had won several high-profile, human rights cases. He left a measured inheritance."

"But you said you were in law enforcement?"

"Yes, I was with the FBI in Chicago for thirty years. I spent an additional ten as in-house counsel."

"This friend whose funeral you came here to attend, was he a local man?"

"He was living at his father's beach cabin on Ocean Drive just past Mile Marker Seven."

With a look of astonishment, nearly choking on his words before getting them out, Tom uttered,

"Steve? You mean, our Steve, Stevie Donaldson? You were a friend of his?"

"Since high school."

"Everybody around here loved that son of a bitch, especially me."

"Respectfully, if I may argue, I'd say especially me."

"You know, for an old cuss, that guy could still really heave a football damn near halfway down the beach. He loved playing catch with the kids, making them run post patterns. Were the two of you once married?"

"Only in spirit."

"He was a Hoover man, you must've known that?"

Michaelene replied sharply, "No, no he wasn't." With her octave level immediately returning to a more even keel, she continued, offering: "He joined the Bureau shortly after J. Edgar Hoover died, making Steve a member of the modern FBI."

Tom decidedly took the somewhat prickly nature of Michaelene's reply at face value, going onto to say: "You know, Steve and I had much in common. Back in the day, when we were both in the service, he was one the Army's most talented bomb makers, often called upon by other branches of the US military as well as civilian authorities for his expertise."

"You mean explosive ordnance expert, correct?"

"Yes, and fortunately for us, he was on our side. While I, in the Navy, was the guy responsible for disposing of the bombs that didn't go off."

"So you two shared a mutualistic, symbiotic relationship, I take it?" Michaelene offered with a straight face.

"Sure, you could call it that." Replied Tom with a raised eyebrow, wondering exactly how to take what was clearly a sharp-tongued taunt.

With a quickly passing, school girl-type giggle Michaelene offers, "Forgive me, Tom. I apologize. I'm sorry. I was thinking of Steve. Years ago, when he and I were working our first case together, we were trying to establish the motive behind a horrific explosion that occurred on the outskirts of Chicago when that phrase popped into my head. At the time, he gave me the same look you just did. Steve and I were always locked in good-natured, verbal banter; each trying to keep one step ahead of the other. Steve's repartee was often far better than mine."

"Oh, I doubt that."

Recalling her state of mind moments before being attacked – as she reflected upon tender moments over the years she'd shared with Steve - Michaelene offers up from a place deep in her heart, "I concluded long ago that Steve and I didn't marry because we were both quite insecure."

"How so?" Tom offers, failing to take into account the true value of this woman's comment.

"Because neither of us dared to be the first to say we loved the other. Steve tried but I…"

"So the two of you worked together?"

"Yes."

"Often?"

"As the need arose."

Tom shrugged off both Michaelene's apology as well as her disclosure, returning with ease wanting to tell the tale of his beach-buddy pal, Steve Donaldson:

"Whenever Steve and I hung out together which was quite often, he'd go on and on about this remarkable *bombshell*, that's what he called her - this talented and beautiful bombshell of a woman who was the Bureau's first - oh Christ, wait, wait just one minute, God almighty, I'm such an ass. You're her! I mean, his. You're *the* Mrs. Westgate, the gal he was always bragging about. I'm so sorry I didn't recognize your name right off the bat. It is such an honor and privilege to meet you."

"It's Miss."

Overlooked and practically forgotten, Tom turns quickly to Nicole. Given the excitement in the air, the young waitress is once again, beaming.

"Nicole, do you have any idea who our friend here, is?" the former sheriff of Dare County, North

Carolina, asks. Unwilling to wait for an answer, with a lilt of fanfare in his voice, Tom offers;

"I will have you know young lady, that this beautiful woman sitting right here with us today was the FBI's very first, modern day, female Special Agent. This is THE Michaelene Westgate."

Nicole offered, "The very first? Oh my gosh, you really are my hero."

"I should have immediately recognized your name. I knew that I read it before but I couldn't put my finger on it right away. This is one hell of a coincidence."

"You read my name somewhere?"

"Yes, I remember reading it in the FBI's *job test/prep pack*. I took the Phase One portion of the Bureau's entry exam, years ago. Never made it to Phase Two."

"I'm sorry."

"I'm not. Life's been great. You're mentioned in the study course's prep pack as the very first, female Special Agent, early 1970s, wasn't it?"

"Yes, 1972 but that statement is not completely accurate. I was one of the first two female Special Agents in the modern Bureau. I was, however, the first female authorized to carry a weapon in public."

"What?"

"Yes, I was the first woman authorized to strap a gun and badge to my hip."

"1972? Really? That late? Well, I'll be damned."

"Mr. Hoover allowed one woman in the 1920s to carry a revolver but she had to do so in her purse. Anything more than that he considered *unladylike.*"

"So you think Hoover was wrong in suggesting that?"

"I beg your pardon?"

"This is what I've been trying to say, "unladylike" that brings us to today."

"I'm sorry Tom, I'm not following you."

"In the 20s, one of your predecessors was authorized to carry a gun in her purse. You come along in the 1970s, and you're authorized to wear a gun on your hip. This woman named Tennessee, I guess she represents the next phase in the evolution of the women's rights movement?"

Tom's attitude had abruptly switched from friendly to a mixture of uncertainty and anger. "Now our country is in the grip of this insane idea that especially woman need to carry a gun but if caught, well..."

"Where are you going with this, Sheriff?"

"That's just it. It's not me. I'm not going anywhere with this. It's Aldridge. That's where this is going. Sure, this woman, Tennessee is at the center of the majority of crime around here. Yes, she's disrupted the local economy. Sure, she is a pain in the butt but she doesn't deserve to be executed on site."

"What? I don't know what you mean, Tom?" Michaelene offered, returning to using the sheriff's first name again in an attempt to deescalate mounting tension. "I'm certain when apprehended, she'll stand trial."

"No, no she won't. No way in hell."

"I don't understand?"

"You're right. You don't, you can't understand. Aldridge is obsessed with her. This gal 'Tennessee,' brought a gun to what could have easily passed for a street fight. Aldridge won't tolerate anyone with a weapon but oh boy, a woman with a gun, for Aldridge, that's just way over the top. He has already put forth a shoot to kill order on her. I'm certain of that. She'll be

hunted down and executed like a rabid animal."

"That's absurd. Perhaps if I offer not to press charges I can..."

"Please, Miss Westgate. This whole mess is way beyond you. Don't misunderstand me. There are a lot of good men here in the South. Still, there are too many around these parts who see themselves as retail and women as wholesale, if you catch my meaning."

"Perhaps if you and I together contact the FBI field office in Charlotte, we can...."

"Let me be clear. When I was Sheriff, this "Miss Tennessee's" crimes were a mixed bag of misdemeanors and third-degree felonies. Even at that point, Mayor Webber ordered me to bring a stop to her "at all cost." I know you know what that means. I told him I'd be delighted to haul her ass in front of a judge. That made him furious. My way, she'd get five years in state prison. That wasn't good enough. Our illustrious mayor wanted more. With Aldridge, Webber will get exactly what he wants, an abrupt end to this crime spree."

"An objective accomplished. The greater good be damned?"

"Political gain will be had by all once her pelt is hanging on the wall. Perhaps that's the future for all women, for women's rights. Some men will allow it to only go so far. Step beyond a certain point, one man then another and soon an angry mob will form, all agreeing that killing is the only way forward."

"As it happened before."

"What?"

"The execution of not one woman but masses of women, it has happened before."

"Like sheep to the slaughter, is that what you're trying to say? Come on."

"By viewing women as inanimate objects like scraps of paper or pieces of wood, the wholesale extermination of masses of woman, has occurred. There is a historical precedent for it."

"Oh, come on. Really? Okay, tell me. I've got to hear this. And while you're telling this tale, keep in mind one thing."

"And what would that be, Tom?"

"I'll be listening very carefully."

"Please, I encourage you to do so." With that, Michaelene starts out, "The wholesale round-up then extermination of a mass number of women did take place...and more than once. It began with the simple belief that the male of our species is inherently superior in all instances to the female. It's called sexism..."

"Yes," shouts Nicole in acknowledgment.

"...a distorted mental imagery that still lingers throughout the world," as Michaelene continues "...and in many parts of our own country, today."

"Like here," Tom whispers awkwardly in acknowledgment.

"The second key contributor, ' as Michaelene advances her argument, "is the warping of religious principles, often used as a foundation to subjugate women as evidenced in this instance. We have all seen the crucifix burned into Tennessee's face."

Nicole's head snap backward, a gesture that captures the years of remorse for her failure to improve the quality of life of the family into which she was born. With that, she interjects:

"For the man is not of the woman; but the woman of the man. First Corinthians 11:8." It's my mom's favorite verse. She recites it daily. It keeps her tied like a slave to that outrageously self-centered, SOB father of mine," offers Nicole without apology. I researched it. At best, it's taken out of context but ..."

"But what?" Tom wants to know.

"It's been ingrained in my mother for so long she couldn't accept the fact that it is a common error, a distortion of the King's James Bible, even when I clearly pointed out to her that it's sort of like 'what came first,' the chicken or the egg?"

"The third key contributor is simple finger-pointing," Michaelene presses on, "blaming the ills of the world on misguided or promiscuous females."

"One gender blaming the other..." Tom interjects, weighing his thoughts carefully this time before offering, "Yes, I've seen many examples of that over the years but not enough..."

"Then there is the fourth and most dangerous additive," Michaelene asserts. Simply put, it's *my-people-are-superior-to-your-people-therefore-yours-must-be-wiped from the face of the earth.*"

Nicole offers, "That's called xenophobia, right? The fear of something foreign to the world you know?"

"Yes. And those four, key contributors blended together provided the foundation for the mass execution by one nation of the female population of another."

"So you never married because you hate men, is that it?" For the briefest of moments, Tom's attitude took an odd and aggressive, slant.

"Whoa," young Nicole interjects, standing up for her new found friend. "Where did that come from, sir?"

Michaelene calmly rallies to her own defense: "I'm simply aware of the history of what certain men have done, Tom. For the most part, I thoroughly enjoy the company of decent guys like you."

"Well, I thought you were well, you know, one of those with a chip on her shoulder—ah?"

"I'm not a lesbian if that's what you're thinking. And as I said, I loved Steve. He was my partner, the love of my life and much more."

Michaelene Westgate was not just the FBI's first modern day Special Agent. She had been appointed, Special Agent in Charge of its high-profile Chicago office following the passing of the Bureau's founder, J.Edgar Hoover:

"I'm simply saying as today's feminists continue to push, redefining the role of women seeking to obtain a more level playing field..."

With that, Nicole leans in, not wanting to miss a word.

"It could happen again?" Tom offers, wedging his thoughts in between Michaelene's, something Steve also had a tendency to do when he and Mike first worked together. "I get it. I see your point. You're looking at this situation here with Tennessee and with Aldridge calling the shots and as one thing leads to another..."

"It is not outside the realm of possibilities that some men, certainly not all, have the potential as you said of Aldridge, to rise up, take matters into their own hands and..."

"...put females back in their place." inserts Nicole once again, reflecting upon her father and mother's relationship.

"It doesn't occur in a vacuum or plotted out in some darkened basement. All it takes is one man with an accomplice or an enabler with a loudspeaker or..."

Tom offers, "booming voice like our mayor? So, you're saying that this kind of targeting of women, a sort of gender genocide, took place at some point in ancient times?"

"No, not at all. It took place in far more recent times. There was a nation of men who targeted millions of women across half the globe for disposal, killing them by the tens of thousands as they expanded their territory by way of standard military aggression and newly weaponized diseases, setting aside a limited number of young females for reproductive and recreational purposes."

"That's sick, offered Nicole."

"I've never heard of anything like this before. So, you're saying this really happened?" former Sheriff Tom Helgesen, offered, having acknowledged the social issue but still circumspect regarding Michaelene's reference to the mass extermination of women.

"Yes, in fact, it did. It was and remains very much a part of the global history of modern-day, womanhood, a portion that has been overlooked for far too long."

"But if it's true and if like you say, it was recent," Nicole inquires, "then why haven't we heard of it before?"

"The simple answer is because many men around the world including our own government leaders at the time, upon catching a glimpse of some portion of the event, turned away from it opting to minimize its further exposure on themselves and the rest of our society."

"But who did this?" Tom railed.

"Yes, who could do such a thing?" added Nicole.

"The Japanese. Specifically, the Imperial Japanese of World War Two. They, both men and women, encouraged their military during the first half of the last century to eliminate by all available means, the female population of the nations they planned to occupy."

"Defeating men on the battlefield, that wasn't enough for the fucking cowards?" Tom asks.

"It wasn't cowardice, Tom. In their minds it was pragmatism. If the Imperial Japanese hoped to successfully occupy and ultimately prosper on the land of their enemies, the goal of reducing future resistance movements had to be addressed up front and with unrelenting fanaticism."

Tom offers, "You mentioned something about a glimpse? Yeah, sure, okay, perhaps most everyone has caught a glimpse or two of Japan's wartime brutality on movie screens, through TV documentaries and such but I never stopped to think that there was more to it than that - that there could have existed underlying atrocities of the magnitude that you're suggesting. A glimpse - a quick glimpse - good Christ?"

"One of the offspring of the two generals who carried out this gender-based, mass extermination," offers Michaelene, "tried to bring such wholesale slaughter to the US. Steve and I had a little something to do with stopping this mastermind and his accomplice."

Just then, without warning, history took its first step towards repeating itself. From down the beach, ripping through the air came the sound of a single rifle report. With that, twenty-eight-year-old Elizabeth Sue Woodard aka: "Tennessee" lay dead, bleeding out on Nag Head's white sand beach.

Oblivious to the sound of the high-powered rifle, Nicole, with eyes beaming wide, turns to Michaelene and exclaims, "Wow, you must have had an explosive career?"

Both Tom and Michaelene, having glanced in the direction of the report turn back as Mike replies, "It certainly started out that way."

CHAPTER THREE

Chicago, Illinois, Thursday, September 7th, 1978: 7:19 p.m.

And so it begins. With fewer than five days remaining, unless a means to stop him can be found, all human life on the North American continent will fall subject to the whim of a rage-prone, psychopath. To uncover this madman's scheme, seeing her way through his brilliant web of deception is the FBI's first, fully authorized, side-arm bearing, female Special Agent, Miss Michaelene Westgate.

As the clock ticks, across town, a maroon-colored, 1977, Ford LTD wood-paneled station wagon exits Interstate 90 At off-ramp 48A, pausing briefly before crossing the intersection of frontage road and the railroad tracks. The driver a young housewife, passing by the vast oil refinery on her right, slips her vehicle aside a gas pump isle at the corner Shell station on the flat-lying, Chicago suburb of Belmont-Cragin. Engulfed in this year's scorching temperatures, the surrounding hillside of this oft-overlooked, mixed-use burb normally a lush green, is clinging long and hard to a dingy, burnt brown.

The driver, a woman in her mid-to-late 20's with cascading blonde locks, steps out of her vehicle. With head ducked to avoid the off-chance of being spotted by a passing neighbor or worse, one of her husband's co-workers, she fills the gas tank, slides back behind the wheel, drives halfway up the block, pulls to the side of the road and stops. With engine running and AC on, she rolling up the windows, sits and waits to rendezvous with Bob, her lover. Bob on the other hand, without notice, had decidedly moved on to a woman of equal age but of a less virtuous nature, true love being the last thing on this young Lothario's mind.

Eight stories up in an abandoned high rise a sniper and his accomplice for the past seventy-two hours, have been camping out, scoping the much-talked-about, newly developed, Shell service station complex and its surrounding acreage, below. The accomplice, the spotter, watches through binoculars as his teammate, a man with dire contempt for women - especially those who birthed the men who humbled his people - exits the front of the building, crosses the street and uses the hilt of a bayonet to break the driver's side window of a wood-paneled, maroon Ford station wagon.

"But, I..." was all the young beauty could utter before the bayonet's cold steel blade passed across her lips, jamming into the back of her skull. With the palm of his hand, her assailant slams the hilt first up then down to dislodge C-3/C-4 along her cervical spine, negating her ability to speak and resist. Swiftly removing the rusting piece of forged steel, he then opts for a box cutter. With its razor-sharp edge, he severs her carotids then begins the process of methodically dissecting her, carving a message - like father, like son - into her forearm. She bleeds out lying across his lap.

Just before dawn, the butcherer removes her body through the passenger side of the station wagon. Hoisting her over his shoulder, he carries her into the tall grass of the vacant field next to where she had chosen to park on this - and far too many previous occasions - allowing a pattern of behavior to be well noted.

As if tears from heaven, a light drizzle begins to fall. Steam rises from the pavement. Across the street from the gas station, a transit authority bus brakes to a stop. A young, black man carrying groceries and draped in the clutches of a middle-aged, white woman, steps onto the sidewalk.

Together they pause to open a stubborn umbrella as the bus's hydraulic doors close behind them. Up the street, at the bottom of the hillside, in a nearby vacant field, a faint glimmer of light, like a cigarette lighter being struck, catches their eyes. Both turn to look. As the flame abruptly disappears, in its place they witness two shadowy figures, one a short, rather stocky man, the other a seemingly intoxicated, near-naked woman. The man is clutching her arms around his neck as together, they fall to the ground, their movements hidden behind a curtain of tall grass. The black man and the white woman, chuckle. Holding hands, together they cross the street heading for the front door of their apartment half a block away. Both drew the same conclusion. Both were wrong.

CHAPTER THREE The next day; Friday, September 8th, 1978: 6:57 p.m.

(the eve of the hottest day in Chicago's history).

On the twelfth floor of a high-rise office building in the heart of downtown Chicago, the stage for the filming of a segment of the CBS Evening News with anchor Morton Dean, is being set. A statuesque, dark-haired, fair-skinned, professionally attired, young woman three minutes early for her scheduled interview is captured by the cameraman's lens as she enters the room. The skyline of America's fourth largest city is spotted behind her. The camera crew is nervously awaiting Mr. Dean's arrival, making last minute adjustments, moving subconsciously to a song on the radio, an oldie but a goodie:

JOHN SEBASTIAN (OF THE LOVIN' SPOONFUL, SINGS)

Hot town summer in the city. Back of my neck getting dirty and gritty...

Michaelene Westgate, or *"Mike,"* as she is known to friends and colleagues is a woman at the forefront of a new age in American culture, a deviation from what had been the norm for more than two hundred years. And if nothing else, she is most certainly a breath of fresh air in the fifty-year tradition of the J. Edgar Hoover-led FBI. Following the death of the gender-biased director five years prior, on May 2nd of 1972, Mike became the first woman since Alaska P.

Davidson in 1922 to become an official, gun toting, Special Agent of the Federal Bureau of Investigation. Proving herself to be an invaluable asset, within her first two years, Agent Westgate's research and analytical skills supplied key pieces of missing evidence in the Bureau's investigation into the largest cash robbery in Chicago's history, the infamous Purolator Vault Heist. Mike determined that the perpetrators used time-delay fuses on gas-filled grenades to serve not only as a distraction but to distort the timeline of the robbery. Employing a stop-watch and a metronome—having estimated the height of each burglar and with that, determining their stride—she rolled back the clock on the surveillance cameras, ably demonstrating to her superiors the actual moments in which the perpetrators escaped and thereby, the route they took. Both were crucial pieces of evidence that ultimately lead to the robbers' capture and the recovery of all but $1.2 million of the $4.3 million taken.

Mike then gained national attention three years later, capturing headlines on August 27, 1975, when she single-handedly disarmed the fourth in a series of bombs strategically placed by

Palestinian terrorists along Chicago's L-Line. Initially reported as a discarded piece of luggage, a large suitcase strategically placed on the tracks outside the main entrance to the Standard Oil

Company's office building contained enough explosives to collapse the entire sky-scraper onto the commuter line. With the bomb-squad reporting four minutes out and the timer readout on the now opened suitcase reading under one, when all around hesitated, Michaelene acted. For her act of unparalleled courage, this self-effacing, rising star was awarded the Bureau's highest accommodation, The Medal for Meritorious Achievement. The story, along with a captivating photo of the "beautiful and gutsy" Chicago FBI Agent, titled "*The Bureau's First,*" was leaked to the press.

The face of one of their own and a woman no less, plastered on the front of a newspaper was an extraordinary breach in traditional FBI protocol. Newspaper accounts that lauded the effort of a specific agent had been banned by Hoover since 1934. That was the year "Melvin

Purvis, The Man Who Got Dillinger," received nationwide fan mail that included more than a hundred marriage proposals. With Hoover's passing, newly minted Director Kelly, a pragmatist, was looking to upgrade the Bureau's stodgy, old-boys-club image. He was looking less for the right person than the right opportunity. Seizing upon her public persona, Kelly offered Michaelene Westgate, a temporary duty assignment as Acting Special Agent in charge of the FBI's Northern Illinois bureau. Mike jumped at the chance.

7:03 p.m.:

As night falls and a light drizzle begins anew across metropolitan Chicago and its surrounding suburbs, CBS News Anchor Morton Dean, arrives.

(THE LOVIN' SPOONFUL)

> *All around people looking half dead.*

> *Walking on the sidewalk hotter than a match head.*

> *But at night it's a different world.*

> *Go out and find a girl...*

> *Been down, isn't it a pity.*

Doesn't seem to be a shadow in the city.

The sound man's Panasonic, portable radio is turned off.

7:08 pm

Cameras roll. Morton Dean's live interview of Michaelene Westgate takes place. In its closing segment, Dean asks the newly appointed Special Agent In Charge:

"The Director is rumored to have said that placing you, a woman as he put it, as head of one of the FBI's most visible posts, was part of a 'grand experiment.' Are you aware of that comment?"

"Yes, I am."

"When you heard it, how did that make you feel?"

"Honored."

"How so?"

"Thomas Jefferson was the first to use the phrase, 'grand experiment'. He was referring to the newly formed United States of America as a Constitutional Republic, an on-going 'grand experiment' in which the rights of all its citizens, regardless of the color of their skin, religious beliefs, or gender will be treated under the law, equally. FBI Director Kelly is 100% correct to use the same phrase regarding me. As a woman now in a leadership role, I am a visible part of that on-going experiment."

CHAPTER FOUR

Fifteen miles away, in a mixed-use community of tiny, single-family-residences astride a menagerie of neon-lit used car lots, a sprawling industrial park, and an infamous watering hole with an upstairs bordello known affectionately as "Mother's," where women voluntarily lounge in cages awaiting their male customers, the same song is blaring on the radio of a brand new, 1978, Chevy Caprice, convertible. Its owner enters the same Shell gas station where, the night before, a maroon-colored, wood-paneled, Ford station wagon had passed through before parking up the street on the corner of Fourth and Amsterdam. Just twenty-four hours earlier a female in her mid-to-late 20's—an innocent young woman searching for love—passed from this earth without notice; her body dumped face down in a gully inside a vacant lot. Surrounded by a virtual sea of long-neglected, long-necked weeds, swaying back and forth in shifting winds, her remains may have rested there for decades if not for what was about to happen.

Pulling in and parking beneath one of the stations well-lit, island canopies, Bob, the egocentric womanizer, jumps out as the rain increases, to re-fasten his *drop top* Chevy's convertible top. Securing the canvas canopy, he dashes into the station's business center, flicks a folded ten dollar bill in the direction of the night clerk and says, "fill 'er up on pump 12."

Splashing through an accumulation of tiny rainwater puddles, the young Lothario returns to his vehicle removing the nozzle from the gas pump's cradle. Unscrewing the gas cap on his cherished "love machine," he inserts the nozzle, squeezes its spring-loaded handle and awaits the sound of flowing, sixty-five-cents-a-gallon gasoline.

(THE LOVIN' SPOONFUL)

Come-on come--on and dance all night Despite the heat it'll be alright.

And babe, don't you know it's a pity.

The days can't be like the nights.

In the summer, in the city.

In the summer, in the city.

It what little time it took for the Chevy's fuel tank to reach capacity, the last chord of the song is struck as Bob retrieves the pump's nozzle from his vehicle. With that, he holds the elongated spout upright in the air to his side as he refastens the gas cap. Residual amounts of gasoline at the tip of the nozzle gush, spilling over onto the pavement. Alas, behold, the long-awaited target.

7:14 p.m.

From the window of an abandoned high-rise overlooking the corner Shell gas station, a sniper's rifle focuses on a weathered gauge affixed to a huge, above-ground, commercial propane dispenser at the side of the newly constructed service center. The shooter exhales as he pulls the trigger. The round from his weapon travels the 650 yards to clip at exactly the prescribed angle, the elevated unit's near, half-century old, thick metal, pressure-release spigot. With a barely audible whoosh, the heavier than air flammable gas breaks loose, flushing to the ground, surging like a giant invisible serpent across the service station's tarmac to the feet of its unwitting, solo patron.

Within the same split-second, the bullet, having its initial trajectory altered by the impact - ricochets - striking the hand-held, metal nozzle, generating a spark. The spark ignites the gasoline spillage at the tip of the nozzle, sending a funnel of flame surging across the pump's handle. The propane tank's invisible hydrocarbonic gas seeks the flame, acting as an accelerant, leaping up the pant leg of the startled patron, flushing what has now become an inferno, down into the hose and into the underground gasoline storage units. The tirelessly rehearsed shot is a spot-on success.

Bob's hand, on a mission to reinsert the nozzle into the gas pump's cradle, fails. It and he disintegrate as the gas station and all that surrounds it erupts into a colossal ball of flame.

The sniper whispers, "Fukushuu."

In reply, his spotter, as a tribute to Imperial Japan's sneak attack on Pearl Harbor, offers a low and confident, "Tora. Tora. Tora."

Of these two men, a naturalized, American citizen and a Japanese national - the spotter and the sniper - the latter having been brought to Chicago by the former by way of falsified documents to be his 'lab assistant.' A more fitting title would have been 'fall guy' or 'patsy.'

Clutching his custom-made rifle firmly against his chest as if holding a religious artifact, the sniper rolls away from the open window of the abandoned high-rise apartment shielding himself from the blazing radiance of the explosion across the street to which he just gave birth. Flushed with indignation, in the grip of his culture's moral superiority, he pauses. Keeping with the customs of his people, the sniper claps his hands twice, summoning forth the spirits of his deceased ancestors to thank them personally for providing him this heroic opportunity.

CHAPTER FIVE

Like a giant, flame-belching, carnivorous animal set free from its bounds, once-interconnected, underground cement-lined gasoline containers burst, shooting skyward from beneath the earth. Erupting balls of gasoline bluster and boil, exploding in ranting gusts as they make their way to the nearby oil refinery. Once merged, oil and gasoline fill the sky with a stunning display of black, red and yellow torrents of devastating mayhem, devouring everything in its path.

The station pumps, the free-standing structure, its tire warehouse, its signage, the tractor-trailer servicing depots, the automated car wash, nearby street lights, the sidewalks, a maroon Ford LTD wood-paneled station wagon - having been relocated to the far side of the Shell *Super Service* Station - and the Chevy convertible, together, form a hail of molten fragments that first shoot up, then rain down across the neighborhood, sparking hundreds of tiny brush fires and igniting wooden roofs. With a single shot, a 2.1 square mile "war zone" of scorched earth has been created over the near four-square-miles of the Chicago suburb of Belmont-Cragin.

"Come on. Get up. Move! We need to get out of here! *Subayaku idō*!" The spotter urges his counterpart, using what little Japanese he knew.

The gloved hands of the sniper pass the weapon to his fellow conspirator. The spotter breaks down the precision-milled, Russian sniper rifle, struggling with its scope, packing the entire unit into a double-paper shopping bag emblazoned with the word "Safeway" across its side. In an exercise of simple yet effective suburban subterfuge, on top was added one empty, quart-sized, milk carton, a head of lettuce, a stalk of celery, a roll of paper towels and a bag of Lay's potato chips. The spotter - the mastermind who plotted this event - picks-up the single shell casing and places it in the right-side pocket of his black, custom-tailored, pleated dress slacks.

"*Deteiku!* Move out!" He shouts.

7:14:02 P.M; September 8th, 1978; Chicago, Illinois

Back downtown, Morton Dean, Michaelene Westgate, the CBS camera crew, together with the other FBI agents in the room, all turn to watch what was later described as the top of a giant matchstick being struck outside their office window. A red and black mushroom cloud formed by the thousands of gallons of exploding gasoline kept beneath the Belmont-Cragin, commercial gas station, having merged with the nearby oil refinery's storage tanks, resulted in a thermal heat wave causing windows fifteen miles away in downtown Chicago's office buildings, to violently vibrate.

"Holy Christ, what was that?"

Up the street, nearing the top of the hill from where the several-acre gas station complex once stood, the mutilated remains of a woman lies in a gully in an abandoned field overgrown with tall weeds swaying in the wind. The roar of the fire and the intensity of the flames turns evening's dimness into early morning light. Lying face down, the flickering light from the inferno frolics over the pale skin of the woman's corpse.

Captured by the evening fire's flickering flames, tiny particles of feces mixed with blood, slowly dribbling down the woman's exposed skull. Her assailant having inserted an elongated blade into her anal cavity used her hair to wipe it clean.

Agent Westgate abruptly ends the interview. Recalling her experience with her own Explosive Ordinance Team, she immediately orders her assistant, Tom Edwards, to *"Contact Agent Steven Donaldson. He's with the Iowa Bureau. Whatever it takes, get him here now."*

Steve is a former U.S. Army Ranger, a member of its long-range reconnaissance scouts. He is now, the FBI's leading explosives and small arms expert, a field agent designed to teach quarterly at Quantico. Steve and Mike have a history, one long ago dismissed but not discarded. On orders from Michaelene, and with the cooperation of the Special Agent in Charge of the Iowa office in Cedar Rapids, an FBI helicopter - a twin-engine AH 1 Bell originally built as an attack chopper for the Marine Corps, now stripped of its armament and heavy plating - is being fueled and prepped for flight. Iowa State Troopers in a three-car convoy with lights flashing and sirens screaming, are making a hole through local traffic to pick up Special Agent Donaldson and rush him to the off-grid hanger near the Illinois/Iowa border where the former warbird is secretly stashed. Since preliminary news of the explosion was first heard, a near unspeakable reality has been hanging heavy over the law enforcement communities on both sides of the border:

What if it were a backpack nuclear bomb—some kind of dirty bomb set off outside Chicago? Was it a solo effort or the first in a series? Maybe it was something else; something less, something more? What if...? What if...?

Answers, both clear and concise, needed to come and come fast.

(that same night on the Iowa side of the border)

Suddenly, like something out of a Steven King novel, the amplified voice of an angry man roared through the shadow-laden rows of passing corn fields as each of the late model, four door police squad cars, now making their way down a darkened country road, are slowed by a gleaming black object swaying from side to side, blocking the path ahead.

"This is the Iowa State police. Move your vehicle to the side of the road, now!"

The order went out over the loudspeaker of the lead squad car. Attempts to communicate via the police band two-way radio and even through standard CB channels failed to capture the attention of the driver of the vehicle blocking the narrow road ahead.

"What the fuck?"

Like a raging wildfire, thoughts of what this may be - and as a result, what may lie ahead - ran through the nine

State police officers and the one federal agent in the ever-increasingly delayed, convoy.

Is this son-of-a-bitch drunk or was this phase one... phase one of the worst case scenario?

To the seasoned law enforcement veterans seated in the convoy, a hijacking to impede police intervention in what may be a series upcoming, terrorist attacks headed their way, was the foremost thought filling the officer's mind as each were abruptly pitched forward then slammed back into their seats as breaks were hit and acceleration halted...then resumed.

The officers in vehicle number three - loaded down with a wide array of military-grade weaponry - were prepped and cleared to take "any and all action deemed necessary to protect the people of their State." The directive was handed down by none other than the governor of Iowa, a tall, handsome, dullard of a man elected by the slimmest of margins by those who'd grown weary of intellectuals running their state. It was the governor who set in motion the idea that what took place on Chicago's outskirts in Cook County, Illinois, could make its way to the Iowan police officer's back doors; jumping to conclusions being the most dangerous of norms in any fluid situation.

The new and very large, shiny black Mack Truck belching exhaust from its Cummins diesel engine as its trailer veered from left to right, provided a wake of billowing dirt and a hail of small rocks to an already tense and sweltering September eve. To those rushing Special Agent Donaldson in the back of car number two, to the chopper's farm belt hideaway, the eighteen wheeler, persistently giving no quarter, was teetering on an act of war.

Inside vehicle number one, the normally patient - able to laugh-off virtually anything - head of the Iowa State Police Swat Team, Sergeant Whitfield Burgess, was boiling over with rage. "Hey asshole," bellowed the sergeant to the big-rig driver through the dust-laden windshield of his cruiser as if such was a reasonable mode of communication, "If you think you've got problems now buddy, wait till I get a hold of you."

As hearts raced, the driver of the tractor-trailer as if deaf, dumb and blind persisted, refusing to allow the state police's, three-car caravan to pass.

"When he swerves right, I'll floor it and move up his left side," barked Burgess to the officer riding shotgun next to him. "When I do, see if you can catch a glimpse of who this jackass is."

"Sarge wait!"

"Whoa! That was close. He damn near ran us off the road." Throttling back, Burgess softly ordered himself to, "Wait, wait, wait…now! Go, god damnit. Go!" "You got 'em now, boss," added the officer seat beside him. With that, Iowa State Police Sergeant Whitfield Burgess slammed his vehicle's accelerator to the floor. Like an Eastern Diamondback rattlesnake focused on its prey, that hot-rodded, siren- touting, two-door sedan with its three hundred and fifty-one, cubic inch *Cleveland* engine – amongst the finest Ford ever made - lunged forward.

71

"Sarge, Sarge. It's your brother-in-law! It's Hammond. I'd seen his reflection in the truck's side mirror. I caught it when he turned back to see where you were at. It's his rig, Sarge."

The mood of Sergeant Whitfield Burgess transformed in an instant from firey to ice cold. He turned to the rookie officer seated next to him and said: "Take out your weapon son, and roll down your window."

"Sir?"

"When I go to pass him again, fire your first six rounds into the air. If that doesn't get that dumb son-of-a-bitch's attention, empty your last six into him."

"But?"

"Don't but me, rookie. That's an order. There is no time - none whatsoever, god knows - for this kind of dumb-ass, tom-foolery. I don't care if he's related to me or not. Lives, lots of lives – far more than his and all of us put together - are on the line. What Hamm doesn't get is the seriousness of the crisis that we in Iowa, our Illinois neighbors and perhaps even the entire mid-section of this country may be facing. Getting our Fed into the air and over the border without further delay is the only thing that matters right now. And for god's sake, whatever you do, don't shoot the tires. We don't want to jackknife the rig. If you shoot Hammond in the shoulder or the head there is a good chance his reflexes will cause him to either hit the brakes or take his foot off of the accelerator."

"What?"

"Either way, that should give time for all our cruisers to get by without further incident."

"But I don't want to kill the man."

"Until we know exactly what we're dealing with, what caused the Chicago explosion and why, all bets are off. Now son, do as you're told."

That and similar commentary flowed openly across both Iowa and Illinois State police radios. Those ordered to react like these police officers, in the absence of solid information were particularly on edge. Time to debate, consider options or to second guess was simply unavailable.

As luck would have it for Hammond, and of course, for the sergeant and his family, the handgun's initial report quickly got the sergeant's impudent, jokester of a brother-in-law's attention. With squealing breaks, he pulled his eighteen-wheeler off to the side. There young Hammond turned on his radio. With his voice cracking, he offered:

"You tryin' to kill me, Sarge?"

"You crazy little shit. What the hell are you trying to prove?"

"How else could I demonstrate to you and the family and especially my big sis, that I'm not a little kid anymore? I can handle a rig this size even out here? I mean these new puppies are so responsive. I just ...."

"You fucking moron. For no damn good reason you nearly got yourself killed."

"Okay, okay. You can't understand how sorry I am, Whit. I'm sorry, I'm sorry, okay?"

"I'll see what I can do to avoid charges against you."

"Charges? For what?"

"See you tomorrow for dinner at Aunt Patty's ...numbskull."

7:19 pm

(On the other side of the Illinois/Iowa border, in a Belmont-Cragin, back alley)

The rhythmic thudding of leather-heeled shoes as the spotter and the sniper scurry down the building's, custodial entrance metal staircase ends abruptly as the two reach the alleyway. Together, they walk unnoticed through the garbage-littered passageway, merging onto the suburb's main street amidst a horde of dazed neighbors staggered by the explosion. The two Asian males; one tall and proportionate, the other short and barrel-chested, make their way to the center of town. There they slip into a State, license-exempt, delivery van parked curbside with the majority of its once prestigious logo, hastily removed. As the spotter slides into the vehicle, the casing of the handmade bullet rolls out of his pocket and onto the street, making its way to the large metal grate of a liter-strewn, drainage ditch. Remnants of a discarded ramen noodle cup captures the brass casing, forbidding it to pass along with other debris washed by the drizzling rain, into the city sewer system, below.

CHAPTER SIX

1944: July 2nd; 10:47 a.m., on the shores of the island of Saipan, outside the barbed wire U.S. internment camp for Japanese POW's:

"Captain, I have no idea. Like you, I just heard the kid screaming and ran over here. He's outside my gate. Not my responsibility. If you..." Frank stops him.

"Enough."

The Marine assesses the situation. The boy is now whimpering, while still pointing to the woman inside the quarantined encampment.

Frank stares at her. She, in turn, stares at the ground, neither looking up nor acknowledging the boy who is clearly devastated by the site of her. Something clicks in the mind of the young Marine from suburban Chicago. Having fought through three previous island campaigns—Guadalcanal, Peleliu, Tarawa, and now on Saipan—the similarity of the Japanese enemy to native islanders is a fact that this twenty-seven-year-old combat veteran is all too keenly aware.

He points to the woman and barks, "Strip her. Now!"

Two very large American MP's are quick to obey. The woman struggles. All watch as the hair attached to a disembodied scalp falls from her head to the ground. The woman is a man: Sergeant Hiroki Yoshida, a member of

Imperial Japan's barbaric military police unit, the *Kempeitai*.

A man once honored by the emperor with a ceremonial bayonet inlaid with Hirohito's own family crest, a golden Chrysanthemum, Hiroki Yohida now stands naked, seething with malice. Disguising himself with the scalp of the boy's mother - the woman he hastily butchered as American military forces approached his jungle stronghold - he's suddenly surrounded by dozens of his fellow captors. His selfish attempt to secure his own freedom jeopardized their safety. Listening to their bellowing scorn, Yoshida loses control of his bowels.

CHAPTER SEVEN

(Friday September 8th, 1978 7:20 P.M. Belmont-Cragin, Illinois)

The sniper, the man driving the van through the streets of the Chicago suburb is the sole descendant of Sergeant Hiroki Yoshida, the butcherer of the young boy's mother and the conductor of the refractory oven massacre on Saipan's sister island of Tinian, some thirty-four years before.

"Stop. Pull over. We've gone far enough. Get out. I'll drive. Go back. Do what must be done. If Jimmu favors you, there will be another American woman and perhaps more on whom…"

The mastermind stopped mid-sentence and smirked as it dawned on him. Still, in the grip of the adrenaline rush he'd experienced moments before, he'd briefly forgotten that his associate's grasp of the English language barely exceeded grunts and groans. Still, the sniper - the diabolical butcherer of women - got the message. The mastermind, the man who planned this epic two-pronged, distraction quickly cuts short his attempts at verbal communication and reduces the conversation to pantomime. Of all things, he offers his associate a parting gift, a tube of *Chapstick* lip balm, making clear through hand gestures, the two can never be seen together again. Inside the well-known consumer product, the mastermind placed a thin, hollow needle. Inside it was an aerosol-based toxin. Demonstrating to his 'lab assistant' that when the product's cap is removed and its base twisted, any being within a few feet inhaling the gaseous content will experience instantaneously paralysis. Thereafter, in exactly twenty-two seconds, the victim's internal organs will shut-down...permanently.

Of course, the mastermind's hybrid was far more effective and less messy than for example, traditional cyanide. Still it shared many of the same properties and indeed, the same goal. In the event of capture, one could use it on themselves or on one who imposed the captivity. Either way, there would be no spasms, no foaming at the mouth, no almond odor. And unless a toxicology screen is performed to specifically look for this unique formula within the first hour, the deadly fumes will have left the victim's system. As a result, no crime.

Like father, like son, both upon mastering one uniquely challenging, scientific discipline could not resist the siren's song of another. Now that the sniper's role had been fulfilled, the up-and-coming, fledgling physics professor wondered if it was time to bid *Sayonar* to his "lab-assistant," a Japanese word carrying a forever connotation. The mastermind concluded, "No, not yet. Best wait."

The professor leaned over and opened the van's, driver side door for his accomplice. "Okay. Go. Go quickly." Such simple direction followed by a reassuring pat on the back was all that was needed to put a smile on his knuckle-dragging assistant's face.

Thirty-three years earlier and half-a-world away, some five-thousand women and tender-age boys collected from island sex-slave dens all along Japan's outer defense perimeter were brought to the Island of Tinian, to have every measure of their tortured lives erased by the ultra-high heat of the Shinagawa Manufacturing company's built on-site, refractory ovens.

As screams grew and cries for mercy in nearly a dozen languages incessantly sounded, hog-tied with barbed wire, laying naked at his feet, the "lab assistant's" father began a callous game of sexual torture, sadistically wheeling himself then his prized bayonet into the vaginal then anal cavities of a horde of hapless women, much to the delight of dozens of Imperial Japan's finest who joined in the bizarre ritual. Over the course of three days and nights, the game intensified as the number of victims multiplied.

On the island, what cattle survived the on-going acts of war, were served to Japan's officer corps. The nine thousand Japanese enlisted, beyond the one cup of rice per day on which each ostensibly survived, were left as they had been since invading China fourteen years earlier, to fend for themselves. The former tormented souls lined-up for disposal in front of the island's refractory ovens garbed only in barbed wire, were quickly recognized as a ready source of much-needed protein. Those pregnant had their fetuses removed, the preferred delicacy of the non-commissioned officer in charge, the lab assistant's father, Hiroki Yashida. While indications of America's military forces approaching the Japanese position grew, processing the remains of their victims together with those still living, became increasingly problematic. The closer the enemy came, the more overstuffed the ovens grew, ultimately leaving many of the bodies half-charred, fingers knurled, limbs traumatically distorted, faces gripped with terror, still dripping residual flesh.

Out of fear of discovery, *Jugun Ianfu* or 'comfort women' better known to the Imperial Japanese as *Zaimoku,* "pieces of wood," were ordered disposed of throughout the occupied territories; such Eastern "indulgences" being abhorrent to the Western mind. Here, on Tinian, captured by off-shore, island winds, the stench of burning flesh from ovens perched high above the shoreline, pass daily, virtually nullified, merging with the realities of war. Still, island winds can be fickle. They can accumulate, strengthen, propagate, and determine their own course. On the morning of July fourth as the sun began to rise above this distant island landscape while back home, Americans were preparing to celebrate their nation's one hundredth and sixty-ninetieth year of independence, asleep aside a mud embankment downwind from the island's refractory ovens, was 27-year-old Marine Corps Captain, Frank Clifford. Awakened by a sudden passing surge of gaseous fumes, he sets out to investigate.

"Sir, wait one. Let me roust the men."

"No need, Sergeant. Stand down. If I'm not back by 0:800, see to it that Lieutenant Bowie doesn't trip up until my replacement is found."

With a nod of his head accompanied by a typical USMC shit-eating grin, Gunnery Sergeant David Olinsky replies, "Roger that, sir."

A man who is disgraced in Western society, over time, can find redemption and rebuild a life, often being granted a second and quite possibly, even a third chance. Not so in traditional

Japanese society.

At war's end, the once-respected, now-humiliated Hiroki Yoshida, is released by the Americans and returns to his hometown of Nagoya, Japan. Overlooked by the international war crimes tribunal, he lives out his days despised and penniless. His sole offspring, nicknamed Sonny, growing-up in postwar Japan, is shunned and embittered, carrying his father's disgrace. With every morsel of discarded foodstuff that touches Sonny's lips from every garbage can from which he is forced to scrounge to satisfy his never-remitting hunger, what compels Sonny to draw a breath each waking moment of his scorn-riddled life is to find a way to find the man who brought about the humiliation of his father, resulting in the destruction of his family's honor, and bring that man to his knees.

Throughout the decades of searching that lay ahead for Sonny, he'd repeatedly fail to understand that in his mind, he was living in a carnival-like hall of mirrors, a biosphere of powerlessness that reflected only the dullness of his senses and the utter futility of his solo agenda. Locked within the confines of such prismed walls, Sonny would be forced to wait for that one special day when someone with and from a far greater field of vision, would reach out to him.

After years of endless practice with a primitive bolt-action rifle - one awarded him for the killing of an enemy of a local fruit vendor - Sonny develops exceptional marksmanship skills. That landed him membership in Japan's organized crime syndicate, the Yakuza, just days before his 18th birthday.

Tenure, however, would elude Hiroki's sole descendant. The following year, in the winter of 1964, Sonny was summarily booted out of the infamous, international crime syndicate for a conspicuously savage, double murder that went unsolved but not unnoticed by Yakuza senior officials—men who encourage shadows over headlines.

In need of solace, Sonny oft retreated to the darkened cellar of his boundless patience. A nurturing companion and formidable ally, he knew no other.

Sonny survives for the next decade as a murder-for-hire street thug, seeking employment while drifting through a series of gangs. Always at his side, the ceremonial bayonet given to his father by Emperor Hirohito, for "distinguished service," during what the world has now come to know as the *Rape of Nanking.*

It was 1937. Twelve days before many living in the Western world would gather in houses of worship to voluntarily take to their knees in prayer to celebrate the joys of Christmas, Nanking once the capital of the Republic of China - a progressive 2,400 year old metropolitan city where art and free trade once flourished - its people were forced to their knees at the tip of a bayonet. During a six-week-long, hedonistic reign of rape and mass murder undertaken by the invading, Imperial Japanese army, no less than three hundred and sixty-nine thousand, three hundred and sixty-six (369,366), Chinese civilians perished, its city's streets literally drenched in the blood of more than eighty-thousand(80,000) raped and grotesquely mutilated women, both young and old, set on display.

Upon the elder Yoshida's passing, Sonny discovered yet another cherished artifact amongst his father's possessions, a tiny silk pouch. In it was a brown stained, barely legible scrap of an American military newspaper featuring a side profile shot from a distance, of a young

Marine as he ambled past the journal's, photographer. Amongst the last of the detainees in Camp Susupe in the post-war era, Hiroki Yoshida lost what amounted to a tug-of-war for the newspaper's front page with a camp guard. The thoughtlessly discarded rag having found its way through the internment camp's barbed-wire barricades by way of an offshore breeze, was torn by the guard from the POW's grasp. Still, the former sergeant of the blood-lusting Kempeitai got what he wanted. Yoshida retained that portion of the tabloid that held the side profile of a young

American's face, the face of the man who had interrogated him early that day, humiliating the Kempeitai sergeant in front of his men, forever casting Yoshida as a 'leper' in his own country.

As a poor man's Jack the Ripper, Sonny would take brief sojourns to Tokyo, where he'd use his father's bayonet to torture and kill prostitutes, favorably targeting the "easy makes" that dress "American." Holding a swatch of their blood-stained garb, he returns home to Nagoya, eagerly demonstrating to his colleagues that his family, the Yoshidas, are worthy of redemption and honor.

CHAPTER EIGHT

1978: in suburban Chicago, 7:22 p.m., as dusk yields to the darkness of night.

By way of the exceptional talents of his hired gun, the mastermind just minutes ago, successfully executed Act Two of his deceptive plan, an epic explosion that exceeded even his expectations. This would lead investigators into a multi-faceted rabbit hole from which he was convinced, they may never emerge.

"And if by some twist-of-fate they do, the swiftness of my actions will have eroded any chance of stopping what I will soon unleash. Jimmu has placed his faith in me. To succeed is my destiny. It is what I alone have been called upon to do."

The mastermind's version of his father's *Operation No Pa,* a campaign thwarted by the Allies during World War Two, aimed at ridding all who want nothing more than to live free, is now set to advance once again. This time without fanfare, on U.S. soil.

Fearful of floating a plan that would disrupt their business interests, the professor - the mastermind - avoided contact with the Yakuza, pragmatic men who prefer to take advantage of American naiveté rather than killing off such capital prey in mass.

Having read Tokyo newspaper accounts of the brutal killing of street prostitutes, he instead reached out to colleagues at the University of Kyoto, the Yale of Japan, whose underground contacts are as numerous as their professional ones.

Like the prize at the bottom of a Cracker Jack box, the mastermind got more for his money than he expected. He got a two-fer" —a barbaric killer whose disdain for women matched his own and a prodigious marksman. He got Sonny.

"Look up my broad-faced, little fellow. You see it? The sky above. That is my canvas." Offers the mastermind to his ward, less to educate than to hear himself extol the virtues of his perceived artistry. "Like a Rembrandt or a Matisse, a successful distraction is a work of art intensely detailed yet delicate; attached with splender to the universality of all things."

Shrouded in the rapture of each word he speaks, with an upward wave of his hand the mastermind continues:

"I cast deepening shadows in real time against vivid colors across the broadest possible canvas to first seize then beguile the eye. In order for my art to enjoy prolonged success, never more than two of comparable design can be seen. In my world, one event must challenge the mind while the other rips through the heart. And that my little Philistine... my dearest Beelzebub, is the art of distraction and I, its master."

Sonny just grinned.

Now, with both his plans successfully executed, the mastermind - the naturalized American citizen - is convinced that investigators will be torn, first trying to determine how such an epic explosion occurred then hell-bent, pursuing what is at the same time, immediately before them a deranged sexual predator, a serial killer whose skill at butchering women has never before been even imagined in western culture. Two diversions have now been successfully executed with the main act yet to follow.

Hypnotized by the diabolical nature of each sinister act, the mastermind is convinced that his arch foes, America's law enforcement authorities, may never stop to think, look in another direction or consider even for the slightest moment, that one game with two faces has been set in motion to cover for a third. Mounting pressure from a fear-riddled public will soon add to:

"The mastery of my illusion."

This architect of deception's paramount objective is to carry out his father's oft-failed attempts, those that began during World War II, to install the Japanese emperor as the ruler over all the world. His father's weapon is his son's tool. Standing in the way then as now is, the earth's most menacing disease, the American people. To successfully eradicate one disease, another is required.

The mastermind is the son of one of the most prolific and diabolical destroyers of human life in the 20th Century. Born of a Japanese father and a Russian mother, the mastermind bears few discernable genealogical features of his paternal heritage. Haunted everywhere he turns as he walks through crowds of young students on the University of Chicago campus, the man on the verge of resurrecting *Operation No Pa* habitually whispers vile denigrations of his father under his breath.

"Ki sa ma (motherfucker), Our men were bomber pilots, not kamikazes." The mastermind, a nuclear physics professor at the University of Chicago with war ever-raging in his mind, periodically mumbles aloud:

"Did you expect them to follow your orders to fly into the enemy's anti-aircraft guns with what most considered your make-believe bombs? You failed the emperor. You failed our people. I am tall and arrogant just like you but I am your superior, you insipid, short-sighted— yowamushi baka ka (cowardly asshole). I will succeed where you failed."

His brain, an ever-churning vortex of admiration and condemnation, love and hate for his father, less so for his Russian-born mother who throughout the vast majority of her life, kept the identity of his father from her son.

CHAPTER NINE

Zurich, Switzerland, 1967

Much to her credit, by her mid-years living as an émigré in Switzerland, Stephani Diconovich

had turned her life around. For decades 'un-living' her past was a minute-by-minute struggle. Finally, this was her year. She had taught herself how to genuinely smile again, how to make friends and allow herself, whenever the appropriate occasion arose, to actually and quite openly, laugh.

It was twenty-three years ago in the summer of '44. She was living with loving parents and two older brothers in a rural Soviet commune near the Chinese-Mongolian border. There while laboring in the fields, Stephani had been kidnapped by four, Imperial Japanese soldiers led by a hunchback Mongol sheepherder and his dog.

"Stop, let me go!" she screamed in her native Slavic tongue. "Why are you doing this? Where are you taking me?"

The soldiers were operating under orders from one of Imperial Japan's most exalted generals, a trained physician - a prince no less - to harvest pre-pubescent females of "sturdy stock" from Russian farmlands for his microbiology experiments. Just six days shy of her fourteenth birthday, Stephani was ideal.

Murdering her father and brothers, then severing her mother's head after repeatedly raping the older woman in front of her young daughter, the four soldiers bound and gagged Stephani and flung her into the back of a horse-drawn cart, but not before each had suffered several, repeated blows to their groins and knees. After all, Stephani had been raised alongside two loving brothers who cherished her, who taught her the value of standing tall in the face of adversity, to stick up for herself, and where to punch and kick.

Orders were that the "harvest" returned to Imperial Japan's, experimental, *Biological and Germ Warfare Complex* in Pingfan, China, contain only healthy, prepubescent females with unmolested hymens. The Mongol herdsman however, didn't see things that way. He had other plans. Unfortunately, he didn't speak a lick of Japanese. His corpse along with his beloved *Bankhar* hound who decidedly turned on Stephani's assailants, were left to rot alongside the young Russian girl's family.

Taken from the pens in which she and nine other Russian girls of equal age and stature were held on the compound in occupied China - the one bearing the Seal of Japanese Emperor Hirohito - fourteen-year-old Stephani, was tied to a four-pointed stake outside the Prince's office in an open courtyard. There in the absence of any measure of humanity, she was brutally raped by the senior, Japanese medical officer, a man who is also a general, a prince and the Emperor's first cousin. His name, Dr. General Ishii Shiro, the father of the mastermind on the verge of terrorizing the United States.

In the weeks since her capture, Stephani had peered through the pen's wooden slats watching dozens of other human beings bound and tortured, listening to their tormented cries for mercy as their entrails slowly slid from the interiors of their bodies to the blood-gorged, earth below. At some point in the hours, days or maybe even weeks to come, she knew there could be no doubt about it. That too would soon be her fate.

The Prince, the compound's Commander and senior germ warfare scientist, took firsthand accounts of each of his subjects through vivisection, the practice of slicing open living human beings to measure - in this case - the pace of deterioration brought about by his latest batch of designer bacterium. The prince, alongside dozens of Imperial Japan's best and brightest in the medical profession who'd gather to take advantage of the opportunity for their own continuing education, kept copious notes. His, written in Konji—classic Japanese script lifted from Mandarin Chinese—were kept in three, 3"x 16" tightly rolled scrolls, replete with diagrams and timelines, bound with catgut and maintained between two, tailored slices of polished bamboo reed. His most prized possession, the prince's notebook never once left his side. That is, until the day Stephani was again, brought before him.

Pregnant with the prince's child and well into her first trimester, Stephani Diconovich didn't kick, spit at, nor curse her persecutors while being tied spread-eagled, between two stakes. As slant-eyed, on-lookers from the upper crust of Japan's medical community gathered with jubilant expectation, preparing to watch their mentor, the senior medical officer cut into Stephani's uterus to extricate her placenta, she fell silent. Young Stephani had a plan. She knew that prayer at such a moment was utter folly, the scheme of someone destined to die. She, by contrast, wanted to live thus knowing that she had only herself on whom to rely. Fourteen-year-old Stephani Diconovich knew that if she couldn't will herself to focus and failed at the last moment to carry out her plan, it would not only be her but her unborn child who'd be the next living vivisection experiments.

The two guards who had brought Stephani to the courtyard posts held out her arms and legs while the senior medical officer performed a final inspection. This was a special moment for the prince. He was a man who stood a good seven inches taller than the average Japanese male. It had been well known by all but especially by the royal court who continually exalted him, that *The Prince with a cherub's face* was by all comparative accounts, a genius. As a physician, he turned his attention early on, to the dual studies of microbiology and bacteriology. Upon graduation from Kyoto University, like his fellow classmates, he took the *Hippocratic Oath,* pledging to do no harm. In spite of that, he became fascinated by the 1920s research of Frederick Griffith, who through his studies, discovered a naturally occurring substance that could convert harmless bacteria into deadly bacteria. Over the next ten years, the prince repeatedly devoured a paper authored by American scientist Oswald Avery, who expanded upon Griffith's finding and identified the interacting, convertible substance, labeling it *Deoxyribonucleic acid* or DNA.

Ever the consummate student of his chosen field the Prince sought to obtain this substance from the placenta of a first term infant that he had fathered to further manipulate it, identifying what exactly it was that made him - in both mind and body - so superior to the average Nipponese of his day. Once identified, his goal was to develop a "master race" - a race of superior Japanese males like himself - who could mold Emperor Hirohito and his successors, into being the sole rulers of the world. Their throne, *The Throne of the Chrysanthemum*, would be that to which...

"...all people, one day, will soon bow," he was often heard with head held high, to vow.

Consequently, to the prince, Stephani was his conduit, his next step on the road to fulfilling what must certainly be his destiny. Greatness was upon him and he knew it.

Unbeknownst to her, Stephani was not just another maruta or "log" that he could rape, torture, infest like the hundreds of young Chinese, Korean and Filipina girls who came before her to then be tossed into a deepened fire-pit where with what life remained, would wither in excruciating pain and die. No, Stephani was different. He had waited patiently for three months since first impregnating this young Russian teen to obtain her infant's placenta, experimenting extensively with various processes in an endless array of petri dishes long before the fact. Now, the moment for which he had awaited had finally arrived.

The Prince and his guards shared in the joy of mocking what had been earlier, a feisty young 'whore.' Now, as she was being brought before him naked, save for her hand maiden's apron, a reminder to all from whence this once stubborn bitch came, she was submissive.

That apron was indeed quite unique and indicative of the Russian clime from which fourteen-year-old Stephani had been abducted. A highly-specialized garment, it was designed with two separate, large pouches stitched together, one in front of the other, extending the full expanse across the front of the wearer's body. Each morning, Stephani's mother had made certain that her child's apron was cinched properly in the back before her daughter was allowed out the door. On the commune, the two pouches allowed maiden farm workers like Stephani, to segregate the tubers they could spit shine for a quick sale or bargain away the less qualified for other daily needs and services.

While being hauled to the courtyard posts, Stephani silently pledged to her butchered family, especially vowing to the spirits of her brothers, that she would not go quietly into the night. When one guard released his grip on her arms to tie her to the pole, she feigned surrender, pretending to collapse, only to rise up, snatch a knife out of the guard's boot, ripping the blade up and through his groin. Whirling, she caught the second guard in the eye. Then as the 6'1," cousin of the Emperor, the exalted Prince of Japan, raised his hand with an audible whimper to cover his face, Stephani leapt up, slicing downward across his fingers through the back of his hand, snatching his notebook. Stuffing it into one of her apron's pouches, Stephani folded one pouch over the other securing it against her hips and ran. Knowing where the bodies cleared from fire-pit lay - wearing only her apron - she burrowed beneath stacks of them, blanketing herself with the remains of their entrails to hide and keep warm. There young Stephani Diconovich hid for four nights. Utilizing the femur of a corpse to her side, she burrowed inches at a time through the bodies and under the camp's barbed wire to at last, make good her escape.

CHAPTER TEN

As a runaway teen, Stephani first fled "The Middle Flowering Kingdom" with the help of an untold number of its warm-hearted populous. Each sheltered her in their homes from the ruthless pursuit of Imperial Japan's psychopathic legions. Then, under the cover of darkness, this courageous adolescent with an inexorable spirit was secreted from one family to the next until reaching the Russo-China border, leaving behind something rather unexpected, a trail of laughter. As it turned out, each of her aides had told the tale of her escape reenacting it in front of their fellow villagers, highlighting the fact that the proud and mighty, hoity-toity Imperial Japanese, especially one of their greatest generals, a prince no less, had been outsmarted and bloodied by a fourteen-year-old little girl.

With a whirlwind of destruction sweeping over her Slavic land from Germany to the West and Japan to the East, finding a safe harbor in which to restore her life and protect her soon-to-be born child, became Stephani's sole focus. On her knees or on her back, as a transient farm worker or a child prostitute, for four years - with a persistently demanding, infant son in tow - she persevered, miraculously making the forty seven hundred-mile trek to the Swiss border with the help of many who by way of nothing more than a quick glance, gleaned her plight. Her insurance policy was the chief medical officer's notebook. Believing that if it was of such great importance to the prince, a surgeon and a general no less, it must contain information for which she could barter if need be, in exchange for the safety of her and her son. As a result, the binder, ever pressing against her stomach, never left the security of the apron, the one never removed except to bathe.

Having made her way to the outskirts of Switzerland, the only nation with a firm stance of neutrality against the forces of tyranny sweeping the globe, she along with the Prince's Imperial Guards who were now closing in on her, were abruptly halted by the no-nonsense Swiss government's border guards... the Grenzwachtkorps.

History is unclear as to whether these stalwart defenders of their nation's virtue coined the phrase, *Shoot first and ask questions later* but there is no group who adhered to that adage with greater resolve than those *Justice League members* who comprised the Swiss, border patrol.

With what was now unfolding before their eyes, no translator was needed. It was evident. The Japanese Senior Medical officer from Pingfin in a borrowed German staff car just breached the horizon. Through its windshield, he could be seen stomping his feet on its floorboard as his Imperial Guards engaged in a one-sided, belligerent shouting match with Swiss border officials outside the neutral nation's northernmost checkpoint. This, while an 18-year-old Russian girl with her four-year-old son, were being quickly escorted through security into the protection of the Swiss countryside. As the pair passed between the dual Swiss sentry's posts ushered in by a half dozen of their finest, the unmistakable sound of metal-jacketed rounds being chambered into three .50 caliber machine guns from three, Swiss watch-towers triangulating the Japanese Imperial Guard's position, ripped through the air. Thus engendering a rather abrupt end to the outrageous demands of the sons of the Rising Sun. Then, as if on cue, a Swiss-built Pz.39 tank moved forward from behind a blind blocking the entry between the two sentry posts negating any last-minute attempt by the Imperial Guards to try and snatch the fleeing Russian and her son. As the giant, metal colossus inched forward its battleship-size,105mm cannon began to rotate, slowly ratcheting downward, coming to a stop aimed squarely at the Prince's staff car. Either a quick retreat or utter obliteration were the only two options remaining for the pompous Jap general and his guards.

As the Japs retreated, Stephani knew she had at last, found peace. She'd soon settle in Zurich.

1967:

On the western side of the valley on the Üetliberg, in the highly acclaimed university town of Zurich...

"Guten morgen, Fraulein Diconovich. Wie geht es Ihnen?"

With a wave and a smile to a passing neighbor bidding her a good morning, Stephani waved back from her porch with an equally full-hearted smile. "Miss Diconovich" had transitioned in the post-war years from living on the street with a growing boy ever-in tow into a tiny apartment on the outskirts of town. Just this year, she had saved enough money as an itinerant scrubwoman to gain the opportunity to resurrect one of her true passions, baking, opening an equally small, window front store next to her apartment. There, lofty aromas of Russian-style, cinnamon-sprinkled buckwheat cakes, brightly decorated Kulich, blueberry "Zefir" confections and other old-world Russian delights soon became all the rage, sweeping the university town. With her son to whom she gave all now a graduate student at the university, she had become by her own hand, an accepted member of her community. Nineteen sixty-seven was indeed Stephani's year. However, following her rather cryptic disclosure of his father to her son, his disdain for her grew, manifesting into a fiery argument.

"You've given me nothing but lies."

"I am not lying. I ran off with you still in my belly. He was your father."

"You're a stupid woman."

"Yes, you're right. I am stupid. I am not educated like you. So, tell me how could a stupid woman like your mother come up with such a tale of human suffering and horror?"

"How am I to know how the mind of a fourteen-year-old, female runaway-turned-scrubwoman, works? You've been nothing but an embarrassment to me."

Setting aside her fears of what diabolical recipes it may contain, her most coveted possession left inside the fold of her apron now seemed more than ever, invaluable and necessary to share.

"Here take this," she told her son. "Take it to your university. It belonged to your father. Have what it says turned into words you can understand. Then you will see. I have only spoken truth to you."

Two weeks later, Stephani Diconovich was found dead on her kitchen floor. After years of suppressing the utter humiliation of being her son, his pain along with hers had finally ended.

Stephani's highly celebrated, grad student son told police that she had slipped and fell on a butter knife. She was, after all, a baker. With that and no evidence to the contrary, now only science remained, binding father to son.

Though legally exonerated, Stephani's off-spring still changed his name. Dropping Asia's grammatical emphasis over the last vowel of the name his father, he then added an "n" to its end. Upon receipt of his doctorate, the twenty-three year old applied for U.S. citizenship, obtaining a work permit and travel visa under the name, "Randolph Shirin, PH.D." Stephani's son was particularly fond of the first name "Randolph," he had chosen for himself. It has that ring of English gentry, something of which he knew the American ear was fond.

Like father, like son—the brilliant young scientist, Dr. Randolph Shirin, carefully secured what was now his fondest possession, three, *3"x 16" tightly rolled scrolls bound with catgut and maintained between two, tailored slices of polished bamboo reed...* with proven formulas, experiments, additives, diagrams and timelines along with its translation from Old World Japanese to the primary language of the Swiss people, modern-day German, a task performed by a young and eager fellow University of Zurich graduate student seeking a doctorate in Asian studies. Believing that the scroll was hundreds of years old and akin to Da Vinci's scrapbook of anatomical musings, Randolph's campus colleague was fascinated by how in depth its highly descriptive exercises into the realm of the theoretical, plunged. The newly anointed Doctor of Nuclear Physics with both confidence and his father's notebook secured, stepped across the threshold of his mother's doorway as authorities nailed the tiny aperture shut behind him.

Young Randolph hopped a trolley en route to *Kloten Flughafen,* Zurich's international transportation hub. There to board a flight to Chicago's O'Hare International where at the nearby university known as the home of nuclear physics, an apprenticeship eagerly awaited him. Between teaching and refining his chosen profession, Randolph was looking forward to time allotted him by the university for research, time which he will use to immerse himself in his father's discipline, mastering it alongside his own. Operation *No Pao* was on its way to America.

CHAPTER ELEVEN

Friday September 8ᵗʰ 1978; as night sets in on the streets of Belmont-Cragin, Illinois.

"Tell those people to get back."

Nearly an hour has passed since the explosion. In that time, a mass of vehicles including local police, fire department crews from four nearby counties and two unmarked black vehicles with government plates have arrived at the scene choking the road at the bottom of the grade. The one-acre gas station complex is gone. The entire neighborhood is under siege by good Samaritans and first responders darting in and out of buildings between billowing tsunamis of smoke and debris as smoldering craters in the asphalt yawn where the gas pumps and underground storage tanks once were.

As the wind shifts, momentarily clearing the air, glimpses of heaping mounds of smoldering trash covering the surrounding area become visible. Nearby buildings on the outskirts of the epicenter yet to be thoroughly attended by firefighters, are still belching smoke and flames. To military veterans in the community, it is reminiscent of a war zone. To the uninitiated, it appears that what some are saying is right. The soon-to-be-updated, nearby nuclear power plant has suffered yet another down-line breach in its operation; possibly a meltdown. With no salient argument being offered to the contrary, that rumor takes hold hard, and spreads as panic mounts.

8:13 P.M.

FBI Special Agent In Charge, Michaelene Westgate appears at the scene standing five-feet, nine-and-a-half inches tall. Her shoulder-length dark brown hair is twisted into a tight bun. Steadfast and statuesque, Mike wears a smartly tailored, dark-colored suit with a white, open collar blouse. Even with low-heeled shoes, she stands a full head over the police commissioner and the local fire marshal to whom she is carefully listening. One of the buildings directly across the street from the once sprawling service station complex was the local post office. It had been literally vaporized by the explosion. In it were two federal employees. Their deaths together with the destruction of a U.S. Postal Service building itself makes this horrific scene without a doubt, a federal crime. Local Cook County Fire Chief Stan Sullivan is pointing:

"Here, Agent Westgate. Step over here, please."

Ringing the scene immediately surrounding Chief Sullivan are a dozen fire trucks with pole lights extended, casting various veins of illumination through the swirling debris.

Chief Sullivan moves to the hood of his vehicle and turns its on its dual spotlights.. From inside a thick, cardboard portfolio, he lays out the official street map of the city of Belmont-Cragin and permits approved over the last 24 months regarding the now, non-existent, Super Shell service station. Offering to share a secondary check for inconsistencies, looking for something that may have caused this unprecedented calamity, both the Cook

County's senior fire official and the head of the local FBI, find nothing.

Special Agent Michaelene Westgate picks up the city's map, holding it out in front of her, studying it against the distorted lay of the land.

"Over there, Ma'am. That was the neighborhood post office. We were told two mail sorters and a security guard were working late. They're missing, presumed dead. Couldn't have known what hit 'em."

"A bombing of a federal post office. Okay," bellows local Chief of Police Thomas A. Willard, stepping onto the scene.

"Well that's it then, that's out of my jurisdiction. Me and my boys will be headed back to the station."

A tall, thin, forty-something Chinese-American male dressed in a tailored, light brown suit, gently nudges the fire marshal aside, stepping in between agent Westgate and the local police chief. The Chinese-American is struggling to speak, coughing while holding a handkerchief over his nose and mouth. He calls out, "Sir, sir!"

FBI Special Agent in Charge Michaelene Westgate intercedes. She barks: "Wait right there, Chief, you're not going anywhere!"

Incensed by the police chief's dismissive attitude, she quickly adds, "Tell your "boys" to finish doing their job. Cordon-off this scene, and who said anything about a bomb?"

Turning back to the Chinese-American still standing to her side? Mike asks, "Excuse me sir, exactly who are you?"

"Agent, my name is Congressman Robert Chin. I live here. I represent this district."

A member of the House Ways and Means Committee, the Congressman shows Mike his identification then turns to Chief Willard.

"I have a responsibility to the people of this community, as do you, Chief."

Turning back to Michaelene, the Congressman submits, "I want to be kept in the loop. If you need anything, my office is available to you 24/7. I've never seen anything like this. We'll see that you get whatever you need."

The skillful Congressman asserts authority calling out to three local, uniformed police officers gathered in front of a crowd across the street. "You officers, tell those people that if they can, they should leave the city until the police and fire officials have this situation under control. This thing may not be over."

Michaelene quickly adds, "Tell those reporters that they have my word. I will brief them once we know exactly what took place here. Make sure they understand that I am asking as politely as possible under the circumstances for their cooperation."

"That's all we need is some chink telling white folks what to do," offers Chief Willard to Special Agent in Charge, Westgate.

"That man is an elected official, one who apparently knows how to secure a crime scene and protect those he took an oath to serve far better than you, Chief Willard. Such racist remarks are a blight on our community. It's my job to rid the Chicago area of blight. I take my job very seriously. Do I make myself clear?"

Yes, ma'am.

Howling at his officers through a cyclone of dust and flames, the Chief steps away, ordering his men to stay on site to finish their job.

"You heard the lady. Get these streets cordoned off now. Move, move!"

Fire Marshal Sullivan approaches Agent Westgate. She is starting to cough. Unbuttoning her suit jacket, one sleeve is smoldering. The smoke and its stench have enveloped her. The marshal gestures to a subordinate,

"Here. Escort Agent Westgate over to one of our trucks and get an oxygen mask on her. She's been out here too long. Make sure she gets a good twenty minutes on that rig. Mrs. Westgate, you can watch all the action from inside the cab. No need to have you standing out here."

"Thank you, Marshal. And for the record, it's "Miss.""

CHAPTER TWELVE

9:31 p.m.

After yet another hour and fourteen minutes on the scene has passed, the Bureau's helicopter couriering Agent Steve Donaldson is spotted in the skies above, making an approach. Donaldson is the high school sweetheart of Michaelene Westgate. Steve stands 6'2", with the eyes of a hunter, an athletic build and an insatiable need to excel at all he does. He is a Vietnam war veteran with a sense of humor that frequently rubs the wrong people the wrong way.

Opening the rear hatch of the fire department's emergency hazmat vehicle, Agent Westgate, waves directions to the hovering helicopter's pilot. Suddenly she stops and turns, noticing a short, stocky man standing motionless less than a foot away from her at the edge of the vehicle's outward swinging door."

"Sir, please, stand back. Sir…sir. Do you speak English? What are you doing here?"

An Asian male had drawn so close Mike sensed his breath. He is staring directly at her yet saying nothing. As he steps backward, he bows respectfully, merging into the clouds of smoke and dust, then vanishes from the scene as if an apparition.

Following Michaelene's commands, the helicopter pilot sits his craft down precariously close to the mass of fire trucks and police vehicles.

Mike, upon exiting the fire department vehicle, hands the oxygen mask back to the young, fireman, inside.

"Ma'am, the Chief said a good twenty. It's been less than ten."

"You've been very kind. I'll be fine. Thank you."

"But…"

"It's okay. I won't tell if you won't."

Wearing his standard, out-of-the-box polyester blue suit and carrying over his shoulder a *Hemingway valise* - a battered, leather tote with ancillary zippered document pouches on either side - Mike meets Steve halfway across a narrow patch of undisturbed blacktop. She shakes hands with her old friend. A mutually shared smile is short lived.

"Agent Donaldson, you always liked making an entrance."

"Nice for a change to get off a chopper Agent Westgate, without someone shooting at me."

"Oh, don't worry, Agent Donaldson. I'm certain the father of one of your latest dalliances will be along soon."

"Witty. Someone once said that such wit is nothing but educated arrogance."

"It was Aristotle, and he was right."

"Good Christ! What the hell happened here? Any idea what caused this dent in the landscape?

And by the way, congratulations on your promotion."

"The promotion's temporary. We're still searching for answers. The heat and the winds have made operations more difficult than usual."

"You know the public is freaked. They're going to demand answers now, not later."

"Agreed. Still, we can't afford a rush to judgment. I briefed the governor. I spoke with your boss and mine. Both a federal and state police presence will be on the streets 24/7. The Governor sent out an APB to the directors of all state agencies ordering them to pull out all the stops - go beyond their emergency budgets if needed to provide every resource the Bureau may require. I asked the State's sanitation workers union to team-up with our CSI units. No one knows these streets better than the men who drive those garbage trucks. I want every square inch of this burb inspected then re-inspected again with maps provided to me demonstrating what ground was covered and what unit covered it. I tasked my office with setting up a public forum as soon as possible. I told them to secure a location large enough to accommodate at least five hundred people, and I want cameras there, as well as every single local specialist they can round up who can look convincing in front of a news camera, people who can help assure the public of well, whatever this is and whatever caused it won't happen again. We need to buy time to run this investigation thoroughly, wherever it may lead. I set all this in motion before you arrived."

"That's my girl. Smart. I especially like the Town Hall bit, everyone meeting in one place. That'll keep both the public and reporters from getting in our way. Hell, we don't even know the scope of this thing we're trying to deal with as yet. We can't afford to have even the slightest sliver of evidence trampled on or discarded."

"Educate rather than inform. Glad you approve."

"We need to demonstrate to the public in no uncertain terms, that the Bureau has control of this situation."

"Roger that First Lieutenant Donaldson—" a reference to Steve's last official rank in the U.S Army, "—and be advised."

"Yes?"

"I'm not 'your' girl."

CHAPTER THIRTEEN

9:58 p.m.

As Mike and Steve walk together surveying the scene, they observe two men noticeably related, standing together across the street, up-wind from the epicenter of the explosion. Like statues frozen in time, the two are motionless, speechless; just staring.

The night's fires paint their profiles. One of the men is tall and rail straight, late '50s, early '60s, sporting thick, white hair combed straight back on top, clipped high and tight on the sides. As the two agents come upon the elder of the two, they note his expression. It's impenetrable. His sharp, blue eyes – ostensibly unaffected by the night and its smoke and flames - are scanning everything within range, seemingly missing nothing. A moment passes. He then introduces himself: "My name is Frank Clifford. This is my son, Bradford." Acknowledging the badge and sidearm on Michaelene's hip Frank states, "You must be the FBI?"

Brad Clifford is slightly stooped with the pallor and softness of form of someone who spends most of his time indoors. As the two agents extend their pocketed ID's, Brad begins to complain, nearly whining to his father who is clearly ignoring him.

"Who could do this to us?"

"I'm open to any suggestions you might have?" Special Agent Westgate, quickly inserts. She receives only a stunned look in reply.

A local police officer abruptly appears on the scene. Officer Richard Sweeney is struggling as he approaches the two agents, trying not to regurgitate the Diet Pepsi and Snickers candy bar he consumed a few minutes before. As he nears, he wipes his mouth using the sleeve of his uniform to remove any possible residue.

Michaelene is the first to speak. "How can we help you, officer?"

Officer Sweeney with a flashlight in hand motions over his shoulder, "The two of you need to see this."

The officer reports finding a woman's body hidden at the bottom of a hillside gully surrounded by tall weeds a block up the street from where the gas station once stood.

Mike turns to Frank Clifford and while making only eye contact with his son Brad, offers to both, "Please wait here. I'll be just a few minutes."

Mike and Steve follow Officer Sweeney. They view the body *in situ*.

"Holy shit! What the...?" Combat veteran Steve Donaldson is genuinely taken aback.

It is clear that the young woman did not die from fire or explosive trauma. At first glance, as now two more flashlights pass over her, there is evidence of genital mutilation, cuts on the back of her arms, legs, and side. Both breasts lay severed, stacked neatly to her side beneath her right arm. An eyeball has taken the place of each areola. The flesh on her face had been methodically removed, her skull crushed, her mandible removed, and the tips of each finger severed, destroying all possible means of identification.

Mike leans down over the body to examine it closely.

Sweeney and Donaldson step away. Officer Sweeney, turning towards Steve, holding out his hand, offers Donaldson a shard of rusty metal wrapped in what looks like, a piece of the officer's uniform.

"One of our techs found this scrap of metal at the scene and tossed it. I thought it may be important so I retrieved it."

"This was beside the body?" Agent Donaldson asks.

"Yes, sir."

"And one of your department's CSIs discarded it?"

"Yes, sir. I asked him if he had any extra evidence bags. He didn't. So, I pulled out my shirt and used my knife to cut off a piece of its hem, just enough mind you, to make certain that there was enough material to wrap around whatever this is so that my fingerprints didn't further contaminate it if somehow, you know, it has something to do with the murder of this woman."

Agent Donaldson stares at Officer Sweeney. He can't believe what he is hearing.

Officer Sweeney continues unabridged "I kinda agree with what the CSI was thinking I mean, the piece is old, it's rusty; it looks like it had been laying in that field for twenty years or more. I didn't want to add to the problem or get someone in trouble but then again, I thought maybe..."

"You're right. You thought. He didn't. I want this bozo's name."

"Sir, I know this guy. He's a good man with a wife and family. He needs his job. If you need a name, I would prefer that you use mine."

"Ah, Jesus H., Officer Sweeney, what are you trying to say to me? Don't you understand? We need people who know how to professionally perform their duties. What we don't need is someone who is going to discard a potential piece of evidence because it doesn't fit his preconceived notions or it's too inconvenient for him to find a secondary means of securing it as you ultimately did. I respect your loyalty to your friend, but..."

"I already ripped him a new one sir and told him I would personally file a complaint to bring him in front of a review board if ever..."

"Unbelievable. Okay. Fine. Here. Let me take a look at that thing", Agent Donaldson offers pulling out a pair of Nitrile gloves.

Steve believes he recognizes what may be a broken or sheered piece of a knife or bayonet with a small, odd swirl with remnants of gold inlaid somewhere near - if it were a knife - the bolter and the heel or if a bayonet, immediately below its hilt.

"It kinda looks like a flower, sir. That swirl, I mean." Officer Sweeney, says. "My wife and I have a garden. She grows flowers."

"And she's a seamstress or fashion designer, right? How else would a grown man like you know that just like a woman's skirt the bottom of a guy's shirt is also known as a hem?"

"Yes, she works at a tailor shop. They make uniforms for us and do alterations when you know, some of us put on a little weight."

Special Agent in Charge Michaelene Westgate, having completed her initial inspection of the mutilated female's body, stands, takes a few steps over to where Steve and the local policeman are talking, and leans over her fellow agent's shoulder. She offers, "Officer Sweeney is right, Agent Donaldson. It's a flower, a Chrysanthemum. Is that paint or flakes of real gold? Let's get it to the lab to find out for certain."

"What?"

Amazed and reacting under the circumstances somewhat holier than thou, Steve asks,

"How would…"

Frank, having left his son Brad standing alone, suddenly appears without notice, directly behind

Agent Donaldson. He passed the mutilated remains of the woman lying face down in the field.

Now he too, is looking over Steve Donaldson's shoulder catching a glimpse of the metal fragment. Steve turns and confronts him.

"Mr. Clifford?"

Inwardly disturbed by the magnitude of the brutalization of the woman's body and now by the sight of what may well be a fragment from the hilt of a Japanese, Model 30 bayonet, one while serving as a Marine in the Pacific during World War Two, the now sixty-one-year-old had seen far too often. This one, however, had been found lying a block away from his former Belmont-Cragin, service station complex, the one he painstakingly designed and subsequently supervised through each phase of its construction. Frank, remaining outwardly stoic subtly exhales.

Officer Sweeney, steps in front of the two agents exercising his local authority, saying to the unannounced stranger, "That's far enough, mister. Turn around and get out of here right now or

I'll throw the cuffs on you."

"My name is Frank Clifford."

"I don't give a damn if you're the caretaker of President Carter's peanut farm. You can't be hanging 'round here."

"It's okay, officer. Mr. Clifford and I have met before. Recently, wasn't it, sir?" Mike feigns. "And I apologize.

117

I should have asked you then. Exactly what are you doing here?"

"I owned the service station."

"Where the explosion took place?" Mike implores.

"Yes."

"I hope you don't have plans to leave town?"

"I do not."

From across the street, Michaelene notices her assistant, Agent Edwards, hurrying to join the assemblage. Upon arrival, Mike introduces the two men to one another.

"Mr. Clifford, this is Agent Tom Edwards. Please surrender your driver's license to me and provide him with your office, home address and a working telephone number. When the two of you have finished, do us all a favor. Go home. I will be in touch with you as soon as I can. I will return your license after you and I have had a chance to sit and chat."

Brad blurts out, "Hey, you have no right to take my old man's driver's license!"

Reaching into his hip pocket, Frank takes out his wallet and removes his Illinois State driver's license.

"That will be fine, ma'am." Having been given nothing, the elder Clifford offers nothing in return save of course, for his cooperation.

Tom Edwards, Michaelene's duly designated assistant, a man rarely not seen glued to her side, as ordered, takes down Frank Clifford's information then turns to Frank's son, Brad asking:

"And you sir, what is your address and how best can we reach you if necessary?"

"My old man lives with me. His address is the same as mine."

Edwards turns to Frank, "Is that true, sir?"

Setting aside the question of actual ownership of the stately northwest suburban home in which both reside, "Frank simply offers, "Yes, that's true."

Before this evening, neither Agent Edwards nor Agent Donaldson had the slightest idea that either walked the face of the earth. At first glance, Steve sees Edwards as a typical bureaucrat, a sub-species of sort. Agent Tom Edwards is convinced that Steve Donaldson is an arrogant ass with an unsustainable ego. Tom, after all, is a guy and although Mike is his immediate supervisor, she is a highly intelligent and beautiful young woman married only to her job with what some would say is an oft-captivating if not somewhat exotic presence about her.

CHAPTER FOURTEEN

10:52 p.m.

That night at the Clifford family residence as both men return, Frank endures the usual struggles with his family. His son Brad's wife, Olivia, a typical 1950s *Leave It to Beaver* housewife, does her best to keep her husband from going off the moment he comes through the door on their precocious, nine-year-old son, Tommy, a violin prodigy whom Brad refers to far too often, as "sissy-boy." Tommy was still up, waiting to see if both father and his beloved grandfather were safe before turning in for the night.

"Hey Olivia, what's sissy-boy still doing up? You just can't stop spoiling him, can you?" Such are the first words out of Brad's mouth as he breaches the threshold of his home, sees his wife and son with looks of relief from worry on their faces, standing in the foyer.

Frank struggles to watch this dysfunctional relationship. It stands in stark contrast to his partnership with the love of his life, his now deceased wife, Mary.

Late that night, Frank is in his study gazing at Mary's photo, processing the events of the day, when he doses off in his high-back, leather chair. In dreamscape, he flashes back to 1944, on the island of Tinian, engulfed in heavy fighting with sounds of shrapnel shredding through tropical jungle vines

DREAMSCAPE:

In yet another, oft-repeated, sleep-stealing, nightmare, Frank sees himself as a young man in battle gear. In the distance he hears the roar of heavy bulldozers - American 'dozers -distorted and out of context, belching between braking and accelerating, a high pitched screech when slammed into reverse, then an unmistakable drone as the gears grind forward. The sound of a young teenage boy's voice heard amidst exploding ordinance incessantly crying, "Nana, Nana" abruptly surrenders to a woman's scream. Gasping, wondering what she had done so terribly wrong to now be forced to relinquish her last breath, the echo of her voice, fades. In his dream, Frank hesitates, determines the direction of the female's voice then hurries in that direction. When he arrives, she's nowhere to be found. In her stead, a choir of women move about him crying in anguish each indistinguishable from the other. Pounding through Frank's dreamscape are the words of one of the bulldozer drivers.

"Over there Captain, those oven doors. Don't stare at 'em long, you hear?' They'll get their hooks in the back of your eyes if you do. Don't let em', sir. Don't let 'em get their hooks into the back of your eyes. If they do, they'll rot right straight through to your soul."

The bulldozer driver's words repeat like a mantra.

Amidst the pulsating turbulence within Frank Clifford's recurring nightmare, a moment of profound clarity appears upon its surface.

"People gotta know what happened here, Sir." says the bulldozer driver stepping off his rig moving suddenly ever closer to young Frank. "My orders are to destroy 'dem human incinerators...to knock them down but I can't. God help me. I won't."

The pock-marked face and tussled, red hair of the bulldozer driver, a Petty Officer Second Class, in the Navy's construction corps -The Seabees - now takes center stage, inches away from the nose of young Frank.

"I'll stand court martial if I must for disobeying orders Sir, but I refuse. You tell 'em. Tell 'em for me. I WILL NOT KNOCK DOWN THESE FUCKIN' OVENS. Some of 'em gotta stand, sir. Who'll ever know what happened here if they're gone? What kind of sick pieces of shit human beings could do this to other human beings, to the innocent, to women? People got to know, sir. This isn't war. This is murder, mass murder, nothing short of that."

As the line between awake and sleep is tentatively crossed, Frank realizes "And there is no statute of limitations for murder, not in my country."

The thirty-two-year-old bulldozer driver stares closely – too closely - into Frank's eyes then suddenly grabs the young Marine's hand. Holding it out, he slowly pours the cremated ashes from inside one of the human incinerators into Frank's open palm. As the ashes flow across each finger, faces of the women whose remains they were, appear, crying out in wanto agony then fade as the last droplet of ash reaches the ground. With that, the driver abruptly vanishes as Frank's dreamscape nightmare moves on.

Triggered by a continual barrage of enemy fire charring the earth, whirls of smoke and dirt fill Captain Clifford's eyes. When briefly it subsides, rows of shiny, red brick structures - the ovens from which the young Marine Corps officer once fled - each some six-feet tall and eight feet long, appear. A young girl in a tattered white shift suddenly darts out from between the row of ovens. Clifford follows the barefoot girl across the dreamscape field wanting to help her though she remains unrelentingly out of reach. A smoldering field of blackened ash stretches endlessly from the oven doors as suddenly each bursts open billowing smoke emboldened with the stench of burning flesh, a sickening perfume that no one asleep or awake can dispel.

Young Frank walks, runs, falls, and picks himself up, noticing that his pant legs are covered with snippets of barbed wire. He brushes them off. They tear his flesh. With each step, horror grips him as his feet crunch over bones, stained and burned—dull grey, pink to black—over small skulls and slim long bones. Sake bottles mixed with shreds of multicolored, blood-stained cloth stretch to the horizon. Fragments of human skeletal remains snap under Frank's boots as he continues to run, searching for the girl. Through the thick smoke and blinding haze of renewed shelling, he can hear her screams but cannot determine where she may be.

Then abruptly, the earth is stilled. The shelling is lifted. The haze is gone. Frank stops. Everything is clear. He looks down. From beneath the jungle mire below his feet, filled with disbelief, he sees the young girl's hand reaching up to him. Thought dead, her body was buried alongside dozens who were by the bulldozer's blade. Young Frank takes her hand in his, struggling to set her free.

Removing his helmet, using both hands to hold onto the metal encasement, he digs, using its edge to extricate her from the earth beneath what is now the Marine Corps officer's bended knees. With ever-increasing desperation, he releases one hand from his helmet while holding it with the other digging furiously, again reaching for her hand to assure her she will soon be free. As her fingers slowly wrap around his, she in turn conveys to him with words unspoken, to hold fast less to her than to his humanity. Through her grip, she assures him that as a result of his selfless aid to her that he will soon be returning from this place of despair and desecration to all that he cherishes, his home, his family and a woman whose love awaits him. With a last, reassuring firm clasp of his hand, she perishes. Startled, Frank awakens.

In the passing moments between sleep to full consciousness, the bulldozer driver's voice echoes in the recesses of the once young Marine officer turned Chicago-based, gas station mogul's mind, "Don't let those oven doors get their hooks into the back of your eyes."

CHAPTER FIFTEEN

Saturday 6:19 a.m. September 9th, 1978 (Now with less than 72 hours remaining).

Early the next morning, while Michaelene remains onsite in the rubble of Belmont-Cragin directing the investigation, Steve crawls out of the backseat of one of the Bureau's four-door

Ford sedans where he'd chosen to crash last night for a few hours sleep. Opening the driver's side door, he slides in behind the wheel.

Substituting a renegade stick of Wrigley's Gum discovered in the vehicle' glove box for the toothbrush he neglected to pack, Steve plops it into his mouth as he checks himself out in the vehicle's rearview mirror. Straightening his tie, he rubs both hands through his hair. Rummaging through the collection of city maps left in the glove compartment, Agent Donaldson locates the keys, the ones secreted away by virtually every agent in the same place. Inserting the proper one into the ignition. Steve incessantly cranks the ignition while repeatedly pumping the accelerator. Along with more than a few expletives, the over-worked sedan finally gets the message, first sputtering then purrs. The Iowa-based Special Agent hits the accelerator and peels out, heading for his chosen destination, the Chicago area's medical examiner's office.

Making his way from the parking lot, Steve removes his credentials from his inside jacket pocket flashes them at security, then carefully sequestered them back from whence they came. Once inside, he stops to use the men's room. As he exits, he asks for directions from a passing intern:

"Excuse me, FBI. Which way to…?"

"The medical examiner's office?"

"Yes."

"Down this hall to your right. When you get to the water fountain make your first sharp left. It will be the first door on your right about half way down."

"Thanks. And I thought the Pentagon was a maze."

Steve abruptly enters the Cook County examination room where he finds Chief Medical Examiner Dr. Elizabeth Vaziri, speaking aloud into a voice recorder. She is cryptically detailing the wounds, abrasions, and an odd set of markings detailed into the anterior forearm of the corpse of a young blonde, female brought to the examiner's office last night with an FBI's *requires immediate attention* tag affixed to the body bag.

While Dr. Vaziri continues her assessment, Steve once again removes his credentials from inside his coat pocket. This time, he holds them high above his head identifying himself from across the room, as a Bureau Agent. Through a sliding glass doorway at the far end of the span of examination tables, Donaldson notices a sign that reads *Waiting Room*. Pointing to it he offers to wait there to be briefed. Dr. Vaziri nods in acknowledgment.

Suspended from the ceiling in this overly air-conditioned, four hundred square foot, four-walled retreat is a nineteen inch, Magnavox, color TV. On it, the morning news is airing footage of last night's epic explosion captured by the local *Eye In The Sky* news helicopter. The scene looks eerily like a nuclear mushroom cloud now seen by way of this broadcast by every citizen in the State of Illinois and beyond. Beneath the monitor, sitting atop a spindly-legged table, Steve eyes a *Brewmaster,* pump-action, coffee dispenser already prepped for the day. In his most cynical of voices, Steve blurts out "Hallelujah, thank you, Jesus," and helps himself to one of two dozen pre-washed, neatly stacked, ceramic mugs. With his valise slung over his shoulder and borrowed cup in hand, he exits the frigid anteroom walking past the entrance to the morgue out into the hallway.

Still struggling to rekindle the majority of his cognitive faculties after less than four restless hours of sleep, Steve happens upon a hallway bench and drops into it. There he opens the zippered pouch of his tote and starts reading through the FBI's hastily compiled CV of the owner of the gas station. Clippings taken from Frank Clifford's 201 file, the Marine Corps' account of Colonel Clifford's military career, have been cryptically edited and inserted into an FBI file by researchers at Michaelene's office. Steve carefully eyes each page.

Clifford, Frank. O-6, Full "Bird" Colonel, Second Marine Division (ret.).

As he reads Steve ruminates, finding himself slowly slipping into Colonel Frank Clifford's shoes.

Second Marines, First Expeditionary Force, Pacific theater led U.S. ground forces in four island campaigns against the Japanese.

"Holy Christ, four?" Steve, the card-carrying atheist barks, aloud.

Donaldson pauses as he listens to his assessment of Colonel Clifford's military career echo down the corridor of spotless white-washed walls and high-polished floors. Remaining locked in thought, without looking up, he lifts his feet as a mop passes in and around where he sits.

"A combat veteran. First in. Tip of the spear. Three years in the thick of it promoted twice, both field commissions, both by General Howland Smith, himself." Steve is enthralled, still pondering, now beneath his breath, "No combat-related wounds or injuries. Recipient of the Navy Cross. No noted R+R. What the...? He never left the field?"

Steve thought of his own tour of duty in Vietnam and recalled hearing that World War Two combat personnel were not scheduled to rotate home every nine months like his.

"Okay, so, this guy survives four of the bloodiest military campaigns in U.S. history, gets out of the Corps, goes to college, graduates in three and becomes one of Illinois's leading businessmen. Okay. I get it. I see. Now I know exactly who you are Frank Clifford. You're him.

You're that guy, the prototype, the archetypical American civilian-soldier. Finish what you start and always keep moving forward. Son of a bitch!"

Dr. Vaziri steps out of the lab into the hallway, asking Steve to join her inside the examination room. She is ready to review with him the autopsy's preliminary findings.

As the two approach the examination table, the lab assistant pulls back the sheet covering the young victim's body. Dr. Vaziri explains,

"At first, Agent Donaldson, I must confess to you I read this woman's body wrong. I considered her to be the recipient of rage but I was mistaken. Upon further evaluation, my conclusion is that this once healthy female in her mid-twenties was the victim of a carefully-executed, meticulously-patterned, highly-sophisticated, non-stop, ritualistic mutilation."

"That's quite a mouth full."

"The attack and subsequent mutilation lasted somewhere between fifteen to eighteen hours. The mutilation was carried out both pre and post mortem. It was concentrated and deliberate, ceremonial but well beyond satanic. Candidly, such focused rage is well beyond anything I've encountered before."

"You're saying that this wasn't this clown's first rodeo?"

"As you noted at the scene, the flesh from her face had been removed with near surgical precision on par perhaps with a first-year med student."

"Studious but not refined?"

"Yes, exactly. The victim shows ligature abrasions, evidence of dehydration, vomiting, and repeated beating again, both pre and post mortem. In addition to the cuts on her arms and neck, her sides and the backs of her legs were vivisected before she died. There is evidence of an inordinate volume of genital and anal disfiguration."

Dr. Vaziri and Agent Donaldson move to the end of the examination table and stare down between the corpse's legs.

"Ah, Jesus Christ," Steve roars. What the..."

Dr. Vaziri offers, "Female, genital mutilation is practiced in the country in which I was born, primarily by the Shafi'i sect of Sunni Muslim Iranians. My parents recognized in their hearts that such acts are barbaric. To save me from that, they brought me here to this country. Traditionally, female genital mutilation is meant to slow the sex drive of young girls before marriage. This is not that. What you see here Agent Donaldson is neither ritualistic nor in the tradition of Sunni or any other religious or cultural sect. What you are looking at is a complete gutting of this woman's sex organs."

Steve grimaces, "This animal used a knife to extract her vaginal cavity with far less thought than was given to peeling the flesh off of her face."

"Yes, but not just one, Agent Donaldson, but rather two types of knives were used. And it should be noted that our perpetrator could be either male or female..."

"Really?" The thought of a female assailant doing something like this to one of their own never crossed Steve's mind.

Dr. Vaziri continues with her description of the knives used to butcher the victim. "A bayonet was first used ...."

"I knew it." Steve stated aloud satisfied for the affirmation of one fact, the rusted fragment at the scene collected by officer Sweeney was, indeed, from the hilt of a bayonet.

"It had been inserted up and into her through her vaginal cavity. In fact, it is the only weapon with the length and firmness of structure to account for the damage to her internal organs. I asked our lead metallurgist to look at the fragment from the weapon you found at the scene. He's from the same lab we share with the Bureau. His preliminary report states that the bayonet was most likely U.S., post Civil War, given that the production quality of the material."

"The production quality of the material? Really... And the fragments of gold inlay?"

"A swirl, not a flower, most likely a section of a far more detailed design like a regimental Union Army's, ensign."

"Intriguing," Steve offers with veiled skepticism wondering how many civil war reenactments this metalugists had attended? Perhaps too many, he concluded.

"A short, single-edged blade with a sharpened tip like a scalpel was then used to inflict the forearm cuts." The medical examiner, continues. "They're too regular, not haphazard. As I said, they're deliberate. It almost looks like a pattern. Closer examination of the cuts to the anterior forearm revealed that some but not all of the interior walls of the incisions were lightly burnt. They were singed at the top of the carving then regular and deliberate, then singed again as the downstroke was made. This was delicate work performed by an exceptionally disciplined artisan someone who for many years, had a lot of time on their hands."

"And experience?"

"Regretfully, Yes!"

"Semen?"

"None and no sign that the body was wiped down. That's one of the reasons I offered that the perpetrator could be female."

"Did your people check for ejaculatory residue around the scene of the crime? Maybe this freak, if it was a guy, got off in a final celebration of his achievement standing or kneeling a few feet away from the body? I don't know which agencies were at the scene before the Bureau arrived but we wouldn't have that fragment if not for the quick thinking of a local police officer. It would be nice to know if we are looking for a man or a woman."

"I'll send my team back out there within the hour."

"Here. Take this card." Steve offers. "The number on the front is the local office of the FBI. If your people find anything, call that number. They'll know where to find me."

"I will."

Steve turns toward the door to leave. Remembering something he abruptly turns back and asks, "Dr. Vaziri, about the marks on the victim's forearm…"

"Yes?"

"My boss, Agent Westgate, thought that it might be writing of some kind? What do you think?"

Nodding, Dr. Vaziri replies, "The incisions did form a pattern. It's likely that it could be script of some sort. I'll have my lab people take a second look. I'll also ask for a series of photographs from various angles to be taken to specifically detail that section of her arm. I'll send copies to your office. Perhaps if necessary, together we can find an expert to provide further explanation of what if anything those marks may mean."

"Thank you, Doctor. And oh, by the way."

"Yes?"

"Glad you made it to States. You're good. We need more people like you." Steve says as he turns and exits the room.

"I had remarkable parents," Elizabeth Vaziri shouts as the door to the examination room clicks shut behind Steve.

CHAPTER SIXTEEN

Saturday, 8:14 AM

Steve arrives back at the scene of last night's epic event to find Mike, looking as if she'd been there all night. She had, pacing back and forth between where the state-of-the-art, Shell, Super Service station had formerly been to the open field where the mutilated body of a young woman once laid.

Steve stops the vehicle a few feet from where Mike is standing and gets out of the car. Like him, Special Agent Westgate doesn't give into distraction. She doesn't look up. She remains fully engaged, sidestepping down the hillside. Dodging segments of the sidewalk forced upward due to last night's epic explosion, Michaelene is headed back to where the Shell gas station complex once stood, darting in and out of the tall fescue aside the road assessing the area, looking for something... anything.

With no one within their immediate vicinity, Steve tries to flirt a little, sarcastically mocking

Michaelene's disheveled appearance paraphrasing a quote he once happened upon.

"Must a beautiful woman always be more accountable for her steps?"

For a brief moment Mike takes a measure of relief from Steve's digression then shakes her head.

"A woman's guess is much more accurate than a man's certainty," she replies.

"Gertrude Stein?"

"Rudyard Kipling."

"Traitor."

Back to business, together they skillfully tread down the hillside. As they reach the epicenter of last night's explosion, Mike offers, "According to the preliminary findings of the fire marshal and our CSI team, a punctured propane tank may have triggered the explosion."

"Imaginative. Do you smell that?"

"What?"

"Unless there was a kennel or horse farm nearby, which I doubt, that very distinct aroma of burning hair, bloated animal carcasses and rotten eggs you've been inhaling, that's gasoline. The smoke that's turning your gorgeous brown eyes red is oil mixed with its fumes. Propane? No way! It's odorless. Do you think maybe someone is pulling your chain, trying to convince you of something other than the obvious?"

"Isn't that our job, to look beyond the obvious?"

"Point taken. Okay, so tell me what you got."

"Neighbors who've been interviewed said that there had been a gas station on this site for decades. It was torn down and sold over two years ago. Left behind was a very large, commercial propane tank. The new owner, our friend Mr. Clifford, purchased the station and the land around it all except several abandoned acres up the street where the body was found. He tore down the old and erected a series of buildings, turning his acreage into an ultra-modern, service facility with a convenience store, a full-service auto and truck repair facility, tire store, car wash, soda fountain, showers and lounge for the truck drivers..."

"Okay. Slow down. I applaud Clifford's entrepreneurialism but let me tell you something. I stopped on my way here and purchased a thermos and filled it with coffee. It's in the car. Come on. Get off your feet for a few minutes. You're tired."

"I'm fine."

"You may recall back in the day, I gave one hell of a foot massage."

"Steve, you're an old, dear and trusted friend and a remarkably talented agent but I need you to stop trying to be my knight in shining armor. Stop drawing conclusions about me. I'll let you know when and if I am tired."

"Noted. I just..."

Mike continues: "The propane tank was exceptionally large and old. According to the officers who conducted the interviews, the consensus was that it was within a few yards of where the new gas pump isles had been installed."

"Brilliant."

"It was a leftover, an anachronism, waiting to be upgraded, changed out or eliminated before the land and the station was sold to Clifford. It wasn't."

"Obviously."

"And the fire marshal bears that out. It's in his records. One neighbor said that the propane tank had a large gauge affixed at its snout that looked to be the size of a home's electric service meter with a brass coupling at its base. The neighbor, an elderly woman, said she was worried that lighting would one day, Quote, *Hit the damn thing and blow the whole neighborhood to smithereens,* Unquote."

"So prophesized the neighborhood seer."

"I know it sounds a bit wild but before we waste time looking for an international terrorist ring hell-bent on blowing up a suburban Chicago gas station and..."

"Yeah right," Steve interjects, with a snicker.

"...and the largest oil distribution center in the state, we owe it to ourselves to start with the simplest of explanations. There was a considerable amount of lightning reported last night. You're the explosives expert. What do you think?"

"Okay. Copy that. Let's start with the elderly woman's testimony; Lightning? Well, Founding Father B. Franklin tied a key to a kite and captured an electrical charge from a bolt of lightning into a Leyden jar..."

"A what?"

"A capacitor in today's world."

"Got it."

"Are you thinking that the brass coupling acted like Ben's key," Steve asks Mike, "and the propane tank the Leyden jar?"

"The tank took the electrical charge but failed to contain it. That's likely, isn't it?"

"What, then boom?" Steve asks, "Is that what you're thinking?"

"The current operating theory handed to me is that fumes from the propane tank were released by lightning. The lightning caused the boom to which you just referred as it penetrated the earth, leading to the eruption of the service station's underground storage unit."

"Ingenious. Don't know why I didn't come up with that exact conclusion myself."

"Quit being a jerk. Focus."

"Roger that."

"In turn..." as Mike continues with the explanation, "...the eruption of the stored gasoline caused a massive fireball that flowed downhill to the oil refinery."

"Any evidence to support this so-called theory?"

"The fire marshal pulled the owner's storage permit. Along with everyday folks, that station serviced interstate trucking fleets. There were plus or minus 40,000 gallons of gasoline beneath the expanse of that Shell service center at any given point."

"That's more than sufficient to result in surface fissures large enough to expedite the downhill flow. I agree, at least as far as that part of the theory goes. What else do you have?"

"Not much."

"Okay, LPG, or what is more commonly known as propane, it's derived exclusively from the refining of crude oil."

"Which was taking place right over there...just down the street, Mike points. "Proximity to the old refinery made it easy for the previous owner to buy in bulk ..."

"... rather than paying for the privilege of returning multiple times for the same amount of product," Steve offers, finishing Mike's thoughts for her. "Okay. Now what? How does lightning or any other natural phenomena fit in? Are you ready to move on?"

"Not quite. We're missing something!"

"What?"

"The obvious. During my Girl Scout days, I knew one thing for certain."

"Where the Boy Scout camp was located?"

"You can't start a fire without a spark. There is one simple fact that seems to be eluding everyone here. Either lighting or some other yet to be determined ignition source triggered both the propane tank and the underground gasoline storage tanks, simultaneously or..."

"Really?"

"Exactly, the likelihood of that happening stretches the bounds of credulity."

"No, it exceeds all manner of logic because first off," Steve interjects, "lighting doesn't penetrate the earth surface and it sure as hell isn't going to penetrate cement storage tank ten feet below it."

Mike, continuing the exercise in deductive reasoning offers, "Or what is far more likely, two separate events occurred, one that independently triggered the propane tank the other the underground storage facility. That is, if we're still considering that tank as the first step in the equation. Two bolts of lightning, however, working cooperatively with each other is quite obviously..."

"Absurd."

"Correct, and that moves us away from a naturally occurring phenomenon to something ..."

"Man-made."

"Precisely." Michaelene acknowledges.

"Bravo. Thank you. So, can any of your brain trust around here describe for us the relationship between cause and effect?"

"I'm not certain I follow?"

"Not the difference, I'm not asking for that. I'm asking for the relationship as in one and one makes two?"

"That's just it. There must be at least three dozen investigators from more than a half dozen agencies including our own here on site. They presented me with what they qualified as a loose-knit theory."

"That's putting it mildly," scoff Steve.

"Yet no one even bothered to offer even a really good guess," Michaelene counters, "if not lighting, what else could have initiated the explosion? What other tools, what other means were on site to set it off...or whether the propane tank initiated the explosion or whether it too was a victim erupting after the fact?"

"Nor how one event could possibly have triggered the other. Where's the connection?"

"Exactly. Mike contends. "You're right. That's exactly it. It's the 'and' in your one and one equation Steve, that no one here is apparently willing to address."

"Okay. Put aside what you've been told. What's your take on all this?"

141

CHAPTER SEVENTEEN (Tick tock)

"I'm an attorney and an FBI 'brick' agent, those of us who pound the streets. What I am not is a high school science teacher. You're the closest thing to that around here. So go ahead. It's still your turn. Give it to me in lay terms."

"Copy that. I'll try." The adult side of Steve's analytical mind steps up to the plate, "Think toxic fumes and gasoline vacuum-sealed in a cement mixer. The two alone can be stirred until hell freezes over with zero effect, right?"

"Until friction is somehow introduced. Sure. Of course. Agreed."

"In order for an explosion to be generated, there would have to have been a third element, an ignition source like friction as you suggested tossed into the mix. But how, and from where? That's the question. Even if the cement walls of the underground gasoline storage units were somehow breached, penetration by fumes from the propane tank alone even under accelerated conditions, would not cause the liquid to ignite."

"You're right. "A" or "one" assumedly, is the propane tank. "B" is the yet to be determined variable, the ignition source. "C" is obvious. The "effect" is "C" and we're standing in the middle of it right now with our proverbial thumbs up our proverbial posteriors struggling to make sense of what, a'loose-knit theory?' It's not enough, Steve. We're missing something."

"Listen, these people around here don't know what to make of you yet. You're a woman in a man's role."

"I'll pretend not to be offended."

"I meant it when I said to you earlier that you did a great job getting everyone suited up and on the same page. You centralized authority and delegated responsibility quickly and effectively."

"I'm grateful for your approval."

"You did what was needed to be done, but now…"

"Now what?"

"So, whoever provided you with this half-baked theory and if it were me, I'd be off in a corner somewhere sweating bullets trying to fill in the blanks. Don't forget, you're the new kid on the block and I'll tell you straight up. You're beautiful, you're strong and everyone here is a bit intimidated by you."

With a touch of feminine guile, Mike offers, "Except you, of course."

"You're not the little girl I once knew."

"I was never the little girl you thought you knew," Michaelene sternly replies.

"This propane theory that you've been handed is most likely just that and nothing more."

"So, where do we go from here?"

"When I was first told of the magnitude of this weenie roast to which you were kind enough to invite me, I began formulating a list of possibilities."

"I'm listening."

"During my flight in, I got on the horn and asked a flyboy buddy of mine, a guy I use to drink with in-country who's now the base commander at Beale, to cross-check Scott AFB, Great Lakes Naval Air Station and with any/all air traffic controllers, military and civilian to identify if anyone lost their luggage over this area last night. He reported back just before my ride touched down that all horses have been in the stable for the last 24 and every stitch of luggage has been accounted for."

"You mentally just slipped back into a time and place where I could not have possibly recognized you. Exactly how would you like me to interpret that litany of macho metaphors?"

"Flyboys are a different breed. They don't know how to get down and dirty but they are exceptionally gifted when it comes to one thing."

"Their numbers are always tight, right? I know. I used to date one. So, no miscellaneous airplanes, engine parts, or bombs falling from the sky, hit ground zero, last night. Okay. Got it.

Finally, one piece of good news."

"Lady, you've graduated from suitcase bombs to whatever the hell happened here. Look around. This whole place looks like the Ho Chi Minh Trail after a handful of our B-52 bombers unloaded on it."

"I can see that."

"So, we're back to square one."

"No, not quite. We haven't left there yet. We do know one thing for certain, it wasn't a bomb casually placed by the gas station pumps."

"And we know that how?"

"It's what the fire marshal said and how he said it. I like that guy. He's been around. I trust his judgment. He said the explosion began underground. That's what I keep hearing, playing over and over in the back of my mind. He said, "It began underground.""

"I agree."

"That was quick. How do you know that?"

"I've been trying to tell you. Our copter passed through a debris field somewhere around 300 feet above the epicenter on the way in."

"And how does that factor in?"

"Ah, Christ." Flushed with exasperation, it hit Steve for the first time since he stepped off the helicopter. He is dealing with a woman he has loved with all his heart since they were kids, now his boss no less, but hasn't touched nor shared more than a few, brief narratives with her over the past decade and a half. Now suddenly without any time to prepare, not even a god damn dress rehearsal, he's been thrust back into her world, a woman who doesn't grasp the short-hand explanation of how a fucking explosion occurs. Recognizing the need to provide the lady he loves a fundamental explanation, Steve stammers, uttering, "Explosions..."

"What? What's the matter with you? You're mumbling."

Now finding his heart, soul and every texture of his being especially his near-exploding brain cavity sucked into a swirling menagerie of mixed signals and memories running through every pore of his being, Steve blurts out,

"I'm trying to explain!"

"Great. I'm here. I'm not going anywhere."

Turning back to his boss, Steve, faces her conjuring up what he hopes will pass as a practical explanation, one he hopes will also explain his behavior:

"It's only been a little over thirteen hours since I got the call from you. I'm concerned about creating another false-positive until we've obtained more evidence."

Mike continues, "Granted, but as you first pointed out time is not our ally. I get where you're going with this. The idea of a naturally occurring event leading to an erupting propane tank above ground that, in turn, resulted in an explosion underground seems far-fetched or at best, leaves far too much room for..."

"Other intervening factors?"

"Yes. Still, I don't want to wind up with egg on the Bureau's face or mine."

"You'd still look beautiful."

"I must know with absolute certainty before considering other alternatives that this whole cataclysmic event wasn't the result of some naturally occurring phenomenon. Is there something else, something we may have overlooked?

With that, the adult side of Steve's brain steps up once again, settling back in for the count. "Okay, let's thoroughly analyze the nature angle. There are essentially two types of naturally occurring explosions," Steve offers. "One is exothermic. The other is endothermic. Simply put, its heat either being released or absorbed."

"Thank you for that."

"An exothermic explosion would cause large particles of debris to be forced upward to considerable heights like an erupting volcano, providing the debris field the Bureau's pilot and I encountered over the scene. Generally, an exothermic explosion is caused by the subject matter or system, in this case, the underground gasoline storage tanks absorbing heat from a concentrated source like sunlight, over a long period of time. The explosion took place last night. Lightning is an impulse of heat and it stops as I said, at the surface of the earth. Lighting alone may have provided cover for some other act but lighting alone wouldn't be enough. Something else caused that "exothermic" style of explosion."

"And the other? Mike asks."

"A naturally occurring, endothermic explosion but that doesn't fit."

"Why not?"

"Think about an egg boiling in a pot of water. As heat rises and the egg is left unattended the egg bursts. Where would 40,000 gallons of gasoline buried ten feet underground in cement vaults gain access to such an inordinate amount of heat to cause it to burst? It wouldn't. It couldn't. There are no active volcanoes or stream of molten lava anywhere around here. It would be impossible. And to go back to the egg, when it explodes, it would burst out not up."

"Wow, I'm impressed. You really do know a lot about how things blow up."

"My point is," Steve concludes, "there is no way last night's explosion was brought about by natural causes, lightning or anything else. We've covered the bases. Now, can we move on?"

"Okay, got it. You're right, no natural causation. I agree. But…" With that, Mike stops then

offers: "Let's do this. Let's stretch the realm of possibilities out all the way." Michaelene is mentally segmenting pieces of yesterday's crimes - those in which she was once deeply immersed - looking to fit any portion that may be applicable into how last night's explosion at Clifford's service complex may have occurred.

"What about a large container of C-4 somehow getting on or near the premises?"

"Towed perhaps, by some innocuous tractor-trailer rig?" Steve inserts trying not to be condescending. Still, he couldn't help himself. A slight smirk flashed across his face.

"With the station's security cameras smart guy, being distorted?" Mike caught the brief smirk.

"And no eyewitnesses on or near the site? Are you serious?"

"Just spitballing here but yes, let's try it on for size."

"Still, more out, less up."

"What?"

"That's how the explosion and the resulting debris field would have occurred. And it would have taken a ton— no, that's not true. Better yet, think of it this way. See those railroad tracks over there?"

"Where?"

"Over there by the remains of the oil refinery?"

"Okay?"

"See the boxcar on the end?"

"Yes."

"Take a guess, Mike. What's its dimensions?"

"I'd say forty-five to fifty feet long by some eleven to twelve feet, high. Why?"

Steve offers, "Think of that railroad boxcar parked on the surface immediately above the gasoline storage tanks filled floor to ceiling with vials of pure nitroglycerin."

"Not a pleasant thought."

"Even that would not be enough to provide the over-whelming amount of downward thrust necessary to first penetrate then force up those sealed, cement storage tanks volcano-style. A shock wave emanating from our hypothetical boxcar would go down but then rapidly dissipate outward. It would definitely not provide a concrete debris field hundreds of feet above the epicenter. Leakage, obviously. Crumbling of the walls of the cement containers, sure quite likely but ignition, hell no. No way."

"And even with that," Mike adds, "What is the source of ignition?"

"And?"

"And exactly how that ignition source entered the gasoline storage tanks ten feet below ground."

"Affirmative! Nothing placed on the surface could have caused this mess," Steve concludes adding, "Respectfully, the fire marshal was only half right. The explosion originated beneath the earth's surface but …" Now Mike finishes Steve's thought…

"…but inside the cement tanks."

"Bingo! Something somehow got inside those concrete storage containers triggering the explosion."

"And it's that 'something, somehow' on which we need to focus. So, now we're there. Now were back to square one."

Musing, Steve mutters the word, "Entropy."

"What did you say? I missed that."

"I said, 'entropy'. With an uncharacteristic deep sigh Steve offers, "It's a word used to describe the level of disorder or randomness in any thermodynamic environment." Shaking his head, he continues, "I've witnessed my share of firestorms in war zones but never... never anything like what were facing here."

"Wow. I haven't heard the term entropy for fifteen years and then it was in a different context."

"I didn't know it fit any other context?"

"Political philosophy 341, Immanuel Kant, in reference to the general pace of the universe rushing to destruction accelerated by man."

"Nature and/or the universe as a whole, as we just concluded, had nothing to do with this thermodynamic cluster fuck. It was clearly man-made. And there was no rush to destroy. This was well thought out."

"But..?"

"And I'm certain," Steve offers as he leans in, placing his forehead against Mike's, "our eighteenth century philosopher Mr. Kant, had nothing to do with it."

Exasperated, Mike places both hands on Steve's shoulders and gently pushes away. "Turn around. Walk back up the hill with me. Maybe we can gain a clearer or even perhaps, a new perspective of this whole 'cluster'…as you put it, from up there."

"I got a box seat view from inside the 'copter. Not pretty, lady…not pretty."

CHAPTER EIGHTEEN

While they continue to walk and talk, Steve reveals to Mike what he discovered in Frank Clifford's military records file... his 201 jacket. Mike pulls her focus away from the dual crime scene - and while listening – begins to speculate, wondering if Frank Clifford could indeed, be their prime suspect.

She turns to Steve and asks, "Give me your take on this guy. He's a vet. He has the training, the capability. He could have pulled all this off?"

"And he could have hired someone else to do it but I don't think so," Steve suggests.

"As I said, he has both the experience and the expertise. Like you, he's a combat vet. He knows how to kill and he no doubt knows how to set a charge?"

"He's methodical and he learned years ago, how to survive. No question about that. He's also someone who, in my opinion..."

"That's what I asked you for."

"Clifford is a throwback to a bygone era. He's someone who lives by a strict moral code—his own."

"Destroying that woman's life?"

"You see. That's just it. I mean, I know this guy. I can read him. To kill a woman, to mutilate her in such a fashion, good Christ, fuck no. No way. That's what tells me it couldn't have been him in either case or if..."

"...The two are somehow linked?"

"And even if they are not, both are acts of a coward. Clifford is anything but. Having read his military record, Clifford is a strictly "by the book" kind of a guy. I don't see him going off the reservation for any reason. If he's facing an overwhelming challenge of any sort, even an inevitable failure, I'm convinced he wouldn't run. He never has. That's who he is. It's in his DNA. I'd bet my career on it. He is not the kind to bring the house down on himself."

Mike and Steve agree that at this stage of the investigation, they don't see Frank as a person of interest, either for the brutal killing of the woman or the destruction of his business. They also agree that on the off chance that they are wrong, to keep Frank on the suspect list as they continue to piece together the cause or causes of these two epic events.

Now overlooking both crime scenes, Agents Westgate and Donaldson are picking at the ground beneath their feet, scrounging about, still hoping to find something they or CSI may have missed.

CHAPTER NINETEEN

Suddenly Steve shouts, "Mike! Get down." Ripping his forty-five automatic out of its shoulder holster he dives to the ground. Hammer backed, locked and loaded, the Vietnam-era combat veteran ends his evasive maneuver in prone-firing position, head up, covering Michaelene who is still kneeling a few feet away. With the sun at his back the man in a dark brown suit encroaching on the crime scene is approaching Donaldson at a determined pace. The abandoned lot's overgrown plant-life has wrapped Steve in a blanket of odorous, long-stemmed, weeds. Clearing his field of vision, he brushes them aside.

"Oh my god, sir! Please don't shoot! It's me, Agent Bowers. You remember me, don't you?" shouts Andy Bowers, Rookie FBI Agent from Iowa, arriving at Illinois' Belmont-Cragin crime scene.

Donaldson rises to his feet. "BOWERS! What the hell are you doing here? Didn't you see the crime scene tape? I SPECIFICALLY told each of the local officers NOT to let ANYONE in!"

"I showed that patrolman over there my credentials."

"Holy shit, Bowers. I don't care if you showed him a picture of your Aunt Betty's titties. I damn near put a round through that thick skull of yours. What the…" As he tries to temper down, Steve offers; "So why are you here, Bowers?"

"Our boss, well, mine too, SAC Gomez, ordered me to hand deliver the contents of this envelope to you."

"What's in it, Bowers?" Donaldson asks.

"I wouldn't know sir. It's addressed to you."

"Do you mean you drove all this way some three hours or more and didn't peek? Not once?"

"Sir, no sir, as I said, it's addressed to you."

Bowers turns his attention to Michaelene Westgate, examining her up and down, failing to recognize that she is the widely heralded Special Agent in Charge of the Bureau's Northern Illinois Office.

"Wow, well, hello there. Where did he get you? You're very attractive. And quite tall."

Donaldson orders, "Give her the package, Bowers."

"But sir, it's marked "Eyes Only." That means your eyes only, sir. I know you know that sir. I don't want to get either of us into any trouble. I read your jacket. You were an Army Ranger. I know that you occasionally bend the rules but…"

Michaelene plays into the scene adopting the role of the helpless heroine. Loosening her elastic hair tie, she runs her fingers through her deep, dark mane. Having smoothed out its tangles her hair cascades, flowing gently, settling gently just below her shoulder blades. With a toss of her head, she offers, "Ah, come on Agent Donaldson, Please sir, can we get back to what we were doing?"

Donaldson steps behind Agent Bowers, turning the 29-year-old to directly face "Mike."

"Andy Bowers, allow me to introduce you to Special Agent in Charge of the Illinois Bureau of our beloved Federal Bureau of Investigation, Miss Michaelene Westgate."

Bowers' face turns blush red. He turns to Steve. Then back to Michaelene then again, to Steve. This time with an "...Oh sh..., I'm so sorry. I thought she was your assistant, a staffer, or secretary or something. My apologies Agent Westgate. I'm a CPA, ledgers and stuff. I don't get out much...I mean for the job, you know? The Bureau wanted me to..."

"Play delivery boy?" Donaldson offers, finishing the young agent's sentence.

"Actually, Sir, to tell the truth, I volunteered. I was thinking that if I had a chance to watch you in action that I might ...."

"Get killed? Okay. You did your job. Mission accomplished. And by the way Bowers, I'm going to insist that Gomez makes certain you attend the next session of our beloved Bureau's new female sensitivity training course at Quantico."

"Oh no sir, I can't."

"Excuse me?"

"You see, sir, I'm in the Air Force Reserve. My upcoming 90-day deployment conflicts with the dates set for that course."

"Don't worry. I have some pull at the Academy. I'll see to it that you get a front row seat at the next scheduled session. And by the way Agent Bowers, there's a new thing out called soap and water. If you ever appear in this State or any other again smelling like a pack of dead skunks, I'll have you written up on charges of Conduct Unbecoming an Agent."

"But sir, respectfully, I—"

"And far more importantly, if I ever hear even the slightest rumor of you disrespecting any women for any reason, in any way again, I'll make it my personal mission to have you run out of the FBI on a rail with your CPA pencils crammed up your ass. Open your eyes. A new world is unfolding. Stop acting like an oversexed Neanderthal. Adapt and overcome. Am I communicating, Rookie?"

"Yes, sir." Agent Bowers humbly drops his head, turns and exits the crime scene, passing by the patrolman who had first lifted the tape to let him in, offering only a brief shaking of his head.

Steve turns to Michaelene. "Do you think I was too hard on the kid?"

"No, not at all. Of course, I can't see it," Michaelene offers teasingly, "but for some reason he actually holds you in high regard. Having handed him a life lesson, my guess is, he'll learn from it. At some point let Bowers know that I will forget that the incident ever occurred."

"Roger that."

"To be honest, I'm rather proud of you, Steevie," offers 'Steevie's boss as she playfully pushes on Donaldson's shoulder.

"I see that even you've matured quite a bit. An "over-sexed Neanderthal," really? Was that a flashback moment for you?" she offers with a smile. "And by the way, you owe that fellow Iowa agent of yours an apology."

"You're kidding. But you just said…okay, for what?"

"The stench you reamed young Bowers for wasn't coming from him. It came from the weeds he trampled through as he made his way over to us. All anyone has to do is brush up against those wildflowers and they give off that choking odor. You, Mr. *Napoleon Solo*, rolled in them, very

Man from Uncle-ish of you, by the way. Thanks for covering my back but please do me a favor?"

"Rub your feet?"

"Stand downwind from me for awhile."

"Cute, sophomoric but cute."

"And, before I forget, thank you." Michaelene pauses then offers, "Good to know that chivalry wasn't canceled along with that TV show. So, what's in the envelope?"

Agent Donaldson removes a pearl-handled, switchblade from his jacket pocket, one he picked up at a Saigon 'gift shop' in trade for his U.S. Army issued, K-bar knife. He snaps open its blade.

"Standard Bureau issue, I take it?" Michaelene snidely asks knowing full well the answer.

Steve replies, "You're not going to report me for carrying an unauthorized weapon, are you?"

"I'll think about it and give you my answer when we put this case to rest."

Steve carefully inserts the knife's blade, tearing open the heavily-padded, 8x11-inch, manila envelope, removing its contents. He hands the note enclosed from SAC Gomez to Michaelene. Upon investigating the contents of the envelope, Steve extracts a padded evidence bag. Inside, stretched out and pegged on a thin piece of plywood, is what is identified in the accompanying correspondence as the forearm flesh of a woman with similar burnt etchings as the first.

The note from Gomez reads:

Steve, Yesterday, I reviewed the inter-bureau memo sent from the Northern Illinois office. In the case of your mutilated murder victim, there has been another with a similar MO. A bag containing the severed breasts of a woman, her scalp, and the remains of her vaginal region, were found on the St. Ambrose University campus here in Davenport. A white van with what one eye-witness identified as a partially removed, University of Chicago stencil on the driver's side door was seen leaving St. Ambrose campus from the service road by the football field. The equipment manager, the son of a South Vietnamese émigré, provided an eye-witness description of the driver. He described him as Japanese, a man in his early to mid-'40's, approximately 5'6"5'8" with a stocky build. The woman's forearm now in your possession, was found hanging from a wired gate near the coaching staff's locker room approximately 500 yards from where the plastic bag containing her remains was found. We determined that the victim is an Angelina Rodriquez, an Illinois resident, a hotel manager in Rock Island, who disappeared four nights ago. According to the memo, the Chicago medical examiner's office has already undertaken an autopsy of your victim. As you know, they are better equipped than ours here in Iowa, to handle any type of extensive, comparative analysis if one is needed. For the above-stated, I had this package couriered directly to you. We checked. There were no prints on either item. My best to both you and SAC Westgate. Good hunting. Signed, Joe.

"What?" Mike starring at Steve, asks. "His best to us both? I heard Gomez didn't have a compassionate bone in his body? Did you get him laid before you left?"

Steve ignores Mike's comment. "We have a serial killer on our hands, Agent Westgate."

"Agreed…but"

"But what? It's evident." Steve is growing incensed.

Mike submits: "Yes, perhaps, but only in part."

Steve notices a sudden wrinkle of curiosity rising across Michaelene's brow as he asks, "What just crossed your mind?"

"An Aesop's fable."

"What, *The Boy Who Cried Wolf*, he derides?"

"No, *The Scorpion and the Frog*."

"You and your father used to love tossing those ancient Greek morality lessons around."

"Dad would say that how human beings interact and why they do what they do as a result, are the hardest of life's riddles to solve. When I complained to him about you or Danny—"

"Who the hell was Danny?"

"Dad never lectured or told me what to do. Rather, he encouraged me to use Aesop's creatures as a guide to discover for myself the answers I needed. My weekly allowance was based upon how well I could analyze those 'morality lessons' and apply them to my life. I could make up twenty bucks a week if Dad approved the conclusions I reached. If you recall, I'm the one who paid for the hotel room we shared on prom night."

Steve is upset. He doesn't get it and frankly doesn't care. "This is hardly the time for a retrospective? Let's focus on what's at hand, okay?"

"I am."

"You lost me."

"It's just a hunch…"

"That female intuition thing again?"

"Okay, let me put it out on the table for you right here, right now." Michaelene offers. "Think back. When we were both kids in high school, I was geeky and withdrawn, right?"

"Good god you really were, but what does that have to do with—?"

"You, on the other hand, were quite frankly, the most gorgeous human being I had ever laid eyes on."

"Oh, please."

"You were All-American, our high school's quarterback and Main South's student body president. Every time you spoke at a pep rally, half the girls in that school would have readily dropped their panties for you."

"I was never into bimbos."

"That's part of what I'm trying to tell you. You're a classy guy. You have a strong moral compass."

"I bet you didn't think so when you came over and sat down next to me at lunch and I blurted out that ridiculous line?"

Michaelene mimics Steve's voice, *"Oh, oh Pardon me miss. Are you playing with my leg?"*

"Yes, exactly. Oh god. Do you really have to remember everything?"

"Having gawked at you for months, I finally mustered the courage to rush across the lunchroom floor and snag an empty seat next to you before some other girl took it. I purposely dropped my purse to the floor between us so I could reach down and brushed my hand down your leg."

"You did that on purpose?"

"I needed to know what kind of young man you really were and I wasn't willing to rely on intuition, female or otherwise then or now."

"Okay, so?"

"When I touched your leg, you didn't freak out. You didn't make a scene or bark out some rude remark to your friends. You were cool. You handled it well. You were respectful."

"I was?"

"You just looked over at me and shyly uttered those memorable words."

"I didn't stop to think. I just blurted it out."

"Under different circumstances, it would have made a great pick up line."

"Okay, well, if we're putting it all out there you must know, I was in awe of you."

"No, wait. Let me finish. I'm trying to make a point here."

"And so am I. When you stood up on that table in the cafeteria the week before and publicly shamed three of my teammates for bullying that down-syndrome kid, I was blown away particularly by how eloquently you put them down. You did the right thing—something I wish I had had the guts to do. And if you must know, I wouldn't let anyone take that chair next to me for the week thereafter." Steve abruptly laughs aloud as a memory from days past enters his mind. "Tall and skinny and those god-awful braces you had to wear, you really were one of the geeks."

"Thank you."

"The truth be told. After that memorable speech you gave, I saw you very differently. Still, like an ass, I didn't have the strength to put aside my rep and come over and talk to you. I was hoping you would finally make the first move and you did!"

"Your interest in me boosted my confidence and sky-rocketed my self-esteem."

"And you made me recognize that the world is a far bigger place than a football stadium. Don't get me wrong, I love the game but when you stood up on a table in the cafeteria in front of everyone and gave it to those guys, I gotta tell yeah…"

"Steve, please."

"No, listen. Don't you remember? In a matter of seconds, the whole place fell silent. Hundreds of kids hung on your every word. Hell, I didn't even know your name then but as I watched and listened to what you had to say, it was like a newsreel playing in my head featuring human suffering around the world, interspersed with President Kennedy's "*One Man Can Make a Difference and Every Man Should Try*" speech. From that moment, I simply couldn't see myself living life just playing a game. I felt a responsibility to help others in every way possible. You really rocked my world that day, little girl. You changed my life."

"Thank you. And that's exactly what I'm trying to tell you. You and I shared at that time what is clinically known as a mutualistic symbiotic relationship. We needed one another then."

"… and we used one another albeit inadvertently, to our own advantage."

"Like the Scorpion and the Frog."

"No predator was going to hassle that frog with a scorpion on its back, right? And if someone hassled you ..."

"…and the scorpion would not have been able to make it across the waterway without the frog?

"Exactly. Okay, I get it, but if I remember that fable correctly, the scorpion ultimately kills the Frog. Ah, shit, am I the frog in this case? Well, if I have to go I feel best that it be at your hand."

"Don't be silly. I'm drawing a comparison. Hear me out. It's pertinent to this case."

"Go for it."

"Within the past 48 hours, we've been handed two grotesquely mutilated bodies and an explosion that essentially wiped out half of a town."

"Granted."

"This whole thing, doesn't it strike you as being a bit too symmetrical... a bit too well-ordered?"

"What do you mean?"

"Two entities, a scorpion and a frog forged a partnership and together became part of a singular process."

"To serve a mutual objective?"

"Yes. In this case, however, it feels like we're being served a pre-packaged scene."

"What does that mean, exactly?"

"It strikes me that someone is intent upon making us see each of the events that have occurred only in one way, separately - one at a time - rather than perhaps, each working together in a collaborative fashion as part of a greater whole."

"You're right. Perhaps that's true if I really understood what the hell you're talking about but if I may be so bold," Steve sets forth sarcastically, "allow me to suggest that we focus right now on what's right here in front of us. I want to end the existence of this psychopath, male or female, before it destroys the life of yet another human being."

"You're a law enforcement officer. You're no longer a soldier."

"You weren't at the medical examiner's office. You didn't see what this—"

"Do I have to send you back to Iowa, Lieutenant?"

"Ah fuck it. No! Okay. Got it. Understood. Sorry, Mike."

"There may be a bigger picture here, one we have yet to see. One we may not be able to ignore. What if the butchering of the two women and the explosion at Clifford's gas station are somehow related but in a different way for a different reason?"

"You've lost me. You've repeatedly argued that they are not related?"

"Officially, no, they are not. There is no hard evidence to suggest that they are but—"

"Where are you going with this?"

"Think of it this way. What if there was a deliberately staged interaction between the three events - the explosion and the two mutilated women - intending to overwhelm the Bureau and local law enforcement drawing our collective attention away from...?"

"You saw the remains of that woman in the field," Steve interjects. "You know that there is no way she was killed by that explosion."

"Remember, that the frog provided the scorpion the means to cross the waterway by allowing it to hitch a ride on its back."

"What?"

"Bear with me. Hear me out. What if the butchering of these two women and the explosion in Belmont-Cragin together are the frog?"

"Working together as what, a unit?"

Yes, that jointly, the women and the explosion are one in the same, a, collective - a collaborative enterprise - forming their own mutualistic, symbiotic relationship."

"To what end?"

"To serve as a distraction to something yet to occur, some greater event?"

"On his back?" Steve is still lost.

"Yes, exactly. Given the bizarre nature of both crimes, I can't dismiss the feeling that someone - person or persons yet known - may be out there pulling our strings, staging all of this, both events merely as a performance in advance of some far greater event...something imminent."

"Something bigger than blowing up half a town?"

"Conceptually, yes."

"What could be more—ah, shit!" As a vision of this morning's news broadcast crossed his mind, Steve answered his own question. "A nuclear explosion—the scorpion's sting."

"I represented the Bureau at an Atomic Energy Commission hearing at the governor's office in Springfield, earlier this year."

"And?"

"The AEC wants to extend the life of the Dresden nuclear power plant by another sixty years."

"That's the one that's been in the papers a lot recently, the one that the locals linked to the Belmont-Cragin, explosion. Seems like it is always having problems."

"Yes but it provides electric service to over a million people here in Chicago and throughout the northern half of Illinois. The AEC's argument was that its safety is assured. Their physical security personnel with whom I directly met, struck me as less convincing."

"Why, because the condescending dickheads didn't like a beautiful young woman questioning them?"

"Because they were a bit too quick to agree with their scientist's assessment."

"How many nuclear power plants are there in Illinois?"

"Three, the Quad cities facility in Cordova, Zion Nuclear power plant off the coast of Lake Michigan, and the Dresden plant, approximately thirty miles from downtown Chicago, and half that distance from Belmont-Cragin."

"Why imminent?"

"How long had the first woman been dead before the explosion?"

"Approximately twenty-four hours, according to the medical examiner's preliminary findings."

"And the magnitude of the public impact of both events?"

"Epic and growing."

"Set aside physical proximity and the state of the woman's body for a moment and consider the timing of both events?"

"One right after the other."

"Thus my definition of imminent. We've got to figure out what exactly is happening and we've got to do so quickly to avert yet another epic disaster; one potentially far more destructive than the first."

"Lady, you know that my admiration for you is endless but I have no idea how the hell you come up with this stuff. We have a killer, a butchering psychopath right here in front of us. We need to focus on that and put the world of the theoretic on the shelf for the time being."

"Okay, but tell me one thing?"

"What?"

"Why did the scorpion kill the frog?"

"I have no idea."

"Simple. It's in his nature."

CHAPTER TWENTY

9:18 a.m.

"Time to have a talk with the man?"

"Agreed, and you're right."

"About what?" Steve, asks.

"It has only been a few hours. Firefighters are still struggling to get each of the secondary fires under control. We need to give our people time to do their jobs. I need to call Fire Marshal Sullivan. I need to speak with him, directly."

"Regarding?"

"Geiger counters. I saw one in the back of the Hazmat vehicle I was sitting in while waiting for your whirlybird to land."

"Whirlybird?"

"I want to know how many Geiger counters Marshall Sullivan has and how many he can get his hands on…and I want a list of when each was last calibrated."

"You're going for an independent evaluation of last night's explosion—nice! I like it. It's underhanded and surreptitious as hell but—"

"And no doubt that's why you like it. I'm confident that the Fire Marshal will work with us on this. We need a preliminary assessment - something tangible, something as independent and transparent as possible - something to hold up to the public that will either validate or dispel the rumor regarding the Dresden nuclear power plant's role in last night's drama. The time needed for the feds from the AEC to show up to provide a thorough analysis is going to do nothing but heighten public anxiety. There is only one readily available means of getting the answers we need before tonight's town hall meeting."

"A few firefighters with Geiger counters under their heavy coats hiking from Clifford's service station to the oil depot and back. If the Dresden plant was involved they won't need to go further than that. Smart. Good call. A plus or minus radiation read, will —"

"Will get us exactly what we need. As you said when you first arrived, the public wants answers now. The Atomic Energy Commission need to take a serious look at the Dresden plant but not today, not before the fact…"

"After the fact if at all."

"Once we have at least a preliminary idea of what we're dealing with we'll know how to move forward. I'm not going to trust the opinion of those responsible for the operation of the plant to provide the answers we and the public deserve."

"If the Bureau gets wind of us stepping on the toes of another federal agency, your temporary promotion may be more temporary than planned."

"Thanks, but my career is the least of my concerns right now. I want each of the two major breaches - the one at the gas station and the one at the oil depot - and every inch in between along the fissure line, to be carefully walked and measured for even the slightest sign of radio-activity."

"Let's hope that all report unremarkable readings."

"It's 9:17 a.m. I'll call the office and ask them to locate Marshall Sullivan, asking him to stand by for a call from me in exactly twenty. I'll also ask Edwards to contact the Clifford residence and set an appointment for both of us with them for twelve noon."

"Don't forget to return Clifford's driver's license when we're there."

"Roger that."

"You may remember, just like you, I grew up around here. Park Ridge at best is no more than twenty minutes away. Why the delay?"

"I want to stop by my place for a change of clothes and a quick shower."

"May I watch?"

"You lost your chance, Romeo, a long time ago."

"I was just a narrow-minded kid, parochial as hell. You can't hold that against me forever?"

"Try me."

Descending the hilltop side by side, Steve briefly stops to remove his suit coat, shaking off the debris from the field of weeds. Tossing it over his shoulder, Steve hurries to catch up with Mike as the two agents jump into one of the now nine, unmarked black sedans at the bottom of the grade and head to the Clifford residence with a scheduled quick stop at Mike's home.

While waiting in the car in front of his boss's house, Steve opens his valise and flips through the borrowed stack of folders from the Fire Marshall, rereading Frank Clifford's 201 personnel file, making notes in the Bureau's folder on both.

10:26 a.m.:

Steve checks his watch. It's been well over an hour. Still no sign of Michaelene.

"Oh come on, woman, geez!" Steve pronounces.

Frustrated, he gets out of the black sedan and bolts up the four flight of steps to Michaelene's front porch, noticing its heavy wood-and-metal framed door is ajar. He stops rings the door bell then knocks. No answer. Drawing his service weapon, he peaks in through the crack offered by the unsecured entryway. Slowly pushing the door open just enough to allow access, he steps in.

Breathing deeply yet playing it calm, Special Agent Donaldson, the Bureau's lead, small arms and explosive expert, peers into his boss's home, a turn of the last century, three bedroom, two bath, eighteen hundred square foot, bi-level.

"Hey, Mike! It's me. Are you okay? Where are you?"

Donaldson inches his way down the first-floor hallway. Entering the kitchen, he stops to turn the volume down on the portable TV sitting atop the counter. At the other end of the kitchen, a kettle is steeping on the stove, its steam permeating the air. With weapon at the ready, Steve turns the corner entering an adjacent corridor. There he confronts a magnificently designed old-world banister, its steps leading up to the second-floor landing. Around it, he notices his boss's discarded clothing, including her underwear. Looking up Steve hears the upstairs shower running. That was soon followed by an all-to-familiar voice:

"What the hell do you think you're doing?" Michaelene screams as she exits the master bedroom's shower wearing a thick white bath towel hurriedly draped around her. "Get out of here!"

Steve turns and looks away. "You left your pager and that new Motorola Dyna-Tac gizmo in the car. They've both been going off continually. I've been out there for more than an hour. I became concerned. I thought..."

"Okay. Fine. Thank you. Now, get out of here. Go wait in the car. I'll be out in a minute."

Another twenty minutes pass before Mike emerges from her home. Sliding into the passenger side of the Bureau's Ford, she is wearing an FBI stenciled, bleach-white, T-Shirt beneath a smartly tailored, navy blue, summer sports coat, khaki pants and black, flat heel, slip-on shoes.

"I dozed off in the shower. Thank you for well—for being discreet."

"Respecting both you and your privacy has never been a challenge for me but hey."

"What?"

"Do me a favor next time?"

"What's that?"

"Lock your front door when you go inside."

"I always do."

"Not this time. That's how I got in."

"Well, that was sloppy. I must have been more tired than I thought. Glad it was just you."

"Yeah, me too." Steve offered, thinking to let the issue drop. After all, Mike was right. She'd been up for the past twenty-four. She was in a hurry. She thought she'd secured her front door. Going through her regular routine she didn't stop to double check. That fit. It was logical. Still, there was something odd, something that troubled Steve. The clothes that Michaelene had previously been wearing weren't randomly discarded. They had been folded and laid out neatly and placed purposefully on the stairs beneath the banister. "Not sloppy." Steve mumbled aloud.

"What?"

At this point, Steve rather wisely didn't want to get into a discussion that had anything to do with Mike's clothes or in particular, how she may have taken them off.

"It's nothing. Let's go."

11:48 a.m.

The heavy traffic of Highway 294 on the outskirts of the Chicago suburb of Park Ridge virtually disappears as the two FBI agents turn onto Grand Boulevard, the upscale community's premiere, residential street.

Steve offers, "That's it. 424 Grand. We're early. Let's find a station and fill this gas guzzler up. I don't trust its gauge."

"The last thing we want to do," Mike adds with a humbling smile, "is embarrass the Bureau by running out of gas in this neighborhood."

Mike and Steve circle the block, passing by the childhood home of Hillary Rodham Clinton, the wife of the newly elected Governor of Arkansas. They stop at the local gas station, a Shell. Mike pumps the gas. Steve cleans the windshield and checks the tire pressure.

Mike offers, "Illinois Bell introduced the first ever Cellular Mobile Phone last month. It's clearer than our standard, Motorola two-way. That was Agent Edwards calling."

"What did he want, help getting his panties out of a bind?"

"He got a message from your boss Gomez, in Iowa. Gomez said I can keep you as long as I need. I don't think he likes you very much."

"Who, Gomez or Edwards?

"Both."

"I'm shocked."

CHAPTER TWENTY-ONE

The serenity of the stately homes along Grand Boulevard disguises the war that wages within.

Brad is at the family home's breakfast bar with a cup of coffee and a newspaper. Its headline reads, **"U.S. bans sale of computer hardware and software to Russia."**

Brad's bathrobe is open, he's slouching. What passes as boxer shorts are draped far too low and loose for a grown adult male even in the confines of his own home.

Olivia enters the kitchen from its patio side door. She has in her hand, freshly cut flowers from the stately, clapboard home's, professionally-cultivated gardens.

"Brad, Brad! Listen to me. I'm talking to you. There must be something wrong. Our next-door neighbor Jeannie Tomlinson, must have forgotten Sparky, that darling little Pekinese of hers. It's been barking non-stop. I wish I had Jeannie's complexion. She's a Grace Kelly, storybook type of a pretty girl, wouldn't you say?"

"Shut-up Olivia. Don't you try to sweet talk me. The problem is you and that kid. Precocious... me-cocious." Fine. Tommy is smart—but he's a little sissy-boy. A real mamby-pamby. You coddle him too much."

Finding a measure of motherhood rage mixed with a dash of self-respect - both suppressed for decades - Olivia stiffens, as she boldly pronounces,

"Did you want our son to grow up to be like you?" An open-hand slap to Olivia's face sent her to the floor.

Back at the Park Ridge, Shell, Mike asks Steve, "So, what's your take on Mr. Bradley Clifford?"

"He and Frank bear a father-son facial resemblance but all similarities end there. His posture—and oh my god, the way he whined like a little girl as you and I approached him. How embarrassing was that?"

"That's a rather quick assessment and a rather tawdry one at that."

"I call 'em as I sees 'em, lady!"

Steve and Mike pay the station attendant, having to collect their respective change. The attendant had never before seen a Federal credit card. He refused it.

"He could have at least tried to run it!"

"Get in the car, Steve. Let's go. Don't cause a scene."

Mike and Steve leave the gas station and head back to 424 Grand Boulevard. The two Agents park their vehicle directly in front of the house, get out and walk to the Clifford family's front door.

"Don't you think parking in the back alley might have been a bit more discreet? "Steve asks?"

"Perhaps, but looking like covert operatives sneaking around would only fuel neighborhood suspicions."

"You always were the considerate one."

12:01 p.m.

Frank, son Brad, Frank's grandson Tommy and Brad's wife Olivia are at the Clifford's, Northwest Chicago's Park Ridge home. Brad answers the door. He is still in his robe and underwear. Both Agents upon invitation, step forward, entering the stately home's foyer.

Steve, overwhelmingly impressed by what he now knows of Frank's military service, immediately refers to the patriarch of the Clifford family as...

"Colonel."

...much to the surprise of the entire Clifford household. Son Brad's face, in particular, contours in doubt and resentment.

Like many veterans, especially those once steeped in combat, Frank has never spoken of his military days to his family.

"Wait. Wait a minute. What did you call my old man?"

As Brad remains frozen in the foyer, still trying to wrap his head around what he just heard, the two agents are ushered by Frank and Olivia into the home's Florida room. A sunroom designed by Frank's wife, Mary, of tall, plate glass windows neatly fitted between sliding French doors surrounding a designer's vignette of lounge chairs and a wrap-around coach, each highlighted with yellow and white, overstuffed pillows setting forth an aire of subtle, springtime, sophistication. Through the windows, the rolling, tree-lined, half-acre, backyard with its recently mowed, emerald green lawn projects adds to the image of cultured living, an image completely opposite that shared by the home's only married couple, Brad and Olivia.

Still wearing a puzzled look, Brad steps into the Florida room bumping into Steve, as the Colonel's only son reluctantly decides to join the collective. He takes a seat on the piano bench in front of one of his mother's treasurers; her whitewashed, *Honky-Tonk* 1930's, upright, player piano.

With the exchange of cordialities behind them, Steve hands Mike Colonel Clifford's bio. As the family sits, both agents remain standing with Mike at center stage.

Reading from the file, Special Agent in Charge Michaelene Westgate gets right to the point wanting to drill down deep in an attempt to extract any inconsistencies that may lead to identifying any component of the two epic events- the explosion and the mutilation of a young woman - to which Frank is somehow tethered. She starts by first telling the assembled Clifford family how their patriarch as a young Marine was twice promoted in the field, first from the rank of sergeant to lieutenant and then lieutenant to captain, both times by lawyer turned four-star, Marine Corps General, Holland M. Smith.

"Is that true, Frank?"

"Yes." The elder bluntly states.

Lifting her eyes off the page, Mike continues, offering,

"Given Frank's many accomplishments in combat and unique proximity to one of the Marine's

Corps' legendary generals, Frank became something of a legend himself. In 1944, a cameraman for the Army Newspaper *Stars and Stripes* captured a photo of your father minutes after the

American flag was raised on Saipan; a Pacific island vital to America's strategic interests during World War Two."

"Oh, *South Pacific*, my how absolutely wonderful," Olivia exclaims as she turns to share her reluctantly with each member of her family. "That film truly captured my heart. Oh, you must have had such a glorious time, Frank. How lucky you were."

"Saipan is in the Central Pacific, not the South Pacific. It lies southwest of Japan, east of the

The Philippines, and I'm not aware of any such photo."

A subtle glow begins to emanate from Michaelene as she turned towards Frank's sole offspring, proposing, "You should know Brad, your father played a decisive role in keeping the United States free from Japanese occupation. Wrestling control of that island was essential to stopping Japan's advancement across the Pacific, keeping their military from gaining a foothold along our Pacific Coast."

Brad offers, "If that's true, I'm certain he wasn't alone in the effort."

"No, you're right. He wasn't but there is something unique about your father," Michaelene continues. "In June of '44, just days before the Marines landed on Saipan, your father received orders from Washington D.C.'s War Department. He was being sent home. He had survived three campaigns. They wanted him stateside to sell war bonds. He had the opportunity to board the next flight home but refused. The job wasn't done, right, Frank?"

"Saipan was the turning point in the war against the Japanese. It was to us what the Battle of the Bulge was to our guys in Europe. It could have gone either way."

"Brad, your father chose to stay, asking General Smith to write—" Michaelene pauses as she scans through the pages in her hand searching for the direct quote," Ah, here it is. An *invaluable to the war effort—must retain* counter order, keeping Frank in place while keeping him from facing court-martial when and if he finally made it home."

"I didn't have to ask. He knew I wasn't going anywhere."

With that, Michaelene's glow rose to a peculiar mix of astonishment and approval, nearly palatable as her eyes widened and warmed. Something long-held, long-consoled, and long-repressed shot forth from deep inside this intrepid woman's soul, an awakening, a reemergence soon to be shared.

"America's victory over the Japanese on that remote island destroyed their ability to further prosecute the war. No..." Michaelene again, abruptly stops. A tinge of anger seeps into her voice.

"No. I'm sorry."

An uneasiness settled over the room as each of the assembled tries to figure out what was coming next. Then, what had been long repressed washed over all.

"It wasn't a war." Michaelene continues, with a decisive shake of her head. It was a pandemic of mob violence and depravity, promoted by the Shinto religion and its Bushido subculture of deception and deceit. Together they preach that the blood of their one true god, their Sun God Jimmu, runs through every Japanese, past, present and future, making them mankind's only pure race giving their armies the right to cripple, kill and subjugate without mercy, every man, woman and child who isn't Japanese. Technically speaking, Saipan ended the war with Japan but it took Hiroshima and Nagasaki to drive the message home."

Frank is now the one taken aback. He couldn't understand how this beautiful, statuesque woman now standing in front of him, a female baby boomer, and a cop of all things, could speak so articulately and in such passionate detail about a war - *his* war - a war steeped in another culture, that had ended on the other side of the world before Special Agent Michaelene Westgate could have been at best, more than a year or two, old?

Mike, on the other hand, is now pondering what and why she just said. For a moment, she struggles uncomfortably, trying to regain an official posture. As Mike collects her thoughts, Steve inserts his.

CHAPTER TWENTY-TWO

"If I may Agent Westgate, no doubt like you Brad, I too was raised on stories of World War Two—the war in Europe. But there was another side to that conflict that few Americans understand - the war that was reshaping the world on the other side of the globe - the war in the Pacific."

Brad angrily inserts, "Yeah, I saw the movie."

"What?" I'm sorry?"

"I said Mr. Agent man, I saw the movie."

"What movie?"

"The Sands of Iwo Jima."

"The one with John Wayne, the actor?"

"Yes."

"Well, the war in the Pacific Brad, was a little bit more than that. It was more than just one island, more than just Iwo Jima. When the Japanese bombed our fleet at anchor in Pearl Harbor on December 7th back in '41, the war that was started by the Japs ten years earlier in 1931 - the year they invaded China - had finally arrived on America's doorstep. Facing a two-front war with a mere 175,000-man army equipped with World War One hand-me-downs, President Roosevelt had a tough choice to make."

"He chose to take on the Nazi's first."

Steve offers, "Likely because it was easier to move across Europe's contiguous land mass than island hop across the largest ocean on the planet. We lacked the technology to do that in '41. The development of the Higgins boat, for example, was still underway in the Louisiana swamp when war broke out. In the absence of landing crafts the Pacific war had to take a costly back seat."

"Wrong! Roosevelt chose to support America's first ally first, Great Britain!"

"Respectfully, Brad, at the outbreak of World War Two 'Great Britain' was not America's first ally, China was. And regarding The United Kingdom, it would be more accurate to say that England and Scotland were America's ally while other portions of Great Britain like Ireland sided with the Germans. Imperial Japan, however, seized more land and destroyed more lives through unimaginable butchery as Agent Westgate suggested, than Hitler could have dreamed possible."

"Yeah, right?"

"Hitler made it to France and occupied Eastern Europe. His advances were cut short at Normandy beach and at the gates of Stalingrad. By contrast, Hirohito and his thugs occupied all of Asia north and south including Vietnam. From there, they made their way across the Pacific, stationing troops and building fortifications in Alaska and targeting California. Like a dog marking its territory, at each step along the way they erected a Shinto shrine. I witnessed firsthand the scars the Japanese left behind throughout Southeast Asia."

"So, what are you some kind of war-mongering history buff or something?"

"Before joining the FBI, I was an Army Ranger. We are schooled in the past. It's the world in which we live, Brad, and how we got to where we are today."

Frank at first, sat silently just listening. A subtle nod of the head validated the World War Two combat veteran's approval of this Vietnam era, Army officer turned FBI Agent's assessment of geopolitical, military history. When he finally spoke, Frank offered "It's hard to plan tomorrow when you don't know how you got to where you are today, son."

Mike reenters the conversation. "I want you to know from all that the FBI has gathered on your father, it is clear that each of us owes this man an immeasurable debt of gratitude. He willingly put his life and the future he once hoped to live on hold to secure each of ours, help-ing to bring that war to its decisive end. It's an honor to stand here in front of you today, Colonel." Hearing that, Steve's eyes well-up.

Olivia, ever the consummate hostess, pops up and asks, "Would anyone care for coffee or tea? I prepared sand-wiches."

Airing her personal insights into America's war with Ja-pan was a step over the line. Elevating the family patri-arch in front of the rest of the Clifford clan was not.

Michaelene was seeking their reaction, especially Brad's. Turning to him, she asks the younger Mr. Clifford to join her in the hallway, hoping to obtain a quick sketch of the Clifford's businesses then set a date to go over the franchisee's books, recognizing that what started yesterday may not be over. Inside the Clifford family's hallway, Brad jumps ahead of any question Mike had planned with a blistering assessment of his father Frank, the family's patriarch:

"He's savvy about the industry, I'll give him that, and of course like most of his generation, he's great at saving money. Mom told me he paid off this house when I was seventeen. But he doesn't know how to make his money work for him. That's the difference between that old dude and me. You put him in a room in front of a bunch of MBAs and he just sits there listening, just like he's doing now. Those guys want feedback, they want data. They're all about the data. I speak data. I don't know about this so-called economics degree. I've never seen it. If he got it, it's outdated, just like him."

Mike asks, "How would you access your current financial situation? Can you give me a thumbnail sketch?"

"We own eleven full-service stations, and last year we experienced growth across the board. Our operational debt is 3% below the industry standard. As far as the family goes, the old man insists we pay cash for everything."

"Do you, or your father, have any enemies? Anyone who might want to do the family harm?"

191

Overhearing Agent Westgate's question as she moves from the Florida room down the hallway to the kitchen, Olivia asks, "Does that mean, you mean, what happened last night wasn't an accident?"

"God, Olivia, of course it wasn't an accident," Brad admonishes.

"Ma'am, the FBI doesn't investigate a crime unless there is reason to believe that something other than an accident may have occurred. My colleagues and I have already reached that conclusion." Mike offers, "It wasn't an accident. That's why we're here." Special Agent in Charge Westgate continues as she strains to contain her mounting disdain for Brad.

"Given the magnitude of the explosion it's astounding that accordingly to reports received thus far, that only a handful of people lost their lives. It's very important that we know if you have any enemies you can name? Have there been any legal issues, lately?"

"I just got through telling you we had one of the best years we've ever had last year, and that was during a recession. Hell, you can't be this successful and not ruffle some feathers, arouse some jealousy, you know that. You know what I mean, right?"

"Is that a yes?"

"No."

Having snatched a sandwich, Steve leaves the kitchen and approaches Mike in the hallway. He interrupts the conversation by asking his boss, "May I speak to you aside for a moment?"

"Yes, of course."

As the two take a brief sidebar, Steve whispers to Mike, "Where did that come from?"

"Where did what come from?"

"From the day I first met you, you had your head buried in your father's law books. How do you know so much about America's war with the Japanese?"

"If you had ever stopped to ask, you may have learned something about me other than my cup size."

CHAPTER TWENTY-THREE

1942,February 3rd: 0:900, Mare Island, Naval Shipyard; San Francisco: (12 days before the fall of Singapore and occupation by Imperial Japan)

"Welcome, Commander. Is this your first time aboard one of our Navy's submersible coffins?"

"Yes, I'm afraid so, Master Chief. I gotta say. This submarine looked a lot bigger in the photographs General Donovan left on my desk."

Respectfully, sir, that's how we get guys like you to try one on for size." She's an S-Class, launched April 1st, 1918. She's a good ol' gal. She'll get you where you're going."

"How about getting me back?"

"Don't know much about that, sir. Can't say for certain. Haven't seen those orders."

"Was that an April fool's joke, Master Chief?"

"You superstitious, Commander?"

"Aren't all sailors?"

"If you say so, sir."

"Not superstitious Master Chief, just cautious. I signed on for this mission because Bill Donovan asked me to."

"General Donovan briefed us, personally, sir. Gotta say, there wasn't much to it. No real details nothing to bite down on if you know what I mean? Now that I think about it, he did say one thing about you that seemed to stick with everyone here?"

"And what would that have been, Master Chief?"

"He said that not only were you the right man for the job but in his view, the only man who could pul it off."

"Did he have his fingers crossed behind his back as he spoke?"

"Can't say I noticed his fingers but now that you mention it sir, his hands were behind him as he went on about you, Commander."

"Let's move forward, Master Chief."

"Aye, Aye, sir. Take in that last breath of fresh air, Commander. We're about to shove off."

A Chicago based lawyer serving as an officer in the U.S Navy Reserve, "Barnacle Mike" Westgate, so nicknamed by his Naval Academy classmates for his ability to dog-gedly stick to a problem despite its magnitude, volunteered in the bristling winter of 1942, to serve in the OSS, the CIA's forerunner.

Later that same morning, somewhere in the Pacific aboard the diesel-powered S-Class submarine en route to the Malay Peninsula:

Gathered around the conning tower, Commander West-gate briefs the sub's senior staff. He begins with:

195

"I don't know much about this mission. In fact, I probably know less than you."

"That would be next to nothing, Commander." spouts the sub's Chief of the Boat.

"What I can say is this. Two years ago, the one they call the *Tiger of Malaya*, Imperial Japanese General Tomoyuki Yamashita, met secretly one-on-one in Berlin with none other than Adolf Hitler and Benito Mussolini."

"That must have raised some eyebrows around DuPont Circle. So, does that have something to do with why you're here, Commander?"

"This guy Yamashita is smart and effective," Commander Westgate continues, "He has adopted Nazi, *Blitzkrieg* tactics in his effort to conquer Asia."

"Blitzkrieg, that means lightning war, right Commander?"

"Yes, it does and make no mistake about it. Yamashita is the biggest threat to the stability of the Asian-Pacific theater since Genghis Khan."

"And he knows how to win!" Lieutenant Commander Greg Nosal firmly asserts, looking left and right, addressing all aboard as he continues:

"The scuttlebutt is sir, that right now Yamashita and his troops are walking all over a joint task force of British, Indian and Australian soldiers defending Malaya alongside their fellow countrymen."

"No need to sugarcoat it, Commander" Replied Sr. Commander Westgate. "It's a fact. As we speak our allies are being slaughtered by the Japanese. Yamashita is working his way south, down to the tip of the Malay Peninsula heading for the industrial port of Singapore. Along the way, the civilian population is also being fed into his meat grinder. The Allies have lost all means of communication throughout the region as a result of this nationwide bloodbath. I was asked to go in, size up the situation and do what I can to reestablish our intelligence narrative. That's all that I can say because frankly, that's everything I know. Your orders are to deliver me safe and sound. In my book, that gives you the right to know why you're putting your lives on the line."

"Our greatest military minds put all this on you—just one man?" asked Sub Captain Reynolds, stepping forward.

"I've heard it said that one man can make a difference," replied Commander Westgate. "Perhaps they heard that too."

In the face of what was a rapidly-depleting flow of reliable intel to U.S Operations Command from its British and Chinese allies regarding the Japanese military's 'juggernaut' steamrolling its way across the entire Malay Peninsula, something had to be done and done fast. Little time remained before the entire area would fall to the Japanese. It was Mike's job to fill in the blanks - a last minute Hail Mary as Wild Bill" Donovan put it, a feasibility study along Malaya's southern border - feeding what he found back to Operations Command. Recruiting native resources to aid his assessment was vital. The Japanese occupation of Malaya threatened the sovereignty of all nations throughout Southeast Asia especially those immediately surrounding it. Controlling Malaya would give Japan's war machine a base of operation from which to strike into Thailand, Vietnam, Indonesia, the Philippines and overwhelm the oil rich harbors of Singapore with virtual immunity. Not having enough manpower and naval resources to thwart an invasion of one without exposing another, the possibility that the Allies would ultimately cede all of Southeast Asia to Japan's dictator Emperor Hirohito, appeared with each passing minute, to be imminent. Mike's boss, none other than the head of the OSS, World War One Congressional Medal of Honor recipient, General William Joseph "Wild Bill" Donovan - the man lionized by President Franklin Roosevelt as his "Chief of Skullduggery" - designed the initiative. Waiting in the wings to be called upon if requested, were the men of the "SOF," the "Special Operation's Force," highly trained experts in irregular warfare who operate behind enemy lines in small groups - often no more than three man teams - relying on speed, surpise, and repetition to disrupt the enemy. Their fate and that of a nation and of those surrounding it, were now resting on the shoulders of one man, US. Navy Commander "Barnacle Mike" Westgate.

On a windswept, cold and rainy Friday afternoon on the 13th of February 1942, following a far too long and uneventful, diesel-fumed voyage, Commander Westgate was transferred under the cover of darkness from a U.S Navy sub - one designated as sold for scrap years before - to a

Malaysian fishing boat outside the occupied port city of Singapore. Donning a British designed, *Davis Rebreather,* a newly devised mechanism that separates carbon dioxide from oxygen inside a sealed unit, keeping air bubbles from rising to the surface, "Barnacle Mike" slipped into Singapore harbor, undetected.

Two days later on the fifteenth of February, in what was the greatest military defeat in the history of the British Empire, eighty-five thousand of England's finest surrendered to thirty-five thousand Imperial Japanese. On the wharf from behind a series of cargo boxes, Mike photographed segments of the event. At the slightest sign of resistance, beheadings rained. Witnessing the humiliating surrender first hand, strengthened Barnacle Mike's resolve.

Living in the surrounding jungle by day and scrounging for food by the docks at night, the following eve as dawn fell on Singapore's eastern wharf, Mike encountered a desperate, nineteen-year-old boy who was after the same discarded bucket of fish as him. A struggle for survival ensued.

Grappling across wooden planks, Mike finally subdued the scrappy kid. Bending him backwards over his knee, Mike, a "JAG" lawyer, a member of the U.S. Navy's Judge Advocate General's Corps, was preparing to stick his serrated diver's knife into the kid's ribs. That is, until the 19-year-old courageously pronounced in a high-polished, academic version of the King's English, "Foolish American. We all look alike to you. Go ahead. Take my life if you must."

"What the…?"

Recognizing that this scrawny teen was by no measure the enemy, Mike released him. On a dimly lit, moonless night on the Singapore waterfront in the Winter of 1942, with waves moving up from the Indian Ocean through the Strait of Singapore, pounding against the dock—and with tents along the shoreline as far as the eye could see filled with Imperial Japan's infamous

Kempeitai and their goons, the exalted 'Imperial Guards,' all under the command of Japan's "God of Operations," the brutal Shinto saber-rattler Tsuji Masanobu—two men, an American and a Chinese stood and faced one another each in desperate and immediate need to understand the other.

"Who are you?"

"My name is Lee Kuan Yew. Who are you?"

"No one you want to know."

"I'll be the judge of that."

Lee Kuan Yew was educated at Raffles Institute, Singapore's oldest and most prestigious institute of higher learning where he excelled in French, English, Japanese, Spanish and, not surprisingly, debate.

Before their chance encounter, Lee Kuan Yew survived Imperial Japan's pre-occupation probes into his homeland by being their lapdog, intercepting and translating Allied radio communications. That kept him clothed, sheltered and barely fed until one day after surviving a scuffle on the docks, Lee began turning his intercepts over to a man he had befriended, an American spy known as "Barnacle Mike," making note of the "minor errors in translation" he passed onto the Japanese.

"What's this?"

"It's a message I received the day before you arrived."

"You know I can't read it?"

"It's a personal message from General Yamashita to Commander Tsuji Masanobu. It was cause for a great celebration by the enemy."

"What does it say?"

"A small group of Shinto warriors killed two hundred unarmed, British patients and doctors in a hospital in Alexandra, a few miles north of here, including one waving a white flag attempting to surrender. He was gutted. That garnished grand laughter throughout the Kempeitai tents down the beach."

Mike asks, "And their nurses?"

"There was no mention of the nurses."

"I hate to imagine why."

"I doubt if the Allies have gotten word of this massacre. So, please take this. Notify your people."

"Why are you giving me this now?"

"Trust takes time but time is not something the Jap is willing to provide any of us. Can I trust you?"

Looking the brave young man he deeply admires in the eyes he says, "You're alive, aren't you?"

Nineteen-year-old Lee Kuan Yew would one day become Singapore's first prime minister, recognized as its Founding Father. A woman called "Beautiful Grace" was Lee's cousin.

Lee Meixiu (beautiful grace) Neo, at age 19, was a tall, light-skinned, long-haired, radiant beauty whose ever-present, beaming smile signified an insatiable love of life - even in the face of the most monstrous cruelty - it seemingly never failed. Plucked by Japan's sadistic Kempeitai from the thousands of Chinese women round-ed up on the docks for "The Cleansing," she was to serve as their concubine.

"The Cleansing," also known as 1942's Sook Ching Massacre, took place from the 18th of February through the 4th of March. Over the course of those eighteen days, no less than seventy thousand Chinese men, women and children living in the port city of Singapore were system-atically lined up and gunned down by Imperial Japanese machine-gun fire.

The daily round-up, killing, and disposal of so many once living beings drained Beautiful Grace's psycho-pathic kidnappers of time and energy leaving only fella-tio as their sexual preference. Forced to engage she nev-ertheless refused to lick their boots. For that, she was beaten and made to kneel on sliver-laden, angled bars of wood. Once in position, her captors wrapped her in barbed wire. Forced by the wire to remain still unable to move without being pierced, they left her there without food or water for three days carrying out their "God of Operations," orders. On the evening of the fourth day, her kidnappers applied electric shock. That ws their undoing.

"I'm very worried, Commander Mike. I haven't seen my cousin in days. I have no idea where she might be. I counted the bodies floating offshore. Hers was not among them."

Lee Kuan Yew, Barnacle Mike's, now adopted aide-decamp, lost track of his beloved cousin in the tumultuous pushing and shoving as people knowing their fate cursing their enemy's cruelty, lined the docks. Without a word from Lee's cousin, three long days and nights had passed.

On the fourth day frantically searching as evening fell, Lee chanced upon a string of Kempeitai tents lit oddly enough not by candles like most others but by an electric generator and light bulbs.

As he passed, one string of bulbs surged. He then heard what he thought was Beautiful Grace's voice in a muffled scream.

Knowing he needed help to subdue her guards, Lee rushed back to the wharf. There he was scheduled to meet each night with his American friend. This night, Lee begged Mike for help.

"You needn't say anything more. I'm in. Do you remember exactly where you saw this particular tent?" Barnacle

Mike once tried to count the number of tents strewn across the shoreline without being seen. He'd reported that there were upwards of eleven hundred.

"Lee paused trying to find the right way to set aside his emotions to say in English what he knew he must. "Yes, I'm confident I can find it again. Come on. Please. Hurry. We must go!"

The sole tent awash with a steady flow of light was evident among the others. Outside, nearby, sat a munitions wagon. Climbing aboard the long, wooden carriage, young Lee hunkered down between its rows of barrels. Upon receiving the last in a series of hand signals from his American ally, the Chinese teen tipped the contents of one of the barrels over the side. Leaping out onto the wagon's opposite side, the brazen teen hid behind one of its large, spoked wheels. Hearing the clickity-clack of cascading bullets hitting the ground, the two goons inside the tent peer out the flap. As planned, with the guard's distracted, Barnacle Mike sneaks in. There wrapped in a corset of barbed wire sat Beautiful Grace, smiling with that infectious smile, up at him. Before they could turn to see, Mike snuffed out the lives of the young woman's captors, taking considerable pleasure in performing the task. While freeing the long-haired beauty, two wires from the generator to the light bulbs were hastily disconnected, touching the side of the tent igniting its thinly woven fabric. As the trio fled, the mounting stench of two burning corpses and the fear of rising flames sent panic through the sleep-deprived Imperial Japanese. For the Shinto devout as the fires danced ravaging the encampment, the fear of being burnt to death never having one's ashes collected and placed in an urn, condemned the deceased —according to their beliefs— to drift alone throughout eternity, never to be reunited with their ancestors. That thought brought forth near mass paralysis allowing just enough time for the fleeing trio without further encounter, to escape.

Eleven years before, the Imperial Guards of the living offspring of the Shinto Sun God Jimmu—the same Imperial Guards who now occupied Singapore—led the savage incursion into China, ultimately establishing the four-square-mile Germ Warfare complex in Ping Fin. Approved by Emperor Hirohito, a vile of his cousin's bacterium, a gas gangrene/sarin hybrid, was couriered to Singapore by one of the most trusted Sergeants of the Imperial guards; the son of the man who under Yamashita, ordered the Sook Ching massacre Lt. General Takuma Nishimura — his son being one of the two men whose life Barnacle Mike enjoyed ending while freeing Beautiful Grace. The vile of bacterium was intended to expedite the genocidal disposal of the balance of the Chinese population along the Malay Peninsula. Unwittingly, it had been broken and considered destroyed by the fire that ultimately ravaged the dockside camp. Of the remaining formula, the sarin would have been diluted by the bucket brigades that quickly formed in an attempt to put out the fire, washing it out to sea thus neutralizing it. Regarding the *Clostridium perfringens* or gas gangrene — if any of that still lingered, it was deemed proportionately insignificant to cause infection.

In the months that followed,'Beautiful Grace,' Lee Meixiu Neo and Chicago lawyer Barnacle Mike, married sharing vows with Singapore's future founding father Lee Kuan Yew, acting as best man.

Eight and a half months into her pregnancy, Beautiful Grace, contacted an unknown bacterium, one rapidly imploding her internal organs.

Singapore's first female physician forty-seven-year-old Lee Choo Neo - the first Chinese female to be awarded the coveted Cambridge medical certificate - tried desperately to save Beautiful Grace but to no avail.

U.S. Navy Commander Mike Westgate, a man who operated as a spymaster behind enemy lines providing counsel and direction to the Special Operation Force, the man whose sense of duty and commitment to a cause had never been known to shrink, held fast the hand of the only woman he knew he could ever love as Beautiful Grace's aunt performed an emergency cesarean, bringing a healthy baby girl into this world. With her ever-present smile lighting the hearts of all around, the infant's mother passed as Barnacle Mike openly wept.

In 1945, at war's end, both father and daughter returned to the United States.

Michaelene's father, Barnacle Mike practiced maritime law in Chicago, focusing on the international crime of human trafficking.

Imperial Japanese General Tomoyuki Yamashita, *The Tiger of Malaya* who was once demoted for suggesting to his superiors that peace with China and the United States would better serve Japan's interests - during his post war internment - never denied his responsibilities. A man of honor he faced the International Tribunal's hangman's noose without hesitation. By contrast, the Shinto saber-rattler Tsuji Masanobu who ordered *The Cleansing* as well as the infamous *Bataan Death March*, escaped and went into hiding in Thailand. He was found dead in 1968 having masqueraded for twenty-three years as a Catholic Friar.

Over the years as his daughter grew, Barnacle Mike shared bits and pieces of his past with her, guardedly answering questions about her mother until one day before Michaelene's nineteenth birthday, Mike ceremoniously sat and answered every question his daughter had. That brilliantly-lit summer day marked the anniversary of when the bold American and the love of his life, Lee Meixiu Neo, 'Beautiful Grace,' first met.

With a star on the CIA's Memorial Wall dedicated to him and his name forever emblazoned on his Chicago law firm's wall, Retired Rear Admiral Michael Donahue Westgate died proudly having lived to see his only offspring, his daughter Michaelene, step forward in 1978 at the age of thirty-five, to accept the responsibility of heading their hometown office of the Federal Bureau of Investigation.

Thanks to the unrelenting courage of both men and women of the Philippine, Thai, Vietnam, Malaya and Indonesian Resistance movements, each fighting alongside the western power's Special Operations Force, the

Japanese military occupied their respective homelands for three years but never conquered their people.

As stated, "Michael" is the given first name of Michaelene's father, Barnacle Mike. "Lee" is the maiden name of Michaelene's mother, Lee Meixiu Neo, and "Ne" in Mandarin, is an emphasis placed at the end of a sentence to indicate a strong resolve or at the end of a name to denote a "strong-yet-quiet character."

No other name, term, tag or handle could better fit the exceedingly brilliant and beautiful Michaelene Westgate, Special Agent in Charge of the Northern Illinois office of the Federal Bureau of Investigation.

CHAPTER TWENTY-FOUR

1978: Back in Park Ridge, Illinois at the Clifford family residence: 1:15 pm

"If I genuinely offer to you my sincerest apology for the asshole I once was, could you forgive me?"

"It would be a start."

Tommy excuses himself, walks over to his grandfather, giving him a big hug, saying, "Love you,

Gramps. You were my hero before I heard any of this."

Tommy kisses his grandfather on the forehead, offering to withdraw to his room to practice a rather challenging Mozart violin concerto, clearly demonstrating that a resolute character can indeed, skip a generation.

Steve retakes a seat in the Florida room, seeking further evidence to support his initial assessment of Frank, one combat veteran to another. He begins by asking, "Colonel, it is our understanding that you own and manage twelve Shell gas stations in the area, is that correct?"

"Eleven."

"Yes, sir, my apologies."

"With that, the delicate task of peeling back onion layers, one man's then the others, is set in motion."

Steve continues with another open-ended question, "How did that come about?"

Shrewdly perceiving the game ahead, Frank decidedly signs on, hoping to discover what he too is seeking to know.

"When I was eight, I got a job cleaning around Mr. De Groot's gas station here in Park Ridge. His was a small operation, typical of its day. If you'd blinked you'd miss it, just two pumps and a lift."

As the discussion continues, Frank reveals that he worked after school for Mr. De Groot for ten years, proudly offering that he never missed a day…

"…Right up to the time I joined the Marine Corps, three days after the Japanese attacked Pearl Harbor."

Steve asks, "De Groot." That's Dutch, isn't it? Shell USA, isn't that a Dutch subsidiary?"

"Of Royal Dutch Shell, yes, and both countries sent boys to fight in the Pacific."

"The Central Pacific?"

"Throughout the Pacific with a large contingent stationed in Indonesia."

"Why Indonesia?"

"To protect their nation's, colonial interests."

"Oil?"

"Yes."

"I thought the Japanese occupied Indonesia during the war."

"They did."

As the game of who is interrogating who continues, Frank finds himself legitimately warming to this kid, this Fed, a former Army officer of all things, at best guess, some 25 years his junior. Wanting the 'game' to proceed along a route of his choosing, Frank tosses the kid a bone.

"I wasn't aware of the photo taken on Saipan to which your boss referred but I am well aware of another of me that gained some attention."

"And what would that be, Colonel?"

"A poster on which my likeness appeared across the U.S and half of Europe."

"Really? Why was that?"

Steve responds with all the enthusiasm of the younger of two brothers wanting to learn from the elder, surprised by the pitch of his own voice.

"It was pre-war, one of those odd, circumstantial events. I was ten. I was attempting to help Mr. De Groot lift a large bucket of water off the ground. It sloshed over both of us and spilled out into the street. Mr. De's daughter Alida, thought it hilarious and captured the moment on her Brownie camera."

"That's one of those old-fashion, hand-held, Kodak box cameras, right?"

"Yes. The somewhat grainy photograph it produced spoke symbolically of the war in Europe spilling into its streets, ultimately, washing onto American shores. The kid in the photo was me but the angle proved that it could have been any ten-year-old. Mr. De Groot shared the photo with a friend at Shell headquarters, stateside. They sent it to corporate. Corporate turned it into a poster. It looked a lot like one of Norman Rockwell's, a symbol of young and the old working together—a large man and a young boy—representing the relationship between the Dutch and the Americans.*"*

"That's right. New York was originally New Amsterdam, wasn't it?"

"The Dutch helped settle our country in the 17th Century and we kicked the Nazis out of theirs in the 20th. That poster became a part of Shell Oil's PR campaign to sell bonds to support of the war effort—two nations with a common heritage and a common goal."

"Survival."

"Exactly."

CHAPTER TWENTY-FIVE

Olivia suddenly shouts, "Oh my god, Bradley!"

Adjacent to the hallway, the Florida room's French doors had remained open since the two agents arrived. The sound of Olivia's outcry filled the entire first floor of 424 Grand. From inside the room, Olivia's irate behavior is edging towards a nervous breakdown.

"Olivia, get a hold of yourself!"

"No, I just don't know Bradley. I can't think. What in the world? I don't know. What if—?"

"Can't you see Agent Westgate, that you are upsetting my wife with your questions? No, the answer is no! I don't know of anyone who wants to end us. Why don't you figure it out and get back to me, okay?"

From off the hallway, the soft, soothing tone of Special Agent Westgate's voice was overheard staying on point, subtly moving the conversation away from the subject of violence, providing Mr. and Mrs. Clifford reassurance.

"I understand. I sincerely do. Let me know if you think of anything else, Brad."

"It's Mr. Clifford to you."

"Yes, thank you, sir. You're right. I apologize. Mr. Clifford, please brings all your records to FBI headquarters by 1:00 p.m. tomorrow afternoon. My staff will be standing by awaiting your arrival. I would also like the names and contact information of all employees, accountants, and subcontractors who have worked for you and your father over the past five years. I'll give you time to compile that with help from my staff over the next few days."

"What about witness protection for me and my wife?"

"I'm assuming you meant your son Tommy and your father, as well?"

"Yes."

"That's an option as we move the investigation forward. Right now, all we have is an inordinately large explosion at a service center owned by you and your father that took place approximately a half hour's drive from here with no member of your family present at the time."

"Who would do this to us?" Olivia asks, her outcries subsiding.

"Mrs. Clifford, we have no way of determining at this point that anything or anyone is directly targeting your family. One of your business locations was destroyed. That's it. That's all we have right now."

Two men representing two different generations both combat skilled survivors, one a soldier, a Vietnam war veteran, the other a Marine who fought against the Japanese during World War Two, both men for the past several minutes have been sitting in the Florida room across from one another behind opened doors remaining respectfully somber. Heeding Olivia's reactions and noting Michaelene's replies, Steve puts down his plate and sandwich and rekindles his interrogation of the Clifford family's patriarch.

"So, how did you wind up in partnership with Shell?"

"I got a letter from my folks while I was at boot camp that Mr. De Groot had passed away. In the letter, my dad wrote that "Mr. De" had willed the station and the land beneath it to me. I was grateful but I thought little of it at the time. In 1945, when I returned from overseas, I was met at the train station by my mom, dad, girlfriend Mary and a representative from corporate Shell. The global oil company kept its word to Mr. De."

"How's that?"

"In exchange for the rights to distribute that poster, Shell offered to provide the use of their brand name free of charge and products at cost to me for the next five years. They said that "the people of both nations need time to rebuild." As far as I was concerned from that point on, Shell and I were partners for life."

"Checking the dates on your GI Bill, you didn't waste much time once you got off that train."

"What do you mean?"

"You applied within twenty-six days of your return to Northwestern University where, exactly three years later, you received a degree in..." Steve looks down at Frank Clifford's FBI file in his hand to make certain he accurately states, 'comparative global economics', correct? That's a thing, right?"

"The GI Bill is the smartest reinvestment in the security of our nation that our government has ever made."

"I went to Iowa State on a football scholarship. Economics wasn't exactly my calling but if I understand correctly, basically, that degree helps one forecast financial trends. It helped you build your business. Is that fair to say?"

"If you wish."

"A character whose integrity had been certified by his superiors from age eight through adulthood, Frank turned one 'two pumps and a lift' gas station into eleven, franchise-branded locations with the latest, number twelve, a commercial complex that was until last night, the largest in the state capable of servicing long-distance truckers and the family station wagon alike."

Steve offers, "You've lived a charmed life, Colonel."

"More than you know, Agent Donaldson."

CHAPTER TWENTY-SIX

From inside the hallway, outside the Florida Room, Michaelene continues her attempt to settle Mrs. Clifford nerves.

"We simply don't know yet, Mrs. Clifford. The Bureau has one of the best forensic accounting staff around and they can call upon outside civilian help if need be. They'll go over the books to determine if there are any patterns—a money trail that may lead to a potential suspect or suspects. Getting answers to what happened last night is the FBI's number one priority. Rest assured, one way or another, we will get to the bottom of this."

A now more steadied Olivia, asks "Sooner rather than later I hope?"

"You have my word," Michaelene replies with a reassuring nod. There was no way was Mike was going to bring up the body of the dead woman they found. Not at this point.

"How do you know you're looking in the right direction?" Brad inquires, with a snide chuckle.

"We don't but traditionally, business records have been a reasonably good place to start."

On the couch sitting across from Frank, Steve presses on utilizing common ground, hopefully without

signaling intent. "Intent" however, had long been recognized.

"Like most of my generation, I've seen a lot of war movies. Lived one too, but the war against the Japanese, I must tell you Colonel, I could never get inside of it—you know, understand how and why it happened."

"Apparently, your boss, Agent Westgate, has a considerable grasp."

"About eight years ago, there was that movie, Tora Tora Tora. It showed political build-up on both the American and Japanese side and some good aerial scenes but the ground war—nothing. When I was in-country, the word was that the Viet Cong learned most of their fighting skills from the Japanese, especially the use of underground cities and tunnels. It's funny, I survived two tours in Nam, rarely coming face to face with the enemy."

Knowing full well where the game at hand was heading, Frank counters, "Rarely was I not face- -to-face with the enemy, being transferred from one island hot spot to another across the Pacific."

"I read that they were relentless, fanatical, the Japs, I mean."

"Agent Westgate is right. For the Imperial Japanese fighting man, it was a transcendent, spiritual campaign like a crusade. Once the lid on Pandora's Box was lifted no Japanese civilian control over its military, even when attempts were made, was possible. Their devout were on a rampage, believing that bombs and bullets were only good for one thing?"

"And what would that be, sir?"

"For clearing a path."

"To what?"

"Our souls."

CHAPTER TWENTY-SEVEN

Frank continues: "Their weapon of choice was the bayonet. The Japs believed they would gain spiritual favor with their ancestors if they could drive their bayonets into our hearts while staring into our eyes, watching us die. We, however, found a bullet through their brain from a nearby handgun quickly dashed such metaphysical enthusiasm."

"Now, that was genuinely funny, sir."

"I didn't intend it to be." Frank counters. "From accounts I've read of your war, the Vietnamese also learned from the mistakes of the Japanese. They rarely sent wave after wave of men into battle."

"Could you consider Khe Sanh and the Quang Tri City Citadel, exceptions, sir?"

"No, Agent Donaldson. I cannot."

"Sir respectfully, I was there—or to be more accurate, I was in the neighborhood of the Quang Tri Citadel when the VC struck in mass."

"I'm listening."

"There were six of us LRP's, 'long-range patrol scouts.' We'd been out in the boonies for nearly a month when the word came down about the Tet Offensive. The Citadel in Quang Tri was less than three clicks away from our position when the outbreak occurred. We wanted to turn around and lend our support but we had orders to stay put. At the Citadel, some 2,400 VC and North Vietnamese regulars swarmed our guys."

"I can point to one essential difference between your VC and the Japs of my day?"

"And what would that be, Colonel?"

"Your enemy had a plan."

"What do you mean?"

"I didn't have to be there to know that none who swarmed either Khe Sanh or the Citadel did so in a wildly indiscriminate fashion."

"I'm not certain I follow, sir?"

"None stripped down to their underwear, picked up a sharp stick or a handful of rocks and shouted *'Bonzai!'* or whatever the Vietnamese equivalent of that would be, and charged headlong into American forces with the only thing approximating even a semblance of a plan being submission to the most expedient means of connecting with their heavenly ancestors—U.S firepower. Nor did your Vietnamese enemy excuse their actions by way of a violence-based, expansionistic religion."

"You're right, Colonel, and as a nation, the Vietnamese people generally shy away from organized religion practicing instead, various forms of spiritualism."

"Like Taoism, Buddhism, or Confucianism?"

"Yes, more inward seeking than outward promoting. I think the average Vietnamese values life more than his

Japanese counterpart. I came to have considerable re-spect for the people of Vietnam."

"I had none for the Japanese. I arrived on Guadalcanal on August 7th of '42. Three weeks later, as a young Marine two years out of high school, some eight hundred Impe-rial Japanese, advanced against those of us guarding Henderson Field. It was surreal. Each Bonzai shouting son-of-a-bitch chose to die. Not a single one surren-dered."

"That's what I mean. That's what I don't get. What dis-rupted set of values and moral decay can cause a person to simply throw away their life?"

"Religion. In this case, the Shinto religion."

"At least the Vietnamese fought on principle."

"And the Japanese fought and died because their mystic God Jimmu - offspring of their storm god and sun god-dess - told them to."

"That's fucked up."

"The largest suicide charge in the history of modern war-fare took place when I was on Saipan two years later. It was 1944. By then, I was a Captain of Marines. My Company reinforced the Army's 105th Infantry backed up to the beach. They had lost almost six hundred and fifty men before my Marines and I arrived but we weren't the ones who save them."

"What happened? Who did ?"

"Jimmu did. He saved the dwindling number of Americans on the beach."

"What? How?"

"Convinced by their fanatic leadership that they will be swept up to sit beside Jimmu by the same *Divine Wind* that saved their ancestors from the Mongol Kublai Khan in the 13th Century, no less than four thousand, three hundred and nineteen human beings (4,319) set aside their rifles and charged half naked, flinging themselves on the sacrificial alter of crushing U.S firepower. When it was over, it was like looking out over a coverlet of red silk. A thick, unbroken mass of steaming corpses of Japanese youth covered Saipan's western shoreline from one end of the beach to the other."

"Mass suicide and why—because some invisible Santa Claus dude said it was a good move?" Steve shakes his head. "Sick fucks."

"What I find ironic is that my generation knows more about Vietnam than you and yours know about my war, Frank offers."

"Why do you think that is, Colonel?"

"Television played a role of course. But there was more to it than that. Somewhere along the way, the American people woke up—and they grew up, with much credit going to their kids, the young people, people of your generation. Young Americans protesting the Vietnam War forced the rest of us to look deep into the monster's eyes. You must have been a student during the antiwar movement?"

"I was."

"Yet, you served in the military?"

"I initially sided with most of the activists on campus. It didn't seem right that we should pay with our lives to interfere in someone else's civil war but…

"But?"

"… I happened to tune-into a PBS News Special that showed kids in Vietnam being caught in the fray. 'Choice' for me, well, at that point there simply wasn't a choice. I volunteered."

"RA—regular army, not a draftee. I respect you for that, Donaldson."

"Thank you, sir."

"War is horrific and perhaps facing it, coming to understand it is what each human being needs to avoid it. Regretfully, war is an inevitable part of the human experience."

"Do you honestly believe that, Colonel?"

"I'd prefer not to, but tell me one thing:"

"What's that, sir?"

"A time in mankind's history when war wasn't waging somewhere on our planet?"

"I heard it said that the study of war promotes its absence."

"...And the absence of its study promotes its propagation. Yes, I heard that, too."

"Exactly. That's why I'm asking."

With that, Frank reveals that he personally killed hundreds of Japanese; as many as possible and many hand-to-hand—something for which he was neither proud nor carries any measure of regret—nor which he would discuss openly under any other set of circumstances with a virtual stranger.

"So, Agent Donaldson, now it's your turn!"

"For what, sir?"

"Go ahead. Ask me, ask me directly. Am I still capable of taking the life of another human being? That's why we're having this conversation, isn't it? That woman in Belmont-Cragin, found mutilated by my station, do you think I murdered her?"

"Both I and Agent Westgate dismissed that possibility some time ago."

"So the purpose of this conversation was what?"

"Agent Westgate and I can't set aside the idea that you are somehow, indirectly linked to the murder. I was hoping that through our conversation..."

"Some material fact may inadvertently arise?"

"Exactly."

"I get it but if I had any idea I would be quick to tell you." "And that's an affirmative, sir. That's exactly the conclusion that Agent Westgate and I reached."

Two American combat veterans locked in the universal quest to understand each other, the world they once endured and indeed themselves, continue the journey. But now as such conversations often do, this one became personal.

In my day, I fought and killed believing if I did, you, my son and members of your generation wouldn't have to."

"And many of my brothers and sisters fought in Vietnam wanting to emulate the courage of World War Two veterans like you sir. We felt we owed you that."

"Owed? What you and yours 'owed' us, you've long since paid, Agent Donaldson. Nothing is more gratifying or offsets the losses I witnessed in battle than to be alive to see a whole new generation of Americans able to lead free and productive lives—able to set their own direction, to create with unbridled thought, a world of their own design. Understand this Agent Donaldson, my generation saw ourselves not only as the first but the last line of defense. We had a job to do and we did it. And this, all this around us— the dynamic of this nation with its many flaws, alive and prospering free from the boot of tyranny, is a monument to my generation's success. This is our reward. Debt paid. Paid in full. Pass the word."

"It was understood by most of us serving in Nam, that if we lost the war, little if anything back home would change."

"And that's my point. That's the difference. During the Second World War to me and mine, it was clear. If we'd lost literally everything back home would have changed. We were defending our families and our way of life against a preponderant evil. Your boss lady was right."

"In what way?"

"The war against the Japanese wasn't a war."

Frank suddenly rises to his feet, a rage clearly building inside of him. "It was as Agent Westgate offered, a plague, a pestilence of insane human arrogance—one that mankind at all cost, had to stop".

The sixty-one-year-old, combat veteran begins rubbing his hands together, intertwining his fingers as visions of the ovens and the carnage they brought suddenly raced through his mind.

"Like the Nazi's. Yeah, I know…"

Frank barks, "No, you don't know!" The Japs were nothing at all like the Nazis." The Marine's eyes close then open, scanning the room, locking down hard on Special Agent Donaldson.

"Hitler's primary focus was real estate acquisition. Hirohito and his thugs were focused on genocide, wiping the world clean not just of Jews but everyone who wasn't Japanese. How many book movies and documentaries have passed your eyes regarding the Nazi war machine, pointing to the five year reign of terror they spread across half of Europe, hundred perhaps?"

"Sure."

"Compare that to Western society's knowledge of the fourteen-year, wave of utter deprivation and slaughter of human life that swept across half the globe from 1931 through 1945, designed by Imperial Japan's leadership and executed by their armed forces. You said it yourself, that movie *Tora, Tora, Tora* was meaningful on one hand yet lacking in substance on the other. Few if any pieces of documented fact have been seen on American movie screens, expressed in newspapers or popular magazines providing an accurate portrayal of the wide-spread barbarity of Imperial Japan."

"I can't say that I ever stopped to consider it but you're right, Colonel. Western society's take on humanity's most epic struggle for freedom is conspicuously lopsided. Most of us only know half of the World War Two story if that."

"Speaking of newspapers, have you read today's Tribune, Agent Donaldson?"

"I've been a bit preoccupied, sir."

"There's a front page article today about a young California girl, a 15 year old Barbara Telling, whose body was found beaten and strangled to death on Torrey Pines State Beach, near San Diego. The headline reads, Shock and disbelief has swept the nation.

"I can't imagine the pain her family is undergoing."

"Why not?"

"What…what are you asking of me?"

"It's just one girl—one, right? As your generation would say, So, what's the big deal?"

"Sir?"

"This repeated emphasis on the Nazis in publications and movie screens, having the Holocaust - though far too real - repeatedly tossed in our face overlooks the simple fact that one half of the world's population, particularly its women, as the Japs preyed especially upon young women—all felt the same pain and wept the same tears as those who suffered throughout Europe under Nazi rule and now this—a 15-year-old, California girl. I want to know how the pain of the Jews and now this young girl's pain or that of her family's differs from the millions of Asian women, the Chinese, Korean, Malaya and Philippine women ravaged by the Japanese war machine?"

"It's not, sir."

"So where is the outrage? Where are the protests? Where are the tears and words of sympathy for all the women whose lives were destroyed by Japan's quest for world domination? And it didn't stop with just Asians. The wives and daughters of Europeans colonists, American nurses, teachers, the Dutch, French missionaries, their nuns, Australians, the indigenous natives of Alaska, female business personnel from across the globe, the Germans? Where are their stories? Where is there 'Holocaust' memorial?"

"Germans?

"Yes. When I was stationed on Saipan, there was a sizable contingent of German citizens who had settled there in the aftermath of the first World War. They lived alongside the island's indigenous families, the Chamarro and Carolinians, in a small town called Garapan. I saw photographs of what their community looked like before war broke-out. It was essentially Main Street America. It had paved streets, sidewalks and various shops with apartments above. Under the Japanese, these shops and homes were ravaged, their belongings heaved into the streets, collecting next to the bodies of the brave amongst its residents who dared to stand up to the Shinto warriors who months before, had offered their friendship to the citizens of Garapan."

With that, Frank momentarily veers off point, his voice taking on an introspective tone.

"Garapan. That was the first time in the history of the Marine Corps that we were forced to fight shop-to-shop, house-to-house. We had no training in this kind of combat. We didn't know how to flush out the enemy. I saw my friends and family here in Park Ridge through the frightened eyes of the people of Garapan. We couldn't save   everyone."

With a screech from a missed note on a violin echoing through the house from young Tommy's upstairs bedroom, Frank puts his hand to his face. From where Steve stood, that jarring sound seemed to have had a profound impact upon Grandpa Clifford's thoughts.

"Are you okay, sir?"

Of course. I'm fine."

"Some may say that Japan's barbarism although horrific, is yesterday's news."

"Their flag, it's still the Rising Sun, isn't it?"

CHAPTER TWENTY-EIGHT

Dreamscape, Tinian Island, 1944: "A daydream."

Sixty-one year old Frank Clifford is suddenly seized by the image of his younger self. As if hovering above, he sees a familiar-looking twenty-seven year old Marine, wearing a sage-green, sweat-stained, World War Two, field uniform with Captain's bars embroidered on each shoulder. An M-1, steel helmet replete with USMC camo net covers his skull. A Thompson sub machine gun lies securely tucked, locked and loaded, under the young Marine's left arm. Disjointed images appear; planes overhead, dirt roads, refugees. Blackness, punctuated by flashes of light, screaming women, mutilated bodies, fires burning, adults holding their children turning their child's face away from the horror of war—the utter futility of such gestures sucking the life out of both. A micro-burst of tropical wind mixed with rain washes across the scene with an impact of a thousand needles—a deluge of soul-saturating moisture departing as abruptly as it appeared. A barrage of cannon and mortar fire, rifles, grenades and machine guns, some off in the distance, some blowing holes in the earth around young Frank now lying face down, beseeching the blackened earth still smoldering, into defying what anyone having once experienced prays never having to experience again, the hellish stench of ... *Napalm.*

Napalm; a burning, gelatinous ooze was first used not in Vietnam as often thought but rather for the first time on

Tinian Island in 1944 to rid the thousands of Imperial Japanese held up in hundreds of the tiny island's, mountainous caves; unwilling to surrender, willing only to continue to fight and die by the Bushido code.

That horrid odor of jellied gasoline and crude oil sets everything it touches aflame. In its wake the stench it leaves still lingers, locked in the back pages of Frank's subconscious. A remnant of days so long ago yet never forgotten had been reawakened by last night's explosion in Belmont-Cragin. While the former combat veteran's neuro-sensors pound at one end of his conscious being forcing him to touch, taste, hear and revel in the same thoughts and feeling he endured more than three decades before, inside him, on the opposite end— as the past and present commingle—the quality of life today still fails to compensate, never being quite enough to offset the horrors of so many yesterdays. But it was he, Frank reflects, as the elder sees himself, that twenty-seven-year-old who ordered what was later determined to be eighteen, fifty-gallon drums of napalm dropped from the skies onto his non-repentant enemy, below. With the resounding peel of bouncing metal barrels now growing ever closer to the forefront of Frank's memory, every sensation once lived is born anew. One of Chicago's most respected hometown sons is reliving with every breath, the anticipation and exhilaration of watching what seemed an endless avalanche of metal containers tumbling down that strategic island's hillside, careening off protruding boulders, passing his troops cloistered off to the side, as each barrel of utter horror burst open hitting its mark, releasing its liquid death.

Then as now, a sense of joy fused with hatred rushes through the sixty-one-year-old veteran's veins.

"Sir?" Steve asks, as Frank's spirit still tethered to his daydream returns if but for a moment to the Florida room of his Park Ridge, Illinois home. "Sir?"

"They wouldn't surrender." Frank states to the young FBI agent. "We gave them every chance." But it wasn't sympathy for the enemy that had given Frank pause.

Recalling U.S. loudspeakers on Tinian shoreline, pointing up the hillside with Japanese interpreters imploring surrender, what provided the sixty-one-year-old combat veteran a moment of reflection was a decision he had been forced at the time to make.

"Was there something else I could have done, something more humane?" He pondered.

Frank recalled being told by an American Army platoon commander who had preceded the Marines up the hillside, that the Japs he and his men had encountered were burrowed several feet down, deep inside each cave preparing to be called upon for a second wave attack.

"Each cave must be explored one-by-one." Frank recalled the Army officer saying, "And there are booby-traps crisscrossing the hillside approach. Most important-ly, if your Marines encounter a civilian at the mouth of a cave begging to be freed, don't. They too are booby-trapped."

Using native women and children as human shields to ward off American probes, or at least to cushion the blow ultimately due the sanctimonious Shinto warriors, was a practice wide-spread throughout the Imperial Japanese military.

For the briefest of moments, the lip of 61-year-old Frank, standing in his Park Ridge Illinois *Florida Room*, curled upward in disdain just as it had some thirty-four years ago when the lids began popping off those drums as he ordered his Marines to take cover. As that torturous, gelatinous compound washed over the caves, the smoke laced with guttural cries no doubt like that from the human incinerators young Frank had discovered just days before, filled the air. Once having made the decision that the lives of the civilians were over regardless of any other option he might have chosen, the thought of losing so many of his men as they searched each individual cave became the deciding factor. Reviewing that moment in his life, Frank determined then as now, that the decision he made at the time was the right one. With that, the elder recited aloud the same words he spoke as a 27-year-old:

"You fry women, we fry you. God help the innocent—and forgive us all."

Frank then opened the double French doors at the rear of the Florida room. Having exorcised yet another enduring demon, he had this once Army lieutenant turned FBI agent and his line of questioning to thank. With his back to 'Steve, staring out across the rolling lawn, Frank smiled. A wafting bouquet from the surrounding honeysuckle vines, the magnificent backyard Magnolia tree blossoms merging with the aromatic fresh cut grass was the elixir that drained Frank's anger. The memory of Tinian Island, its human incinerators and the toxic stench of a hillside set aflame by the napalm he ordered, all settling back into his subconscious, Frank turned to face Steve. Standing razor straight, his mind and body now a reunited front, the World War Two combat veteran offered:

"What far too many people throughout the Western world fail to recognize is that unlike the Nazis, the Imperial Japanese did not want to share this planet with anyone. Though fanatical to the Western mind, the singularity of the objective was highly practical to the Imperial Japanese.

Killing men on the battlefield wasn't enough. Their goal was to eliminate their target's reproductive resource, their women, and whatever number of revenge-seeking offspring they may generate. It was unfettered, autocratic madness. It had to end."

"They didn't see a world of other nations standing in their way?"

"Just stepping stones in their minds to us. The Japs recognized early on that their biggest obstacle in their quest for world dominion was us, the United States. Imperial Japan's war college in 1907, adopted the Sato-Akiyama Plan. It was a plot to invade the continental United States and destroy the lives of every human being living within its borders. The "plan" was sanctioned by the Imperial court thirty-four years before the Jap's sneak attack on Pearl Harbor."

Steve counters, "Ambitious. How did they intend to pull that one off?"

With that, Steve glances over to the home's hallway, hoping to catch Michaelene's attention, wanting to buy more time. She subtly nods in agreement.

"They had devised a strategy."

"Care to share?"

"You know your boss Agent Westgate appears to know more about the war against Japan than she is letting on. I hadn't heard the name Jimmu for decades. And coming from a young,

American woman?"

"She is complex. I'll give her that. So, what was their scheme?"

"The scheme, as you call it, began as a command that came from the mouth of Jimmu. When you're fighting an enemy it's invaluable to know the source of their motivation."

"Get inside of that, you can defeat them. I know. That's what I tried to do." Steve offers using his own experience to subtlety rekindle his probe:

"I came to understand the mindset of the Vietnamese, how they think, how they rationalize."

"I did the same. I came to understand the Imperial Japanese fighting spirit by reciting to myself

Jimmu's divine proclamation as often as possible."

"Something like the Lord's Prayer."

"Not quite."

"So, what was the ancient command?

Let us extend our capital until it covers the eight corners of the world under one roof.

"What? That's it? That from some god? *Let us extend our Capital*? Sounds more like a dictator's creed."

"And that's what frightens me to this day. Wars begin and end. Religions seemingly have no end. Their belief systems are rarely challenged and their most devout continue..."

The front doorbell rings at 424 Grand Avenue.

CHAPTER TWENTY-NINE

"I'll get it," Olivia shouts, her senses somewhat restored.

Back inside the Florida room, Steve continues: "So, are you saying that Japan is still our enemy?"

Frank offers: "Japan is an island, plagued by a scarcity of resources. The vast majority of their food, clothing and even their culture, is imported. Whenever ' Bushido,' the feudal-military code that places *might* over the right of human life rises, it's like a hallucinogen pushing the people of that nation to breakout, exceed the limits of their island boundaries and conquer the land of other nations, particularly those immediately surrounding them. It is much easier to envision Japanese militarism raising its ugly head again than to see the people of that island dwelling in an Athenian-like state of peaceful coexistence; philosophically introspective and humble to the rest of the world. Yet that too, is Bushido, a false façade, a veil of humility behind which a world of treachery is hidden. Until that changes somehow, the Japanese nation and its people will always be an uncontrollable variable on the world stage. "

"There are factions within every society willing to play the long game to advance their agenda."

"For the Japanese, that is an inherent part of their culture."

"And they believe they can still somehow, conquer us, conquer the world?"

"All eight corners. That's what Shinto, Bushido and the Samurai legend is all about. Myths and legends all rolled into one and adhered to with unfettered devotion, forming a religion, one devoted not to the betterment of mankind but rather to its enslavement then ...selective elimination. Occupy, control and destroy; war by every means possible."

"Industry, real estate, but they're so damn polite."

"Again, that's part of the veil. Keep your enemy off balance, welcome him into your home, study his practices, learn his weaknesses, especially his excesses, then use what you've learned to destroy him. That's bushido, the art of deception. With every Japanese Shinto practitioner following the Bushido code every moment of their lives, theoretically, inch by inch,

Jimmu's proclamation that Japan's Emperor, their living god, will one day be the sole ruler of the eight corners of the world will come to pass, at least in their minds. Time as you and I know it is irrelevant."

"Sounds more like a fucking cult. So, that's what World War Two in the Pacific and the death of what, some thirty-five to forty million people boils down to, religious ideologues hell-bent on conquering the world because some invisible Messiah-dude told them to?"

"Essentially, yes."

"Fanatics always have some secret weapon in development ready to overwhelm their enemy. Any idea what Imperial Japan might have had?"

Olivia walks from the front door into the Florida room.

"Excuse me, gentlemen. Frank, it's our neighbor, Mr. Dawson, from across the street. He'd like to talk with you. He's quite upset. I told him we had company but he insisted and…"

"Please excuse me for a moment, Agent Donaldson."

"Of course."

Frank walks to the front door. He greets his neighbor.

"Good afternoon, Wilfred. As Olivia mentioned, we have company but I can give you a few quick minutes. What's on your mind?"

"It's your next-door neighbor, Mrs. Tomlinson."

"Jeannie?"

"Yes."

"What's the problem?"

"Have you seen or heard from her recently?"

Frank turns to Olivia, standing to his side. "Olivia?"

"No gentlemen, I have not. I did hear her dog barking this morning. It sounded awful, like the poor little thing was frighten to death for some reason."

"A few minutes ago I walked across the street and knocked on Jeannie's front door." Dawson offered. "You know how she is. She's a nut about conserving energy. The lights throughout the house have been on for the past two days and the sprinkler in her rose garden in the front yard…"

"Did you call Burt, at his office?" Frank asks.

"Yes, they said he was out of town. I didn't want to sound alarmed, so I just left my name and number."

"Tomlinson is an international investment banker. It makes sense that he's out of town."

"It seems he's always out of town." Wilfred admonishes. "I don't get it. What is he, some twenty-five years older than her? She's a very nice young woman, very polished, very polite and she genuinely loves that station wagon of hers. And the funny thing about that…"

"A funny thing about her station wagon?"

"As you know, I own the Belmont-Cragin hotel on the other side of the freeway from—well, where your service station once was."

"Thanks for the reminder. And as I said, I have company. If you have a point Wilfred, please get to it."

With a look of downright bat shit confusion, unable to grasp the dispassionate nature of his comment and Frank's stinging retort, Wilfred Dawson continues, "I often like taking the back roads home, you know, to avoid all the noise and freeway traffic."

"Please, Wilfred."

"The night before last, I believe I saw Jeannie's station wagon abandoned near 4th Street and Amsterdam. I thought to call the police but then again, I thought I'd check with you and your family first. You live next door, after all."

Unable to avoid eavesdropping from the adjacent hallway, Special Agent in Charge of the FBI's Northern Illinois office, Michaelene Westgate, steps forward entering the foyer.

"Hi, Mr. Dawson, is it? I'm sorry, I couldn't help but overhear. Perhaps I can be of some help?"

Michaelene extends her right hand with a greeting smile soon followed by her left with credentials in hand. Together, hand and credentials stop within a comfortable reading distance from Mr. Dawson's nose, forcing him to look up, taking his eyes off of Michaelene's exceptionally taut, female form. At seventy-eight, Dawson, the neighborhood watchdog and consummate gossip, still considers himself something of a lady's man even though no one who knew him could even begin to fathom such a possibility.

"Oh yes, I imagine you're here to investigate last night's explosion at Frank's gas station?"

With that, Frank shakes his head then Wilfred's hand, cordially thanking him for stopping by and returns to the Florida room. There, Special Agent Donaldson has been politely waiting, waiting intensely, actually, to further probe Marine combat veteran turned successful Shell gas station franchisee Frank Clifford's life, both past and present, looking for any link to any person or event that may lead to the party responsible for last night's monumental explosion and brutal murders. Clearly, the most "explosive" part of Frank's life was and 'is' his war with the Japanese.

Michaelene takes over. "Mr. Dawson, would you be kind enough to join me outside for a moment. I would like to get your impression of last night's events. Oh, and by the way, regarding the station wagon you mentioned..." Mike is about to engage in a game of connect the dots – one of her favorites - exploring the possible interconnectivity of each event of the last twenty-four hours. "Was anyone with the vehicle? Did you happen to notice its license plate number?" Typical "cop" questions but how they were answered and the body language used had captivated Michaelene's highly disciplined mind...especially the dots that were left out, those that the average person would have included.

Frank sits down on an overstuffed chair across from Agent Donaldson and rekindles the conversation seamlessly picking up where he left off:

"Japan is essentially a rock; mountainous and heavily forested. Eighty percent of Japan's entire land mass is unsuitable for any kind of agricultural, industrial or residential usage. Starting from such a geological and resulting economic disadvantage, if you were in their shoes, how would you go about starting a global war?"

"Be the bully on the block, the kid who lies the most and shouts the loudest, all as a precursor to a pre-emptive, first strike into the economic heart of a neighboring country, preferably one ill-prepared to militarily defend itself."

"Like the Japanese sneak attack on the city of Mukden?"

"Hey, now you're talking. You're referring to the *Manchurian Incident.* I'm very familiar with that one, Colonel. That was part of a homework assignment for a mandated, Ranger school class I attended. At the time, Mukden was China's leading trade center. It was a textbook-101 move. So obvious it worked."

"Go on."

"That's where a select team of Imperial Japanese saboteurs secreted themselves across the Chinese border, blew up the train station at Mukden, murdered the governorship, blamed it on a Chinese warlord then insisted that they had to stay to protect the railroad depot that was then rerouted to feed goods to the Japanese homeland. I mean, it almost makes you want to sit back and applaud— if it hadn't been the start of the second Sino-Japanese war."

"...That evolved into World War Two.*"

"Exactly!"

"In the 1930s, if Japan truly wanted to put all of East Asia into what they referred to as a *great, co-prosperity sphere* and eliminate western colonialism as their propaganda machine touted, they would have forged a peaceful alliance with China, The Father of All Asia. Instead, they decided to butcher him."

"Over the years, I've tried to pound Mukden into the heads of many of my stubborn friends," submits Agent Donaldson, "those who insist World War Two began in September of '39 when the Nazi blitzkrieg rolled into Poland. It began in September alright, but eight years earlier at the Mukden railroad station at the other end of the world."

"The Manchurian Incident in 1931 was to China what the bridge at Lexington and Concord in 1776 was to the American Revolution. Both were *shots heard 'round the world*. Both evolved into cataclysmic global conflict and both resulted in horrific social upheaval."

"According to the West Point Major who conducted that Ranger school class, it all could have ended right there, right there at Mukden, if the Japanese foreign minister who rushed to the city seeking to re-establish civilian control over his military, wasn't driven out of Mukden at bayonet point by his own people."

"And from there, as the world's superpowers especially the United States, did little but write letters for a decade protesting Japanese aggression, Hitler and his henchmen watched and learned. Ten years later, once the Nazis so-lidified their control over the German nation, Germany declared war on the United States, believing we would once again, act as we had with the Japanese. That same afternoon however, the Nazis received a surprise. By way of a unaminous vote of Congress, the United States declared war on Germany."

"December '41, was a busy month. The day after the Japanese bombed Pearl Harbor on the 7th, we declared war on them. Why didn't the U.S. and our allies see the Japanese juggernaut coming and intervene in the '30's before it gained momentum?"

"A key reason is that the Imperial Japanese launched their invasion into mainland China neatly wrapped in a blanket of anti-communism."

"Okay, Oh sure. I get it. The enemy of my enemy is my friend, the 'Arthashastra,' fourth Century, Hindu, political theory."

"Good. You read."

"I try to keep up."

"The Japanese informed the Western World by the late 1920s that they too were fighting the spread of Communism."

"Yet another veil behind which the Japanese pursued their own agenda. That's all our government officials needed to hear, that one simple word 'communism,' and poof, just like that, the U.S. was kept at bay."

"No one in the Pentagon or State department dared to lift Japan's anti-communism veil to study their real goals. There was one exception to that, a fellow Marine, an Intelligence officer, a man by the name of 'Pete" Ellis."

"Yeah, I remember hearing that name before. Ellis, yes, as I recall, he studied the Japanese for years immersing himself into their culture ultimately becoming a spy at great personal peril. Then one day he was never heard from again."

"That's him. In 1921, Ellis wrote an operational initiative describing how the Micronesian islands, especially Saipan and Tinian, could be used as giant stationary aircraft carriers from which to counter Japanese aggression when it arose. His superiors still dazzled by Jap' anticommunist veil, shelved it. Twenty years later, shortly after Pearl Harbor, someone happened Ellis's initiative, dusted it off and insisted that the Chief of Naval Intelligence read it. As a result, it became the blueprint for rolling back Japanese aggression across half the world."

From what you've said, the Japs had a global initiative in mind from day one?"

"A global, military initiative devised at the onset of the 20th Century, propagated by extreme xenophobia, based upon a pseudo-religion that preaches genocide and subjugation."

"Letting the Imperial Japanese do their thing without consequence. Wow. You gotta hand it to the little fuckers, they learned how to play the entire global community like a cheap violin."

"In 1904, As the Japanese celebrated their victory over Russia prior to World War One, it became clear to their Imperial court that their military's ability to fulfill Jimmu's proclamation of world domination by means of conventional warfare alone would be impossible. So, while the Allies and the Nazis struggled with nuclear fission to develop an atom bomb, Japanese leadership decided to focus on a more, readily obtainable resource with far greater killing potential."

"What?" As yet another piece of the onion skin begins to peel back.

"Germs."

"Germs?"

"Specifically, a bacteriological WMD—a weapon of mass destruction capable of being unleashed without notice."

"And spreading before detection."

"Wiping out a countless number of people without destroying homes or infrastructure."

"No need to rebuild. Just infect, disinfect and occupy. Efficient. Holy shit!"

"Assigned to head the development of this program was a Jap Lieutenant General, a man by the name of Dr. Ishii Shiro, a surgeon, and a microbiologist."

"A medical doctor? Never heard of him," Steve offers.

"There's a reason for that."

"What do you mean?"

CHAPTER THIRTY

Frank continues: "In 1931 when Imperial Japan first invaded China - the land known for thousands of years as the father of all Asia- millions of innocent men, women and children, especially women, lost their lives to the Japanese invaders. Of the number of senior Jap generals who engaged in a deliberate and coordinated effort to take China by destroying its female population, two spear-headed the effort; the 'pragmatist,' General Yasuji Okamura, the senior commander of the Japanese military occupying China, and the psychopath, Dr. General Ishii Shiro. For them, the ability to kill masses of people evolved into a game of one-upmanship, a form of amusement, a competition. After being responsible for ordering the deaths of a recorded three million civilians, General Okamura…"

"What?" The reality of such an enormous toll of human life destroyed on orders from one man hit Steve hard. He interjects, "Three million—Holy fuckin Christ, are you certain, sir? Is that a hard number?"

"Indeed, it is."

Still stunned, Steve offers, "That's like what—every man, woman, and child in the State of Oregon being wiped off the face of the earth?"

Frank continues, "Following General Okamura's well-documented assault on humanity, he then ordered the taking of young girls from their homes across all occupied territories in what he labeled his *comfort women program.*"

"I heard that term before but I thought it was a random thing. You're saying it was a general order like a battle plan?"

"That is precisely what it was, a battle plan."

With his core values and every measure of his being whipped into a fury, Steve offers, "Oh fuckin A. How can…?"

The second, our psychopath Dr. General Ishii Shiro, sought to prove to his uncle the Emperor and the people of Japan that his methods of exterminating vast populations were superior to Okamura's. Ishii began by targeting mothers and elderly women, infecting them with cholera, bubonic plague, and simple malaria. These women, in turn, acted as delivery systems, unwittingly spreading the disease to their families, fellow villagers ultimately impacting entire communities."

"This piece of shit medical doctor you're describing makes the Nazi's Dr. Josef Mengele look like Russian poet Dr. Yuri Zhivago."

"During Ishii's first few months of experimentation, some twenty thousand Chinese died while lingering for up to ten days in excruciating pain. Ishii and his staff were outraged, deeming these efforts an unmitigated failure. They then began to mix and match keeping copious notes, inventing new, far more deadly bacterium assuring more efficient and a greater number of deaths per dose."

"This sounds like science fiction...?"

"Unfortuntely, it's not. For example," Frank continues, "*Claviceps purpurea*, more commonly known as ergot, a fungus that grows on wheat shafts and given to women throughout history to expedite birth, was blended by Ishii with gas gangrene. At first, when ingested, these two ingredients combined take on the appearance of a simple yeast infection. Within a few days, the infection grows deadly, causing the fetus to burst inside the mother resulting in the deaths of tens of thousands of more women. At war's end, the U.S Army torched Ishii's headquarters in occupied China."

"That must have been a real fuckin' rat's nest."

"You're right. Quite literally it was. Before Army flame throwers destroyed some 26,000 caged rats, each infected with an advanced version of the bubonic plague and other designer pathogens, they snagged a literal bounty of empirical medical records."

"The Black Death, the god damn plague? That's what he was cooking up? That was there, too?"

Steve is struggling to process what kind of sick mind would be willing to once again, unleash such an uncontrollable, deadly pathogen on humanity?

"Are you talking about the same germs, those same microscopic parasites that.. ?"

"Yes, the same bacterium that killed-off a third of Europe's population in the 14th Century but in this case, it was a hybrid."

"You mean, a more advanced version?"

"Unfortunately, yes. A review of the seized documents showed that Ishii was tirelessly working to improve upon whatever his most recent concoction provided. After the war, I met a General Tom Sackton, one of yours, a U.S. Army officer at a fundraiser for then Presidential candidate, Dwight Eisenhower. Tom as a Colonel, led the team that first entered Ishii's lab. He told me that once they torched the cages, his men blew off the locked door of an adjacent room. Inside they discovered a stockpile of an additional two hundred and fifty, plague-filled test tubes inside rows of incubators ready to be applied to a soon-to-be-arriving, new batch of rats. The time of delivery and what to do with the rats uon arrival, was spelled out quite neatly on a nearby chalkboard. The distribution date and the effectiveness of this second stockpile was stated in a mathematical formula. It read…"

"Ah, do I really want to know this?"

"One mcg over twenty-four equals one K minus. This program was set to be released throughout mainland China."

Steve deciphers the formula: "So what you are saying it reads that one microgram of this shit in twenty-four hours would kill a thousand people? Just one—just one, just one millionth of a gram?"

"Yes, that's how the theorem was designed to play out."

"Real sweethearts."

"Before the U.S Army arrived, upwards of quarter million Chinese women and their tender-age children died at Ishii's hand."

"And after we arrived, a quarter million lives were presumably saved. I wonder how many people know that the US Army took such great risk to save so many? I mean, if one of those rats got out and bit one of our guys or an incubator exploded releasing its toxins before the flamethrower could finish its job the result would have been catastrophic."

Steve wraps-up his educational immersion into weaponized bacteria, using now what he learned to peel back yet another skin of the onion. He asks, "Gas gangrene? What the hell is that? And respectfully Colonel, how do you know so much about all of this?"

"While on Saipan during the war, my Marines and I happened upon ceramic bombs laced with what turned out to be a prototype version of the gas gangrene bacterium. After the war, I learned that this was Ishii's concoction. For a period of time, I became rather obsessed, wanting to find out all that I could about him. When I asked through official channels, I was told that the answers I sought were above my paygrade. So, I turned to a friend who wasn't bound by such restrictions."

"And you got answers?"

"Model 50 Ceramic bombs, to be precise."

"And you actually came across one of these things?"

"One of my Marines did. He picked up a piece of a ceramic shell."

"Army Rangers are schooled in past wars to give us an idea of what to expect both militarily and politically, when we're out in the field. Why am I hearing about bacteria-laced, ceramic bombs as a weapon of war now for the first time?"

"Most likely because it failed miserably."

"What? I don't understand?"

"That failure defined Ishii for what he is."

"And what would that be?"

"A true genius."

"I don't get it. How can you say that?"

"Once you set aside his fanaticism, you can see why the Japanese people revered Ishii as a visionary, a hero. But like so many other geniuses throughout history, Ishii was so intensely focused upon obtaining his end result that he failed to thoroughly take into account key steps along the way."

"What do you mean?"

"Ceramic explosives laced with gas gangrene or rats doused with bubonic-plagued fleas are highly effective as a weapon of war when unleashed directly onto the land. Contained within thin ceramic shells and dropped like bombs from the sky, was thankfully, highly ineffective."

"This guy Ishii may have been some kind of genius in your book but to me, he sounds more like *Blofeld*, a villain right out of a James Bond novel."

"Except, in this case, our villain is real. Ceramic bombs were air dropped over Saipan in June of '44, as the U.S attempted to retake that island. Most of the rats, fleas and adjoining bacterium died in the rarified air before hitting the ground. What hit the earth was consumed by conventional weapons of war."

"And you were there?"

"I was. I was on Saipan and its nearby neighboring island of Tinian throughout June and July of 1944. Along with my men, I was a potential victim of a *Fugos, a* grand experiment, a trial run."

"And I thought I was the guy forever in the wrong place at the wrong time."

"It was Dr. Ishii's attempt to wipe out all living beings on the island, theirs, ours, and some 13,000 native islanders by dropping ceramic bombs across the entire land mass. If it worked there, no doubt the concept was it would work anywhere."

"Like on the sunny beaches of Southern California?"

"That was the idea. I learned that the Japs had specifically targeted California, as the war neared its end in June of 1945. Under Ishii's orders, the Japs were prepared to unleash their bacterium off the San Diego coast. They called it *Operation Cherry Blossom At Night*. From there, the intent was for the bacterium to spread inland. Like the flu, it was easily transferrable. Unlike the flu, its kill ratio was upward of 85%."

"It would kill 85% of the people who came in contact with it?"

"Conceptually, yes."

"I guess all the Japs on Saipan would have been grateful?"

"Frank asks, "For what?"

"To be the first in line to feast at Jimmu's table!" Steve is still wrestling with the idea of a madman so detached from reality and so eager to place himself above others that he would kill his own and everything and anyone around them to achieve his objective.

"Gas gangrene? What the hell is that, anyhow?"

"Basic gas gangrene seeps into the body, building toxic gas beneath vital organs, causing them to rapidly rot. From my research, I learned that death is inevitable if not treated within 48 hours."

"So, not only does he want to kill off his enemies," Steve cites, "he wants to make sure they suffer before they die."

"Ishii was an exceptionally talented micro-bacteriologist, a prince, a surgeon, a three-star general, and medical prodigy who, guided by Emperor Hirohito's hand, failed to recognize the simplest of facts. Imperial bomber pilots were highly skilled and bright young men, not ideologues. They were reluctant to fly low over Saipan and Tinian, directly into our anti-aircraft guns to drop a weightless payload of what they considered to be mad scientist's experiment. Some pilots persevered only to be *splashed* offshore by our heavy cruisers before ever eyeing the shoreline. But most of these single-engine bomber pilots simply dropped their loads at the standard ten thousand foot elevation then headed back to their carriers."

In his head, Steve is doing some quick calculations, "At ten thousand feet, the average temperature is plus-minus, negative five degrees Celsius or approximately 22 degrees Fahrenheit. The bacterium immediately froze as the bomb bay door opened. What fuckin idiots."

Frank gave the young FBI agent a puzzled look.

"I use to drink with a lot of flyboys in Nam. I liked them for details. So, that Marine of yours, what happened to him?"

"Corporal Edmondson? He survived. Got a Christmas card from Kevin and his wife Amanda, this year.

"How? I mean, how did he survive?"

"Maggots from fly larva. A Navy corpsman grabbed a handful of maggots and jammed them into Corporal Edmondson's rapidly festering wound."

"How did he know to do that?"

259

"He didn't."

"So what, he just grabbed a slab of slimy goo and slapped it into a Marine under your command, and you just stood by and allowed it?" Steve is trying to mellow out but his anger over the deaths of so many millions of people on orders from just two men has his guts twisted."

"Maggots were eating fly larva. My corpsman thought they may eat whatever infected Corporal Edmondson. They did and it worked."

"One of my men in Nam once said for every evil the devil creates, God provides an antidote. I'm an atheist so I never gave it much thought but perhaps there's something to what he said."

Michaelene breaches the threshold of the Florida room and steps inside. Steve and Frank stand and turn towards her. "Agent Donaldson, may I speak to you for a moment," she asks.

Together, Steve and Mike move to a secluded section of the Clifford family home's hallway. Mike is the first to speak. "I just called my office and got an update. The meeting to address last night's Belmont-Cragin explosion is set for 7:00 pm tonight. CBS, NBC and ABC affiliates, channels 2, 5, and 7 respectively, will paste select segments into their news telecasts throughout the night and into their early-morning broadcasts tomorrow. PBS affiliate WEIU-TV will broadcast it live, uninterrupted and commercial free. They also offered to drop a copy off at Bureau headquarters. Chicago Mayor Bilandic, secured a church near City Hall, St. Margaret's of Scotland, it's a Parish on S. Vincennes Avenue. Our governor, James Thompson will be the first to speak at exactly seven, then-Mayor Bilandic, followed by me and finally, the state's, leading nuclear physicist a Dr. Randolf Shirin, from the University of Chicago."

"Sounds impressive. Who's this Shirin guy?"

"I was introduced to him once at a State function. He's pretentious as hell, always smiling. He makes my skin crawl but from what I understand, he's one of the best in the country. I encouraged an open forum following our initial delivery. The mayor agreed but said he'd have to run it by the governor. While on the phone, Edwards informed me of a bank robbery in progress with a non-fatal shooting in Belmont-Cragin. He said it was amateurish. Nevertheless, I ordered him to throw everything we have at it, making a show of it to contain it quickly and set an example."

"If you hadn't locked down that community as effectively as you did, we'd be receiving more news like that."

"I gave the assignment to Agents Haskell and Wilson, two of the best in my office. How are you making out with Mr. Clifford?"

"Christ, this guy is a walking encyclopedia. I got to tell you, I'm fascinated by him."

"Where are you with him right now?"

"Still probing. I ask questions. I can see he's legitimately trying to answer but he's struggling. I'm convinced he considers himself a link to both crimes. He just can't figure out how."

"No doubt he's still shocked from last night."

"No. Not this guy. He's been suppressing something that goes back much further than that—much further than last night. He simply doesn't know how to bring it forward."

"Look." Michaelene begins, "Someone who…"

Frank steps out of the Florida room and into the hallway abruptly facing both agents. Without offering Michaelene an opportunity to transition into the conversation that he and Steve were having, Frank blurts out,

"When the ceramic bombs failed, the Japs sent scientists to Saipan with test-tubes in hand filled with a collection of hybrid bacterium. They were part of Unit 731, Dr. Ishii's group. They never made it to shore. A U.S Navy sub sunk the troop carrier they were aboard. Only one survived.

We had him contained in an internment camp outside a village called Susupe on Saipan's shore. He spat on me when I was outside its gates interrogating another prisoner, one who tried to escape disguised as a woman."

Frank rambles on. Both agents turn to the former Marine combat officer and carefully listen.

"This guy, the one in a dress, a muumuu, he was Kempeitai, Jap 'Secret Police'—psychopaths the lot of them. This one was especially fond of butchering women, carving them up. Once stripped of his disguise, he danced about the compound like a mime employing an invisible blade. Satirizing the agony his female victims had endured, he spread his legs inserting that same invisible blade. The other guy, a medical officer from Unit 731, he....

Olivia enters the hallway next to the agents and her father-in-law.

Steve implores, "What about this guy from Unit 731?"

"Excuse me, Agent Donaldson, someone from the Medical Examiner's office is on the phone for you. She said it was urgent. You can take it in the kitchen if you'd like."

Frank's eyes dart to one agent then the next. He is well aware of what he said and he wanted to say more. What Frank couldn't read was the impact his words had on the two young agents.

Michaelene looks at Steve and insists, "You and Frank need to continue your conversation."

"Roger that, boss."

CHAPTER THIRTY-ONE

Olivia hands the telephone to Steve. He takes the call. "It's Dr. Vaziri," Steve offers to Mike, then listens intently, to Dr. Elizabeth Vaziri

"I'm calling to first off, extend my apologies. I jumped ahead without first discussing the matter with you."

"No apology necessary. What've you got for me?"

"An Asian linguistics expert is coming to the morgue to view those suspicious marking on the victim's arm. The extent of the torture this woman endured has made it difficult even for photographic evidence to accurately capture the message if any, of the cuts on her forearm. I thought you would like to be here when she arrives. Can you be here in an hour?"

Steve conveys the conversation privately, to his boss. Mike listens then turns to Frank.

"I would like for you to accompany Agent Donaldson with our driver to the medical examiner's office. While en route, the two of you can continue your conversation regarding the Unit 73 envoy. I would particularly welcome Frank, your firsthand assessment of any features or anomalies you may witness concerning our victim. Are you up for that?"

"Happy to help any way I can."

Mike turns to Steve, "Agent Donaldson, from this point forward, I am asking you to take the lead on the murder investigations. We will continue to treat the two crimes, the murder and the explosion as unrelated incidences until further proof if any, arises. I've called a meeting at four pm this afternoon at Bureau headquarters. I'm asking all state and city agencies involved in both cases to have a senior representative on hand. I want preliminary reports no matter how preliminary they may be. Once received, I'll have a few hours to review and analyze the data before tonight's town hall address."

"Agent Westgate?"

"Yes, Frank?"

"No need to have someone pick us up. I have a Dodge truck. It's new. I can drive Agent Donaldson downtown. The examiner's office, that's the new building on 18th and North Clark Street, isn't it?"

"It is."

"I know the area well. I grew up around there. My parents would take me to a diner across the street from that building when I was a kid."

For the briefest of moments Frank fell melancholy. "You know, my dad was an optics engineer. When he finally landed a job with Bell+Howell, we moved from there first to Des Plains then to Park Ridge. It's been too long since I've been back to the old neighborhood."

"Okay, but you'll need this."

"Oh yes, my driver's license. Thank you, Agent Westgate.

"No. Thank you, *Colonel*."

COOK COUNTY OFFICE OF THE MEDICAL EXAMINER – EXAMINATION ROOM.

Dr. Vaziri steps forward to meet Steve and Frank. She offers her hand and smiles, politely.

"Dr. Vaziri, this is Marine Colonel Frank Clifford, a combat veteran. He's here to observe the body. I'm hoping he may be able to provide some perspective."

Dr. Vaziri looks a little skeptical, but nods pleasantly enough.

In the examination room, the lab assistant has prepared the body now face-up on the examination table. On hand is language expert Professor Meredith Chang who has already begun her analysis. Steve enters the room slightly ahead of Frank. Both men take the mask and gloves handed to them by an assistant. Slowly approaching the examination table, a grimness befalls the World War Two warrior's face as he sees something he thought he would never see again.

Drawing a sudden and deep breath, Frank views the dead woman's forearms up close for the first time.

Dr. Vaziri offers, "Agent Donaldson, this is Dr. Meredith Chang. She is an Associate Professor of Phonology and Sociolinguists at the University.

Steve replies, "Ms. Chang, it's a pleasure to meet you. We appreciate you driving all the way up here. What have you got for us?"

"Do either of you know what Kanji is?" Professor Chang asks, her eyes smiling behind a surgical mask, reminiscent to Frank, of a beautiful, young Nun, a French woman, he once knew.

Frank who has said nothing up to this point, abruptly takes the initiative, offering, "It's an ancient form of Asian script."

"Yes, very good." offers Miss Chang. "Its roots are in the Chinese character system. However, this particular character is clearly Japanese."

"How can you be so certain?" Steve asks.

"If you initially thought the inscription was Chinese, a mark of the Triad for example, you would have been right except for one thing?"

"What's that?" Asks Frank.

"The uniqueness of the incision. This is not the work of a Chinese, male or female. When the artist inserted the blade and started to carve, he—"

"You know that for a fact?" Steve inquires.

"Know what, sir?"

"That it was a man?" Steve was desperate to have one piece of solid evidence at long last. on which to rely.

"Yes, there's no doubt," Meredith acknowledges. "When the man who fashioned this design went from a highly delicate touch at the top to a bolder flair at the bottom, that's the same as an American saying, "In your face, dude."

An effervescent, Chinese-American female, both young and attractive, using the word "dude" combined with expressive mannerisms uniquely American of hands on the hips and head cocked to the side, elicited a chuckle from Steve.

Meredith continues, "Such 'boldness' is characteristic of the male dominant Japanese culture of the Meiji period, 1867-1910. Your perp is a Japanese male. No question—and he is no taller than 5'8".

"And how can you be certain of that?"

"The weight of an arm of a taller man would not have been able to make these delicate strokes. His thoughts captured on her arm are very old school. Your perp is a victim of an introspective and sorrow-laden life. This is a highly disciplined and insufferably patient anthropoid, someone who has spent a great deal of time alone."

"How can you tell that?" Steve probes.

"What he wrote and how he wrote it speaks to a human being stripped of emotion devoid of even the most basic of interpersonal relationship skills—a real dud on a date if you know what I mean?"

"So, what does it say?"

"Fukushū."

Steve and Frank look at each other. Steve looks startled, but Frank's eyes reveal recognition.

"I'm certain I misunderstood you. Will you say that again, please?" Steve asks.

"Fukushū."

"You're laughing and telling *us* to go fuck ourselves, is that it? I'm sorry, professor, but I don't get the joke? The FBI is seeking evidence regarding a murder investigation. If you can't be of any further assistance, I will ask Dr. Vaziri to ask you to leave. And I suggest you take advantage of this offer within the next ten seconds before I decide to arrest you for interfering in a federal investigation."

The ever-bubbly Meredith struggles to keep a straight face. "No, Agent Donaldson, I apologize. Not at all. That's not what I'm saying. In fact, I expected your reaction. What you are hearing and what I am saying are examples of what language experts refer to as "cultural bias." In other words, who you are, in what time period you were born and raised and where and to what extent you were educated, influences what you hear. In this case, we are translating a written word carved into this woman's arm, into a spoken word across three different cultures and hundreds of years. Misinterpretations are bound to occur."

"So, what does the carving in this woman's arm actually mean—in English?"

"Revenge."

Silence draping heavily, fills the room.

Dr. Vaziri, Ms. Chang, thank you both for your help. I need to get back to the office. Colonel Clifford, will you walk with me?" Steve leans in and whispers to Frank, "Now!"

Frank and Steve exit the Medical Examiner's office. Slamming aside the building's double front doors they enter onto North Clark Street. Wanting to get to FBI Headquarters across town on West Ogden for the 4:00 pm briefing, they hurry down the cascade of cement stairs with Steve taking the lead. He barks at Frank, "What the hell was that?"

Frank purposely grabs the side-railing at the bottom of the steps and stops. Steve, having made it beyond to the sidewalk below, abruptly turns back.

"Are you okay?"

"You need to stop asking me that." Frank sucking up a virtual lifetime of war-induced, emotional trauma, replies, Give me a moment to think."

Steve takes a seat on the stairs next to Frank. It's evident on the faces of both men. Their minds are reeling, trying to piece together a puzzle that's still in the box, a box on which both share a grasp but have yet to finds the means to open. The bustle of both pedestrian and street traffic shields their conversation.

Frustrated, Steve ask, "What was that all about back in there? You gasped when you saw that woman's corpse. That was not the kind of reaction I would have expected from a combat veteran who *killed hundreds of Japanese, many hand-to-hand?*"

"Before we left my house, your boss assigned you the 'murder investigations" Frank asserts. "She said 'investigations.' That's plural, meaning as you know, more than one, more than one victim. It's your turn, Agent Donaldson. You tell me. What the hell is going on here?" demanded the Colonel in no uncertain terms. After all, once a Marine always a Marine.

"Yes, okay. There has been two female victims, at least as far as we know of at this point... the second more barbaric than the first if you can imagine that."

"Believe me, Agent Donaldson, I can," offered less as a criticism than a statement of fact. "But your count is still off. There has been more than two."

"How could you possibly know that?" Had he'd been wrong all along about this man? Steve felt his gut beginning to churn. Was he about to hear the confession of a murderer?

"The first wasn't that young woman back there on medical examiner's table," Frank asserts. The first was more than thirty-three years ago."

"What are you trying to say to me?"

CHAPTER THIRTY-TWO

Cook County Office of the Medical Examiner – front steps

"I saw the shard of metal you were holding at the crime scene. I simply didn't want to believe that a rusted souvenir from a war that took place on the other side of the world more than a quarter of a century ago could have anything to do with the murder of that young woman on the coroner's examination table we just left or the destruction of my service station complex. I don't believe in coincidences, Agent Donaldson. That shard being in that place at that time, it wasn't an accident. If you have any information that links the destruction of my service center to the first murdered woman and now the second, you need to share it with me. There is a good chance I may be able to help but I need to know the facts – all of them. I need the truth."

"We have nothing except proximity to your service center to connect the first murder victim and nothing to connect it to the second. So, until we arrive at another conclusion or you can help me fill in some of the blanks, we are treating each of these crimes as Agent Westgate said, separately. And perhaps you can start to help by telling me about that murder you referenced, the one that occurred on the other side of the world, thirty-three years ago?"

"Somewhere, there's a missing piece to this puzzle. There has to be?"

"Good god, not you too?"

"What?"

"First Agent Westgate, now you! You're both trying to latch onto some kind of common thread that magically links the explosion at your service center to the murders. It may exist. I can't say for certain. What I do know is that right now we have the bodies of two grossly butchered females for whom I have been tasked with the responsibility of apprehending their murderer or murderers."

"The first, at least the one I knew of, happened during the war." Frank goes onto to relive his dreamscape nightmare in real time. He sums with, "I did all I could."

Steve checks his watch. "You and I need to get to Bureau headquarters, pronto."

TIME 3:28 P.M.

"Ah shit, we're going to be late. Let's hurry. Agent Westgate will have us both castrated if we miss the four pm briefing."

"Earlier, your boss Agent Westgate inferred that what is missing in both cases is motive?"

"From what we just heard it's revenge but for what?"

"I don't know why or even how but I may have some idea, who." The once relentless jungle fighter of World War Two turned upscale, 70's, Illinois businessman is inwardly struggling, trying to formulate a salient argument; one regarding a horrific event in his past – one

273

more troubling than any other - that may aid the FBI in their current investigation. He could lay the groundwork. Of that he was confident. Reliving the memory, struggling to find the right place to start well, that may take a little more than what the aging Marine Corps combat officer may be able to give.

"Agent Donaldson, I..?"

"Frank, I think it's time we dropped the formalities. You've allowed us to call you by your first name repeatedly without correction. My name is Steve. Please, call me 'Steve'."

"Steve?"

"What?"

"I'm hungry."

"Ah shit Frank, we can't stop. We've got less than thirty minutes to get to Bureau HQ. If we hurry, we may make it with a minute or two to spare. As I said, if we're late, Michaelene will have us both..."

"Oh Michaelene, is that her name? That's very pretty."

"Come on Frank. Let's head for that pick-up truck of yours and get the hell out of here."

"Steve, you're right. It is my truck. I have the keys and I'm the one driving. I'm also the one that's very hungry. You see that diner across the street? That's the one I referred to earlier."

"You mean that shithole, dive bar over there? Oh, great. I'm going to die from salmonella poisoning and get kicked out of the bureau all in the same day? You're getting me in a lot of trouble, Colonel."

"Or Army Lieutenant Donaldson, this Marine may be the one to lead you out of it."

CHAPTER THIRTY-THREE

It opened as a nightclub in the 1920s, before the Great Depression. It transitioned to *Mighty Mike's Juke Joint,* a bar+ grill, Blues club in the 1930s. Throughout the 1940s and into the 1960s, it was a sock hop diner catering to the hamburger and milkshake crowd. A few years back, it failed as a disco. Now, it's this.

Special Agent Steve Donaldson passes through the brightly painted red door of a near dilapidated building into a high-ceiling, dimly lit, elongated room with Frank two steps ahead.

Once inside, Steve was shocked.

"Damn, Colonel."

The place was clean, one might even say spotless. The no smoking sign Steve noticed over his left shoulder as he breached the entryway, was clearly in force. The massive, hand-crafted, back bar with beveled mirrors, a throwback to the establishment's *Speak Easy* days, bristled with decades of polish and care, highlighted with a rapidly depleting array of spirits from *Jack Daniels* to a barely touched bottle of *Dolin* Vermouth. Red leather bar stools stood like *Royal Guardsmen* at parade rest in front of an elongated countertop. In the absence of the stench of stale smoke, the aromatic enticements of grilled steak and onions with just a hint of bacon, wafted through the bar's interior emanating from a kitchen to the rear. Such taste bud titillations were egged-on by a series of interconnected, ever-in-motion, belt-driven, ceiling fans strategically placed above the entire establishment.

The floor beyond the bar and main entry was old but clean. On it, were a series of no thrills, wooden tables and chairs each with a stand-up menu-card. Noticeably absent on each menu was a listing of salads and desserts. Looking down into the cavernous recesses of the room past the jukebox and a series of four, green felted pool tables was a high polished wooden dance floor.

"This is my kind of joint," Steve announces enthusiastically. "Thanks for bringing me here, Frank but I gotta tell ya..."

"My mom and dad frequented this place back in its hay day. I was just a kid then. I'd sit right here and watch as my parents Matt and Nancy, danced the night away right over there. On Thursday nights, the jukebox's coin mech was by-passed and the songs were set to free play one right after the other."

Frank turns in his chair, pointing to the aged, barroom dance floor. His mood and the tone of his voice take on a more balanced resonance as he talks about his parents.

Agent Donaldson sat silent and attentive. He is a man who learned long ago, when to talk and when to listen. His instincts were telling him that ultimately something of value regarding the events of the last forty-eight hours was going to come out of this. When and how was still up for grabs.

"When my parents and I came here, it was always a special night. I'd order a cheeseburger and a glass of milk. The bartender served the milk ice cold in a tall, frosted glass. I'd savor it. It was delicious. There was never enough money for all of us so as I ate, my parents just danced and held one another. When we arrived back home, mom and dad would still be dancing and singing. Dad whistled a tune. Mom struggled to hum along. I'd be picked up and swirled around. The three of us would then burst into laughter as together, we'd plop down on the couch grinning ear to ear. Just to watch my parents, always holding hands, unashamed to show affection for one another regardless of time or circumstance, provided a joy that I would do anything to share once again even for the briefest of moments. They genuinely loved and nurtured one another till the day they died—just two days apart. Looking back, I've often wondered how they could have been so happy?

"How's that, Frank?"

"When we lived in this neighborhood Dad could barely keep a roof over our heads."

"I've heard it said that true love can conquer all," Steve offered as he remembered as a teen, looking deep into Michaelene's eyes as she gazed back into his.

"I found the answer to my parent's happiness for myself. She was sitting right over there." Frank turns in his chair and points to four chairs and a table next to a window near the front door, the window and its frame looking noticeably newer than its interior counterparts.

"Her name was Mary Townsend."

To Steve, the Colonel seemed to be on his way, edging ever closer to what may well be something invaluable, a pieces of information... a piece of the puzzle.

"I can still see her, my Mary. She was radiant, full of life. I loved to call her Maggie, like "Maggie" from the *Jiggs and Maggie* Comic Strip? It was popular when she and I were kids. When I called her that, when I called her Maggie, it made her cheeks blush and nose twitch at the same time. It was the dandiest of things. Like her comic strip namesake, there was a joyfulness and an ease about her, something my Mary never lost. I guess that made her seem vulnerable to some."

"As I said before, you're a very lucky man, Frank."

"It was the spring of 1940. We were both in high school, sixteen or seventeen years old, I don't recall exactly. My utter contempt towards men who abuse women began that year."

Steve adjusts himself, sitting straight up in his chair. He had a hunch where this may be going.

"Three of our classmates came in, pushing and shoving, loud and boisterous with no regard for the other people in the diner. You know the type."

"Regretfully, yes."

"One was a kid named Max Mitchell. He was our school's most prominent athlete. The others were his en-tourage, enablers who gained their self-worth simply by

279

standing alongside him. Together, they surrounded Maggie and began to tease her, lifting her skirt. Mitchell, believing his reputation gave him a free pass, slipped his hand down the front of her blouse."

Steve offers a mumbled, "ah shit" under his breath.

"I caught Maggie's soft blue eyes darting around this room. There was genuine fear in them. I don't know what came over me. I wasn't a very big kid, then. I rushed Mitchell, body-slamming him, catching him by surprise, pushing him through that window over there. I then positioned myself by the front door between Maggie and the other two. I shouted,

If I ever see any of you around this woman again, you better kill me, quick. If you don't as God is my witness, I will hunt you down and destroy every shred of evidence that you were ever born."

"So, Colonel, you were a real badass before joining the Marines?"

"Years later, Maggie relayed the story of how she and I met to another young couple at a dinner party reciting word-for-word what spewed out of my mouth that day. Mary told our young friends that she knew at that exact moment that I was the man with whom she'd spend the rest of her life."

"How so, Frank?"

"When I asked her that very same question she smiled, reached for my hand, kissed it and said:

"Because you were the first person who ever referred to me as a woman."

"She sounds damn near angelic, sir."

"In part, no doubt but she was also very down to earth and keen-witted."

"If I may Frank, you were about to tell me who...?"

Suddenly Frank's voice and posture took on an unbending, steel-like presence. Agent Donaldson decidedly backed off. It wasn't the right time to tighten the investigatory tether, not just yet.

"What I don't understand Agent Donaldson, is why? Why so many young boys start out life bullying adolescent girls?"

Steve set aside his direct question, keeping it in reserve, offering in its place, "Not me. I was scared crapless of them." *Until Michaelene introduced herself to me,* Steve thought, reflecting once again upon his high school days.

Frank offers. "Boys are awkward. I get that. They try to get a girl's attention but bullying is too often their first choice."

"In my book Colonel, bullies are the same no matter how young or old or from under which rock they may crawl."

"They're cowards, the lot of them," Frank adds as disdain leaves its mark upon his brow. "They don't understand that a real woman respects a man who demonstrates respect not just for her but for others as well."

That comment struck a nerve in Steve. Now his temperature takes a sudden rise. "For me personally, any low life, shit heel that assaults a woman or molests a child should get down on their knees and be damn grateful that I swore an oath to enforce the laws of our country without prejudice."

"My parents never sat down and explained such boy-girl relations to me. They taught through example. Still, by the time teenage years roll around, too often girls are seen as nothing but playthings. For those carrying that same kind of moral imbalance into adulthood, especially in a culture where checks and balances do not exist…"

Steve offers to himself, "Okay, here we go." As Frank continues:

"…and the popular religion of a militant nation encourages the segregation of genders, matters often escalate, raging uncontrollably with all sense of humanity gone, washed away."

Steve thought to himself. "Now we're getting somewhere. We're back to the Japanese."

"I mean, that girl, butchered in Belmont-Cragin, that fifteen-year-old butchered on a California beach, a French nun, thousands of women from various nations, incinerated and how many more…"

"Sir?"

Frank trembles. Steve leans back in his chair. The veneer of the successful Illinois businessman abruptly vanishes. In its place—at least for the moment—is the "badass"

Marine. Suddenly Frank pushes back his chair and abruptly takes to his feet. Striding towards the bar, his eyes fixed on the man behind it. As the jukebox plays *What Will My Mary Say, a song sung* by Johnny Mathis.

I must be going (Don't go)

My heart is showing (Don't go)

I better hurry away

If I don't leave I'll be sorry

What will my Mary say?

With the voice of an outraged drill sergeant, Frank barks, "Turn off that damn thing!"

"What?" asks a startled bar keep.

"That jukebox! Turn it off, now."

With that, Frank turns away from the barroom counter and walks to the corner table, that very same table where his Mary first sat. He leans with one hand against the frame of the once-shattered window and holds his head with the other, weeping openly.

The sound of Steve's chair being pushed back as he starts to stand, wanting to reach out, wanting to help, elicits a nod from Frank, a gesture requesting a few moments alone.

DREAMSCAPE; "Mop Up" another daydream, July 1944:

As Frank continues to subtly weep, his mind recaptures the image of his younger self standing amidst the rubble that was once the town of Garapan, Saipan. Outside, on its pile of steaming bodies and debris-filled streets, stands Sister Maree Bertrand's billowing white tent with its giant, *Red Cross* on top, fluttering in the offshore breeze. Flushing through the sixty-one-year-old's mind, he sees her face…

"So beautiful, and I thought, so wanting" muses the elder, as he relives the moment chastising himself aloud for having wanted her. He'd been abruptly lured off guard by a French nun as she removed her habit and frock in front of him. The sudden appearance of her full, white, supple breasts as she fell to her knees, burying her face in the waistline of Frank's stench-ridden fatigues, as she cried out, *Il n'y a que le dieu du tonnerre. Il n'a pas de dieu de la lumiere* (There is only the god of thunder. There is no god of light) confused him.

"Seeing her there, all I wanted was to wrap my arms around her, carry her into that tent and burying myself deep inside of her…" With words barely audible Frank's voice could still be heard echoing through the bar. The dozen or so other patrons in the establishment politely took no heed and turned away.

"Haunting me, restraining me, were thoughts of my Mary sitting alone back home, waiting day in and day out, wondering if she'd ever see me again."

Like most real warriors, those that fight for a cause, Frank's heart was seething with passion.

"I couldn't see what was happening right there at my feet. I misread everything. How could I have been so blind?"

The song "What would my Mary say" continued playing ever louder on the barroom jukebox. Trying in vain, the bartender is unable to properly manipulate the machine's volume control.

Your lips are thrilling

My arms are willing

I know that I shouldn't stay If I don't leave I'll be sorry
What will my Mary say?

Instead of picking her up and taking her into her tent as it appeared that is exactly what she wanted—mad as hell—asking about the young boy they had encountered outside Camp Susupe, Frank reached behind the near-naked, young nun catching a fist full of her flowing, dark brown locks, pulling her off of him demanding:

"I left the kid in your care? What happened to him? Where is he?"

But it wasn't a sexual desire that caused the beautiful French female to disrobe in front of this war-weary, American. Bending her backwards, forcing her to look up, the nipples of her breasts staring up at him, Frank, a twenty-seven-year-old from the suburban streets of Chicago, didn't notice the tousled and darkened earth between her knees. It had been tainted red with blood, her blood. Disrobing, shedding her last remnants of worldly possessions was her way of demonstrating that she'd given her all and had nothing more to give. She was ready to meet her lord. The lovely young pacifist, a woman from a far off land who devoted her life to providing goodwill and medical care to all in need, had been scalped between her legs, her pubic hair now an Imperial Japanese war souvenir.

On her knees in front of Frank, as she bled out, she struggled to answer his question. Gesturing to a rope dangling off of the main gun of a nearby American tank, a Sherman that now sat idle having arrived belatedly to help the Marines clear the village of Garapan, she gasped and said: "Le Cordage."

"What? What the hell does that mean? Where's the kid?"

"THERE," She exclaimed in captured English.

Looking up at the barren rope, seeing nothing, Frank looked down. That's when he saw the boy's body.

Still hearing Sister Maree Bertrand's voice as he stood by the window in the downtown Chicago bar, he choked on his tears, repeatedly offering, "Mere, mere, mere."

'Mother, mother, mother' were the last words the mesmeric, French nun uttered as she passed from this earth. Her outcries were not, however, for the woman who brought her into this world.

Steve looked at the barkeep, wondering why the music was still playing. Having heard Frank's voice barking orders, the bar's, middle-aged owner emerged from the kitchen, rushing, nearly delirious, as he struggled to find the Jukebox's reject button. Finally, he opted to simply pull the plug.

As the barroom music abruptly ended, "Mere, mere," Sister Maree's last words like a broken record, played over and over again through the sixty-one-year-old's episodic memory, haunting him as he thought:

"What would my Mary have said? What would she have said if she knew of the horrors suffered by this woman, one with whom I had forged an alliance, an alliance of mutual reassurance? Would my Mary have understood? And the mutilated bodies of so many women? Would she see Max Mitchell's lust-filled eyes in the Japanese— repulsed by what she would be quick to label their demonic pleasure? Would all this lead to her one day seeing me as repulsive as they?"

What the Catholic nun was attempting to tell Frank before she passed he'd soon learn from the natives who suddenly appeared, surrounding him. As he held the beautiful French woman's now lifeless body in his arms, he turned from one native to the other using what bits of the Chamorro language he had learned, pushing the dead woman's body into the chest of one man, then another, snarling like a wild beast, demanding to know...

"Why?" What had taken place right where they stood sheer moments before? To each man he turned he encountered an empty vessel devoid of purpose—men staring back at him withered and broken at the site of their deeply beloved, guiding angel. With that to Frank, the truth slowly dawned.

From beneath the boot of a roving band of Imperial Japan's elite, scavengers who dodged the Marine Corps "mop-up" operations refusing surrender, the fourteen-year-old boy who had previously seen his birth mother butchered as her scalp was removed cried out…

"Mere, mere"

… to Sister Maree Bertrand, the woman who had taken him in, his adopted guardian, as she reached out to him with her last full measure of motherly love as the flesh between her legs was abruptly removed.

Carrying out blanket orders from the general staff to eliminate any female capable of producing a future enemy, a pack of unconscionable savages suddenly appeared outside the Red Cross tent having literally, slivered down the hillside on their bellies like snakes to avoid detection. Ultimately reaching Sister Maree, the four held her down. One Jap with a hastily made shiv crafted from one of Garapan's broken window panes penetrated the flesh between the care-giving French woman' thighs.

Set free in the immediate aftermath of the grotesque butchery, with no other way to free himself from the site and sounds of the last moments of now the two women he cherised, the fourteen-year-old climbed atop the U.S Army's, thirty-one ton, mobile killing platform, throwing a rope over the tank's main gun. Cinching it tight, he fashioned a noose at the other end then slipped it over his head. Looking down at Sister Maree Bertrand, his adopted mother's desecrated body overwhelmed and now all alone, the boy whose name was never known, jumped.

Frank brought his hand off the window frame of the downtown Chicago bar and abruptly straightened up. Of course he never talked about his wartime experiences. There had been no need to do so. That is, until now.

Frank's mind-wrenching attempts to relive segmented memories of his past opened far greater wounds. Racked with pain to which no less of a man could endure, each reawakening brought Frank closer to the unrelenting truth he had suppressed since war's end. Stitching together first this memory with that—inwardly assuring himself of an accurate sequence of events—transparency, first within himself was now all that he sought, all he could see. It was his "cleansing," his path to freedom.

And there it was, finally exposed. Frank had long felt himself a coward, a treasonous coward at that. He never reported the site of the ovens to his superiors. Navy Seabees with their bulldozers already on site provided a fragile excuse.

"What good would it have done?"

That's what he told himself then and lived with since, night after night.

"Why didn't I step forward? Why didn't I report it? The dozer driver was right. It wasn't war. It was mass murder." The sixty-one-year-old whose outward appearance misleadingly speaks to someone content within his own skin, mused:

"What would my Mary have said if she knew that I allowed those soulless beasts to get away with it, allowing each to live on, never to be held accountable for ending the lives of so many innocent women and young boys, burning them alive?"

Knowing how and why those refractory ovens were used, Frank envisioned his Mary, having learned that her husband happened upon the truth then turned and ran from it, would say those words - words he so deeply feared - words that would stagger and drain him, raising doubt in her heart regarding the character of the man to whom she devoted her life. Just three words, so simple and direct;

"How could you?"

Then there was that other issue, the one that compounded the matter. American bulldozers covering up a Japanese war crime in the immediate aftermath of battle, that too was a war crime in itself, Frank alleged.

"Who gave those orders," he often pondered?" Afraid to ask, presuming he knew the answer. Still, a Marine Captain doesn't buck the chain of command without hard evidence in hand, especially when his mentor resides at the top of that chain. Still, knowing USMC Marine

General "Howlin Mad" Smith as he did—a man who frequently lectured his Marines to *protect the lives of civilians at all cost*"—Frank wouldn't allow himself to believe that the one-time general in charge of all U.S. military forces in four of World War Two's most horrific conflicts; the taking of Saipan, Tinian, Guam, and Iwo Jima, was capable of issuing such an order. It just didn't add up.

But in Frank's mind, as he stood staring out the side window of the *Crucible Bar+Grill*, all that was moot. It was he and he alone, who failed as a man, a Marine, and according to a life lesson provided by his fourth grade, homeroom teacher, Miss Carol Lucas, Frank Clifford knew most of all that he was a failure, a failure at being what she had long ago labeled, "a true American."

It was the image of Miss Lucas that first flashed across then, twenty-seven-year-old Frank's mind as he bolted from the human incinerators thirty-three years ago. Failing to do his duty to report the presumed dual war crimes—the incineration of thousands of human lives and the resulting cover-up—that's what former Marine Corps combat veteran turned Illinois industrialist had burning a whole inside him, perpetually festering, erupting at will in the form of nightmares and daydreams ever since. Those damnable ovens and the bodies that surrounded them were not something about which he had read in a report or came to understand through research after the war. They were something once right in front of him, right there at his feet. And so, no matter how far Frank chose to run or what corner of the earth he would ultimately settle, those ovens, those iniquitous human incinerators—their choking stench and the distorted faces of its victims lying all around—were inescapable.

Frank could hear Miss Lucas's voice beaming with purpose as if, at this very moment, she was standing next to him. In a flash that voice transported him back in time, seeing himself sitting one row back from the front of the schoolhouse classroom, eyes wide open.

As a purveyor of lessons-to-live-by, Miss Lucas was exemplary, frequently breathing life into historical characters to make her point.

"Among the several thousand who were present that day, only two didn't hide, only two didn't cower."

Miss Lucas's reconstruction of the British seige during the American Revolution of Ft. McHenry in Baltimore harbor on September 13th, 1814, had a profound and lingering effect on Frank. Even today he could see the event play out just as it had on the day his elementary school teacher painted the original image on the canvas of his nine-year-old mind.

As the massive 42 foot long, Baltimore harbor flag, America's *Stars and Stripes,* took repeated hits from offshore British naval cannons, the pole that held it began to waver.

Royal Navy Admiral Cochrane, an honorable man in the strict British tradition, offered salvation to the citizens of Baltimore. All they had to do was lower that flag and pledge allegiance to the King of England. With that he assured them, the bombardment would cease and all still living, would be spared. News had reached Baltimore that the month before, the British handed American forces the "greatest disgrace in their history" at the Battle of Blandensburg, along Maryland's eastern border with Washington D.C. That defeat left the door open for the British to march into the District of Columbia, capture the nation's capital and burn the White House. Upon hearing such news - not just in Baltimore but throughout the Colonies - many lost all hope that the rule of law would ever find a foothold to protect the rights of the individual over the whim of a tyrannical despot.

Of the Americans who died during the uninterrupted, twenty-five-hour siege on the Baltimore City garrison two amongst the frightened crowd were a teenage girl and boy. Together, both stood and ran forward into the exploding fray to hold the giant mast with its *Star Spangled Banner* waving high, saving it from touching the ground. As rockets burst and cannonballs erupted tearing into their flesh, the pair never wavered. They stood tall. Frank remembers his teacher asking the class:

"Why? Why did these two young people rush forward knowing full well they may die?" asked Miss Lucas. As the obvious spewed forth, Frank's fourth-grade teacher explained to her class:

"No, boys and girls it was not to save the flag. The flag is simply a piece of cloth. No piece of cloth is worth a human life." She exclaimed as she held up a rag she frequently used to wipe the classroom's chalkboard.

Frank recalls, "Then she pointed to me," and I gave the answer that put a smile on her face. I said:

"They did it because it was the right thing to do."

"Yes," said the preeminent molder of sound, young minds, "That's right, Mr. Clifford. You're exactly right, young man. As Americans—as true Americans, that's what we do. We always strive to do the right thing. We may fall and we may fail but we must always keep in mind what we know in our hearts to be right as we move forward."

With that, Frank's most beloved, elementary school teacher picked up from off her desk a portrait of two nineteenth-century teenagers, one Black, one White and held it high over her head for all to see. It depicted both young people to whom Miss Lucas referred as amongst America's greatest unsung heroes, wounded, bleeding, with arms wrapped around a giant flagpole, holding fast less to the wooden pole than to their convictions.

"If you think long and hard about these two young Americans when you someday are facing a difficult decision, even one that may take your life," offered Miss Lucas as the school bell rang, "you'll always know the right thing to do."

Sixty-one-year-old Frank Clifford looked inward, still mumbling, punishing himself:

"And I didn't. Both crimes, the mass murder of human life and its cover-up were literally at my feet. Once I realized how those ovens were used, turning away from them, not reporting it regardless of the outcome was un-American. I did it once…"

With that Frank turned and looked over to where the young FBI Agent was still sitting. "Never again," he submitted aloud.

If he was to help the FBI, if there was even the slightest chance that his past may somehow be linked to the crimes currently erupting all around the Chicago area, he had to make clear what he knew. Not only did this once formidable warrior, this successful industrialist, this husband, father, this keeper of a compassionate spirit had to speak up, demanding of himself to fully reinvigorate fragmented memories, piecing them back together in proper order to ably describe them in exacting detail, he had to first off and far most importantly, lay himself bare.

As Frank pulls out a chair taking a seat to rejoin the young, FBI agent, Steve asks, "Sir, can I get you a glass of water ?"

Frank blurts out, "Unimaginable horrors—horrors so diabolical that only if one happens upon their aftermath as I had, can one understand the level of inhumanity that men are capable of reaching—and all it takes is one deranged mind and one enabler."

"And if a god is that enabler?" asked Steve, the devout atheist.

As he hesitates, struggling to piece together an answer for the young federal agent, a rapid succession of images rushes through Frank's mind. Sister Maree Bertrand is seen aside a snapshot of 'Maggie' as a teen. That's immediately followed by rows of half-charred pink corpses of women lying motionless, some half buried, strewn across an expanse as long and wide as an American football field, then back to 'Maggie,' as an adult mother holding infant Brad, then to the site of the butchered woman in the abandoned lot in Belmont-Cragin, Frank replies,

"There would be no god."

Finally, with the lasting image of his beloved Mary, her smiling face and soft blue eyes guiding him, Frank offers:

"I loved my wife with every measure of my being. It's for her sake, for my Mary, AND IN HER HONOR, that I need the FBI to understand what I believe is happening here today. I have seen that forearm carving before. I don't know why or how it is even possible, but the man who did the same thing to another woman thirty-three years ago is somehow here today."

Reaching into his shirt pocket, Steve unfolds a written document with the Seal of The State of Illinois, emblazoned at the top. He slides it across the table.

"Before you say anything further Frank, you need to read this. It's an official apology from the metallurgist retained by the medical examiner's office. He admits that the conclusions he reached in his preliminary examination of the shard found in that vacant lot up the street from your service facility were wrong. That piece of rusted metal was from a World War Two, Japanese bayonet, one made for pageantry, not service. As a result and with Japan's limited access to iron ore throughout the war, the bayonet was not manufactured to any known exacting standards thus its unusually rapid deterioration… and it was a Chrysanthemum, finely detailed in 18-carat gold into what remains of its hilt. The metallurgist's note goes onto read that the gold inlay…"

Steve quotes from memory "...*distinguished it from the thousands of bayonets found in Army/Navy Surplus stores around the world.*

"No shit Sherlock." Steve admonishingly adds, "And if you had identified it accurately the first time, we may be closer to determining the identity of our murderer by now. Did you catch that last sentence, Frank? The Illinois Governor's office reached out to the Japanese Embassy in D.C., officially requesting any records that may ..."

"Deceive?" Frank picks up and carries the conversation forward, "As Japanese Ambassador Nomura once did."

"You know what, I remember reading about that. Nomura, 1941, right?"

"That son of a bitch stood face-to-face with US Secretary of State Cordell Hull, in his DC office offering a peace proposal while Mitsubishi dive bombers over Pearl Harbor sent 2,400 Americans to a watery grave. That same day, two hours later – two hours after the fact - the Japs declared war on us."

"Steve focused on the present, half hearing what Frank had said, scholding the metallurgist in absentia. "You doofus. You cost me precious time."

"Agent Donaldson, I have a confession to make."

"What's that, Frank?"

"I identified the shard the moment I saw it in your hand."

"What the hell, Frank? Why didn't you speak up ?"

"Before approaching you at the crime scene, I passed the corpse of that young woman in the field. There she was lying on her stomach, face down, her forearms in the earth. Across the street at the medical examiner's table, she was on her back, face-up. It was only at that point for the first time, I could see the cut patterns on her forearm. Prior to that I had no way of knowing the relevance of the shard. The message carved in her forearm bore an uncanny resemblance to the same carving on a young girl I tried to rescue during the war some ten thousand miles and three decades removed from here. I held that girl's outstretched hand as she died. My eyes couldn't turn away from her forearm. Her carving wasn't fresh and it wasn't random. It had been cut into her days before, and it was intricate. I can't explain—I don't know how the hell it could be possible but as I said, he's here."

A soft, gentle voice towering above the two men sitting at the table asks, "Who's here, Frank?"

4:14 pm

Steve looks up, "Mike, ah, Agent Westgate, what the…? What are you doing here? How did you find us?"

Good afternoon, gentlemen. I hope I'm not intruding.

"Ahhh, no not at all. We were just…"

"I called Dr. Vaziri's office. Her assistant said she saw both of you leave rather hurriedly. You didn't show up at my office. Steve, you had a sandwich at Frank's house. Frank, you didn't. I remembered what Frank said about growing up around here. I put two and two together and here I am. Now, may I join you, gentlemen?"

Both men stand and remain so until Mike takes a seat at the table. "Sure, of course."

"Did you cancel the four o'clock?" asks Steve.

"I turned it over to Edwards."

"Oh yeah, Edwards."

"You need to cut that man some slack, Agent Donaldson. Edwards is a gifted researcher. He'll compose what I need for the seven pm meeting—a meeting that neither you nor I will miss, agreed?"

"Yes, ma'am."

"He volunteered to share his preliminary notes with you. Here. This should bring you up to speed."

"I'll remember to thank him."

"Do that."

As the three sit together in the noiseless, dimly lit bar, Frank tells Mike about his encounter on Saipan and Tinian Islands in June of 1944, with the Ovens, the microbiologist from Unit 731, and the butcher Yoshida:

"As I was trying to tell you both back at my house, this particular Kempeitai sergeant, in charge of a series of human incinerators on Tinian Island in the Mariana Archipelago, liked to whittle on the forearms of the women waiting to be processed. One escaped. I found her. She was presumed dead and half buried by the blade of a bulldozer assigned to level the area. As I neared, she reached out her hand to me. Her forearm like the woman in the morgue, was delicately carved. She died while I held her hand. I don't remember much after that. I only recall breaking through a wall of jungle vines to find myself on the beach. But today, what I saw on the forearm of the young woman on the medical examiner's table my first thought was it's him. I had humiliated Yoshida in front of his men during an interrogation, exposing him as a coward to his people and I assume, he's seeking revenge against me but if it is him—I don't see how...?"

Steve offers for Mike's benefit, "According to the linguist hired by the medical examiner's office, the word *revenge* in an ancient Japanese language was carved into the forearm of our murder victim."

Mike asks, "So you think this manYoshida is seeking some kind of reprisal after all of these years? How does he fit the picture, today?"

"He doesn't," Frank offers... "He can't. At least not logically. And that's what's troubling me. Yoshida and the Kempeitai..."

Steve interjects, offering an explanation to Michaelene, "The Kempetai were Imperial Japan's version of the Nazi's Gestapo and SS henchmen rolled into one."

"Thank you, Agent Donaldson," Michaelene extolls, "I am well aware of who the Kempetai are."

Frank continues, "Yoshida and the Kempetai were not serial killers as we use that term today. They were mass

300

murders who preyed on the weak and the unarmed especially women and rarely one at a time. Knives, swords and especially bayonets were their weapons of choice, not explosives. Targeting me by blowing up my service station, that's one of several things that simply doesn't fit."

Michaelene and Steve turn towards one another and then to Frank as Mike asks, "Give me a chance to get on the same page with you two, gentlemen. I need to make certain I understand precisely what you are telling me. Please start from the beginning Frank, and provide me a capsulized version of what the two of you have been discussing."

Over the next twelve minutes, Frank succinctly relates all of the details he learned from being a Marine on the scene and what he researched and discovered at war's end. All the details that he and Steve shared were highlighted accurately without exception. Frank then sums:

"According to the Shinto religion, Japan's wartime Emperor Hirohito, as you know, was said to be a living god, a direct descendant of Jimmu, born of Amaterasu, the Shinto sun god."

Steve the consummate atheist, rolls his eyes.

"In order to fulfill Jimmu's proclamation, killing men on the battlefield alone was a labor-intensive task that impeded the objective."

"And that objective was?" Michaelene asks Frank as if not knowing.

301

"World domination with Hirohito and his offspring seated on the Throne of the Chrysanthemum as rulers over all the world."

Michaelene inserts. "My father would say that Hitler had his thousand year Reich. The throne of the Chrysanthemum was Imperial Japan's equivalent. Neither however, managed to live beyond their hype."

"Targeting civilians specifically women, reduced the population of the country the Japanese intended to occupy at a far greater pace."

"Are you saying that this Yoshida character is here today in the United States—somehow preparing to exterminate a mass number of American women?" Michaelene, asks.

Steve offers, "Could our two butchered women be a precursor or some kind of sign?"

"Like *post-it notes*" Michaelene adds, "Using their bodies to send a message, baiting you, baiting us?"

"You see, and that would make sense, wouldn't it?" Frank offers.

"It would be linear at least" Michaelene adds.

"But you see that's what I mean. It's not." Frank goes onto explain. "Back during the war while on the island of Saipan, my Marines and I captured Yoshida and his band of psychopaths imprisoning them in a high-wired compound. I had an interpreter, a Nisei with me throughout the interrogation process."

"That's a—" Steve began to offer.

"An American born of Japanese ancestry. Thank you, Agent Donaldson." Michaelene, asserts. "For the record, so we're clear, I am well aware of the Nisei. I am particularly aware and damn proud of an all-Nisei, U.S. Army unit the 442nd, who fought in Europe. To this day, they remain the most decorated, combat unit in U.S. military history proving once again what I have said many times, that Americanism is an ideal and being an American is not now nor has it ever been a matter of race, color of one's skin or ancestry. So gentlemen, are we now good to go? Can we move forward?"

Both men acknowledge.

"Good. Go on, Frank." Michaelene directs.

Frank continues. "This interpreter was a psychologist, a recent doctoral recipient from the University of Michigan before the war broke out. He couldn't make sense of Yoshida. According to Lieutenant Pike - that was his name - Yoshida talked in incomplete sentences and broken thought patterns, changing subjects numerous times while attempting to answer the simplest of questions. Pike pressed him to determine if Yoshida was playing games. He wasn't. In other words, Pike diagnosed Yoshida as a moron, an adult who, clinically-speaking, has the mental ability of an eight-year-old. Even if he was still alive and somehow had the means to come to Chicago for the purpose of continuing his rampage, killing a mass number of American women then blaming it on me, he couldn't pull it off. Brutally killing those women, dissecting them, carving messages into their arm yes, that's him at least that's his …?" Frank pauses, searching for the right term.

"His modus operandi?" Michaelene offers.

"Yes, and it would take a real mastermind to plot the destruction of my service station and half that town. That doesn't fit Yoshida. Not the Yoshida I knew."

Steve offers, "Perhaps a copycat?"

"Or someone who learned at Yoshida's knee," Michaelene counters, "an offspring seeking revenge for something. Something…?". Before completing her thought, Mike turns to Steve and asks, "Why that look on your face?" Knowing full well the answer.

"A moron and a mastermind?"

"A frog and a scorpion—the two working together?"

"Forming an alliance of convenience, or what was that phrase you used, earlier?"

"A mutualistic, symbiotic relationship."

"While attempting to achieve a mutually beneficial objective?"

"Like crossing a pond!"

"Precisely." Now I get it. Steve acknowledges with a nod."

Frank stares at both agents for a moment then asks, "Exactly how long have the two of you known one another?"

CHAPTER THIRTY-FOUR

"It looks like your one-and-one theorem, Agent Donaldson, makes two after all. Though there is still no hard evidence" Michaelene makes clear, "it's likely that we've got two perpetrators who have joined forces placing two very divergent and catastrophic crimes in our face at the same time in an attempt to pull the Bureau in two separate directions, leaving their actual objective – something far bigger and far more devastating - somewhere in the middle unfettered and…"

"And unexposed, free to move forward without impediment." Steve offers.

"The bodies of the women and the explosion that started Frank, at your gas station," Michaelene reflects, "are conjoined—one in the same. Our scorpion, this mastermind, I have to hand it to him, he's good. He's been playing us and he's been winning so far. So now I'm redirecting this investigation. You and I, Agent Donaldson, are back on point moving forward, together."

"Perhaps you didn't notice?"

"Notice what?" Michaelene responds rather sharply.

"I've yet to leave your side."

"What our 'mastermind' failed to recognize" Mike concludes, "is that he actually made our job easier."

"Because when we find one of these assholes…" Steve offers

"...we'll find the other."

"Bingo. Now what we need to do is put names and faces to our deceptive duo."

"And determine exactly what the next move in their masterplan will be."

"You were right, Frank." Steve offers.

"How's that?" replies the elder amongst the three.

"The true genius—one so intensely focused on his objective as you said earlier, invariably overlooks the obvious, that thing that catches the eye of most everyone else."

As the front door opens, sunlight penetrates the darkened recesses of the Crucible Bar and Grill, temporarily impaling the vision of the three sitting at a table directly in its wake. As the door closes and eyes adjust, Agent Ron Israel is seen standing at the barroom counter, waiting to be invited to the table. He probes with a subtle, "Ma'am?"

On the drive over from the FBI's downtown office, while Michaelene was on the mobile phone - the one built into the backseat of the Bureau's four-door Ford Granada - answering questions and giving direction, Agent Ron Israel, who'd volunteered to man the wheel in Agent Edward's absence, had been waiting outside, keeping the engine running to charge the car's phone.

"Pardon me for interrupting, Agent Westgate, but I thought you'd want to know. The phone is now ready. To make certain, I picked up the receiver. As I did, a call came in for you. I believe it's the one you've been waiting for, ma'am—a Mister Langston? I placed him on hold."

"Fine."

"He's on the line now. If I may say, boss, he's not very happy."

Michaelene turns to the two men sitting beside her and says, "Frank, Agent Donaldson, please excuse me. I need to take this. I'll be out front."

As his boss stands to leave Steve offers, "Be nice." It was one of those things one says then immediately regrets. The look on Michaelene's face as she passed by, looking down at her former high school lover, said it all.

Mike exits the bar + grill and plops down in the back seat of the Ford Granada as Agent Israel takes up a position on the sidewalk by its right rear door, guarding the entry.

"Mr. Langston, good afternoon." Offers Agent Westgate, her voice calm yet ripe with purpose.

"Well hello there, sweetie. I've read about you in the papers. You're quite a gal. Whatcha' got going on? You should know that I've been on hold for almost three minutes now waiting for you."

"Mr. Langston, what we both have "going on" is a city on the verge of a complete meltdown with you and your facility in the crosshairs of its rumor mill. The Dresden power plant, as I explained to your assistant with whom I left an urgent message asking you to call more than four hours ago, is not—repeat, is not—being investigated by the FBI. That's not our job. What is our job and of immediate concern to us is the prospect of a physical attack on your facility...possibly, eminent."

"Preposterous."

"Perhaps and I hope you're right but I'm asking you to increase plant security and maintain it until further notice. We have no idea at this time who or how such an attack may occur but..."

"Well when you do little lady, let me know."

With that, William "Willie" Langston, Chief Administrator of Northern Illinois' most controversial, nuclear power plant slammed down the receiver on his desk phone hanging up on the person he had read was *the temporarily assigned, Special Agent in Charge of the FBI's Chicago office.*

Mike immediately calls back. Langston answers with a blustering, "Now you listen to me, young lady. I don't like anyone telling me how to run my facility, especially some short-term, bureaucratic skirt. I've had more than twenty-five years as head of this facility and I—"

"Michaelene interrupts, "Willie, that's what everyone calls you, right?"

"Well yes, but—"

"Willie, please understand," offered Michaelene, taking a page out of Steve's playbook, "I don't give a rat's ass who you are or how many years you've been on the job.

My job—and right now, that's the only job that matters—my job is to protect this city and its people. All I'm asking for is your cooperation."

"You've got quite a smart mouth on you, little missy."

"Thank you. Yes, I do. And the next person with whom this smart mouth will be talking is a gentleman you may know, a Mr. Mark Franke?"

"Look, young lady, if you're trying to intimidate me...?"

"Your boss Mark, do you know where he is at the moment?"

"Now listen here..."

"He's at 601 Pennsylvania Avenue, just down the street from the White House. Are you familiar with Washington's, *Capital Grill*, Willie?"

"You know damn good and well I'm not."

"Too bad. It's a very swanky restaurant. Mark and Donna, that's Mrs. Franke, are having dinner this very moment with my boss Clarence and his wife Shirley." If I have to interrupt Mr. and Mrs. Franke's dinner in front of the Director of the FBI and his wife to inform them that due to your lack of cooperation I have been forced to ask the governor of Illinois to call out the

National Guard to protect the Dresden facility, that's not going to go over well with their collective digestive systems, wouldn't you agree, Willie?"

"You're bluffing."

"He's your boss. You must have his number. Call him."

With a huff, Langston offers "You've made your point, Agent Westgate."

"Thank you. And thanks for acknowledging who I am and of course, my role in this matter. The governor's office had already sent notifications to all State agencies authorizing them to exceed their budgets. Look on your desk. I'm certain it's there, somewhere."

"It read, 'if deemed necessary.'"

"So you have seen it? Deem it necessary, Mr. Langston, and double the number of plain clothed security staff on site. I don't want a military presence on or near the Dresden plant any more than you do."

"Fine."

"Thank you. I'll be standing next to our governor on television in a few hours. You may want to tune in. I'll be informing him in front of what I believe will be a rather large viewing audience that you extended your fullest cooperation to the FBI in this matter."

"That's quite generous of you. Thank you."

"As soon as I have any concrete information I'll immediately pass it on to you. Enjoy the rest of your day, Chief."

Mike motions to Agent Israel to stand aside and free the door. Instead, he opens it for her as he asks, "You were bluffing weren't you?"

With a sterling look of complete satisfaction, Mike replies in her best Southern drawl. "Why, whatever do you mean, Agent Israel?

"Yes, ma'am."

No sooner than Mike is out of the car placing her hand on the Crucible's front door than the car phone rings again. "Please take that, Agent Israel. "I need a moment. I'll be right back."

Reentering the distinctive, barrelhouse watering hole, Mike makes her way to the table where Steve and Frank are still seated. She turns to Frank and declares in a most heartfelt manner,

"Colonel Frank Clifford, you are an exceedingly decent and honorable man. We are eternally indebted to you but it's time Agent Donaldson and I officially move forward on our own."

"I understand. You know where to reach me if I can be of any further assistance."

"Be assured, we'll be back in touch with you and your family, soon."

As Mike and Steve jump into the Bureau's vehicle to head to St. Margaret's Parish for the evening's telecast, Agent Israel offers,

"That last call was from the head of the State Sanitation Commission, a Mr. Ken Porter. He was genuinely flattered that you asked his people for their help. He said that they have already gathered some pieces of debris that may interest you."

"Any further details?"

"As you know, Mike, the sound quality on the car phone is pretty bad," Israel states, as he flips the turn signal on, looking both ways, waiting for an adequate breach in the traffic before pulling out. Continuing with his report, Agent Israel recalls Mr. Porter saying something about one of his drivers reporting a 'funny thing,' an oversized brass button with a hook on it getting wedged into one of his garbage truck's tires in a Belmont-Cragin back alley this morning. As a breach in traffic presents itself, Agent Israel presses down on the vehicle's accelerator. "He also made mention of ..."

CHAPTER THIRTY-FIVE

5:09p.m.

WHAM!! The sound of screeching tires, buckling metal, and busting glass fills the air. The Bureau's Ford Granada is slammed back into the curb, hit head-on by a DHL delivery van cutting across traffic. Even with Agent Israel executing an evasive maneuver ultimately minimizing impact, the government vehicle nonetheless, is launched skyward, landing on top of a parked car - an old Buick - rolling off of it and onto a parking meter, spreading several hundred dollars-worth of nickels, dimes, and quarters across the adjacent sidewalk. In the backseat, the impact hurls Michaelene upward before coming down hard on Steve. Hearing the crash, Frank, the barkeep, the Crucible Bar and Grill's owner, and a cluster of patrons and passersby, immediately rush onto the scene, some peering into the backseat to determine the condition of its two passengers, seen in a rather compromising position.

As the cobwebs clear, Mike pushes herself off of her former high school lover saying with an appreciation of how the situation must appear: "Spare me any of your cheesy remarks Agent Donaldson. I know what you're thinking."

Recovering quickly, Steve replied with a dubious smile, "Don't worry. I wasn't going to say a thing. I'm not that brave."

Michaelene reached forward from the backseat to check on Agent Ron Israel. Touching his forehead, she asks, "Are you okay?" The physically intimidating, six foot, four inch, former collegiate hockey player, his team's enforcer, uttered:

"I'm fine. Let me help you."

The deep cut Mike felt across Agent Israel's forehead spoke volumes to the contrary.

Rolling off of Steve, Mike places an exacting kick to the base of the backseat passenger door forcing it open allowing both to exit. Curbside, with Frank's assistance, both agents work to bring the third, Ron Israel, out from behind the wheel and onto his feet. Securing him upright on the sidewalk leaning him up against the government's totaled, Ford Granada, they closely check him for additional injuries. Bob Mapes, the bar + grill's owner, ducked inside his establishment to call the police. For a CPD cruiser to make an appearance in downtown Chicago, one doesn't have to wait long.

With their vehicle coming to a screeching halt, Mike, Steve, and two of Chicago's finest walk over to the overturned DHLvan as its driver on hands and knees, makes his way out. Physically unscathed, the thirty-one-year-old, couldn't stop talking, blaming his pager. He admitted taking his eyes off the road looking down to see who was trying to contact him. Then, as if Scrooge's midnight nemesis, Jacob Marley's ghost began rising from the steam grate at Matt Sorensen's feet, DHL's Employee of the Month turned suddenly pale as his eyes lock onto the guns strapped to the hips of two handsome, plain-clothed strangers standing in front of him. In less than a heartbeat after the female of the two presented her credentials—-as if bearing his soul to St. Peter having already arrived at the Pearly Gates - Sorensen mutters, "I screwed up, didn't I?"

"Here. Look at me." Steve asks Mike as he turns away from the DHL driver. "You've got a slight cut above your brow line," Steve continues examining the face of the undeclared love of his life. "And a bruise along your left eye is starting to form but I think with a quick touch-up with some of that girly make-up of yours you'll be fine, at least for tonight."

"We need to get moving, Steve. We're running out of time.

Mike looks into the backseat of the Bureau's vehicle. The base of the phone is dangling over the rear seat's center console. Snapped loose from its mooring by the impact, it was undoubtedly the source of damage to Michaelene. More importantly at least at the moment, it was inoperable.

"Any suggestions on how to get out of here?" Michaelene asks aloud of all still standing about.

Mike turns first to the Chicago police sergeant standing nearest her. While on the phone to dispatch requesting back-up to clear the streets, the sergeant categorically refuses to request a fellow CPD officer to provide what amounts to a taxi ride even for the FBI. A taxi itself is of course, out of the question. The two feds need to talk

315

privately to piece together what they've already learned to determine how best to move forward. Mike then turns to Bob Mapes, asking to use the phone in his bar. Before the head of the local office of the FBI can get a word out, Marine Colonel Frank Clifford once again, steps forward offering:

"You said tonight's telecast is scheduled to start at seven?"

"Yes."

"It's now 5:48. You two are running out of time. On a Saturday night, traffic down here is brutal. At best, it will take forty minutes for one of your agents to get down here, another forty to get from here to St. Margaret's. Why don't you let me drive? I promise to keep my mouth shut and not repeat anything the two of you may say in front of me."

"Do you know St. Margaret's Parish on South Vincennes Avenue?" Mike asks.

"Everyone listening to the local news for the past several hours now knows exactly where that parish is."

Steve acknowledges, "That's right, Mike. We asked the bartender to turn the sound up on the television behind the bar when a public service announcement was being aired."

"They're calling it the Dresden Town Hall Meeting," adds Frank, "letting everyone know where and when it's being held."

"And inciting a riot by publicly validating an unsubstantiated rumor, the idiots! When we've wrapped this case," Mike is uncharacteristically infuriated. "I'm going to make it my mission to determine who—"

Frank interjects; "Michaelene, please.

Momentarily taken aback hearing Frank use her given name, 'Mike' quickly regains her composure attempting to finish her sentence. Before she can, Frank drives home his point:

"Please. We don't have time to waste. I can get you to that meeting but we need to go—now!"

Mike turns to Steve, "You good?"

"I'm good."

"Okay, Frank, you win. Let's go."

Steve's knee was hurt in the collision, rekindling an old war wound. He starts out with a hobble. Frank takes hold of the young Agent's arm placing it over his shoulder. The three hurriedly make their way to the parking lot at the rear of the Crucilble Bar + Grill. Frank, orchestrating the seating arrangements, offers Michaelene first choice. With a quick acknowledgment of Frank's, old school, *lady's first* charm, she opts for center position. Sliding in, Mike fastens one of three sets of seat belts around her waist. Steve squeezes into the passenger side of Frank's, two-tone, brown and tan, half ton, pick-up. With passengers secured, Frank climbs in behind the wheel and starts the engine. Steve, the Vietnam War vet, a man keenly attuned to his surroundings regardless of the type of 'jungle' in which he might find himself, turns to Frank and says:

"Your truck's side emblem says this baby is a diesel. It sounds more like a V-8. Nice."

"It came from the manufacturer as a diesel. I had that engine ripped out and replaced when I heard."

"Heard what?" Michaelene asks, wondering if Frank's incongruous comment had anything to do with the case.

"That the 1978 Dodge diesel engine was manufactured and installed by Japan's Mitsubishi Motor Car Company, the same people who built the tanks and aircraft my Marines and I faced in the jungles of the Pacific."

CHAPTER THIRTY-SIX

Remaining on point, turning to Steve, Michaelene asks, "Where are we on this case, Agent

Donaldson? What do we have on perp number one, our frog? Sum it for me."

"We have two matching accounts, both from reliable sources, both identifying perp number one, our butcher, as a Japanese male. The first source. you may recall, was an eye witness interviewed by our fellow agents in Iowa; a Vietnamese equipment manager at Davenport's St. Ambrose College. Shortly before you arrived, I obtained our second account directly from Dr. Meredith Chang. She's a Professor of Phonology and Sociolinguists at the University of Chicago. She described our perp as a Japanese male by way of the carving he etched into the forearm of the woman on the slab in the Cook County morgue. Although Professor Chang did not specifically mention age, our Vietnamese émigré at St. Androse, identified the suspect being in his mid-to-late forties. Both, however, made it clear that he stood no taller than five feet, eight inches."

Hearing that, Michaelene recalled the Asian standing next to her in Belmont-Cragin, as she exited the Hazmat unit. The description fit but she thought to keep the encounter to herself until more evidence if any, regarding its relevance presented itself.

"And now"—Steve offers as if Frank isn't sitting behind the wheel at the other end of the pick-up truck's cabin— "we have Frank's testimony that you heard for yourself. The carving on the arm of at least one of our female victims matches that of the carving on the arm of another by a Japanese soldier he captured thirty-three years ago in the Mariana Islands. It's safe to conclude that our butcher, perp number one, our frog, is Japanese and related in some significant way to Frank's prisoner Kemptei Sgt. Hiroki Yoshida but I think we'd be safe to take this Yoshida prick off the list of possible suspects. However…"

Mike quickly inserts, "Okay, Yes, I know where you're going with this. I know what you are about to say but reaching out to the Japanese consulate concerning two of their fellow countrymen and waiting for a reply is…"

"…a time-burning proposition, serving as a roadblock to your imminent theory," Steve inserts. "But if our scorpion stings within the next several days and it's proven long after the fact that the FBI didn't bother to alert the Japanese consulate regarding its concern for two male Japanese suspects active in the U.S.—"

"Who knows? We could get lucky. Maybe we'll get fired," Michaelene offers, "but we're not going to sit around and wait, play politics, tip our hand or ask permission. No. Not on my watch."

Frank shoots an approving glance in Mike's direction.

Mike quickly adds, "How reliable is the Vietnamese identification of another Asian?"

Steve and Frank look across Michaelene, eye-balling one another, with Steve offering, "A Vietnamese being able to pick a Jap out of a crowd is like either of them being able to identify one of us on a downtown Tokyo street."

"Okay, so we got a physical profile of our frog," Mike presses on. "Can we build an abstract of the scorpion off of it—a quick sketch of our so-called mastermind so we have some idea of what or possibly who we may be looking for?"

"He's no chump." Steve quickly puts forward. "He's not someone who's going to get his hands dirty working alongside the frog murdering women, leaving their mutilated corpses lying around."

"Nor blow up a commercial gas station" Mike emphasizes. "His ego sets him above such mundane acts of violence—no offense, Frank."

"None taken."

"And our scorpion is a dude." Steve continues as the three come to an abrupt halt at the intersection of South Vincennes Avenue and Beverly Street. The traffic light ahead is green but every vehicle in front and to their side is at a standstill.

"I can't conceive of our frog taking orders from a female. No way." Steve persists. "The carving on the forearm of the woman in the morgue was very 'old school' according to Professor Chang, readily identifiable to use her words, to a traditionally male dominant period in Japanese culture. Both the frog and the scorpion are dudes. I'm confident of it."

"And he's educated. Our so-called Mastermind, the scorpion is an educated man" adds Mike, as she leans forward looking out over the hood of the Dodge pick-up. "Highly educated would be my guess. And he's meticulous—and if we're lucky, to a fault."

Frank offers an affirming grin.

"Setting aside how the initial spark was generated, combining the destruction of Frank's place with the oil refinery," Mike presses on, "took not only creative perception and imagination, it took extensive research, geophysical analysis of the surrounding area and access to meteorological, weather forecasts. Those are not fields of interest here today in 1978, readily accessible to the average guy on the street."

"So what kind of douche bag would have ready access to that kind of information?"

Mike takes a moment to weigh her thoughts, "a government official or someone who works in a local elected, official's office or—" a thought of a guy she once dated, a likable sort but not long term material crossed Michaelene's mind as she proclaims:

"... a college professor, a pleasant, non-threatening type, an amiable guy who administrators in each department would openly provide whatever information he requested."

"I can see that, especially the latter scenario. Nicely done," says Steve.

Mike then asks Steve, "So revenge? That's our motive?"

"That's what has me confused. I keep asking myself if a pair of renegade Japanese dudes are seeking revenge on America for dropping atom bombs on their cities—that is what we're talking about, isn't it—the scorpion's sting? Then why all the hoopla? Why not just make Strike One a direct hit on the Dresden nuclear power plant or for that matter, on any other in the State?"

"You're right. Nice work. Something doesn't add up.'

"Exactly. There's a missing piece of the puzzle out there, somewhere" Steve adds.

"And that's it." Mike persists. "Revenge. It's only half the story. It's safe to conclude that our frog is most likely seeking revenge for Frank's actions during World War Two but the scorpion? There's something else up his sleeve. Although the two are working together, what motivates each is quite distinct. Our scorpion, our so-called mastermind, when it comes to him, I'm convinced of one thing."

"And that would be what?" Steve asks.

"He has yet to make his first move."

Steve adds, "It doesn't feel like any of this terrorist shit is in any way, state-sponsored. It's too isolated. We've heard zero news of similar events unfolding anywhere else in the US, just here in the greater Chicago area."

"At least thus far." Mike adds.

Frank breaks his silence, "Do either of you know who Enrico Fermi was?"

"A hit man for the Capone mob?" Steve chides, his mind still whirling.

Mike asks, "Enrico Fermi, isn't he the scientist credited with building the first nuclear reactor?"

"He's also considered the Father of the atomic bomb. In 1942, he built the world's first nuclear reactor out of wood and bricks under a set of bleachers at the University of Chicago's squash court."

"Hopefully, some asshole who put the moves on Fermi's gal, was sitting in the bleachers when the old boy threw the switch?"

"From an article I read, when he activated it, less than one watt of electricity was generated. The point is the crude reactor worked. If you were a well-educated Japanese male seeking revenge for atomic bombs being dropped on your country, where would you start, especially if you want to attach an indelible message?"

"The home of Enrico Fermi."

"Chicago." Michaelene concludes.

CHAPTER THIRTY-SEVEN

6:08 pm

Like a string of red Christmas lights struggling to stay lit in a windstorm, brake lights flash on then off as motorists in front of Frank's pick-up attempt to inch forward as dawn sets in and traffic stretching to the horizon, remains at a virtual standstill.

Steve offers, "This is NOT good."

"Steve's right, ahh, Agent Westgate." Recalling that he hadn't asked Michaelene's permission to call her by her first name - the tradition of 'good manners' remaining his benchmark - Frank stammered. Turning to his wristwatch he then offers, "We've got less than fifty minutes Ma'am, to get to the town hall meeting."

Just then, as if the tornado that swept Dorothy to the Land of Oz decidedly plopped down on the Dodge's rooftop, a helicopter bearing the markings of the Illinois State police zoomed down seemingly inches from the truck's hood then banked hard left, heading to the front of the 'parking lot' of family sedans with engines running, stretched out as far as the eye can see.

"Whoa!" As the pick-up bounces and the blades of the helicopter pass by the passenger side window, instinctually Steve ducked his head. Frank at the other end of the truck's cab remained upright failing to flinch even a muscle, clearly demonstrating the distinction between a combat veteran and a man once deeply immersed in combat.

"It's going to be some time before there's a break in traffic."

"How far out are we, Colonel?" Mike asks.

"Three miles, maybe more."

With nothing more than a reassuring nod between them, both agents exit Frank's pick-up. Steve gingerly sets one foot then the other on the ground.

"Motha f— "he screeches, abruptly aborting his choice of expletives, noticing the number of families with children nearby, making their way up South San Vincennes. Struggling to stand, he puts pressure on both knees. Though throbbing his right knee holds.

With thoughts of the days when his adopted motto was "Die Silent" Steve cautiously hoists his injured leg onto the pick-up truck's passenger side running board. Holding fast to his Ranger creed- without a whimper - he sucks up the pain shooting through him from a second, head-to-knee stretch.

Looking up at Mike, Steve put on his best *I'm okay,* grin. "Go ahead. Take off. I'll be fine. I'll catch up."

As Mike nods in agreement, turns and begins to walk away, in that fleeting instant Steve fought it… I mean, he really fought it hard. He didn't want to *go there* but his mind had a mind of its own, allowing the man himself, no reprieve. Steve couldn't help but to recall the first time Michaelene walked away from him.

It was his right knee, the same one that suffered a torn ACL in '69, as a then Lt. Steve Donaldson was washed down a thirty foot, jungle embankment amidst a torrential Cambodian downpour as his men on the ridge above were slaughtered in one of those rare encounters with the enemy Steve had spoken of to Frank earlier in the day. The one member of the North Vietnamese Army platoon infiltrating the sovereignty of the Cambodian nation who bothered that afternoon to look down the river of mud and debris, failed to distinguish the young American Army Lieutenant from the sludge-covered rocks and branches below.

"Get going. You need to be there. I'll be right behind you." Steve assured Michaelene.

Bone-cold and shivering, it was ten years ago almost to the date that Steve recalled, lying at the bottom of that Cambodian ravine having the flesh just below his right knee punctured by a broken branch from a sumac tree, the resin canals of each of its slivers full of a foul-smelling toxic sap. For several hours Steve dug through his wound with his government-issued, wide-bladed, *Ka-Bar* knife, probing deep with an instrument ill-suited for the task, to remove each sliver. Late that evening the cold subsided and his shivering stopped. Steve Donaldson of Park Ridge Illinois, the most celebrated quarterback in local high school history, a shoe-in for the NFL, now a soldier lost and alone thousands of mile from home, had reached that uniquely rewarding if not somewhat awkward point in the human experience when one realizes it's okay, it's over. As an ethereal blanket of warmth wraps around, an easy route to surrender one's life to one's immediate circumstance often with a smile, ensues. Oddly enough however, in this instance, it was that acceptance and relaxed state of mind that kept Steve alive. The following morning as the sun rose and he opened his eyes, of course, it was the thought of Michaelene that reminded this badly injured young American he wanted to live but it wasn't his love for her that helped him climb out of that slimy wash. With his wound drained and his knee cinched tight using his once rolled up sleeve as both a bandage and a tourniquet, it was rage—a rage that made his muscles strong, knowing no pain—an all-consuming hatred for the woman who once nourished him, who gave him life, his mother Angela, and her contempt for "Mikey," Michaelene Westgate, the unequivocal love of her son's life.

Regardless of what obstacles may lie ahead or befall him as he made his way across the Vietnamese-Cambodian border to the nearby American basecamp, he was going to live, a fact he knew without the slightest doubt. He had to live for one very special reason—to set the record straight. As he climbed, "Just try and fuckin' stop me now" became his repeated mantra.

Standing on the sidewalk on S. Vincennes Avenue, still locked in thoughts of yesterday, Steve was reminded how the jungle's dank, early morning chill returned the instant he decided to climb, cursing god and his parents, their self-righteous indignation and their rejection of anything that didn't fall steadfast into the narrow boundaries of their Christian beliefs—like his teenage love for a young woman in whose soul he found refuge. Their willingness to set aside in a blaze of hypocrisy, his love of Michaelene—that thought burned deep even today as Steve surveyed the scars that still remain across his knuckles brought about by thrusting his hands often up to his elbows, in mud and shards of rock to gain the support he needed to continue his upward ordeal. Each scar was a reminder of his love for a certain young woman. Two things in his life he knew would never fade.

The morning after prom night Michaelene had walked to the Donaldson's residence to thank "Stevie," wanting to let him know that, "I will love you with all of my heart for the rest of my life."

At last night's hotel getaway upon Steve's insistence, they simply held each other and talked *Like Bogie and Bacall* till they fell asleep smiling, in each other's arms.

But the morning after as fate would have it, Michaelene didn't get a chance to say the words she wanted so desperately for Steve to hear. Steve's mother Angela; a hands-waving-in-the-air, Jehovah's Witness who transitioned seamlessly into a full-fledged, Bible-thumping member of the Mormon Faith during Steve's sophomore year, "...had no right to speak to Michaelene that way." His mother's words still reverberate making the teeth of the now FBI Special Agent steeped at present in an explosive murder mystery, grind.

329

"You whore! You're a godforsaken, motherless whore. Look at you." Steve could still hear his mother scream. "And that father of yours, he's never around. He too must have rejected you."

Near spellbound with mounting anger, it took Mrs. Angela Donaldson a few moments to recall a term she felt fit the occasion. Babbling on... "You, you..." it finally came to her. Having repeatedly pointed her finger in Michaelene's face, Angela finally blurted out... "...You consecrated harlot!" Although the phrase meaning "a holy prostitute" even in Biblical terms is something of an oxymoron, it made Angela feel something she had rarely felt before—smart.

In reply, the young gangly teen with captivating dark brown eyes hidden behind thick-rimmed glasses held her ground, defending both her parents and her principles.

"Mrs. Donaldson, please. My mother died with my father by her side, giving birth to me. Although their time together was short each day just like this morning, he takes a few moments to sit and talk with her. Your son is like my father. Both are good and decent men. My dad never remarried. He made a vow to my mother and he kept it. It's that kind of love like my parents had for one another that I have for your son Stephen, Mrs. Donaldson, something forever binding, ma'am."

"Oh, hooey. Stop your drivel. I don't believe a world you say, you, you tramp! I know what you want. You want to bear my son's child so you can live high on the hog off of his future earnings as a pro ball player."

Quarantined in his bedroom down the hall from the front door of his parent's tiny tract home, Steve could only hear one side of that conversation; his mother's bellicose barking. Angela's disparaging condemnations were laying waste to the love of his life as Luke Donaldson, Steve's father—wanting a vehicle through which to regain a measure of self-respect for his own litany of life-long failures— blocked the doorway to his offspring's bedroom, attempting to retain his trophy son until Michaelene once utterly belittled, would voluntarily turn and leave.

"Listen, young man. This is for your own good. Your mother and I know what's best for you."

With mere weeks before his emancipating eighteenth birthday, seventeen-year-old Steve Donaldson broke free of his three hundred pound father's restraints and sprinted down his parent's hallway. Nothing meant more to him that his love for this girl who'd captivated every measure of his being. Arriving at the front door of his parent's home as Michaelene began to depart, he shouted after her, "Let's runaway and build a life for one, together."

Pure and unrehearsed, it was the most romantic thing he would ever say. But "Mickey" refused to turn around. With tears now staining the front of her blouse - something for some reason she didn't want Stevie to see - she shook her head. Her pragmatism taking precident, she just kept walking.

As Steve struggled to take his first few steps down South Vincennes Avenue, the memory of that day with little in between then and now save for a "Welcome Home" telegram from her upon his return from Vietnam, a congratulatory phone call from him to her when she made Agent, the same from her to him when she later found out his career decision pre-dated hers; a dozen birthday greetings sent to her with merely three in return, then an out-of-the-blue official Bureau request for his assistance, all of which seeming so incongruous nearly fanciful when combined with the memory of a distraught teenage girl walking slowly down his parent's driveway, shouting back without turning around:

"It's okay, Stevie. You're a great guy. You'll be fine. Someone else will soon come along to take my place."

"No way, no, no! No! Don't go!"

The scene at the front door of his parent's home still infuriated the now thirty-five year old FBI Agent as he stood on the sidewalk watching Michaelene, now his boss and no longer the gangly schoolgirl his mother unwittingly loathed, take her first steps in route to St. Margaret's Parish but this time something different happened:

Over the sound of honking horns and squealing breaks Michaelene, striving to emulate the motivational tempo of an Army Drill Sargeant, turned and shouted back at Steve "Come on soldier, get off your ass." Then she added in a more even tone, "Hurry up. I need you."

Whether the "I need you" comment was momentary or had deeper meaning didn't matter to Steve at this point. He was moving forward with his reclaimed mantra, "Just try and fuckin' stop me now."

Two quick slaps on the Dodge hood both thanked and dismissed Colonel Clifford. The huge smile on Agent Donaldson's face assured Frank that the role of 'this Marine on this

mision' at least for the forseeable future, had been successfully fulfilled.

CHAPTER THIRTY-EIGHT

Outside Chicago's St. Margaret of Scotland's Parish.

"Hey, Mike. Mike!" Tami Swanson was the first to notice Agent Westgate as she arrived on the scene. Jumping up and down waving her arms above the crowd, the hard-driving, on-the-scene news reporter was doing everything she could to get Michaelene's attention.

"Hey, Mike, Mike. Over here!"

The stunningly beautiful redhead, a former member of the University of Chicago's Varsity Cheerleading squad and a standout student in its political science department left campus life her junior year to pursue a dance career. Summer stock brought her local fame and persistent comparisons to high-energy actress Ann Margaret, ultimately leading to a job Tami was destined to have, *'on stage'* and in front of a camera, a featured gig at the local ABC news

affiliate.

Moving through the hordes of people on the Parish front steps then down through the multitudes gathered on its lawns and into the streets, Tami continued shouting, now using Michaelene's official job title as she and her cameraman worked their way through the tumultuous crowd:

"Agent Westgate! Agent Westgate! Excuse me, sir. That's Michaelene Westgate. She's the head of the FBI here in Illinois. Please step aside," Tami's voice is barely audible over the bemoaning fears and protests of the hordes of people all around. "We've been expecting her. Oh, come on pal. Do the world a favor. Get out of the way, okay?"

Michaelene and Tami are close. They met when Mike was a newbie working on the Purolator heist. Though Tami has an eye for the ladies and Michaelene clearly does not, both are die-hard professionals. As a result, a resolute bond developed between them.

"Hi, sweetheart. You finally made it. Everyone has been looking for you. Agent Edwards is here, somewhere. I saw him a few moments ago. He was coming unglued trying to find you.

Holy shit. Have you seen your face? Did someone hit you?"

Swinging her microphone about as if the rapier of Enyo, a female warrior of Greek mythology, Tami sticks it into the face of a perspiration-laden big guy limping up to them as her cameraman follows intending to capture the moment.

"No, no wait." Mike orders. "Kill the camera. This is my partner Agent Donaldson."

Tami's assessment of Michaelene's named counterpart takes on an overly protective air. "Haven't seen you around before."

"Agent Donaldson is from our Iowa office," Michaelene offers attempting to mitigate Tami's automatically activated defense mechanisms when it comes to meeting men - any man for that matter - for the first time.

"A little over an hour ago Agent Donaldson and I were in an automobile accident. He damaged his knee. I got hit in the eye."

The former dancer, now growing cautiously empathetic, kneels down to investigate the damage to Steve's engorged leg.

"Agent Donaldson is it?" Tami asks. "Your knee is ballooning. It's bad. You should see a doctor right away."

"Thanks for your concern but it's not a big deal. I can fix it in a jiffy when we have time."

Granted, it had been ten years. The wound just below his right knee cap had held with little concern until today.

Tami turns back to Michaelene. "I have to talk to you right away. I have good news and—"

"Wait," Mike orders. She puts her hand into the small of Steve's back

"Don't turn around. Act like you're starting to walk away from me."

"What have you got?"

"See that young, black woman in the blue, polka dot sundress over there?"

"I noticed her the moment I arrived."

"Look just beyond her. There's a stocky Asian guy in the crowd standing behind and to the right of her. Do you see him?"

"Son of a bitch."

"What?"

"I've seen that guy before. He's Japanese. He was standing across the street in the front yard of that neighbor of Frank's you interviewed."

"Wilfred Dawson, the hotel owner?"

"Yes, he was staring at Jeannie Tomlinson's house. I thought at the time, perhaps like Dawson, he was considering crossing the street to turn off her sprinkler. When he caught me looking at him he quickly picked up a rake, loaded it onto the lawn crew's truck and pulled himself inside its cab. It seems he too, has a bad leg."

"Damn"

"What?"

"I didn't put it together at the time. He was the only Asian in an all Hispanic yard crew."

"And he's the same guy that was standing by the Hazmat truck when I got out to give directions to your helicopter pilot."

"Ah shit..."

The thought of the unattended front door to Michaelene's home and her discarded clothing neatly rearranged on the banister leading upstairs to where she had been standing helpless in the shower, sent a cold chill rushing down Agent Donaldson's spine, a chill known only to those real men – the kind willing to go to any length to protect the women they love.

"Now what?"

"I'll tell you later. I'll try to flank our guy."

"A meandering crowd always makes a good cover. Move as they move."

"I got this."

Tami was relentless, continually repositioning herself in front of Mike trying teo secure her attention:

"Mike! Mike! Michaelene! Agent Westgate, please."

"Not now."

"Yes, now. Listen to me. Just before I saw you running up the street I was standing with Governor Thompson and Mayor Bilandic." Tami is talking as fast as she can. "They both love you by the way, 'Big Jim' Thompson in particular. I heard him say that he admires your *Damn the torpedoes*, leadership style. Anyway, what you did, I mean stepping over Willie Langston, getting the firemen to take the risk to provide a quick assessment of possible radiation leakage following last night's explosion, I mean, asking them to stick a Geiger counter under their coats and simply take a stroll. That was brilliant."

"There was never a risk of radiation exposure to the firemen or to the public."

"What?"

With her attention divided, Mike chooses to address what brought forth the surrounding tidal wave of humanity first, one that has been growing exponentially over the past several hours; a crowd restless and unrestrained into which the Special Agent in Charge of the FBI's Chicago office has now found herself completely immersed.

"There was never a link between the Belmont-Cragin explosion and the Dresden Nuclear power plant. Fire Marshall Sullivan and I knew that from the beginning.

"But…?"

"Far more importantly, Marshall Sullivan and I also determined that the time needed for the Atomic Energy Commission to round up and send their agents to the scene would only heighten public concern and potentially turn crowds like this into riotous mobs. Hard evidence gathered particularly by local authorities - those of us more likely to be trusted by the public at large -would enhance credibility and off-set the alarm caused by rumor mongering. In particular, labeling tonight's live telecast as *The Dresden Town Hall Meeting* and using a public service announcement to do so was arrogant beyond belief, and if I have anything to say about it – and I will - it will be subject to a full-scale, federal investigation. I'll soon be making an announcement in front of this crowd that no radiation leakage from the Dresden plant was found."

"But…?" Tami tryingly insists.

"That's it. Nothing more. Not now." Michaelene insists. With that, she turns her attention away from Tami to Steve:

"Go for it. You and I need to talk to that guy. Hopefully, he won't recognize you and make a run for it."

"I won't let that happen, boss."

"There are two uniform police officers standing less than a yard away from—"

Pushing her agenda, Tami reinserts herself into the conversation:

"I agree and I apologize. I protested using that tagline with my station manager, letting him know—well, exactly what you just said, okay?"

"Fine, okay. Apology accepted." Mike exclaims. "Now let us do our job."

"Okay but you need to listen to me. The governor—"

"I can't listen to you or the governor right now."

"Why not?"

"Because Agent Donaldson and I are trying to catch a frog."

"A what?"

CHAPTER THIRTY-NINE

As he stood beside Michaelene on the sidewalk outside St. Margaret's Parish, at 6'2", Steve could from time-to-time, peer above and between the meandering multitudes tramping by on the adjacent Parish lawn.

"Our frog is stationary," Steve shouts, "but hang on—damn, something just spooked him."

"What?"

"Wait." Steve abruptly leans between two passers-by. "Holy shit. That's Agent Edwards up there."

"Where?"

"On the stairs right above our frog."

"What is Edwards doing?"

A momentary breach in the passing crowd provides Mike a clear view of the Parish steps: "Oh my god. That did it."

"What?"

"The Jap just saw Edwards waving at us."

"Worse." Steve quickly adds

As the crowd once again closes ranks, Mike turns back to Steve, "Now what's going on?"

"Edwards just flashed his credentials at a uniform police officer. Now he's pointing, asking the cop to help him make his way through the crowd over to us."

"Busted," offers Mike.

"The cop is refusing. Their arguing. The cop won't leave his post."

Looking behind her, Michaelene finds herself face-to-face with an elderly Sikh, Tami's, turban-headed cameraman, Aatma Singh. Making use of what little time she could afford to spare, Mike puts both hands together in basic prayer position offering them forward with a slight bow of her head,

"Singh the lion, I call upon you for help. I need your camera. Please hand it to me—now!"

Michaelene's father, Barnacle Mike, had often spoken highly of the Sikhs, referring to them as "Peaceful Warriors" who fought only as a final resort but then with ungodly fury.

"Every Sikh boy as a Rite Of Passage is given the name "Singh," He once told her, pledging in return, "to always live life with the heart of the Lion."

Aatma looks to Tami. "Go ahead." Tami forcefully orders. "Give it to her."

Reading the situation, anticipating his role, without a word, Steve moves forward. Giving out with a groan, he sticks his head between Michaelene' legs and hoists her onto his shoulders.

"What are you doing?"

"Hurry, I can't hold you all day."

"What about your knee?"

"Take the shot. Get that son of a bitch on film before he slips away."

The frog couldn't help but notice the camera's light pointing right at him. With but a moment's hesitation, he turns and slowly steps into the crowd. But a moment's hesitation was all the camera and the FBI needed.

Suddenly, the acrobatics outside of St. Margaret's Parish came to an abrupt halt as Michaelene looking down, falls forward, shouting at Steve, "Got him!" She lands on Tami with Aatma lunging headlong like an NFL wide receiver, to catch the station's video camera before it hit the ground.

"Got it!" shouted Aatma. "It's safe."

Steve was shouting too as he watched Michaelene fall as his knee gave out. Collapsing onto his side, this time Steve's expletives were not restrained although barely discernable through clenched teeth. On the ground, behind a row of people each looking the other way glaring at the front entry of the Parish awaiting the official word on when if ever they can safely return to their homes— an explanation scheduled to be given right at seven pm, just a few minutes away—Steve quickly wrangles off his coat and tie.

Loosening his belt, he unzips his fly, pulls down his pants, placing his suit jacket across his waist and pulls out his switchblade, the one he traded in Saigon for his over-sized, government-issued K-Bar blade. With the Ranger motto of *Die Silent* reinvested in his psyche, he jams the knife's blade into the ballooning flesh just below his right knee cap. Swiftly and silently, he yanks it out. Grabbing his suit jacket—the one he pretty much treated like a rag anyhow— he cuts out its lining then wraps his leg with it as nearly a pint of white-yellow pus - an enriched protein sent by the body to abscess areas to fight infection - oozes out. Like pressing down on a tube of toothpaste to gain the last, Steve compresses his leg wound forcing out the last remaining glop; the lining of his suit jacket capturing all. With his necktie, Steve fashions a tourniquet around his knee. Mission completed, he pulls up his pants.

All three... Mike, Tami, and Aatma, each with jaws open-wide, unconsciously formed a semicircle around Steve. Speechless they are looking down at him with Aatma the first to speak:

"You sir have the heart of the lion."

"Thanks. Give me a hand. Help me up."

"Does the Bureau know about this reoccurring abscess of yours?"

Once again Steve offers, "It's no big deal." With a deep sigh, he takes Aatma's extended hand, starts to stand, smiles at Michaelene and says:

"It only swells and begins to bulge when a beautiful woman in the backseat of a car flings herself on top of me."

Michaelene shakes her head, offering a rather reserved smile. "Good thing that doesn't happen very often," she teases. This isn't the first time you've performed this parlor trick with a knife, is it, Agent Donaldson?"

Steve wanted to say , "How the hell do you think I made it out of that Cambodian jungle?" But of course, she never knew nor could she—even as a senior FBI Agent— that like his VC counterpart, Steve was illegally trespassing upon a sovereign nation. And as an

American soldier, if caught before crossing the Tinh Bien/ Phnom Den border, U.S. Army Ranger Lt. Donaldson, would have been stripped of his uniform and labeled a spy, causing a major international incident ultimately leading Main South's one-time, most promising quarterback to the front of a Cambodian firing squad.

"Thanks, Aatma. I'm good. Let me walk to that city trash can over there so I can dump this jacket and ..."

"And its lining?"

"Yes, especially its lining. By the time I get back you'll never know anything was wrong with me."

As Steve first hobbles then begins to take on a normal stride, the two women huddle exchanging whispers as Mike sums, "Do this exactly and I'll sit down for an exclusive one-on-one interview with you within the next seventy-two and fill in all the blanks, agreed?"

"Agreed."

"Don't forget. Wait for my signal."

Now in the absence of a suit jacket, Steve's under-the-arm weapon was exposed. He thought to secure the holster's quick-release strap negating the possibility of an overly impatient member of the assemblage coming up from behind wanting to change the tempo of this evening's events. As he reached, Michaelene put her hand on his shoulder, insisting, "Keep your .45 but give me your sidearm. Without your jacket, wearing two pistols makes you look like one of the James gang out to make a bank withdrawal."

"You're right. Thanks. Here."

Steve hands Mike his Bureau issued Smith and Wesson then pulls the dog tags he still proudly wears out from under his shirt. To its chain, he first attaches the small Bureau's ID badge, the one he removed from his billfold-size, folding credentials. He then explains:

"This is exactly what I was talking about when I first got here. People need to recognize who we are especially in a crowd like this. The cops have uniforms. What do we have? They need to know the Bureau's here and we got this. Look at this thing." Steve grips the tiny Justice Department badge between his forefinger and thumb, holding it up to Mike. Noting the exasperated look on her partner's face, she knew exactly where he was going with this. When Michaelene and Steve's are in sync, the spoken word becomes redundant.

"Here Steve," Mike offers pulling a bobby pin out of her hair, "Use this."

Steve again turns to his ever-reliable switchblade. With its stiletto-fine point, he cuts a tiny hole into his folding credentials at the top of its bind, refastens the tiny Justice Department badge to the right of the large letters that read, "FBI." Then shaping Michaelene's bobby pin into both a hook and a brace—the hook to connect to his dog tag chain, the brace to hold the credentials open as they dangled from his neck across his chest—he offers,

"Now that's more like it."

Mike adds, "You may be onto something."

Tami suddenly shouts, "Oh no, we're in trouble." She looks down at her Piguet Royal Oak wristwatch. "I've been trying to tell you since you got here. Now, you've only got four minutes."

"Tell me what?"

"You're up first."

"For what?"

"For tonight's telecast."

"What? No. I'm second to last just before Dr. Shirin, that nuclear physics professor."

"Not anymore, you're not."

"I haven't had time to brief my notes. In fact, I haven't seen my notes. Speaking of which, where is Agent Edwards? What happened to him? By the way, nice watch."

"The order of appearance for tonight's telecast has been changed. Because of what you and Fire Marshall Sullivan did, Governor Thompson decided not to waste time and give the people what they want to hear from the two people they need to hear it from the most, you and Marshall Sullivan, without a lot of 'political mumbo-jumbo.' His words not mine. The mayor agreed and stepped aside. As I said, they both genuinely admire the heck out of you."

"I didn't do anything but ask. It was Stan Sullivan, who—"

"Come on, hurry." Tami grabs Michaelene by her arm. "My purse is in the news truck."

Michaelene stopped dead in her tracks. Scanning the string of local and national mobile television reporting vehicles with various sized antennas parked and double parked along the street, on the sidewalk and on the parish front lawn, she asked, "Which one?"

Raising up on the tip of her toes, Tami points: "That one over there. I've got a new foundation that will work wonders to cover up your bruise. It will also highlight your eyes" As if such highlighting was necessary.

Michaelene - before moving forward - looks over to Steve, now standing upright and ambling near normal under his own steam. "Will you be alright?"

"Go on, get up there." Steve insists. "You've got the Governor and all these people waiting for you."

"Don't worry about our Japanese perpetrator," Michaelene offers. "I was able to zoom in. I got a full facial. If
he's left the area he won't be a fugitive for long" she
submits, with an affirming nod to Tami.

"Go, do your thing. I'll move through the crowd, cover
your rear and see if I can find any trace of the frog. Maybe he hasn't fled the scene yet."

"And see if you can locate Agent Edwards."

"Roger that."

With tension in the air ever-mounting and now nearly
palatable Michaelene adds, "And when you locate him—
"

"What?"

Reflecting upon his previous declarations regarding Edwards, Steve sighed, expecting a quick dressing-down
with an emphasis on FBI protocol from his boss—in
short, how to get along with coworkers you can't stomach. Instead, he got...

"Be nice."

CHAPTER FORTY

Oh, you just can't imagine how much Steve wanted to say something clever, something worthy of the moment, even something pithy that would convey to her the value of their relationship, like

"Way to go. Good one. You got me. Payback's a bitch." Even such treadmill clichés would have found more fertile ground. Instead in reply, all that came out of Steve's mouth was a cordial,

"Yes, ma'am."

As Michaelene eyes dropped to ground she shook her head. When she looked up, Steve was gone.

"Come on, Hurry." Tami is tugging at Michaelene, we gotta go!"

When Aatma - with lights and camera rolling - began walking backward up the Parish stairs, Michaelene commenced her ascension with Tami, as planned, stationing herself one flight below and to the left of the Catholic sanctum's massive front doors. Noticing that some official activity was finally underway, other news reporters with their camera crews in the lead, began pushing their way through a gaggle of independent photographers to capture the well-recognized head of the FBI's Chicago Bureau, each jocking for 'front row' seats. From atop the steps a sudden breach in the hovering masses caught Mike's attention. Preparing for the worst, she took a deep breath. Then she saw him, a familiar face stepping up and taking control of the media personnel. It was Belmont-Cragin police chief, Thomas A. Willard. Willard and his men had been called up to perform security duty at the Parish. The Chief glanced up at FBI Agent Westgate as he stepped towards Tami. He was about to ask the stunning, Ann-Margaret look-alike to move away from the Parish doors. Mike caught Willard's eye, read his intent and shook her head. He got the message. As of that moment, an ease arose between the two police officials. For her part, Tami was left hassle-free while Chief Willard ordered his men to keep all others at bay. As for Mike, no celebrity on Hollywood's red carpet could have drawn more attention.

Moving parallel to Tami and several feet behind, Steve was scanning the crowd. As he passes through the masses his credentials performing as intended, aid his movement. Steve was looking not only for the frog but for other agents, and especially Edwards but no one in sight stood out as a Fed.

Steve spots a dozen or more people sitting on a cement rise along the eastern side of the Parish. There, both young and old are exhausted from the heat. Towards the end of the row, Steve notices three men each in various phases of the prone position taking more than their fair share of the cement ledge. As he closed on the rise, a tall, middle-aged man abruptly emerges from the crowd on a right angle, intercept course.

"Excuse me. I see you're with the Bureau. You must be Agent Donaldson."

The man raises a large, double-thick, Marshall-Fields shopping bag with handles on either side, presenting it to Steve. "Your office said I might find you here."

"Sit the bag down over there and step aside."

Not living every day in the world of crime and criminals, it took Ken Porter a few seconds to register the reason for Donaldson's abrasive command. After all, from Porter's viewpoint, the state's sanitation commissioner was pulling double-duty, doing the Bureau a favor. He had made a few calls, was pointed in Agent Donaldson's direction and was personally, hand-delivering a bag of potential evidence.

"Sir...now."

"Oh, gosh I'm sorry. I neglected to properly introduce myself. Agent Donaldson, my name is Ken Porter. I'm the state sanitation commissioner. You're a Vietnam vet, right? Okay, me too." On this record-breaking, sweltering September eve, Mr. Porter's awkward attempts to warm himself to Agent Donaldson continued to be met with the coldest possible reception.

"You should know that my entire department and I —" Porter continues, "were quite flattered that your boss, Mrs. Westgate called upon us to assist in this investigation. She was right, you know. No one knows the streets of these Chicago burbs better than my guys, many of whom have been up since we got the word sifting through their latest garbage runs looking for anything that seemed out of the ordinary, anything that may somehow be connected to last night's explosion. In the bag is what's been found so far. It may be relevant. I don't know. Go ahead. Take a look."

Steve glared at Director Porter. "Your credentials, please. May I see your credentials, sir?" No quarter was being given by the Bureau's leading explosive and small arms expert, not in a crowd of this magnitude, one already on the edge of eruption.

"Again, I apologize, Agent Donaldson. What's been going on has all of our nerves a bit frayed including mine. I should have shown you my ID right away. Sorry. Here."

Rubbing his cheek with his right hand, the one nearest his shoulder holster, Steve takes Porter's photo identification badge with his left, looks at it, slowly comparing it to the man standing in front of him, grunts in acknowledgment, then hands it back to the state commissioner. Steve, still skeptical, having seen fake ID's before yet with zero time for an in-depth analysis of this one, picks up the fashionable retail department store bag, steps to the side, and peers in. As if shot from a cannon, all of a sudden Donaldson's right-hand flies to the top of his head then cascades painstakingly slow down his face, ultimately coming to rest clutching his chin as the Army Ranger turned FBI Special Agent concludes to himself: "Fuck me. I'm losing it."

No bomb or female body parts were in the oversized retail department store shopping bag. What was, however, were pieces relating to the simplest of explanations regarding how last night's, ruinous explosion may have been accomplished, an explanation that only a handful of men like Steve would know. Thus his reaction. To his way of thinking what he found in the bag "Was so disproportionate to the *effect,* that offering it as the *cause* never crossed my mind."

To himself Steve muses, "I'm the so-called expert. I should have thought to at least pose it as a hypothetical to Mike, but I didn't."

Steve shakes his head gauging the likelihood of what now seemed evident. "Sure, okay but damn. It's embarrassing to think that the sanitation department's garbage collectors pieced together something that I never even stopped to consider. A single shot fired from a sniper's rifle at the exact moment a series of supporting conditions fell into place, yeah—it's possible. In fact, we've seen it before, haven't we, Stevie?" Agent Donaldson says to himself.

With that thought in mind, former First Lieutenant Donaldon recalls how one of his Army colleagues with a single shot, torched a Royal Dutch Shell oil tanker on the outskirts of Saigon, it's driver a South Vietnamese civilian, an RDS employee. As the driver was hauled down from the truck's cab to allow the Viet Cong at its rear to collect their "liquid taxes," one shot by a sniper to the oil tanker's metal dispenser burst it open soaking the enemy with the tanker truck's contents while the spark from the bullet ignited it... the exposed valve then acting like a flame thrower. Within a millisecond, the flames leaping off of the bodies of the North Vietnamese "tax collectors" fed back into the tanker truck blowing it, the surrounding jungle and the VC platoon of twenty or more hiding in it to smithereens, saving the life of the driver.

Porter asks, "You recognize this stuff?"

"Yes," Acknowledged the Iowa-based FBI Agent in a somewhat less surely fashion than when his conversation with the State Sanitation Commissioner first began. Steve reaches into his hip pocket to retrieve his last set of sanitary gloves as the two men turn and huddle together at the side of building.

"We thought you might." Porter states. "Those pieces had us scratching our heads for a while until one of our guys just picked them up and stuck two of'em together. That's when we decided to call the Bureau. They directed us to you. Best we could determine that stock was found on a street of household waste disposal cans in Des Plaines, somewhere between East Algonquin and Lee Street. That piece, the one you now have in your hand, was found at the University of Chicago in the engineering department's dumpster. Apparently, it had been tossed in rather hastily. It lodged in the lid mechanism. My driver had to get out of his cab, remove it, and then close the dumpster's top before tipping its contents into his truck's hopper. Remarkable, don't you think?"

"What's that?"

"That both pieces were found miles apart yet they fit so well together...*lock, stock, and barrel* as the saying goes."

With the two men still huddled away from the crowd at the side of the Parish to reduce exposure to any passing lookie-lou whose curiosity may precipitate additional unwanted attention, Steve extracts another item from the bag, the so-called, "brass button." He holds it up in the air and examines it from all angles.

"Oh gosh, I'm sorry," utters Porter, his voice barely audible over the hubbub of the churning crowd. "I forgot that was there. I was at my office heading out the door holding this bag of remnants for you when I noticed that someone left that thing on my desk with a note saying it was a button off of my grandmother's chastity belt. Funny guy, right? The building's maintenance crew were already down the hall. They'd snatched my waste paper basket so I just swept it into this bag. My driver, Dick Francis, a former horse wrangler, found that button wedged into the tread of one of his garbage truck tires going through a back alley in Belmont-Cragin."

Porter then notices a sudden shift in the look on Agent Donaldson's face. He misreads it. The Agent's locked jaw had nothing to do with Porter or his garbage truck gang.

"It's not a button. It's a shell casing Mr. Porter, one that's been flattened. Its rim formed a hook apparently when your Mr. Francis, wrangled it out of the tire with what looks like from these striations, a pair of over-sized, utility pliers."

In Steve's mind he's struggling to fit the pieces before him into last night's explosive puzzle.

"A spark from a well-aimed round triggered from these assembled pieces, a collapsible sniper's rifle. Sure, of course! It fits. It all fits together. If successful only the results would be evident. What caused it would be untraceable. Brilliant."

Steve holds the flattened brass "button" up once again and spins it slowly between his forefinger and thumb:

He notices as he continues to himself, "There's no manufacturer's mark on this casing. It's unidentifiable save for the dimension of the firing pin that struck it. Clearly Russian. They overdo everything."

Not wanting to expose the more potentially recognizable items contained in the oversize Marshall Field's shopping bag to the masses milling about, Agent Donaldson stretches wide its top then sticks his nose back into it saying aloud as he first notices, "The tip of an Apex revolving barrel. Wow. Cool. I haven't seen one of these since Nam."

"We weren't certain what that was or even if it had anything to do with the other parts," offers the Illinois State sanitation commissioner. "One of my guys said to throw it into the bag. Let the experts figure it out. That's you and you just did."

"Check this out." Steve proudly pronounces, fully immersed in the likelihood that what he now has in front of him touched off last night's epic explosion. Steve extends the top of the retail shopping bag in Porter's direction, nudging the shortened barrel inside, forward. Reaching in, he giving the four-inch extender a twirl.

"Sweet."

Glancing up, he sees Porter with an *I'm not on the same page with you yet,* look on his face. Steve, the Bureau's lead "Small Arms and Explosives Expert," as if in front of a class of newbie agents at Quantico, begins with:

"Okay. Look. See this? It's an extender. It's placed at the end of a shortened rifle barrel. It spins as the round passes through it, exponentially increasing both distance and accuracy. Simple in design, it's ideal for a round fired from a lightweight, custom-made, collapsible weapon like this one." Steve holds the rifle stock found in a residential curbside garbage can at the top of the upscale shopping bag, offering: "Impressive, wouldn't you agree? And nicely tooled."

Again to himself, thinking of the shooter, Steve bids the sniper a, "Thank you for the clues dumbass, whoever the hell you are. I greatly appreciate the trail of evidence you left behind for me. Next time – as if they'll be a next time - just write me a note. In terms of your marksmanship abilities, I have to give it to you. You're in a class virtually by yourself, no surprise but using this kind of Russian built weaponry tells me a lot about who you are. You're well moneyed that's for certain but my guess is it comes from your douchebag teammate who no doubt, insists that you not wave this stick around fearing a trail that would lead back to him. Thanks again. That saves me a trip. I won't have to personally check out the local shooting clubs. Your appearance at one of them with weaponry like this would be as memorable as a hooker with a "free for the taking" neon sign strapped to her waist. Still, just to be safe, I'll ask the local cops to do the rounds. Maybe some neighborhood shooter or club owner may know of a contact or possible connection leading to how your butt-fucking partner was able to lay hands on this kind of military-grade sniper booty. And you my deranged shadow warrior friend, you and this rat-bastard partner of yours – disposing of the evidence hither and yawn - tells me even more. This guy who's leading you around by your nose is an amateur, new to the killing business. He's keeping you alive, intending to throw you to the wolves – that's us - if the main attraction, this scorpion's sting - whatever the hell that may be – runs into a roadblock requiring more time to develop. You're failure to recognize the simple fact that you're like a used condom unable to be tossed into the bedroom's trash for fear of being found by the wife's jealous husband makes you mind-numbingly naïve, a point-and-shoot carnival act, intellectually starved and morally deprived and as a result, soon to step out of the shadows, slip up, and get caught preferably by me. The other half of the picture you've been kind enough to paint says Mike is right. Whatever you're fucking piece of shit handler is planning, it is imminent otherwise far more care would have been given to disposing of the sniper tools... including you dick wad, you wouldn't be around."

Appreciating the quality of effort set forth by one's adversary together with such flaws, ultimately leads to discovering the identity of one rival, knowledge once spoken by Army Lt. Donaldson to Marine Colonel Frank

Clifford, both men knowing full well how to hunt, capture and when necessary, terminate the prey.

"And this..." Steve offers aloud, as he reaches in and lifts to mid-level height the last item in the bag. Believing that every American who served in Vietnam was immersed in combat, Steve asks,

"Remember this? Sure you do. It's a quick detach, Soviet PSO rifle scope...bitchin', right?"

Ken Porter was a quartermaster, a rear echelon supply officer rarely in the line of fire throughout his tour of duty.

"It's the ideal choice for a clear shot at sunset." That triggered Steve's recollection of the string of abandoned, high-rise buildings towering over the Clifford service station site and the oil depot.

"Oh my god, yes," Steve laughs aloud. "Yes, yes, very good." The event that rocked a state and put the entire Midwest on alert, begins taking shape from the shooter's perspective in Agent Donaldson's mind.

"Now I see it. Shit, yes." He mumbles aloud, "Brilliant, just fuckin brilliant." Steve takes two steps away from Porter and lowers his head.

With eyes closed, the Bureau's most highly regarded Explosives and Small Arms expert begins counting down the sequence of events, those that led to last night's epic explosion, snapping his fingers at the end of each, validating the conclusion reached.

"The sniper's lair, six stories up, no higher or lower. Compensating for wind and humidity a round fired from a .50 caliber rifle using a 750 grain bullet from that elevation, would travel approximately 2,700 feet per second reaching the target in 4.5 seconds. The speed of sound is 343 meters per second. That's…that's 1,124 feet per second. The rifle's report, would have never been heard. It would have been lost in the sound of the explosion. Good, yes, very good." SNAP.

"Projectile to the propane tank, why not? Sure. No need to recreate the wheel. Use what's available, minimizing the retracable footprint of the event." Smooth, very smooth. SNAP.

"The accelerant seeping out, seeks the ricochet's spark. Yes of course. How beautiful is that?" SNAP.

"An unsuspecting customer at the station's pump is transformed into a candle wick, the means by which the heavier than air propane gushes up his pant leg reaching the gasoline spillage at the exact moment the ricocheted round strikes. Perfetto!" SNAP.

"The spark, now a flame, the two together by the weight of the accelerant, are flushed down ten feet through the gasoline's hose into the first of four ten thousand gallon gasoline, cement storage containers." SNAP.

"With interconnecting valves open at the end of a busy day, the explosion of the first storage tank sets off the second, the third, then the fourth. Then Kablooey. Welcome to the midwest's first volcanic eruption since the Stone Age." SNAP

Steve turns back to Porter and says aloud, "Hell yes, definitely doable. Now it's a matter of who? Who today is that good?" Ken Porter left unaware of the thought process that preceded the remark, simply nodded in agreement.

While Special Agent Donaldson was going through the mental machination of reconstructing last night's devastating explosion, The Illinois State Sanitation Commissioner is staring over Donaldson's shoulder at the wide open, double front doors of St. Margaret's Parish as Michaelene having arrived at the top of the staircase, reaching the governor's side.

Captivated, Porter offers, "Wow, she really is beautiful—even from a distance."

"Whoa, wait one!"

There, now over Porter's shoulder, Steve sees the last remaining man of the three once lying prone at the far end of cement rise, attempting to move. The unidentifiable male stiffens then suddenly rolls off into the Parish flower bed on the opposite side of where he once laid.

Pressing in front of Ken Porter, Steve peers through the masses to see he was right He snickers. There, standing next to where the man who had disappeared into the flower bed, was the sole offspring of the diabolical butcherer of women at the Tinian refractory ovens, 'Sonny Yoshida.' The Frog is still on the scene.

Steve brings the two handles of the oversized Marshall Fields' shopping bag back together and hands it to the Sanitation Director. "Ken is it?"

"Yes."

"I need your help."

"How can I be of service?" said the state sanitation commissioner with all the enthusiasm of a kid dying to play G Man.

"Get one of your people to take this bag and its contents to Bureau headquarters."

"My office is nearby. I'll do it."

"Even better but make certain when you walk through the front door that you have your credentials prominently displayed."

"Lesson learned, Agent Donaldson. No problem."

"And give the bag to the agent sent to greet you with explicit instructions that it's a gift to "Miss" Westgate from me, Agent Donaldson, got it?"

"Consider it done."

"You're okay. I've got to go. Move out. And thank you."

Steve, still spying Sonny, went for his gun then hesitated recalling what Mike had said. The Bureau now had full facial recognition of this guy, a "close up" captured by a State of the art television camera no less.

"No need to risk starting a riot," Steve concluded as he released his grip. The Jap keeping his eye on his American adversary, offers a half-ass, military style salute, laughs then waves, finally pivoting on a stiffened left leg and vanishes into the crowd.

CHAPTER FORTY-ONE

Donaldson looks over the cement rise to determine the identity and condition of the man who fell behind it. The man was Edwards and there was no doubt about it, he was dead.

"Shit!" It was times like these that Steve regretted having never learned how to stick two fingers in his mouth and give off one of those great, *train's a-comin'* whistles—something to rise above the petulant crowd and turn the heads of the two uniformed police officers that Mike had pointed out earlier.

In the absence of any means to hail the two officers no more than a dozen yards away, Steve reentered the flow of people making their way to the Parish steps. Shortening his stride, nudging his way, not wanting to draw undue attention, he neared the two uniformed policemen.

"Officers?" The youngest of the two turned. "Officer Nash?" Steve inquires, having taken notice of the officer's ID badge on his chest.

"Yes?"

"Special Agent Steve Donaldson, FBI. I need one of you to come with me."

"What's the emergency?"

"I'll explain when we get there. We need to move—now!" That said, Agent Donaldson recalled one of Michaelene's oft-repeated rebukes. "You're an FBI

Agent, not an Army Ranger anymore." So with that, he quickly added, "Please."

Officer Nash turns to his fellow police officer, "Let me see what this guy wants. I'll be right back."

"No, you won't." Agent Donaldson shouts, making certain to be heard over the crowd. "You'll need to stay put."

"Okay, it's serious?"

"Yes. Come on. Let's go."

As the two insert themselves back into the flow of former residents of Belmont-Cragin and its surrounding communities—those wanting to hear their governor and his quickly assembling associates explain last night's earth-shaking event and how they plan to put the lives of their fellow Illinois residences back together again— Steve turns to Officer Nash upon covering the necessary distance and says simply:

"We're here," The two arrived at the spot where Agent Edwards, tucked out of sight, is lying face down in the garden.

"Get a hold of your dispatcher. Have them send an ambulance immediately and stand here until it arrives. If any civilian approaches you with questions say this man had a heart attack, got it? Or make something up. I don't care. He's one of ours, a Federal Agent. Do you understand?"

"Yes, sir. Sorry for your loss."

"Listen. Do you know who Special Agent in charge, Westgate is?"

"Who in law enforcement in this state, doesn't?"

"Hand me your pen." Steve orders as he takes out one of Michaelene's business cards. "When the ambulance arrives, make cer0tain that the driver knows to take the body directly to the Cook County morgue and hand this card to Chief Medical Officer Dr. Vaziri. She'll know what to do from there."

"And who are you again?" The young officer asks.

"I'm Agent Steve Donaldson, Michaelene Westgate's partner. Thank you. I gotta go. I have to get over to her."

As Steve moves away, Officer Nash says aloud to no one in particular, "Lucky guy."

As the collected multitude stared up at Governor Jim Thompson, Fire Marshall Stan Sullivan, and FBI Special Agent in Charge Michaelene Westgate standing side-by-side facing the cameras atop the Parish steps, amongst the crowd, a calm settles in. Now standing before them were their community's very own Super Heroes—two men and a woman whose reputations for leadership and caring for the people and the communities they serve had been long cast.

From the audience, a woman with four kids attached to her spontaneously shouted, "We're going to get through this thing, aren't we Big Jim?"

Such an unprompted accolade elicited a rousing round of cheers mixed with friendly, supporting laughter. The woman's unconstrained outcry was captured and later played as part of the national news coverage of this earth-pounding, midwestern event.

What was particularly heartwarming to all who noticed was the extemporaneous hand-holding between the three public servants. Not upward as in a victory celebration but kept low and subtle emphasizing a bond amongst the *Super Heroes* and a commitment to the people they swore to serve. It was heartening and perhaps far more importantly, it wasn't staged.

"Yes, you're right," echoed Big Jim as he broke ranks and stepped forward to respond to the middle-aged mother. "Yes, we're going to get through this thing with your help and with all of us working together." Such a sanguine comment had political *Ho hum* written all over it, especially if offered by any other elected official but from Big Jim, it was different. His words, less the specific content than the sentiment they conveyed, spoke to a solemn pledge to do everything within his power to get Belmont-Cragin, the surrounding communities the City of Chicago and indeed, his state back on its feet moving forward once again. And everyone who heard him knew without reservation he meant it.

With a hand now set free, Michaelene subtlety points to Tami Swanson. With that the reporter's exclusive on-the-scene broadcast begins with:

"The FBI believes that they have a person of interest in a recent murder who may also be connected to last night's explosion. He is this man:"

With that, the face of Sonny Yoshida featuring his *Grade A*, vile-disregard-for-human-life grin is flashed across every television set in the State of Illinois and most prominently, on every monitor in every news truck's open door currently surrounding the congregate outside St. Margaret of Scotland Parish.

"He is believed to be a Japanese national or of Japanese descent. If anyone knows the name of this man or where he can be located, please contact the FBI."

As if his trademark beaming smile was cast by an esteemed Hollywood director to be seen by television viewers in contrast to Sonny's sunken-eyed, disdain ridden, Boo Radley expression, every square inch of Governor Thompson's face— as Tami presented her on the spot newscast—radiated both pleasant surprise and support as Aatma Singh's camera lens zoomed-in on the nattily attired governor. Turning away from the spotlight, Big Jim leaned into Michaelene:

"That was quick? You're too much, young lady. A prompt action from a public official? I better be careful, you'll have my job. Go ahead, step up. Tell these people what you told me. Tell them what they came to hear:"

Michaelene places her hand on Fire Marshall Sullivan's shoulder ushering him forward alongside her as she sets forth in no uncertain terms to all present and viewers throughout the state by way of hastily set public announcement system, that last night's epic explosion had zero impact on the Dresden nuclear power plant. "It was not involved in any way."

When Mike was through, Stan Sullivan seamlessly added his comments to hers offering that he personally walked the trench line formed by the explosion. On paper in front of the huddled news reporters with rocks from the staircase garden holding down each side, Stan laid out on the steps below the Parish canopy a summary of the radiation detector's readings taken by him and twelve of his firefighters.

"Three sample sites were compared to the Dresden power plant and Mr. Frank Clifford's former auto-truck, service center. The one whose readings measured similarly to the epicenter of the explosion was the Green Garden Grocery Store down the street; each hovering on a scale of 1-1000 at *18-22 uR/hr* on the Geiger counter's analog readout, indicating the presence of radiation to be 'normative,' or put another way, presenting zero threat to the public."

Then, Michaelene wanting to head off what could turn into a time-consuming question and answer period, offered to the assembled before her:

"I wish to thank everyone here on behalf of the Bureau for helping us and indeed each other deal with this crisis. At this point we've given you all the information we can. Please keep eyes and ears tuned to local newscasts. The FBI has a person of interest. We're seeking his whereabouts. If you happen to see the man whose face appears on your TV screen, do not approach him. Get to the nearest phone and call the FBI's office, immediately."

As Mike completed her thoughts one man in the crowd looked over his shoulder, catching Tami's broadcast on the news truck's monitors. He taps the shoulder of the man next to him. He turns. Soon dozens more follow suit capturing a glimpse of the last segment of the news report with a full facial of Sonny Yoshida, the suspect at large, a name yet unknown to the FBI. The young black woman in the blue polka dot dress recognizing the face on the monitor nearest her screams out, "Oh my god." Pushing through the crowd to find Officer Nash's partner, she's compelled to offer to the police what she knows about the man.

While Michaelene and Stan were conveying to the assemblage their assurances, a podium was being put into place behind them with a permanent sound system with attachments for news reporters microphones. Behind that, inside the Parish, pews were being shuffled about and tables in their stead, were being set in line. It was surprising to all even those in the crowd that few questions, save for the obligatory, *What happens now* and *When can we return home*, were raised. Cynical comments were no doubt in the minds of some but given the remarkably speedy and very tangible forthcomings by the community's three Super Heroes, not a single disparaging remark was publicly aired.

To secure the answers to those *What's the next step* questions, Governor Thompson had been on the phone this morning since 5:00 am. While stepping on board the

State Police *Command and Control* helicopter that would transport him from the state capital at Springfield to Saint Margaret's Parish in Washington Heights — he was still talking with a bevy of pertinent parties when at 6:15 pm, as the chopper settled on the east lawn of the Parish, an incoming call from Washington D.C. was patched in. Jimmy Carter, the President of the United States was calling to personally express his support. Now, in front of the TV cameras, the Chief Executive of the State of Illinois offers to the crowd:

"Good evening. I'm Governor Thompson. First, I would like to thank the Catholic dioceses and the fine people of St. Margaret of Scotland Parish who upon recognizing that a large majority of the displaced from Belmont-Cragin and the surrounding community are here this evening, offered this holy sanctuary to aid the state in distributing its food and temporary housing vouchers to all in need."

With that, from all around, an audible sigh of relief filled the air.

"You'll notice the Red Cross is here working alongside our state's Office of Emergency Management's Disaster Relief Teams setting up tables to the left and right of us." Spotting the head of the local Red Cross in the field of humanity below the stairs to the right, the governor waves and shouts,

"Mr. Bernard Atwater, thank you."

In reply, the Red Cross executive raises his hand and waves in acknowledgment.

Thompson then goes onto say to the crowd: "If you left your home with nothing but the shirt on your back, we'll try to get to you first. I can't imagine how despondent you must feel but I'm asking for your patience. Forms will need to be filled out, so don't hesitate to do so and please, be accurate. That's the best way for our team of social workers and volunteers to quickly fill your short term needs while working to provide a full range of services to assist every person here, over the long haul. We have the resources but we need your help to effectively distribute them. Through our joint State and Federal Emergency relief program, construction crews have already set up along the outside perimeter of the fire line in and around the Belmont-Cragin area awaiting an all-clear from Marshal Sullivan before moving forward. The initial target will be infrastructure. Work is expected to commence at first light."

Governor Thompson, wanting to deemphasize any tie to last night's explosion to the Dresden nuclear power plant, made a point of pronouncing with considerable emphasis, a new name for this catastrophic event :

"For those directly affected by the BELMONT-CRAGIN ERUPTION, local hotels and eateries have already received phase one of State funding to provide you with their services. Make certain you hold onto the voucher you're issued. Getting what you deserve in its absence will be impossible. All the major insurance carriers have been notified and will be here on site to help their policyholders and…"

With that, Stan turns to Michaelene, "Two insurance companies dug their heels in, insisting that their customers make an appointment and come to their offices to address their claims. The Governor called the CEO's of both companies, personally."

Often referred to as Lincoln-esque, at six foot six and two hundred and twenty pounds, *Big Jim* Thompson is a politician whose tone and rhetoric is as smooth as they come but as those who misjudged him then tried to play him were quick to discover, having one's face stomped into the ground by a Chicago Bear's linebacker was preferable to being the subject of one of Governor Thompson's 'voluble rhetorical admonishments.' From the former, one could recover.

From the latter, a lifetime of self-reflection was inevitable.

Eager to get back to his legion of firefighters, Stan shakes hands with Governor Thompson then leans in behind him to receive a kiss on the cheek from Michaelene. Exiting to the rear, the fire marshall noticing a rather "odd duck"—someone he thought he recognized but couldn't quite place—standing inside the Parish off to the side of its front row pews primping... nervously.

Outside the Parish, having made it to the base of its elevated steps, Steve is forced to snuggle closer than the social norms of the day would recommend to a CBS cameraman. The video artist had been basking in the heat and sweltering humidity for several hours carrying a heavy Philips, Electronic Field Production camera on his shoulder. Both men were covered with sweat and exceedingly uncomfortable in each other's presence, the cameraman most notably, given that within such crowded confines, the FBI was literally looking right over his shoulder.

Steve caught Michaelene's attention. Her body language expressed relief knowing he was near. Steve knew he had to tell Mike of Edward's death but this was not the time.

With long strides, as Governor Thompson gestured for him to step forward, the clean-shaving nuclear physicist with an aristocratic bearing Dr. Randolph Shirin, Ph.D., emerged from inside the Parish sanctum and took to the podium. Upon arrival, Michaelene offered him her place next to the governor.

The temporarily assigned Special Agent in Charge of the FBI's Northern Illinois Bureau, received her undergrad degree as a foreign exchange student from Francis's Sarbonne in Behavioral Psychology. Mike was determined to take full advantage of this opportunity to carefully study the nationally heralded nuclear physicist with the hope of seeing in him what she may have missed during their first and only, brief encounter.

With slick backed hair exposing a widow's peak, Mike was struck by the way Shirin's movements as he approached the podium, seemed almost ritualistic as if each was separately rehearsed. Basking in his own limelight, his head cocked high looking from side to side like Mussolini giving his 1936, "Italian Empire" speech from the balcony of Palazzo Venezio, she couldn't help but notice Chicago television's most frequent talking head on nuclear power seemed to be two people—one somewhat miffed as he looked through what was now a measurably thinning crowd—the other uncharacteristically apprehensive as if wanting to point a finger to expose a secret he dared not.

With a dismissive back-handed wave, Shirin acknowledged to the remaining live audience and the vast array of television cameras still in front of him that the female cop and the fireman were, "Right."

That was it. That was all he had to say about them. He even failed to mention their names. In his view, the "cop and the fireman" were two amateurs from whom the masses could have been spared if he a true, learned academician, a leading expert on the subject of nuclear science had been granted his due and called to the podium, first.

Displeased yet trying to hold it together, Dr. Shirin abruptly turned his attention to the young people who'd remained in the audience—students mostly from the University—as he craftily moved away from the horrors that were swirling through every other attendee's mind, to comments on the innocuous subject of setting one's goals and steadfastly sticking to them until…

"…reaching their inevitable conclusion."

From his *front-row* vantage point, Steve thought to himself "What the hell has any of that got to do with what's going on around here?"

Listening carefully, something beyond the out-of-sync misdirection of the professor's comments caught Mike's ear. She heard several words in Shirin's opening comments that contained a hollow, phonetic resonance as if they were chosen to please the audience, yet unfamiliar to the orator. Delivered in iambic pentameter less Shakespearean and more in keeping with a throwback to the 1950s, Greenwich Village scene, the highly rated academician was clearly unaccustomed to speaking to a lay audience, especially one—it dawned on Mike— composed of everyday, working class, Americans. Shirin's long formal pauses—the caesuras within his speech patterns—intonations interspersed with formidable hand gestures like an orchestra conductor whose woodwind section abruptly missed a cue, all appeared somewhat Mannequin-like, scripted and if rehearsed poorly so—and if delivered by anyone else in any other set of circumstances—downright laughable.

One catching Dr. Shirin's act from the side, the other near center stage, Steve and Michaelene had the same thought at the same time but given the surrounding circumstances, were unable to directly share.

Steve caught a sideways glance, a subtle sheep's eye from Michaelene. "Where is this guy from?"

Steve could only shrug his shoulders in reply.

Dr. Randolf Shirin was growing noticeably uncomfortable. Coming on stage having to play second fiddle to a woman was bad enough. What was now digging deep into his psyche he could he barely contain. He had entered St. Margaret's Parish from a side gate passing by the opened, sliding door of a news van, one that arrived late finding available parking only to the rear of the building. Inside the opened van door on the TV crew's monitor, Shirin saw a close-up of his "lab assistant." There was no doubting it and clearly no way to sidestep the fact. It was Sonny.

Sonny Yashida of Nagoya, Japan; the Yakuza crime syndicate reject that the University of Chicago physics professor imported to help carry-out his highly choreographed scheme of annihilating the American people by way of a mass bacteriological infection of its female population. Seeing his "fall guy" on camera hit Shirin like the fat end of a baseball bat thrust into his gut. Dr. Randolph Shirin's co-conspirator, his dupe, his sidekick, an international butcherer of women, the son of the man who whittled while he waited for the bodies that he and his men cast atop the fiery rungs of a refractory oven melted as they cried for mercy. A marksman indeed, "in a class by himself," there he was, Sonny Yashida the inheritor of his father's chosen discipline now on television for all the world to see.

With his brow furled the University of Chicago's nuclear physics professor, wondered "How long will it take for investigators led by this treacherous woman now standing so close, to connect me to him?"

"Ha." Shirin said aloud, offering reassurance to himself. "What worry should I have? These stinking simians, these pale monkeys are no match for me. They're bureaucrats the lot of them, intellectually weak puppets of the state unable to see the abstract I created, let alone decipher it."

From Caesar to Sun Tzu, to modern day warriors, the refrain *know thine enemy* has passed through history with many laid asunder who failed to heed it.

Indeed, how long will it take for those led by Michaelene to work backwards, determining that the professor is the *Scorpion* to Sonny the Frog; the butcherer of women, Randolph's *two-fer,* the initiator of all that has befallen, the trigger man, the sniper?

CHAPTER FORTY-TWO

Still standing behind the podium, Dr. Shirin looked out of over the Parish steps. Few of the temporarily displaced were still about. Thanks to the state of the art sound system recently attached to the podium all could still hear the professor of nuclear physics rambling on about "the history of nuclear power," its modern failsafe systems and its future-linked economic advantages. Frankly however, the vast majority who could hear no longer gave a damn. The angst had settled and interest's shifted. With assurances established by the governor, the Cook County Fire Marshall, and the FBI - that what had happened last night wasn't going to happen again - people were now focused on their individual needs as they lined-up in front of dozens of Red Cross tables. There a slew of volunteers shook hands, handed out cups of water, and periodically hugged a displaced, fellow human being. Once a Red Cross staffer had taken down the needy soul's information and filled out the form on their behalf, it was handed back with encouragement to proceed into the Parish to the *State Office of Emergency Management's Disaster Relief* teams where, as Big Jim promised, immediate relief vouchers were being handed out.

As calmness continued to mount, Dr. Shirin's resentment grew. From the podium, looking at the few still gathered who periodically glanced up at him and snickered, he snickered back, filled with a godlike sense of knowing that it was just a matter of time before their lives and all around would soon fall to his will.

"Fools! Each one of you will soon pay for your arrogance." Fortunately for Shirin, his comments were only partially audible. They spilled forth as unintelligible babble, partially spoken, partially retained as thought.

Seizing the blackboard in his mind, as perspiration ran down his face, Shirin reassessed a mathematical formula, one handed down from father to son, one with a most delicate of timelines. He needed to make sure, absolutely sure for as prescribed in his father's text, "No margin of error can be suffered." There would have to be enough time not only for each element to rise like yeast in a controlled environment, comingle then blend with the others but time to distribute the newly formed pathogen before its limited shelf-life expires. Once gestation was reached, the pathogen needed a host to prolong its survival. Finding the best possible environment to nourish the newly born substance outside of an incubator was essential. That had brought him to Chicago. The "windy city" also provided a veil behind which Shirin could carry out his deceptions. After all, he was indeed, a nuclear physicist. Who would think that such a learned man steeped in such a demanding science would be the criminal genius behind yet another, one capable of far greater, and the more wide-spread annihilation of his fellow man than the other? Having learned one and inherited the other, making Chicago his home provided Dr. Randolph Shirin a kind of 'rebirth,' as it was not only that place where his primary science was born but now 'his soon-to-be new life as the exhalted one who'd brought Jimmu and the throne of the Crysanthmum to their rightful place on the world stage,' began. By contrast, Shirin would boast to any who would listen, how proud he was to be called a citizen of the great city of Chicago. That made the formulation of his deceptive plans taste even sweeter. Still, there was something far more sinister to his long studied, choice of residency. His exit strategy.

Built in stages beginning in 1803 along the banks of Chicago River, the city of Chicago- Algonquin for "Onion Weed" rests atop an enormous, backwater, swamp. There could be no better, nurturing environment for a developing airborne viral contagion than the vast Chicago wetlands. Born anew with each contact with a seed, root or even a houseplant, it matures until deadly to humans. Shirin concluded that if his "patsy" could conveniently turn himself in or better still, continue...

"Yes, yes! Far better. Continue, yes!" For the briefest of moments Randolph again spoke aloud. This time he caught himself. His ruminations having retreated back inside, his body setting forth a brisk, self-congratulatory shiver upon reentry, straightening his backbone, standing him upright.

"Yes," he now whispered to himself, "continue to draw the police and FBI's attention away from me for the next forty-eight hours," he mentally summed, "with that, *Operation No Pao* can proceed."

To make certain his mental mascinations were spot-on he needed to get back to his laboratory, to its blackboard to recalibrate.

And just like that. There it was. You could see it on his face. Reality had set in. Complicated schemes, regardless of how successful they may have been in the past, were now moot as windows of opportunity were closing fast all around the gifted young scientist. Yet, stopping to take his own measure, pondering all that he'd accomplished to stand where he stood today - including killing his mother to blur his pedigree - Dr. Randolph Shirin, the bastard son of Shirō Ishii, drew a measure of solace. And so to maintain his façade he decided to carry on like an automaton, continuing to prophesize the glories of a nuclear-powered future to the now clearly disinterested, dwindled masses. On the verge of fulfilling his quest, he knew that the police and the FBI were no longer his enemies. Time and time alone was his inescapable nemesis. And he needed all he could obtain.

While he stood behind the podium contemplating in what order the events he controlled must take, shadows of doubt eclipsed every attempt at formulating a constructive way forward. As his mind seethed with hatred, his body froze. Rising to a crescendo his focus suddenly flip-flopped, shifting back to Sonny, now punishing himself for keeping his pet troglodyte alive.

"Was it wise after firing that extraordinary shot to allow him to live?" asked Randolph, the studious scholar of death.

"Should I have given Sonny the *Chapstick Balm* without explanation? He always points to his lips, complaining how the climate irritates them. Yes, rather than sending him off on his own, I should have given him one last task to perform, ending him as he ended it. Why didn't I? Leaving Sonny's body in a Belmont-Cragin back alley, would that have slowed authorities or would it have brought them sooner to me," mused the *Scorpion* questioning the value of his *Frog*.

With the arrival of a sudden gust of wind, the professor closed his eyes, stepped inside himself, and reinvested in his objective. In short, he pulled himself together.

"I will succeed. This I swear on my soul to you Jimmu. I will succeed."

No question the man is a genius. Still any person divested of direction and drawing into question one's previous decisions is in the throes of designing their own downfall.

Governor Thompson, seeing that his efforts had resulted in the outcome he had hoped to achieve, was escorted pass the grateful lines at the tables to the police helicopter - the one in which he arrived - to be taken back to his home and office in Springfield.

Nearly losing his make-shift ID while pushing through the crowds as he left the cameraman's side, Steve placed it back into its original folder then stuffed it into his right front pocket and walked up the Parish steps heading for Michaelene. As he neared four agents from Mike's office who had no way of knowing who this stranger was, stepped from the wings and closed on him to protect their boss.

As introductions proceeded and tensions by way of cordial exchanges receded, Susan Sykes, the only other female agent in the bureau's Northern Illinois office, a recent Boston University grad just eight months out of the academy, handed Mike a closed frequency walkie-talkie. Turning to Steve as she did, she said, "I'm sorry. I didn't know to bring two."

"That's okay." Michaelene countered, "Agent Donaldson and I will share. What's the status of Agent Israel? How is he?"

"Ron is home now. He's recovering well," Agent Skyes submits. "Haskell signed him out in your absence."

There were a countless number of things about the Bureau's founder, J. Edgar Hoover, that didn't sit well with many of the younger agents in the early 1970s, including Michaelene. But the basic protocols and the level of decorum on which he insisted she felt had merit. Always referring to a fellow agent for example as just that; as *Agent Israel* or *Agent Haskell* provided a homogeneous atmosphere, a sense of belonging, of camaraderie, of shared respect and responsibility. Guys wearing dark suits, a white shirt, and a no-frills straight black tie complimented such protocols. Mike remembers her war with Hoover over his desire for her to wear a skirt while on duty. Less in defiance than in the pursuit of simple, god damn practicality she wore the most finely tailored slacks she could afford. Hoover didn't like it but said nothing and with that, a tradition for women in the Bureau was born. But hearing young Agent Sykes drop the most basic of protocols while reporting on the status of two of her fellow agents, especially under present circumstances, grated on SAC Westgate's nerves.

"Mike, I—" Steve attempts to report to his boss but his efforts were thwarted. Agent Sykes simply couldn't find a way to throttle down her enthusiasm. Thrilled to be working in the field with the Bureau's eminent Michaelene Westgate, the young rookie couldn't help digging herself into an even deeper hole. Stepping in front of Steve, she inserted herself and her thoughts to Mike ahead of his.

"Before arriving here on the scene," Skye's offered, "I must tell you that all of us back at HQ saw the *Hue and Cry* you set in motion using Miss Swanson and her TV camera. Modern technology meets jolly old, 19th Century England police work. Invigorate the public. Use them to point the direction to the bad guys. Brilliant call, Mike."

Having allowed himself a brief moment of sympathy for Agent Sykes, Steve was actually glad she asserted her comments before his. Having done so would either get her summarily removed from this detail or properly focused. There was a murderer on the loose. There was no time to waste sucking up to the boss. Susan Sykes clearly knew who Michaelene was and was comfortable using her boss's nickname—no problem there—but she hadn't been around long enough to gain any actual insight into the person. If she had—if her tenure had been more than just under a year—Mike, upon hearing Susan's fawning commentary, would have opted for option number one, sending Agent Sykles immediately back to the office, dismissing her from this public venue to await an official reprimand, possibly even a transfer. In Mike's world, wasting time for any reason was unacceptable. Wasting time with kiss-ass remarks in an attempt to curry favor not only turned Mike's stomach but was damn near, unforgivable. The look on Michaelene's face as she glared woman-to-woman at Susan, wilted the young agent. Steve had seen that look on his former girlfriend's face only once before. It was in that moment just prior to "Mickey's" ascension to the high school's lunchtime, tabletop to address his bullying teammates. As it was then, it was now. Hell's fury rose and then abruptly ended replaced with a more decisive desire to free her mind from emotion to better deal with whatever the problem at hand, required.

The problem at hand was that guy now standing a few feet from Mike gripping the podium as if needed to steady himself. The FBI's, Special Agent in Charge and the University of Chicago's nuclear physics professor, the hunter and the soon-to-be hunted, standing so near yet unaware of the direction the next few minutes will set them both upon share similar character traits. Both are highly educated and highly accomplished. Both are passionate. Though Michaelene had little interest in science, she had studied abroad before settling upon Northwestern for law school. There she was selected as editor of the law review. But perhaps one key difference sets the two apart. One had a father who did everything to support his offspring, providing guidance, backing, and that one so vital of an ingredient, unconditional love. As a result, Miss Michaelene Westgate knew herself. She was grounded. The other quite obviously, had no such upbringing and that was about to show.

On every field of human endeavor wars erupt. *Know thine enemy* is rule number one. If set aside, one soon discovers that thine enemy is thee.

That glare from the woman who blazed the trail for other female Agents in the FBI, brought Agent Sykes in line, her priorities in lockstep with her fellow agents.

Mike, having never uttered a word up to this point, asks Sykes, "Damage assessment?"

"Eight stitches to close the laceration across Agent Israel's forehead. He also had two broken ribs."

Steve, the man better known as Special Agent Donaldson, finally gets his chance to report. "

"I had eyes on the frog minutes ago. He's still around here. I'm confident of it."

Mike orders the four agents on her team to fan out, "Get names and contact information from anyone who even brushed up against our Japanese suspect." She quickly adds as they turn to descend the Parish steps, "And Find Agent Edwards." Steve seizing the moment, steps to the side, his back to his fellow agents and that oddball still standing at the podium and whispers to Michaelene, "That won't be necessary. I know where Edwards is."

Hearing that and the tone of voice in which it was given Mike shouts: "Belay my last." Her father, after all, was a Navy man. "We got Edwards. Focus on the public."

CHAPTER FORTY-THREE

As he rambled on still glued to the podium, making hand gestures to indicate something indeterminable yet of great social import was on the verge of being announced, 'Randolph' deliberately remained a few feet away from what he'd rightfully determined was a bevy of federal agents hovering around their Bureau chief. Shirin lingered there, at the top of the Parish steps eavesdropping, hoping to obtain any tidbit of information regarding the direction their investigation may be taking.

Three of the Bureau' finest, following orders, started down the Parish stairs high stepping over the congregate of reporters, cameramen and their equipment. At essentially the same time, Sykes, Donaldson and Westgate in near unison hesitated, turned and looked in the direction of the podium each having the same thought in mind. A thought that began with:

"What the hell is that guy still doing here?"

From the base of the stairs at St. Margaret Parish, a voice with a lively baritone pitch climbing towards them was heard offering…

"Oh, shit, dude. Seriously? Do you mind? Come on. Let us through here, okay!"

Four grad students from the University of Chicago whose parents had been displaced by the *Belmont-Cragin Eruption* discovered a pathway between a coven of thirteen cameramen as each were packing-up their image-robbing devices in "show's over" fashion. Three of the four students were Shirin disciples, each a rising star in the world of nuclear physics.

"Hey you kids," one cameraman replied, "Go on, get out of here. Skedaddle."

"Well gosh darn-it" said Oliver the kid in the lead with the baritone pitch mocking the cameraman's use of an outmoded expression. Making the sign of the cross, the Westinghouse Science honoree ended the Catholic Church's ritualistic blessing in a most unconventional fashion...with a middle finger raised in defiance towards the cameraman.

It took little time for the eager young scholars to reach the top of the Parish stairs and surrounded their celebrated professor. Noting their enthusiasm, Mike turned to Steve along with Agent Sykes, and said,

"Let's hang back for a few minutes and see how Shirin interacts with these kids."

Outside the classroom it was easy to label this self-aggrandizing virtual mockery of himself an awkward geek, ill at ease in a public forum, flawed in the absence of lecture notes or a crib sheet. However, to imagine him inside the classroom, wrapped-up in the authority of four walls lined with blackboards each scribed with theories that push the boundaries of known science... heart-pounding, feasting off his audience as they rise to keep pace, intellectually nourishing him with their questions, frankly, was not that difficult for the three agents - themselves not that far removed from their own daliances with academia - to grasp. Here was a man not much older than the eager minds who filled his lecture hall who was idolized, fundamentally, a demigod to his students.

"Look at those kids." Steve says to Mike. "They love that son of a bitch."

From the standpoint of these young scholars who have now settled in around the physics professor, this was the chance of a lifetime, a chance to get a little "one-on-one" time in an unstructured forum with their mentor; youthful ambition having long ago set aside their hero's eccentricities. In the world of nuclear physic, the University of Chicago's Randolph Shirin Ph.D., was miles ahead of all the somber elders in the field. In the classroom before a captured audience, Shirin was brimming with new and exciting ideas, dynamically offering innovative and challenging new ways of looking at old concepts and breathing fresh life into them. Out here in an unrestricted space, who knew what this remarkable man of science would have to say? No way were these young scholars going   to   leave.

Mike, believing that the appearance of a woman - one who in this case is eight years younger than herself - may be best to move this unconventional oddball and his base of followers off the stage and out of the area, gave the nod to Agent Sykes. As the blonde-haired, pony-tailed, mid-west-raised agent took her first step toward Shirin, he reached for something inside the portable speaker's podium.

Mike grabbed Susan's arm:

"Wait!" She ordered.

The esteemed professor of nuclear physics was reaching for something that no one apparently including himself, could see. Shirin was trying to locate the controls to the speaker system. Struggling, he wanted to turn the speakers off. As he fumbled about, their volume receding, he continued to ramble on, no longer to an inattentive crowd but exclusively to his body of collegiate admirers. As he reached he inadvertently bumped the castor-based podium, repositioning it in the direction of the FBI.

"Did you hear that?" Mike asks, looking at Steve.

"Hear what?."

"Exactly."

It's what Mike didn't hear that caught her attention. She didn't hear the "click," the sound of the volume indicator as it reached its final "off" position. The speakers attached to the podium had been reduced but were still "on" and fully functioning. Voices from inside the huddled sanctum of young scientific minds led by their adopted guru could still be heard albeit in hush tones privately expounding upon the theoretical, the "x" factor --- and as young people often do amongst themselves--- on virtually everything else under the sun. Now too, three members of the Federal Bureau of Investigation were free to judiciously over hear.

"Let's give this a few moments. Let's see where it goes." Michalene orders.

A white noise hum from the speaker's receiver provided the students on the floor behind the podium surrounding Shirin, with the sense that their voices were being drowned out. Such was true to their ear. However, the audio output from the podium's microphones was still perceptible a good twelve to eighteen feet down wind, in the direction of Mike and her fellow agents.

As Steve, Mike, and Susan turned intentionally looking away from Shirin, the professor made a clearly audible statement. One that ended with...

"What? Are you sure?" Steve turns staring at both of his female colleagues, both with furled brows and jaw agape.
"Now that was bizarre." Skyes whispers to Michaelene, Agent Sykes being closest to clearly hear Shirin's voice.

Dr. Randoph Shirin, Ph.D, was so deeply immersed, answering questions left and right from his students that he forgot for far too long the identify of the people standing at the other end of St. Margaret of Scotland's grand staircase.

"...first reduce the female population."

"Context?" Michaelene calmly asked.

"No, none. I'm sorry. Didn't get it." Skyes replied.

CHAPTER FORTY-FOUR

Shirin's comment exploded onto the scene resulting in both he and the FBI shifting positions.

For Shirin, to stimulate critical thinking amongst his students, he'd relinquished his role as the Oracle of Delphi allowing instead for Socratic debate, offering his flock the chance to ask and answer questions among themselves as he guided the discussion.

The conversation amongst the academics evolved into, "the proliferation of nuclear powered energy resources will bring an end to war." Hearing that gave the FBI trio pause, their first of what would soon be, many. Mike in an attempt to locate the best possible position to determine exactly what was being said and its context, casually took a few steps to the left, then a few to the right.

"Come on. Move over here." She gestured to her two colleagues having found the best possible place from which to overhear. When they arrived, she whispered, "I want each of us to hear what is being said, directly."

With deafening cries of anguish laced with horror-filled yelps, just then came a pudgy-cheeked, tear-stained nine year old boy dressed in his best Sears and Roebuck, summertime rompers running through the crowd at the base of the Parish stairs. Knocking over chairs and signage he was stirring the once settled nerves of the mass number of displaced gathered around. The feds on stage heard the boy's screams but couldn't tell from which direction they were coming. Local Police Chief Thomas A. Willard was the first law enforcement official to lay eyes on the frantic

young boy. Hindered by the crowd and in this heat, the chief couldn't reach him.

"All wars boil down to "resourcing cheap energy." Shirin, the self-perceived purveyor of all wisdom, unable to sustain his role as a sideline coach, couldn't help tossing his thoughts into the ring. A comment regarding war by a nuclear physicist especially this nuclear physicist, gave the Bureau trio pause yet again. It was heard in part by Mike and Agent Sykes but clearly heard by Steve as he bent over to actually retie his shoelace. Remaining bent over longer than necessary, he heard:

"Nuclear generated energy may bring an end to war when every man can access all the energy needed to heat or cool his home and factories for pennies a year." With advancements in nuclear power being the subject at hand Agent Donaldson overheard one student asked a counter question, arguing that:

"If an abundance of nuclear energy brings about an end to war, wouldn't overpopulation result?" It was that question that set forth the comment that Syke's overheard the tale end of a few minute before: ",,,reduce the female population."

"Father Dan, Father Dan." Shrieked the bawling nine year old as he climbed the Parish stairs searching for the man he believed could help him, his Parish priest.

Bounding upward, one side of the boy's Buster Brown suspender snaps gave way falling between his feet, causing the overweight child to trip and fall backwards down the stairs. His outbursts now even more intense, animated the crowd about him.

"I got this," offered Skyes, looking to Michaelene for final approval.

"Go," ordered Mike. She and Steve remained focus on Shirin.

Susan Skyes was one of those women who without knowing, was a gifted mother. She grabbed the arm of the ten year old, offering repeated reassurances while being lambasted by the boy's flaying fists that everything will be okay. Managing to sit him down next to her at the bottom of the staircase until what fears he harbored were overshadowed by exhaustion - through his blubbering and screeching - Sykes ably pieced together what the boy was trying to say.

"What? Where?" asked Agent Sykes.

The kid's reply was barely audible.

"Okay, take me there. Let's go!"

Being restored to all within the immediate surroundings was a sense of calm as they witnessed a now somewhat Quieted young boy holding up his summer shorts with one hand take the hand of the sprite, young, pony-tailed FBI Agent in his other as together they walked off, heading to the basement steps of the Parish.

With an ear affixed to Shirin and his crew, Michaelene watched as her agent - one whom she planned to mentor - vanish to the rear of the massive Parish hand-in-hand with a fidgeting little boy. Mike didn't like what she saw but there was nothing she could do about it. The two way walkie-talkies distributed earlier had hastily left the office without being fully charged. The one Mike held, the one given to her by Agent Sykes, was now dead. Once again, there was no way for her to communicate with her fellow agents or to reach Skyes to order her to wait for another agent. Mike turned to Steve.

"No! No way. Don't you dare ask. I'm not leaving you!"

Just then State Police Lieutenant Timothy Keating, the man given charge of all the uniform Illinois police officers on the scene, enters the sanctuary at its furthest end through the Parish vestibule enroute to face the Agent in Charge. Threading his way through the folks crowded at the State's *Office of Emergency Management's Disaster Relief* tables, the Trooper is carrying what looks like a briefcase held high, pressed to his chest.

As Shirin and his students continue clamoring to support their respective positions, Chief Willard and two of his officers are diligently holding back the tide of folks wanting to ascend the stairs to talk directly with Agent Westgate. From their standpoint she is standing alone. To keep the calm and to provide a viable excuse for staying put – aside from eavesdropping - Michaelene offers Willard to let a few in at a time. The locals chat briefly with the well-recognized head of the FBI and walk away grateful, knowing that someone of importance in their eyes took the time to listen to their personal concerns. Each having approached Mike from the front, the on-coming state trooper with a briefcase still held high was approaching Mike from behind her.

That set off all the bells and whistles of former Army Ranger turned FBI Special Agent Steve Donaldson, the keeper of what he perceived was an unrequited love, one for which he was now determined if circumstances required, to gladly lay down his life to protect. Locking out all the world around him, the FBI's lead explosives and small arms expert, focused every measure of his being on the on-coming, quick-paced State Trooper. Removing his handgun from his underarm holster, Steve held it to his side, muscle down. While Michaelene continued smiling and hugging members of the citizenry keeping the calm in play, Steve moved on an intercept course to the State Trooper. Before Lieutenant Tim Keating could clear the sanctuary and broach the expanse of the Parish front stairs, he was met nose to nose by a very, single-minded man. If there was a bomb inside the case Steve knew his body would shield Michaelene from its initial blast.

"Stop right there. I need you to open that case!"

"I'm Lieutenant Timothy Keating of the Illinois State Police."

"Good for you. Now, open the case."

"You don't understand. I've been ordered by the governor to deliver an important message directly to SAC Westgate."

"Clearly, you don't understand me. I said …open the case."

It was not uncommon in Steve's experience for an enemy to approach wearing the garb of a "friendly."

"If you don't get out of my way right now I'll have you arrested?"

Steve gave his best "fuck you" snicker, followed by, "I said, open it."

"Out of my way, cowboy." With that, Agent Donaldson's thumb slipped back the hammer on his forty-five.

"What? Are you going to shoot me in front of all these people?"

"If need be."

"You'll start a riot, asshole." Taunts from trooper Keating were schoolyard, the opposite of professional. All they received in return was a cold, unyielding stare.

With that, the proverbial flight or fight syndrome rose in Keatings eyes. They darted about, a precursor of trouble for Steve if either were to erupt. Knowing better than to try and step around the man in front of him, assessing his surroundings, Keating came to a conclusion and asked:

"You a fed?"

A good question but asked far too late. Needing to know the employment history of a man standing with a locked and loaded weapon in front of you is edging towards the definition of professionalism but in the context of the real world, it was just a plain and simple, god damn asinine thing to do.

"Open the case."

Keating was clearly frustrated and growing impatient but he was not a man lacking in reason. It dawned on him finally what he must have looked like holding a nondescript briefcase up against his chest moving through the crowd in the Parish sanctuary being neither stopped or slowed by anyone. Too, he realized that the "message" he was ordered to deliver had nothing to do with what the man in front of him was asking to see. Consumed by the obvious, Trooper Keating reached up and released one of the two clasps that held the suitcase closed. It sprang open with a metal to metal clang.

With that, Steve moved half a step forward bringing his Colt .45 up slowly, jamming its cold steel firmly into the ribs of the State Trooper.

"Now the other one...slowly."

Quickly assessing how best to deescalate the situation and live to carry out his orders, Illinois State Trooper Lieutenant Timothy Keating, looking steadfast into Steve's eyes, reached to release the second latch. As he did, the barrel of Agent Donaldson's vintage, U.S. Army hand gun dug an inch or two deeper into the State Trooper's ribs.

Inside the attache case now opened, was a Motorola portable phone. This one fully charged.

"The Governor is on the line. He's been waiting." Explains Keating. "He has a patch through call for SAC Westgate. It's very important. The patch is from the fire marshall. Now are we good? May I walk over to her?"

Reholstering his .45, Steve calls out to Mike, "Agent Westgate. This trooper needs to speak with you. Shall I send him over?

Mike holds her hand in the air, signaling she needs more time, giving only half measure to the uniformed trooper who is standing by, waiting.

Mike is in her element. Handling the kind of pressure that would buckle the knees of the world's strongest man was second nature to this woman. Her talent both innate and honed, she had taught herself years ago to proficiently handle two dissimilar tasks at the same time. In this instance that meant consoling those who desperately needed reassurance while keeping an eye on Shirin. For people who can effectively multi-task, two is the limit. A third, the task of keeping track of the agents under her command, knowing where and under what conditions they may be operating - the most fundamental of responsibilities of the agent in charge - was eating Michaelene up inside. Since Steve provided a quick-take report on Agent Edwards, she knew she had to completely jettison one task in order to fully focus on another.

Inside the attache case now dangling half-open, the phone rings. Illinois State Trooper Lt. Keating answers it, nervously offering an explanation for the delay in fulfilling his assignment. Governor "Big Jim" Thompson doesn't wait to hear the Trooper's full explanation. Instead, he cuts to the chase :

"Don't press that woman. She knows what she's doing. We'll wait. Give Agent Westgate all the time and space she needs."

"But, the fire marshall said…"

Yes, I know, Fire Marshal Sullivan said he has information that may be vital to last night's explosion. You needn't lecture me on what I already know. When she's ready, hand Agent Westgate the phone. She'll call us. Sync your wristwatch with mine. What time do you have?"

"8:43pm, sir."

"The Marshal and I will be available again at precisely 9:30 and then again, every half hour on the hour until sunrise if necessary. Let her know that. That's one lady worth waiting for."

Trooper Keating replies with a level-headed, "Yes, sir. Will do."

Helping to reassemble the chattered nerves of a young couple with a newborn on the way who purchased their first home in Belmont-Cragin days before the epic explosion, Mike summed her recommendations to the expectant couple with a three party hug as cameras both civilian and professional enthusiastically captured the moment… and as J.Edgar Hoover rolled over in his grave.

"Trooper, hold fast." Michaelene implores. "Give us a few moments. Agent Donaldson, join me over here, please."

As the young couple exits the Parish by way of a path through the crowd created by city police, Steve walks nine paces to Michaelene's side. At the far east end of the cascading stairs, Belmont-Cragin's police chief Willard ushers the couple forward lending the expectant mother a hand.

As the thought within Steve of permanently losing Michaelene to a briefcase bomb – to never again hear her voice - begins to lessen, looking down from the Parish steps onto the crowd below, he catches Chief Willard's gentlemanly gesture:

"Hey, that's him, right?" Nudging Mike with his elbow. "That's the local cop you were telling me about, isn't it? He's the one who wanted to pull himself and his men away from this gigantic cluster fuck when it became clear it was in our lap? Seems like you may have gotten through to him?"

"He's a good man. It was hard for any of us to think straight at the onset of this investigation. His priorities were temporarily muddled but I didn't ask you over here to talk about Chief Willard. I want to know about Agent Edwards? What did you mean when you said you knew where he was?"

Steve's mind raced looking for an appropriate way to lay out the truth regarding Agent Edward's 'absence.' But as close as they'd been since their teenage years, Steve forgot something about his boss. Indeed, Michaelene West-gate was not "his girl" She was 'his boss,' the Special Agent in Charge of this "gigantic cluster fuck" and there was one good reason for that. The woman is effective. She takes in information, discerns its significance, envisions a way forward and then clear-headedly act upon it, setting aside any and all emotional considerations until all necessary measures surrounding the reality of the incident have been addressed. This is not to say that Michaelene was, by any stretch of the imagination, devoid of emotion while on the job. She just automatically knew in what order of importance to place such matters.

"He's with Dr. Vaziri."

"The Cook County Medical Examiner?"

"Yes."

"Why?"

"I sent him there."

"Why? Oh, are you telling me...?"

"Yes. He's dead."

"How?"

"That's why I had him rushed to the morgue. There was no exterior signs of trauma. From what I could tell, he simply stopped breathing. I asked a uniform to get a hold of an ambulance and to downplay the scene, telling anyone who might inquire that this "man, identity unknown," had a heart attack, perhaps brought on by heat prostration. At that point Agent Edwards had my sympathy but not my concern. That I focused on you. I had no idea other agents were on site. Further, I had no idea if Edward's death was a one-off or the first in a series. I had to get over to you."

"And Agent Skyes? Where's she?"

"No idea. She hasn't reported back to you yet?"

"No." Michaelene looked out over the crowd. She could see the back of the heads of Agent's Gillespie and Fontaine carrying out their orders, interviewing members of the crowd but Agent Sykes nor the little boy with whom she was last seen, were no where in sight.

"How long does it take to calm down an hysterical kid these days? Steve admonishes. "Sykes should know…"

"She does, Agent Donaldson. Agent Sykes knows the importance of the circumstances we're facing. She may be a rookie but she's nobody's fool. I don't like this. I don't like this at all. We need to locate her, now. Trooper, I'm sorry. What was your name again, please?"

"Lieutenant Keating, Timothy Keating, Ma'am."

"I've used one of those attache phones, before. It was demonstrated last month at my office. An AMPS, correct?"

"Yes, Ma'am, Motorola's Advanced Mobile Phone System. It's being market-tested by federal law enforcement agencies before being offered to the public. This one has a band width of…"

"Of 800 megahertz. Yes, I recall. How much time is remaining on the charge?"

"Exactly eighteen minutes, Ma'am."

"Excellent. And you said that the fire marshall had an urgent message for me, correct?"

"According to the governor, yes Ma'am."

"Nine thirty is the next scheduled opportunity for the patch-through. Did I overhear that correctly?"

"Correct, Ma'am."

"Lieutenant, you and I are going to exit these Parish steps together, down through the sanctuary and out through the rectory to the back of the building. Agent Donaldson assures me you know the way?"

"I do."

"Does that walkie-talkie on your hip work, Lieutenant?"

"Charged and ready, Ma'am."

"When you and I turn to leave, get on it. Call two of your men. Get them to come here but make certain they low ball their approach. When they arrive, they're not to talk nor make eye contact with either of us. I want them to simply take our place when we leave. Tell them once they arrive to put forth their best *'smoke 'em if you got 'em'* attitude, to dilly-dally. They're uniforms not trained detectives so advise them to lighten the air with casual conversation and some laughter. Their primary purpose is to keep a watchful eye on that group over there by the podium. That's Dr. Shirin sitting in the middle. Did you hear him speak a few minutes ago?"

"I did."

"You're assessment?"

"May I speak, openly?"

"Of course."

"He freaked me out Agent Westgate. He strikes me as a rather disturbed individual."

"It doesn't look like he and his followers are planning to leave anytime soon so I don't want them spooked. Make that clear to your men. Got that?"

"Affirmative, Ma'am. Roger all."

Mike walks over to Steve. "The last I saw Agent Sykes, she was headed to the rear of this building with that child leading the way. Go. Leave now, head down the stairs."

"Got it." Steve could easily slip down the front of the Parish without raising suspicions. Michaelene could not. Her rear exit strategy, keeping Lt. Keating by her side, was ideal.

As Mike and the State Trooper made their way through the sanctuary Steve had made his way through the crowd to the side of the building.

"Hey, what's going on here? Steve shouts. "You two. Get your dicks out of your brains and grow the hell up. Go on girls, get out of here. Hey! Yes you. I'm talking to you. Last warning."

While keeping young girls from being lured by the news crews into their vans, Steve was rooting about asking everyone he encountered if they'd seen a blonde-haired, pony-tailed woman with an hysterical child clinging to her. The latter gained far more traction that the former with comments ranging from *"Yes, I saw them come by"* to *"Well, I don't know maybe I did, I mean, who hasn't seen a screaming kid clinging to its mother before, right?"*

It was at this point that a twenty-something gofer for one of the encamped TV crews abruptly appeared on the scene. Having noticed Steve Donaldson, a man standing 6'2" with an exposed shoulder holster, Buzz, decided to chance warming to this apparent cop. If his asshole fellow TV workers were about to be swept up in a statutory rape police raid, he wanted to be clearly seen standing apart from them. From behind a van door, Buzz approached Donaldson. Steve posed the same question to him:

"Yes, Buzz answered. The kid was screaming. Your friend, was she a cop?"

"FBI. Go on."

"Well, she also screamed or maybe, I don't know, she just raised her voice but I presumed it was to counter the kid, to settle him down, you know what I mean right, and it did."

"Then what?"

"That was it. As I said, it worked. I figured, game over."

"Where did this raised voice or scream come from? Do you recall?"

"Sure, over there by the Parish basement's stairwell. You can see from here. The Dioceses installed that metal door last year to keep kids like me out."

"So when did you see the agent and the child come by here?"

"About twenty-five to thirty minutes ago. The basement door was apparently unlocked. After the screaming stopped, I saw it open then shut. I guess your friend and the kid went inside. Come on. I'll walk over with you and show you."

"First, may I have your name for the record?"

"I guess. I don't see any harm in that."

In fact, that is precisely what Buzz was desperately seeking. He wanted to be officially recognized as having nothing whatsoever to do with the alcohol-based seduction of three under-aged teenage girls by two cameramen well beyond the age of being excusably dimwitted to let their dicks get in the way of common sense. An employer ID and nothing more linked Buzz to his camera crew and he was eager to keep it that way.

"Everyone calls me Buzz but my real name is Nick, Nick Willard."

"I'm Agent Donaldson. You related to the local police chief, Chief Willard?"

"He's my dad."

"You stay here, Nick. I'll check it out. But I have one question before I go. How did you know about the Parish installing that metal, basement door? You work for the news station? I fail to see how that could have been a news worthy item?"

"I came to worship here with mom and dad since I was a little kid, but I stopped coming when he did."

"How's that?"

"Well, since mom died. Gosh, let me think. It's been almost been a year and a half now. She had breast cancer. Her passing was the best thing for her but damn near destroyed my Dad. They had a good thing going. They were close, very close. It would have been thirty-nine years next month. Now he wants to retire. I'm afraid if he does he'll die soon thereafter."

Steve volunteered aloud, "You're a good kid, Nick. Stick by your Dad" Having gained a measure of respect for Chief Willard by way of his son, Steve thought to himself,"Walk a mile in another man's shoes? Too often there's never a chance especially in this line of work..." he mused "...to take even a few steps before becoming judge, jury and sometimes even executioner."

"If you need me for anything, I'll be around. Just shout for 'Buzz.'"

With a passing thought that he would have been better off with a father like Chief Willard who apparently did something right to turn out a kid like 'Buzz,' Steve left the parking lot at the rear of the Parish and walked over to the building's basement stairwell. Before reaching its handrailing Donaldson was met by a multitude of house flies and a mounting stench, one a former combat veteran knows all too well.

Unlike many of his fellow Vietnam vets who suffer from Post Traumatic Stress Disorder, Steve was among a number on whom the war had the opposite effect. He had been diagnosed with Post Traumatic Growth. Even when staring directly at it, death purchased for him less hatred than compassion, less coldness than concern, less a desire for revenge than for mercy, lifting him above the putrid nature of war, all this no doubt the result of his love for Michaelene. Now nearly a decade later, perhaps that's the reason why it is taking Special Agent Donaldson more time than usual to determine what he is looking at, there at the bottom of the stairwell.

In its depths, death has been waiting. Wrapped in each of its rank odors, vile, abhorrent, yet even more so in this instance, more monstrous, more inexcusable and well beyond the boundaries as Steve was about to discover, that any sane person would allow their mind to venture.

From the top of the Parish basement's stairwell looking down some ten feet to the landing below - a slab of concrete the size of a child's wading pool - Steve was first struck by the volume of blood accumulated there. The steel door was ajar. Crisis-crossing, blood-splatter patterns across it spoke to multiple victims. Soon, this would be the first in a series of observations that would sling-shot Special Agent Donaldson, back to a time as a young Army recruit when hatred of his parents especially his mother, her God, the enemy he'd soon be facing and hatred of himself for failing to secure Michaelene as an integral part of his life, dominated his soul.

It didn't take much from this point forward for Agent Donaldson to recognize that this had been the Frog's butcher shop, perhaps just minutes before.

"But what was keeping the door from closing?" Steve couldn't see. He had to find out.

Removing his socks and shoes then tying both sets of shoelaces together, Steve fashioned his footwear high and dry over his shoulder prepping for his descent into this subteranneous 'hell hole,' below. A fortress steeped in the practice of extending good will to all ironically, the Parish now had a large, sticky 'welcome mat' of blood outside its basement doorway. Rolling up the pant legs of his polyester suit to just below his knees - while swating away flies - Agent Donaldson cautiously takes his first step on his journey to the bottom of the darkened stairwell.

Holding fast to the surrounding hand railing, the sting to barefeet of each hot metal stair onto which Steve ginger-ly placed one foot then the other, is offset by the pool of blood on each. The two inch rise along the base of the metal door together with something Steve couldn't see but his bare feet repeatedly brushed up against was clog-ging the storm drain he was now straddling, forming a catch-all, basin. Bending over to take a closer look at what had kept the large metal basement door from closing - as the proverbial sling-shot began being pulled back – he paused and belched out:

"Son of a..?" Unable to finish his thought and unable to agree with what his eyes were forcing him to see still, there it was. Rusted and chipped, having never been meant for service was an essentially in tact, artfully decorated, ceremonial replica of the hilt of a World War Two, Type 30 Japanese military bayonet. Five inches in length, the bayonet's hilt had kept the metal door from sealing tight. Wanting to see what if anything to which its total fifteen inch blade may be connected, Steve, inched forward, sticking his face into the crack left by the opened basement door. Making certain not to touch it or anything else with his bare hands, from inside the Parish underbelly nothing but darkness stared back at him. Still, the ghastly odor that the opened aperture produced caused Steve to abruptly straighten up and take a step back. As he did, something once again brushed the side of his bare foot. As he raised it to look to see what was so playful, what light-furry haired object was so determined to pester him, he suddenly noticed something he wished he'd never seen.

"What the hell ?" Steve stared captivated by a less than six inch long, greyish-looking creature. Animate or inanimate, alive or dead, Agent Donaldson was unable at first to tell. Soon he discovered it had eyebrows, then fingernails. As he gazed, the metal door behind him crept open. From behind it, having recognized the voice of her fellow agent, Susan Sykes pushed with all she had remaining to widen the gap. As she did, she exposed much more than an increase in the asphyxiating smell of death. Three bodies, that of the pregnant woman with her belly cut open, that of the little boy who witnessed his mother's butchery then ran screaming for help - his throat cut so deep his head bobbled - and herself, Rookie FBI Agent Susan Sykes, with the fifteen and a half inch long blade of the Imperial Japanese bayonet protruding from between her legs. Witnessing that, the proverbial slingshot let loose hitting Steve right between the eyes. Hatred; pure, unadulterated and targeted, surged through every corner of the former All-American quarterback's exceedingly focused and determined being. Abiding sympathy for Susan, honoring her desperate struggle not to leave this world without a fight, empathy for her parents back home forever so proud of their accomplished daughter, her missing blonde pony tail and the picture in his mind first of the Frog waving at him standing near where Agent Edwards lay then that up close shot of the mug of that same murderous freak captured on video tape by Michaelene, pushed former Army Ranger turned FBI Special Agent Steven Donaldson, to unleash his anger upon the world, beginning with that which was right in front of him.

"You soulless mother fucker! You're going to fucking die." He screamed pounding his fist against the Parish basement door. "I'm going to kill you in the most merciless way possible you detestable piece of human slime." This from the guy who told Marine Colonel Frank Clifford that *Any low life, shit heel that assaults a woman or molests a child should get down on their knees and be damn grateful that I swore an oath to enforce the laws of our country without prejudice.* Now of course, that was yesterday's news.

Steve grabbed his Bureau ID and with a bellowing, "Fuck this shit," heaved it up and over the stairwell's handrail. The ten foot Parish walls, the murmuring of the crowd still gathered out front and the increase in the volume of the night's winds, contained Steve's outrage to his immediate locale.

"Damnit, we had the pieces of the puzzle? How did we fail to put them together?" Steve thought of the faceless woman in the Belmont-Cragin field, seeing her again on the slab at the Cook County morgue. Then he remembered the name *Angelina Rodriquez,* the woman from Rock Island mutilated on St. Ambrose campus. Steve saw himself staring at the inscription on her forearm, its flesh staked out, bagged and hand-delivered with his name *Agent Donaldson/Eyes Only* scrolled across the top of the envelope.

"Yeah, okay. It was Iowa SAC Gomez's call. He decided to keep the investigation within the Bureau okay, but..." then his eyes opened wide. The thought they signaled staggered him. For the first time in his life he did something he would never have thought possible, he questioned Michaelene's judgment.

"Having read the letter Bowers delivered from Gomez, she turned it into a joke. Then this whole Aesop's fable nonsense began. The Frog and the Scorpion, well hell Mike look..." He ordered her in absentia, "This is what I've been trying to make you understand. Here is your so-called Frog's handiwork. Right here, right in front of us and where the hell are you, still off chasing your hypothetical Scorpion, somewhere? Damnit woman. Open your eyes. He doesn't exist. These bodies...This is real, not something imagined or about to happen. This, this has happened. They're fuckin dead...god damned, butchered to death for christ's sake." Steve's recriminations end with a thud as he again, slams his fist into the Parish basement's steel door, blaming Mike for the deaths of the three now lying literally, at his feet.

Knowing nothing about the man they'd labeled 'The Frog,' his real name, where he works or where he lives - known best as "Sonny" in his native Japan - has now over the last two hours, taken the lives of two more woman who 'dress American'- because they are American - Agent Sykes and the unidentified pregnant woman. Add to that, the life of a nine year old little boy and most likely that of Agent Edwards, Michaelene's long time business confidant. And then there was this...

Like his father before him - a member of Imperial Japan's barbaric *Kempeitai,* Hiroki Yoshida, a man once honored by the emperor with a ceremonial bayonet inlaid with Hirohito's sacred family crest, a golden Chrysanthemum - now his sole offspring Sonny, no more than twenty minutes ago, saw an opportunity to honor the spirit of his father and seized it. With an abrupt insertion of the Type 30's, 15 inch blade into the pregnant woman's stomach followed by an arching upward swing Sonny tore the fetus from its mother's womb hoping like father-like son, to soon feast upon it. Instead, it's tiny body had slowed the blood emptying into the storm drain.

Facing away from the Parish basement door, Steve turns to rescue it. Unaware of exactly what it is, nevertheless he makes his move. As he does he slips and falls, banging his forehead against the inner stairwell, landing face down in the pool of blood. The fetus at the end of its second trimester had survived outside its mother's womb for perhaps a full twenty minutes, ultimately drowning in her body fluids and that of her big brother's... and that of the brave young woman who sought their rescue. It had died before Steve had made his way down into the stairwell. It's animation resulting from his moving about.

Some twenty minutes before Steve took his first step down those stairs - crouching beneath the tall bushes on the approach to the Parish basement stairwell - Sonny had laid hidden. As Susan approached, springing from behind, he quickly overpowered her. As the rookie agent fought back, she felt a boxcutter's blade slash across her thoat. Fending off her assailant with one hand, she tried desperately to stop the bleeding with the other. Weakened having lost track of the boy save for his screams, Sonny pushed her down the stairs landing on her side, the one that bore her weapon. As she struggled to reach it, Sonny pulled his bayonet from its scabbard, the one sewn into his pant leg – the one that gave him his sympathetic limp – and inserted it into the young agent intending to end her life in the most heinous fashion any woman could imagine.

"Steve, Steve! Good God" Michaelene abruptly appeared at the top of the staircase gripping the handrail, her knuckles white. Looking down she shouts, "Don't you dare die on me you son of a bitch…" meant not as an explicative rather as a statement of fact. At that moment, she wanted to proclaim her love for him but the "I love you" forming on her lips was dashed by the need for restraint in front of the State Trooper and some kid now standing next to her, who just happened to show up out of nowhere.

Hearing his name being called by a voice he knew all too well, Donaldson struggles to regain his bearings and stand. As he does, he trips and falls again, his feet taken out from under him by the accumulation of body fluids in the 'kid-size, wading pool' between his feet.

As she starts down the stairs to help Steve to his feet - "Here! Ma'am. No. Wait!" - Keating grabs Michaelene's arm. "Let me get him out of there."

In that tone of voice that would make the devil himself stir, Michaelene turned to State Trooper Timothy Keating saying slowly, "You must know what trouble lies ahead for you if you do not immediately let go of my arm?"

"Ma'am, please. Let me. I'm wearing these things…patrolman's boots." Lt. Keating raises his foot to demonstrate his footwear's heavy tread. "…and respectfully Agent Westgate, you're the last person anyone around here needs to see with blood on her shoes and clothing."

Mike, having taken a deep breath, says, "Fine. Go."

Before setting off Trooper Keating, notes the time, "We've got just under eleven minutes if you want to make the call to Governor Thompson at 9:30?"

"Acknowledged."

A twenty-something kid with an energetic disposition positioned himself a few minutes ago at the stairwell's hand-railing next to Michaelene, as he heard her shout. As Keating makes his way down the stairwell, the kid says, "Hey, I know who you are? You're that famous FBI lady?"

"You need to move on, young man. You don't need to see this," said Mike, keeping her focus on Steve.

"That's Agent Donaldson, right?"

"How would you know that?"

"Hi, I'm Buzz. He and I were talking a little bit ago. Here. This is his. I found it over there." Buzz wipes Donaldson's ID on his jeans, cleaning off blotches of blood. "He's okay, right?"

"We're about to find out."

"He lost a lot of blood."

"It's not his. Buzz, was it?"

"Yes, Ma'am."

"You're pretty cool about all this. Why?"

"Well, I guess I get it from my dad. I'm Chief Willard's son. You met him at the site of the explosion."

"You haven't answered my question."

"One of the things that makes my dad different from others is that when he comes home at night he talks openly about his day to the whole family. The mind paints picture you know. They can often times be as vivid as the real thing. Through that, I can't say I've seen it all but I've certainly heard most. So, if you'll allow me, I think I can be of some help to you?"

"Not now, Buzz. Stand aside."

Lt. Keating brings Agent Donaldson to the top of the stairs. As he does, Steve gives out with his obligatory, "I'm fine."

"Oh, drop the act, Agent." Mike tried to play it tough but there was no way. The lilt in her voice filled with love for the man now standing two feet away, drenched head to toe dripping vile, red body fluid, betrayed her.

Donaldson is anything but, "fine." Like the character played by Sissy Spacek in the movie *Carrie* that Michaelene caught when first released two years ago on her third and final date with Professor Teddy Winfell, the sight of so much blood covering any person let alone the one she loved was at the very least, off-setting.

As if more drama needed to be added to Michaelene' day, from behind her, several voices are heard heading her way. She turns to see six members of the encamped TV camera crew now running towards her with three, clearly under the age of consent young woman bringing up the rear. Rearranging cut off shorts and tank tops as they struggled to keep up, not wanting to miss out on what excitement there was to see, Steve nodded to Mike to *Go, take care of business* and of course, she did. Turning to greet the onslaught, she saw Buzz with the Parish garden hose out of the corner of her eye. To keep the calm and to avoid by every means possible a TV news camera crew capturing the basement stairwell with three mutilated corpses now lying in plain sight with a federal agent standing at the top of the stairs drenched in blood, no other course of action was immediately at hand and certainly nothing more effective.

Mike looked over at Steve. Seeing Buzz with the garden hose, Steve nodded his approval. Michaelene then turned back to Buzz and shouted, "Let it rip."

"Hey, what's going on over by dere?" Shouted the young, lead cameraman as he approached the Parish stairwell. "Say, what? Is that blood all over that dude? Let me get a picture of that?"

Dutifully stepping forward, spreading both arms out to each side in an effort to halt further advancement, Illinois State Trooper Lieutenant Keating took action to protect the crime scene. Beginning with an aire of pleasant reassurance he offers, "There's nothing for you folks to see here. Please go back to your van. We sincerely appreciate your cooperation. Thank you."

"No way, man. We gotta right to be here and pigs like you can't keep the truth from us."

Michaelene having heard from across the parking lot some mid-twenties, overly aggressive, keeper of First Amendment Rights shout about "the truth," she left Steve in mid drenching supported by the stairwell's handrail and walked over to Trooper Keating still facing the six with his arms outstretched. She stopped immediately behind him.

Leaning back over his shoulder Trooper Keating whispered, "We don't have time for this, Mrs. Westgate. What do you think we should do?"

Releasing the snaps on the auxiliary pouch of the Lieutenant's, utility belt, Michaelene removed its contents.

"Oh, here it comes." Shouted the young lead cameraman. "Hindering and obstructing a what, a Federal Investigation? Well, before you pull that out of your ass pretty lady, let me tell you something."

With its fully automatic shutter and most significantly, given the hour, its integral pop up flash, Keating's Minolta Hi-Matic, 35mm viewfinder camera was ideal for capturing the moment.

Click!

The young lead male turns to the girls behind him and says "I told you. I told you didn't I? I told not to follow me. Now see what you did? You got us all in trouble."

To this young cameraman who could not keep his mouth nor his zipper completely closed, Michaelene made it clear, "No, just you. Lieutenant may I now borrow your walkie-talkie?"

The lieutenant responds in a loud, stern voice. "Of course, Mrs. Westgate. Just press its squelch button rapidly, three times" That's our emergency *officer down* signal. The backside of this Parish will be crawling with my men and every uniformed officer in the vicinity before these three child molesters can get to their van and exit the parking lot."

Carrying on with their newly-forged, impromptu shtick, Lt. Keating confesses, "You know," as he looks down deep into the eyes of the youngest of the under-aged girl, "I got a daughter about your age. She's fourteen."

"You see. Just like Johnny here says, you cops don't know shit. I'm almost sixteen."

"Shut up, Betty."

"My name is Bonnie you imbecile and don't tell me to shut up. You told me you loved me Johnny or was that just to get your hand inside my panties?"

"I think we now have all the evidence we need. Thank you for your cooperation," Michaelene offered to the ban of six as she fought back the urge to grin.

"Okay, okay, we got the message. You made your point. We're leaving."

But Johnny couldn't win the fight for control of his ego. It convinced him that if he were to obtain footage of this gruesome incident - scooping all the other stations - his boss would back him 100% if the State punitively filed statutory rape charges against him. So the former third string, high school halfback breaks to the right of Trooper Keating and heads for the stairwell.

Agent Donaldson thoroughly enjoyed the late night shower. It was almost as much fun as watching some kid with a news camera being soaked til stopped dead in his tracks by Steve's new found sidekick, Buzz.

"Jagggggofffff." Screamed the thoroughly drenched Johnny Petrucciani, slumping back, soaking wet to his TV station's van. "You'll never find work in this town again buzzard head, never!"

"Wrong again, Johnny. I've already passed the policeman's exam. I start the academy next Monday morning, seven a.m, sharp."

Lt. Keating having now dropped his arms turns, looks back at Michaelene, Steve and the stairwell. Steve is wobbly but standing upright, his bad knee apparently unaffected by his repeated slips and falls. Off to Steve's left stands Buzz with the Parish garden hose in one hand and the lieutenant's rescued, briefcase phone in the other.

"It's time."

Walking over to Buzz Trooper Keating offers a sincere, "Thank you, young man." and takes the briefcase from him.

"We've got less than three minutes. Ready Ma'am?"

"Place the call."

CHAPTER FORTY-FIVE

9:27 pm, Saturday Evening, September 9th, 1978.

The first words out of the governor's mouth expressed concern for the assemblage outside the Parish.

"My staff estimated that the crowd on site has swelled. They're now saying that there is between twenty-eight to thirty thousand people still congregating in and around the Parish. Getting everyone at least through the first sign-up stage is expected to continue until sometime before noon, tomorrow. A Parish official informed my office that their doors will remain open until the needs of the last person are met. I've been in repeated contact with the mayor. He advised that dozens of restaurants across the city including upscale Wing Lee's over on Lincoln Park and the Gold Coast's Pump Room are closing their doors early, prepping food and working with the Teamsters under the direction of my State Troopers to cut a path when ready, through all the traffic to get within walking distance of the Parish. The Catholic dioceses offered reimbursement to all participating restaurants. Not a single dime was accepted. The Marshall Field family dropped off a six figure check at my office, their way of giving back to what their executive referred to as *the Field's extended family, the fine people of Chicago*. With no outbreaks to report, everyone acting peacefully, my chief of staff told me that you had a lot to do with that."

"Thank you, but..."

"Oh, before I forget and turn you over to Marshall Sullivan, an American working for Interpol in London called asking for me referring to himself as 'Juicy Fruit...'"

"Oh my God, how embarrassing, a former Army buddy of my fellow agent Donaldson, no doubt."

"Yes, how did you know?"

"The handle fits a pattern."

"It seems our mid-western drama has been deemed newsworthy by the BBC. Donaldson's colorfully named friend said something to the effect that when bullets and explosives are involved *Hop-along Cassidy* the Bureau's top explosive ordinance expert would be on the scene. He couldn't reach you so he called me."

Playing along, Michalene replied, "Yes, *Hop-along* is here" wondering when and how Steve's nickname never known to her until this very instant had come about? She witnessed a demonstration of his affliction earlier in the day but now something unusual had risen inside of her. It took a minute for the head of the Illinois bureau of the FBI to determine what it was but then it hit her. It was jealousy mixed with a core level of resentment towards Steve, knowing that some guy from England who referred to himself as a brand of American chewing gum knew more about the man whose love she could never set aside - and in her mind never live up to - than she.

"Take down this number. Give it to him. When Agent Donaldson's friend stopped giggling, he stressed that he had been selected by the leader of the Brit's Conservative Party, a woman by the name of Margaret Thatcher, to determine if a current experiment by a British scientist named Jeffreys, could somehow be applied to law enforcement. He said he liked the idea of the Brits helping the Yanks for a change and if he could help his ol' pal in the process he'd sleep better at night"

"Anything further, sir?"

"He politely pointed out that I was not a law enforcement figure in the eyes of the British government and although what he had to offer was a potential investigative tool it had been tagged by the Crown with what the American intelligence community would call an Eyes Only classification. He got permission however from Thatcher to share it strictly with one Bureau colleague he named and trusted. That was your Agent Donaldson."

"Eyes only?" Mike repeats and affirms. "Roger that." She reaches for the pen in Trooper Keating's breast pocket, takes it and inscribes Interpol's, international, back channel phone number on the State Trooper's citation book."

"This should prove interesting," Keating light-heartedly confides to Mike as he stares at the large numerical scrawl.

"What's that?"

"The conversation I'll be having with my captain."

"Regarding?"

"Who scribbled these numbers on my citation book and for what purpose."

"Tear out the carbon paper or better still, here, give me that whole thing." Mike tears off the bottom half of blank citations, those on which her scrawl may have transferred and hands the top half back to Trooper Keating. "If your captain has a problem with that have him call me or better still, have him call Big Jim Thompson for an explanation."

"Oh very good, Ma'am."

"Trooper Keating?"

"Yes, Ma'am."

"From this point forward, please don't call me 'Ma'am.' Call me Mike."

While Governor Thompson and Mike were talking, Buzz rounded up Tony Valenzuela, the spry, seventy-one year old Parish janitor. Tony had become a fixture at the community's sanctuary long before Buzz was born. Both were close friends. Together, they located an old window screen to the long abandoned basement office and collected canvas tarps and duct tape from the storage room. The window screen was ideal. It would fit perfectly over the grate at the bottom of the stairwell. The canvas and duct tape were on hand to secure the three bodies until officials from the morgue arrived.

"Good timing. Here's the fire marshall. Go ahead, Stan."

9:30pm, precisely.

"Hi, Agent Westgate. How are you holding up?"

"Still standing, Stan. What do you have for me?"

"You recall I left the Parish after I spoke to the public about my department's findings."

"Yes, of course."

"After saying goodbye to you, I exited through the sanctuary. That's when I saw this guy."

"What guy?"

"He was standing off to my right nervously fidgeting, talking very angrily to himself in a foreign language. I think it was German. I knew I had seen him before but I couldn't put my finger on where or when."

"I know what you mean. That happens."

"It didn't dawn on me who he was until I was back here in Belmont-Cragin."

"Fires still rampant?"

"Happy to report fires are better than sixty-percent contained."

"Good. Go on."

"As I was saying, I'm out here in the field so I don't know what's been happening since I left but this guy, I guess it was three or four days before the explosion, he came to my office. He sought me out."

"Do you remember his name?"

"He showed me his credentials. He was a professor at the University of Chicago. He claimed to be a nuclear physics expert. I admit. I was mildly intrigued and I guess I got a little caught up in his questions. I wrote his name down after he left. He said he was looking to buy a home in Belmont-Cragin and was curious about my department's capabilities."

"What did you tell him?"

"I told him as a potential homeowner not to worry. I have the resources of the entire Cook County at my disposal to handle any kind of emergency. That's when he went a bit off the rails."

"What do you mean?"

"He started asking about the Clifford family's filling station. That's what he called it, a huge filling station. Who refers to a gas station as a 'filing station' anymore?"

"What was his question about the 'filing station'?"

"Well, this is where it really got a bit strange. I could tell he was putting it on."

"Exaggerating his emotions, is that what you mean?"

"Yes, he got kinda worked up and went onto to say that the giant propane tank and the two abandoned high rise buildings across the street from it were not only eye sores but potential health hazards to the community. He was particularly miffed about the propane tank. He wanted to know the precise date when it would be removed. I said I'd look into it and let him know. When he turned to leave, he made a passing reference to the Chicago quake of 1968, asked if I knew of any fault lines in the Belmont-Cragin, area. I informed him of the Madrid fault but the last time it was active the War of 1812 was going on. I told him I respected his concern for the safety of his family but told him there was no need to worry. He said he could be reached through the University. I stood up, we shook hands, I jotted down his name and he left. That was it."

"Until the explosion."

"Yes, Agent Westgate, until the explosion."

"What was his name?"

"Randolph Shirin., PhD. He made a point of emphasizing that he'd earned a PhD therefore his concerns should be taken seriously…no, no. That's wasn't it. He said his concerns should be 'heeded.'"

Trooper Keating, holding the portable phone, takes on a concerned look, "Governor, Marshall, Agent Westgate, excuse me for interrupting. I apologize. I hate to cut the conversation short but the battery is about to die."

"Wait. Hold one, Stan. Shirin said he had a family?"

"Yes."

"He's a liar. Westgate, out."

"Shirin was scamming the fire marshal," she confirmed to herself, "gathering information on his target." Mike was particularly grateful that Governor Thompson was party to that conversation.

Having replaced the handset back into its briefcase charger, Keating walks with Mike over to Steve. Agent Donaldson is now sitting on the ground with his back against the stairwell's railing. The Parish janitor, Tony Valenzuela, managed to get utility towels wrapped around the dripping wet agent, ultimately providing one of his freshly laundered, back-up work shirts from his basement locker. Before Michaelene sat down next to Steve, she looked over to Buzz telling him that once the window screen was secured over the grate to, "Please thoroughly hose down the stairwell." Boldly wading through the red sludge, Tony set the aluminum wire mesh in place. With a 'go-ahead' nod from Mike, Tony stepped aside as Buzz let loose once again with a torrent of water, washing away the exposed blood pool with remaining evidence if any, captured by the window screen.

Steve looked up at Michaelene and asked, "What did the fire marshall have to say?"

Before replying, Michaelene quickly retrieved the torn page from Trooper Keating's citation book on which she'd scribbled the phone number of Steve's pal. Pulling it out of her pants pocket, she handed it to him. With that, she repeated verbatim what Stan Sullivan had told her about his rather unusual meeting with 'Dr. Randolph Shirin, Ph.D'

"Holy shit. You were right all along. You nailed it. I'm sorry I doubted you."

"I didn't know you did." With highly directed finger-pointing, Mike summarily states:

"Down there at the bottom of that stairwell, that's the frog. That's his handy work. Up there on stage, that's the Scorpion. Dr. Randolph Shirin is the Scorpion. Now all that's left is to collect the evidence to support those allegations."

"Should be easy, enough," As an attempt to lighten the load, Steve's wisecrack, fell short.

CHAPTER FORTY-SIX

"Lieutenant, get the governor back on the phone as soon as you can. Tell him it's an emergency. Ask him to order Langston to shut down the Dresden….No, no wait."

And so, there it was, the road ahead and Mike's role in it all became perfectly clear. The Dresden nuclear power plant, the mid-west United States being laid to waste by a series of oncoming, nuclear explosions or the subject of nuclear energy as a whole, wasn't it.

With her gorgeous eyes wide open, ablaze, with insight Mike turns to Steve, "You've heard it, right? Anyone having any contact with Shirin has heard it."

"Okay. I get it. Yes, I know exactly what you mean. The drumbeat, right?"

"Yes, that drumbeat…his drumbeat being pounded into our heads at every opportunity to…"

"…guide us away from his real objective."

"Exactly. Remember, I told you? I told you how Shirin over-emphasized his skill set to Marshall Sullivan?"

"And how he persisted with his nuclear power rants while on the Parish steps in front of all of those people. He wanted to make absolutely certain that everyone including us, when thinking of Dr. Randolph Shirin, PhD, we think nuclear science and nothing else."

Steve, you said so yourself. If Dresden is the target why didn't Shirin just go for it?"

"Yeah, It's his thing, right?"

"Then Michaelene nimbly offered, "If not something nuclear, then what?"

"If not a nuclear-based incident what else could there be?" Steve pondered, aloud.

"What other tool or means could this egotist have at hand to best himself?"

"...To create a bigger bang than what he pulled off at Belmont-Cragin? I think we can safely say he's not going to deescalate."

"Yes Steve, exactly." Michaelene turns to the State Trooper. Tim, right?"

"Yes, Ma'am, ah Mike."

"Step over here, Tim. Join us. You not only have a professional obligation but a personal right to know what's currently under discussion. We need to determine expediency and accuracy what we're facing and how to put an end to it. And you look more wide awake and bushy-tailed than either of us. Perhaps you'll pick-up on something we may overlook."

"I've been filling in the blanks since I first met the two of you. I have a wife of nineteen years and two teenage children, a boy and a girl. They're the reason I do this job. Thank you for allowing me to directly link in. I won't let you down."

"Look this way while I go that. That's the game at hand, isn't it?"

"I see it. I would have to agree." Offers Keating.

By way of her epiphany moments ago, Michaelene is shot full of adrenaline. "You see, that's exactly what Shirin's been doing. It was never his goal to set off a nuclear devise, cause a meltdown or set off some radiation fallout scenario. To do so in the first place would be obvious and as I see it, this guy is anything but. He's challenging us. He's thrown down the proverbial gauntlet."

"And you're just the woman to pick it up and smack him upside his fuckin head with it." Steve offers, "Besides, if nukes were the issue, it would lead right back to him given his persistent…

"Drumbeat." Adds Tim. Michaelene was impressed. The State Trooper she just met fit in seamlessly, using the same word and grasping the same concept she and Steve had reached. That was followed by a "Please, hold one" as the walkie-talkie on Keating's belt, sounded off.

"He just stood up? Is that what you said?"

The two State Troopers assigned to watch Dr. Shirin are reporting in. "They're saying Shirin's milling about trying to leave. The kids are grabbing onto him, encouraging their professor to stay. Wait one. They want to know if they have permission to follow him if he breaks free?"

Mike quickly offers to Tim, "No, don't let them do that. Get a team of plain-clothed detectives locked onto him. If that's not possible I'd rather loose him than spook him.

We don't want to provide Shirin with an excuse to advance his time table."

Tim Keating adds, "You believe he has one?"

"I'm convinced of it."

Keating continues, "No doubt he's fearing being caught before being able to carry it out."

"Lieutenant sir," the voices on the other end of the walkie-talkie, state, "we need to inform you of something."

As the squelch from the walkie-talkie signaled the opportunity to exchange transmissions, Lt. Keating offers, "Go, Billingsly."

"This guy Shirin is a real fruit loop. He fucking hates women. He outright says that he wants to destroy as many as possible, as he put it, to save the planet."

"Language Sergeant. There is a lady present."

"Well, Ma'am, my apologies whoever the hell you are but I tell you one thing, if you heard what we heard you'd…"

Keating speaks up on behalf of his new found ally and for women of his generation, everywhere, "You're speaking in front of Michaelene Westgate, the FBI Special Agent in Charge of the Northern Illinois Bureau. Understand one thing. It's her not me or anyone else who holds overall responsibility for seeing this investigation through to a successful end. That means she's your boss and you will listen to her, follow her direction, and be very cautious of using any form of profanity in front of her or any other women within earshot. You may not in-cur her wrath but you will definitely incur mine. Do I make myself clear, Sergeant?" A hint of Tim's southern upbringinging leaked through his tempered voice.

"My apologies, Mrs. Westgate sincerely, I meant no of-fense. You should know as Lt. Keating will confirm that both Corporal Lipkin, the man here with me, and I are combat vets. Generally it's bombs and bullets not words that get our attention but we overheard Professor Shirin saying to those kids around him that if they are con-cerned about overpopulation due to the increase availa-bility of..."

"... cheap energy from an increased number of nuclear power plants," Corporal Lipkin is wired up. He inter-jects.

"Yes, exactly, that if they're worried about over popula-tion they should research a Japanese scientist, some World War Two wack job who attempted to control the world's population by way of some chemistry set he got his hands on, something that would wipe the world clean of a large number of women, those currently alive and..."

"...Yeah and then it got really spooky." Corporal Lipkin again inserts himself into the conversation.

Hearing that, Mike sticks her face up close to Keating's walkie-talkie and abruptly asks,"What are you saying, Corporal?"

"Well, with an abundance of essentially free energy everywhere, as the professor put it, there would be no wars anymore."

Sgt. Billingsly steps back in: "When wars end, more babies are produced. Respectfully Ma'am, we've all seen that and many here are a result of it, the Baby Boomer generation, the post World War Two generation, you know what I'm talking about, right? Shirin was saying that an abundance of low cost energy will reduce the likelihood of war, resulting in a drop in the mortality rate but as long as there are…"

"Right, right." Corporal Lipkin jumps in once again. "…As long as there are an equal number of women to men population's will rise ultimately exhaust the resources of the planet, ending life as we know it."

"Reducing availability on one end of the equation…" Michaelene extrapolates aloud.

Keeping with tradition, Steve finishes Mike's sentence for her "…Reduces the volume of conception on the other."

Sergeant Billingsly recalls Shirin saying, "That mankind has no choice. It's either clean, free unlimited energy or reduce reproduction resources. He actually said that, he called women 'reproduction resources.'"

"That's how the overpopulation question came up?" Mike asks.

"Yes. And the fact that Shirin had a ready answer gave me the creeps. Wait one," Billingsly added, thinking aloud. "I have a grandchild. I get Jimmy to laugh counting his toes. It goes eenie, meanie, minie, no, no. That's it. Eenie, the mad Jap scientist of World War Two, that was his name. It sounded like 'eenie'. His name was Ishii."

"What?" Steve is bewildered. "Are you sure? That's the second time in forty-eight hours I've heard that name."

Sorry, sir we know our report is incomplete but we were trying not to fall over each other while leaning in to catch every piece of what Professor Shirin was saying."

"Good work, Troopers. Thank you. Return to your regular assignments. Keating out."

"Like the scorpion in Aesop's fable, our Scorpion used the frog as a..."

"Decoy," Steve, asserts.

"Precisely, Averting our attention."

"And in the case of Shirin," Steve admit, "I fell hook, line and sinker for his bullshit. In the fable, the decoy bought the Scorpion safely to the shore. With that, his objective was fulfilled."

"And that's exactly what we cannot allow to happen here." Michaelene follows through. "We cannot allow our Scorpion to get to shore."

Steve reminds all, "But how do we stop him? Legally, we can't prove he has done anything wrong yet."

"And that's my point. We can't wait until he does. So let's add it up. What do we have so far?"

"A steaming mound of circumstantial evidence linked to the Shirin shit show but that's it."

Michaelene continues, "Yes. Exactly. Although hard evidence has eluded us thus far..."

"If we ever get our hands on it."

Michaelene persists, "...when we add Fire Marshall Sullivan's comments to the profile we've already developed on Shirin, are we safe in concluding that he masterminded the Belmont-Cragin explosion? Can we start there?"

Steve remains silent while Tim sets forth, "Given the enormity of that atrocity and its repercussions, Shirin's primary objective..."

"Must be a real doozy." Adds Steve as he brings himself to his feet as both Mike and Tim follow suit.

"And we don't have a motive?"

"Granted."

"Nor do we have probable cause to arrest him."

"But we could haul him in for questioning on 'reasonable suspicion' and hold him for 24 hours?" Tim offers.

"We'd have to have good reason to do even that" Mike sets forth, "and we don't. We can't say Illinois State Troopers under the direction of the FBI eavesdropped on the guy and didn't like what was heard. According to your troopers Tim, Shirin didn't state that he was going to destroy the lives of anyone or order others Manson-style, to do his bidding for him. Shirin merely directed the scholars under him to investigate the population control research of a Japanese scientist who lived more than thirty years ago. I don't see a crime in that?"

"There isn't one." Keating, asserts.

"Exactly." Mike affirms

Steve continues with his interpretation of Aesop's Fable. "When the scorpion killed his transportation vehicle he must have been what, just shy of the shore, wouldn't you think? Just close enough where his feet wouldn't get wet?"

"Okay?" Both Michaelene and Tim are wondering where this was going?"

"It's your 'eminent' argument, Mike. You called it. If the Scorpion is going to act it's going to be soon."

"As far as we know, your Scorpion hasn't killed his frog yet. With this Japanese guy's mug splattered all over the news media the Scorpion must know he will have to get rid of him before launching his primary assault."

"You're right," Steve acknowledges, "Good point." A seed of mutual respect between the Fed and the State Trooper just found fertile ground. "The Scorpion can't afford to risk the Frog being captured."

Tim underlines that message. "And interrogated."

"You're referring to Dr. Randolph Shirin?" Mike corrects. "Now that we believe we have identified one of our two suspects, let's call him by name."

When the TV camera crew led by Johnny Petrucianni, packed up and made a run for it, the Parish rear parking lot was left with a gaping whole. Through it and the darkness all around, a familiar voice shouted:

"Agent's Westgate and Donaldson, I had hoped to run into the two of you again."

"Oh my gosh, Frank. What are you doing here? It's great to see you but we're in the midst of an investigation. I'm sorry," Michaelene extends, "but we don't have time to talk right now."

"Don't worry. Agent Westgate I'm not here to talk."

"Frank please. It's Mike, remember? Call me Mike or Michaelene but please no more formalities, okay?"

"I'm here to give you both a ride home. You didn't think I was going to drop off my two favorite FBI agents and just leave, did you?"

"That's very kind Frank, but Agent Donaldson and I have no plans to leave anytime soon."

"Did I ever tell you that Governor Thompson and I have known each other for years? We play poker twice a month at his nephew's house in Park Ridge over on Prospect Avenue."

"Frank, sir, respectfully…"

"You're people are still hunting and canvassing and they'll be doing so well into the morning. Thanks to the Bureau, the State Troopers all the volunteers and especially you young lady, with the peacefulness that has been instilled here, Big Jim thought to ask of you to turn over control of this scene - not the investigation mind you but just this scene - for the evening to Lt. Keating. Come home with me and get a good night's sleep. It's a five bedroom home. We only use three. You and Steve can have the two next to my study. The governor has my private number. It only rings in that room. If you agree, I'll give that number to lieutenant Keating before we leave. If either call, you'll both hear it. I will have you...

The grating sound of walkie-talkie squelch penetrates the air. "This is Keating, go. Excellent. Good work, gentlemen. Thank you. I'll pass the word. Keating, out."

Frank continues, "I will have you up, showered and fed and on your way to downtown Chicago Bureau headquarters with shoes shined, clothes cleaned and pressed no later than 0:700 guaranteed." For Mike, aside from the quick nap she took in her shower, she hadn't slept in two days.

Keating turns to Mike, "That was Detectives Malloy and Donovan, reporting in. They're our best surveillance specialists. Trained at Quantico. They both have teams under them. They'll pick up and stick to your suspect until ordered to stand down."

"Thanks Tim. Can you give us a moment? Colonel, I agree with you. At this point a strategic retreat for a brief respite sounds nearly too good to be true. We accept." There was of course, one exception and she voiced it.

"We'd welcome the ride but respectfully decline your generous hospitality offer. If you'd be kind enough to drop us off at my house, that would be greatly appreciated. Steve can bunk on my coach."

Heading towards Frank's pick-up truck The three, Frank, Steve, and Mike, walk and talk as Keating follows a few steps behind.

"Agent Westgate, umm, Michaelene. After the two of you left me I made it back home to Park Ridge. While there on the phone with Governor Thompson there was a knock at my door. When I answered I was handed this file. Here, take a look at it. Special Delivery on orders from Big Jim. The data inside the file was recently compiled by local police. You have a neighbor by the name of Mrs. Wilkinson, correct?"

"Yes. Why?"

"As you'll read, Mrs. Wilkinson saw what she described as the same Japanese male featured in your Parish steps broadcast, enter your home shortly before noon today. A few minutes later, a man who she described as a White male detective-type, drew his gun and entered your home."

Mike turns to Steve, "When were you going to tell me about this?"

"The Jap returned a second time around four p.m. See, right there in the second paragraph, Mrs. Wilkinson said she'd 'swear on a stack of bibles' it was the same man. The local authorities now have your home staked out. Big Jim and I agreed you'd get a better night sleep under my roof. In truth, he sent me back here to find and cordially persuade you. How am I doing so far?"

Mike looks back at Lt. Keating, motioning him to join her. "This unidentified Japanese male whom we've labeled the frog has killed at least one and possibly two of my agents…" As she spoke, Michaelene cringed. Guilt, anger and frustration filled every corner of her being. "I want this…"

"Mike, Ma'am, please stop there. You needn't say more." Offer Lt. Keating. "The word will be passed. We understand. Frogs can be slippery but that doesn't mean they can't be…"

"Okay." Mike acknowledges. Tim, thank you. Bidding goodbye to Trooper Keating for the evening, the three remaining continue their walk towards Frank's Dodge pick-up.

"Damn, I really stink." Steve volunteers. "I'll stretch out in the back. You two share the cab." Frank gets in behind the wheel and starts the engine.

Mike grabs hold of the truck's side-railings and swings herself up and into the truck bed. "Oh no you don't." She knew exactly what Steve was up to. Trying to postpone the inevitable wasn't going to work. Michaelene sat straight up with her back against the rear of the cab, her feet keeping Steve at a comfortable distance. A heavy dose of fresh air would soon wash away a good portion of the stench surrounding this guy she's known the vast majority of her grown-up years but that alone would not be enough. Michaelene stared at him. With his sheepish boyish grin, he tried to look back. That caused her to roll her eyes.

"Did you think you'd get away that easy? You've *got some splainin to do, Lucy*, Michaelene said giving it her best Desi Arnaz accent. You're first going to tell me what really happened when you broke into my home earlier today and then – this one I can't wait to hear" She was now at full throttle - "I can't wait to her about some gung-ho G.I. buddy of yours who has the utter audacity…no. Let me take that back. Who has the balls to call the Illinois Governor and leaves a message for you referring to himself, as 'Juicy Fruit'?"

"You swore!"

"It was an anatomical reference, grow up."

Steve relates his encounter with Mike's clothing neatly laid on her banister.

"Well, that's a piece of information I could have lived a lifetime without knowing."

"That was my hope."

"Thank you. I'm glad you acted when you did. I'm grateful. Remind me never to keep you waiting again. Now tell me about Mr. 'Juicy Fruit' and it better be good. As she said that her suspicions rose Mike asks, "Are there any national security issues tied to this story"

"A few perhaps but I can skip over those parts."

"Great." Mike slides open the dividing window behind the driver's seat so Frank can listen in. "Go for it, big guy. Let's hear this!"

CHAPTER FORTY-SEVEN

"I'll start by saying that I was in a place where I shouldn't have been."

Michaelene smiles, "Imagine that?"

"It was sixty-eight. I was in country. I was alone. The day before I took a bad fall and got a tree branch jammed through my leg. I had coordinates for a Special Forces camp nearby. I headed for it."

"That's all well and good hot shot," Mike offered teasingly, "but I want to hear about a guy who dares to call himself Juicy Fruit. Get to it."

"It's really not like that. Juicy Fruit was Captain Robert Preston, the biggest Black man I'd ever seen. At first glance he was at least seven feet tall and over a thousand pounds."

Peaking through the sliding glass partition separating the truck's cab from its bed, Frank asks, "What happened to change your mind?"

"I hit him."

"You belted this guy?" Mike implores. "Why?"

"I'd approached the camp on my belly. I was in excruciating pain. The jungle humidity had zapped what little energy I had left. I was hollering out my name, rank and serial number at the top of my lungs. I shouted I was an American, I grew up in Park Ridge Illinois, I went to

Main South High School, I played quarterback for the Iowa Cyclones. I was throwing out everything I could think of. I didn't want to be killed by one of our own. I had taken every precaution. Still, I'd been followed. When I crossed the camp's perimeter Captain Preston spun and leveled his M-16 at me. Behind him a VC had snuck into the camp, his weapon inches from the back of the Captain's head. I don't know where I got the strength. I didn't slug Preston, I tackled him. When I did he let loose of his weapon and…"

"And what?" Michaelene probes.

"A big wad of Juicy Fruit gum flew out of his mouth."

"No way." Michaelene reared back, bubbling over with laughter.

"He spat it out as I tacked him. It stuck to my forehead."

"Oh my God. I can see that. Too funny." Michaelene's chest muscles deepened. She was now laughing wonderfully hard and her laughter was good for all to hear. "The next thing I realized" Steve continued, "this huge man, a former defensive tackle for Princeton University, now closer to six six and some two hundred and sixty pounds, was kissing me on my forehead."

"Recovering his gum?" Mike surmises between fits of laughter.

"Yes, And in that instant, I saw this Vietcong teenager shift his focus to me. I picked up Preston's weapon and shot the kid in the head." With that Michaelene's laughter abruptly ended. So too did the brief reprieve from reality that each had been enjoying."

"I had been in a few fire fights but that was the first and only time that I watched a fellow human being die as a direct result of my actions."

Frank offers, "You were lucky. So was Preston."

Mike prods. "That was ten years ago. Apparently, he used "Juicy Fruit" as a name you'd recall when he left a message with Governor Thompson."

"This guy Preston was wicked smart and wicked funny."

"How so?"

"I was in triage waiting outside his base camp's infirmary. It was hot and there was a countless number of men ahead of me. 'Juicy Fruit' took a knee by my stretcher for the duration creating a unique system of keeping the infirmary staff aware of me."

"How's that?"

"He told jokes."

"What? I don't get it?"

"Nor did members of his audience. That was the trick. He'd leave off the punch lines. Each of his witticisms were more gut-wrenchingly hilarious than the first and he was making the stuff up off the top of head. When it dawned on the doctors and nurses that they'd been short changed, they'd come back around begging to know the ending of their particular tale. When they did, Preston would say, "Hey, while you're here take a look at my boy. How's he doing? He saved my life." The MD in charge was a full bird Colonel but there was no doubt, Captain 'Juicy Fruit' was running the show. While waiting I couldn't get the kid I killed out of my head."

"That's understandable," Mike offers. Frank nodded in agreement, adding, "Does anyone mind if we stop? I know of a gas station up ahead. We're running a little low on fuel."

"No, great. That will be fine." Mike acknowledged. "They'll have a phone. I can check-in with my office."

Steve continued seamlessly recalling his first encounter with 'Juicy Fruit', "My leg was swelling. Waiting for the doc was torture. Morphine was out of the question. Draining the wound had to come first. Thrashing around I was asserting that the United States was the aggressor in Vietnam, asking how the Vietnamese teen I killed was any different from some rural Virginia boy two hundred years ago fighting for his country, our country, against British occupation? What makes us any different from them, I argued? Modifying his joke telling style, Preston distracted my bitching and moaning by taking my thoughts instead on a sweeping retrospect, comparing Hitler's loudly barked rationale for invading his neighbors *WE MUST HAVE LIVING SPACE (Wir mussen haben lebensraum)* and Japan's "All The World Under One Roof" (*Hakko ichiu)* Right Frank?"

"Yes. That's right."

"...to America's Manifest Destiny. People forget that our *Sea to Shining Sea* bit was just that. We never sought to gain dominion militarily, over others beyond our ocean borders. The United States had no intention for example, of invading Canada after the war of 1812 when the Great White North was being used by the British as a launching base into ours. Although we fought for two years in the 1840's with our other neighbor to the south, Preston said that in a settlement, we paid Mexico fifteen million for California and Oregon, thereafter never setting foot militarily in their country. And I guess that $15million went a long way."

"How's so?" Mike is now riding along on Steve's retrospective journey.

"Mexico at the time, was on the verge of economic ruin."

"Yes, I recall hearing something about that." Frank contends. "Mexico's military was fighting against us with weapons purchased from a French arms dealer, leftovers from the French Revolution."

And get this, 'Juicy Fruit' calculated off the top of his head that $15mm USD in the 1840's was about $325 million in 1968 dollars. He finally capped his 'round the world comparative military retrospect by saying we're here in Nam not to occupy or subjugate its people but to save the country both north and south if possible from Sino-Soviet overlords. We created a lasting peace in Korea in the 1950's. Maybe there's a chance we can do the same here. Oh, and get this?"

"What?"

"Juicy Fruit said that the United States needs to add the letter 'N' to its name?"

"I don't get it?"

"That we should strike a deal with other nations within the north American continent and come together as one, calling ourselves, The United States of North America. Catchy, huh?"

"A lot of hard work, Frank offered."

"Yet logical perhaps even inevitable." Mike adds.

"Frank sums, "Good neighbors learn to share. Best way to avoid a fight."

Wait." Shouts Mike. "There's a phone booth up ahead!"

"It's outside the gas station I was looking for," Frank affirms. "It's not quite ten pm. Looks like the owner locked-up early." Unable to contain her enthusiasm at finally having a means to directly communicate with the world, Michaelene leaps out of the back of the truck before it stops and dashes to the free-standing, outdoor, telephone booth. While still within earshot Frank hollers after her:

"Here. Let me give you my change. I have some quarters and…" That's as far as this illustrious member of the "Greatest Generation," got.

"Thanks Frank." Mike hollers back. "No need. I got a free-be code"

"Hey everyone, it's Mike." Mrs. Clayfield, the Bureau's receptionist announces to all that their boss is on the line. "Hold on, Mike. Agent Haskell's coming. Good to hear your voice. You okay?"

"Still standing."

"Glad to hear that. Okay, well, here he is. You take care." Haskell and Mike were cut from the same 'no bullshit' cloth. He gets right to the point remitting all frills and one crucial fact:

"Gomez sent over a half dozen Agents from Iowa. Your conversation yesterday morning with Governor Thompson prompted the release of State budgetary constraints allowing troopers from each of Illinois' forty-one police districts to deploy here. This is no doubt, the largest dragnet this part of Illinois has ever seen. Together with local police, troopers with squad car lights flashing have lit up this community scouring every alley, stopping outside of every residential home, grocery, video and convenience store. The face of our Japanese suspect provided by that newscast left an indelible impression on the citizenry making our intrusion into their evenings welcomed. I spoke with Lt. Keating. The two detectives he tagged to Professor Shirin followed him to a dilapidated trailer park, McKinney's, third row in, second unit on the right off of Day Street, North. Two plain clothes units have been stationed at each end of the street, one foot patrol, one, two man team behind the wheel. There's no way the good professor is going anywhere or receiving any visitors tonight without us knowing. I quietly reached out to the university. Shirin is schedule to report for class Tuesday afternoon at two pm.

"Good. Anything else?"

"Director Kelly called wanting an update. I told him that you were still in the field. I also told him that as a result of your efforts this Bureau has been looking hard at a University of Chicago physics professor named Randolph Shirin. The Director informed me that Shirin is scheduled at the end of next week to participate in a US nuclear defense symposium in D.C. That our boy is highly regarded not only among his peers but throughout the military community as the next up and comer. To quote the Director, *If Shirin is involved in any way with a crime make certain that the Chicago Bureau packages him up neat and tidy, secured with everything we have and anything else we can muster. A good number of questions will be asked. Our answers must be incontrovertible.* End quote."

Haskell, the former Command Master Chief of the US. Navy's Truman Strike Group, a gruff on the outside softy on the inside double-dipper, now second in command of the Bureau's Northern Illinois office knew Mike needed a good night sleep, something she wasn't going to get it if he was one hundred percent forthcoming with her. So the hardcore realist transitioned to a pragmatist and seamlessly withheld a critical piece of information, one that could wait till morning. In its stead he stresses:

"I'd fielded calls from the RCMP and Mexican State Police. All wanting to know what the hell is going on. All willing to lend a hand. I graciously acknowledged and closed with a will advise, moving forward."

"Command Master Chief, you gracious?"

"Just like your dad, nothing gets by you. By the way, thanks again for allowing me to say a few words at his funeral. He was the most honorable man I'd ever met."

"Thank you, Agent Haskell." With thoughts of her beloved father filling her mind, Mike's eyes began to dampen. "Westgate out."

"Oh hey Mike, Mike, wait. For the record, you need to know the following. Per Agent Donaldson's directive, Sanitation Commissioner Ken Porter brought a bag of Russian sniper rifle parts to our office. I immediately signed them into evidence and walked the bag and its contents over to our fingerprint lab. The only thing we found was a smudged partial print on the scope. It matched nothing in our records. So I reached out to Interpol and filed an official report with them. Copies on your desk."

"HQ Lyons, France?"

"Yes, but before I could make it to our coffee machine to grab a cup of joe their office called back."

"For what?"

"Someone within their organization apparently with a hell of a lot of pull, put in a special request to have the weapon including its scope couriered immediately to their London office. At exactly 4:54 this afternoon, that scope was jet bound to Heathrow."

"So it's been there for the last several hours?" Mike asserts.

"Roger that. I was contacted the moment it arrived. They have some kind of new, experimental lab under development there. That's all I was told."

Seeing Steve walking over to her, Michaelene points the phone's receiver into the air. She shakes her head in mock disgust at Steve's still rolled-up pants. While he attends to his trousers, she conveys to him the why and whereabouts of the Russian sniper rifle and its night scope.

"Juicy Fruit!" Steve hollers. "Oh my god. Sure, of course, Interpol. Alright. Now it makes sense. A global intelligence gathering and information coordinating organization meets a guy whose brain works like the board game RISK twenty-four/seven. Perfect fit. As you know, Interpol is contracted to consult with hundreds of countries including the US and..."

"Japan. Yes, I know."

"It's 10:10pm here. So that makes it..."

"Four am, in London." Mike quickly calculates. Let the big man sleep for a couple of hours."

"Ahh, the hell with that." Steve abruptly pronounces. "He's already got a good four to six. I've had zero. Give me a couple of minutes and your Bell Telephone pass code. I'll make it quick then set a time when he and I can talk further."

Bending over to roll his pant legs down, a Chapstick dispenser with a mere dribble of balm dangling from its lip drops out of the left cuff of Steve's pants. Crushed either by Tony, Lt. Keating or Sonny himself, its cap had popped off, its content neutralized by blood and water.

"I'll get that." Michaelene offers. She then returns the phone's receiver to her ear, "Haskell, we done?"

"Get some sleep, Mike. Haskell out."

"Shall do."

With a quick jog back to the Dodge, Mike retrieves a pair of work gloves beneath the passenger side seat and a Coke bottle from the station's trash container. Taking a dime out of her pocket, Mike puts it into the outdoor newspaper stand and removes the nightly edition of the Chicago Sun Times. Dropping the Chapstick container into the Coke bottle, she stuffs the paper's advertising section into the empty soft drink container, securing its contents. With Frank's permission, she places the glass bottle into the Dodge glove box, saying to Frank, "Don't worry, I won't forget it. Then to Steve she offers: "We'll take it to our lab and have it dusted for fingerprints." Hopping in the back of the truck, she continues, "Maybe nothing but.."

With the truck's sliding glass window that separates its bed from its cab still open, Frank holds up the front page of the Chicago Sun Times.

HEADLINE: "PEOPLE OF NORTHERN ILLINOIS GRATEFUL FOR GOVERNOR, FBI AND FIRE MARSHALL."

"Thanks Frank. I saw it. The governor, the fire marshall, they've earned that accolade, They've each done their job. I talked, I hugged. That was it. There's a vacuum I need to fill. All I need is a good two hours. Then I'll be recharged and ready to go."

"Moving out."

In the back of the truck Steve relates to Mike his evidence-laced assessment of exactly how the epic explosion a little more than twenty-six hours ago, occurred. The collapsible Russian sniper rifle, its Apex revolving extender, the 'human wick,' the pump handle's flame being driven down by the heavier than air propane through the hose into the underground tanks, a brief reminder of the term entropy, topped off by his retelling of how an Army sniper in Vietnam with one shot, blew a Shell oil truck to smithereens while simultaneously killing an enemy platoon surrounding it.

"You knew people who could actually do that, people who could make that kind a shot?"

"I did."

"Okay, Let's get on that. Let's track them down. Where do we start?" Mike asks.

"The jungle of Vietnam. Their bodies have been rotting there for decades."

"There must be others."

"Damn few. I'll make some calls but we're looking for someone with a nearly unobtainable pedigree. There are a lot of sharp shooters out there who read books and magazine articles even hire coaches to improve the quality of their shot. But it takes someone living virtually in isolation, practicing repeatedly without distraction and with an ungodly amount of ..."

"Patience? Is that what you were about to say?

"Yes."

"Steve, Wait! That's exactly how you told me the medical examiner described the perp who carved "revenge" into our first victim's forearm, someone with a lot of time on their hands."

"And patience up the ass."

"The frog butchers a woman then takes the time to carve a message into her forearm. He's cold, disciplined and at some point in his life in order to survive, he's erased the concept of time from his mind. The profile fits. The butcher is also our sniper."

"Its likely he pulled the trigger, its likely he developed the discipline to successfully make the shot but to plan this whole thing out, to play hide and seek games with us, with me, no way. To carry out a plan of action once laid out for him okay, of course, I see that but to set each domino in place and calculate how and when each will fall, no. That's not the same kind of cat who sits in the dark reliving the results of each of his butchering deeds while exercising his trigger finger or..."

"...sharpening his blade?"

"Correct. That's not brain power that's..."

"...rote behavior." Mike sums. "Welcome Dr. Randolph, Shirin, Ph.D, professor of nuclear physics, brain power plus. And our thanks to Fire Marshall Stan Sullivan who helped us tie those two together."

Arriving back at the Clifford home while the family sleeps, Grandpa and his two guests down the best part of a bottle of *Crown Royal Canadian Whiskey*. Each as a result including Michaelene, sleep a solid six.

Sunday morning, September 10th, 1978: 5:45 a.m.

Seven bathrooms compliment the Clifford family's five bedroom home. Steve and Mike meet in the hallway outside one freshly showered, wearing furnished bathrobes. Waking up to the enticing, wafting, aroma of bacon, eggs and fresh ground coffee from the kitchen below, both required a few yawns and a good stretch to realign with reality. The family's housekeeper Sylvia, had been awake since four voluntarily washing and ironing FBI Agent's Westgate's clothes and preparing the morning meal. What remained of Steve's wardrobe was trashed. It was replaced courtesy of Frank's closet, with a pair of straight-legged black slacks, fresh socks and a freshly starched J.C. Penny, short-sleeve, button-down white shirt. Steve had gone commando since his teens so need there.

Mike asks, "May we use your den, Frank?"

"Of course."

Mike dials her office. Agent Haskell answers. In traditional fashion, the old sea dog foregoes pleasantries and gets right down to business.

"The crowd was peaceful last night. No issues arose."

"That amazing." Mike extols.

"Mike?"

"In what other city could twenty thousand plus people be forced out of their homes to stand in line throughout the night with little to eat and drink without at least one fistfight erupting? I truly love the strength and character of the people of Chicago and its communities."

Haskell moves on: "Our motorpool is exhausted. All resources are out. We leased a vehicle for you from the local Ford dealership. It will be at 424 Grand in twenty minutes. Agent DeMille will be behind the wheel."

"Shirin? Anything?"

"No movement. No visitors. Nothing."

Mike orders, "Get a hold of Keating and the two detectives he assigned to the professor. There's a liquor store around the corner from McKinney's trailer park. We can convene there behind the store in its parking lot. Set the meet for 0:700. I want a good look at the surrounding neighborhood along with the state detective's assessment before they're relieved. Now would be a good time Agent Haskell."

"For what, Mike?"

"To brief me regarding what you decided not to tell me last night."

"How did you know?"

"I didn't until now."

"The frog carved up two more victims late last evening. No question. It was his handiwork. Both teenage girls, eight blocks apart and unrelated. Both assaulted with a box cutter. One survived. One did not. He's still at large."

Mike sets the phone down on Frank's desk. Then, with both hands placed securely over her mouth she screams the word "Fuck!" into them. Admonishing herself for waking from a good night's sleep knowing that yet another girl never will, she places her head on Steve's shoulder. Picking the phone's receiver back up, she places it to her ear. Michaelene then says to Haskell,

"I should have been out there."

"One more person could not have made a difference… not even you."

"You told me that last night amounted to the largest dragnet this part of Illinois had ever seen. So how does a 5'8" Japanese male whose face has been repeatedly splashed across the air waves and by now every newspaper in the State, slip by at least a hundred armed police officers taking two more lives without being captured or seen? Tell me Agent Haskell, how is that possible?"

"By three am that count was nearing seven hundred, Mike. We had choppers in the air, dogs on the ground and teams covering every inch of the sewer systems. And we've been cutting deals with every Asian drug lord and pimp in the area. No leads. Not a scrap of evidence. Nothing."

"And no eyewitnesses?"

"Everyone, I mean everyone Mike, is terrified. There's been talk about vigilante gang forming. Good people Mike, not gang bangers, just wanting to protect their neighborhoods.

"That can't be allowed to happen."

"It's been contained. Two local detectives brokered a forty-eight hour standdown but the word on the street continues to get uglier by the hour. Some people are beginning to see a relationship between the explosion and this barbaric slayer. They want whoever is behind this shitshow in shackles."

"So you're telling me that we have had an epic explosion that leveled half a community and a serial killer on the loose and still, as of this morning, we have no hard evidence pointing to the identity of the perpetrator in either case?"

"Affirmative."

Steve asserts, "I might have something. I've been asked to London."

"When were you going to tell me?"

"You picked up the phone before I could get a word out. There's a round trip ticket to London waiting for me at O'Hare. The return flight is scheduled for tomorrow evening. Preston believes he has evidence that will determine the identify of the person responsible for the explosion."

"When's your flight?"

"8:34am. Don't worry Frank has already volunteered to drive me."

"When you get back fill out a voucher for $500 in Frank's name. I'll have Haskell standing by to sign off on it for you. Colonel Clifford has done that and far more for us. I want him to know that we greatly appreciate his friendship and support."

"Done. Where will you be?"

"Where I'm needed."

Both Steve and Michaelene are standing drinking coffee, passing on the bacon and gobbling down eggs, one order for Mike two for Steve.

6:20am Sunday

At the front door a knock is heard. Frank answers it. A half step behind is Mike.

Agent DeMille presents his credentials to the homeowner, first. He then says to his boss, "Ma'am, whenever you're ready." Michaelene turns to Steve with a heart-warming gaze - the kind poets would argue can melt an iceberg – as then she says to him, "Safe travels Agent Donaldson. Stay close to a phone."

CHAPTER FORTY-EIGHT

It started out as a dark overcast Sunday morning with light rain forecast for later in the day but as Mike and Agent DeMille pulled away from 424 Grand Boulevard to West Touhy Avenue heading northbound for the 294 Tollway, crosswinds began to howl. A light morning drizzle suddenly turned into a deluge. Puddles along the roadway had already formed. Trees lining Touhy Avenue were swaying with several beginning to touch the sidewalk bordering the popular neighborhood thoroughfare.

"Ma'am, the bag at your feet, there's a hooded plastic rain coat in it. I brought it for you. I stuffed it between the two thermoses to keep them from rattling. The tall thermos is full of ice water, the other hot coffee. I asked around and found out how you like each."

"Do you know where we're heading?"

"Yes Ma'am. Agent Haskell gave a point by point briefing this morning."

"Are you bucking for a promotion, Agent DeMille?"

"Yes, Ma'am, I am. Got another child on the way."

"Good answer. I like that. Honesty."

7:02 a.m. Sunday morning, September 10th, 1978.

In the parking lot behind the liquor store around the corner from McKinney's, sat two unmarked sedans, Mike's and that driven by the two State detectives. The others, including FBI Swat who arrived in their personal vehicles, parked randomly throughout the surrounding, four block radius. With car phones and Motorola walkie-talkies fully charged, all are standing by waiting the 'go' signal from Mike.

She knew Shirin and he knew her. She was going in alone. No vest - too telltale - too constraining, especially for someone skilled in using their body as a weapon. If Shirin or the Frog were present Michaelene knew, Shirin would be more likely to stash him to greet her if she was alone.

Still, to arrest an up-and-coming nuclear physicist connected to the U.S military apparatus on suspicion of being responsible for the reported deaths of now eighteen locals who perished as a result of the Belmont-Cragin explosion- in the absence of irrefutable evidence to support that allegation - would end Mike's career and stain Director Kelly's. Far more importantly Shirin would be exonerated, his status and credibility enhanced. If he deserved it, he'd have to earn it. She wasn't going to hand it to him. But arresting Shirin or anyone else save of course for the Frog if he were to leap forward, wasn't on today's schedule. The obtainment of hard evidence - any kind of tangible proof - that's what this morning called for. And that's exactly what Michaelene Westgate, the Bureau's first side-arm bearing female Special Agent, was about to uncover.

A 1949 Spartian Manor dual axle, twenty-five foot travel trailer sitting off the beaten path in a tumbledown, near-vacant, trailer park community, was the target of this early morning probe. Backed up against a patch of woods ripe with stinkweed a half mile from the southern banks of the Chicago River, the elongated, wheel-less, aluminum habitat is the one to which last night, Shirin unwittingly led two state police detectives. They witnessed him open, enter, then close its door behind him. Inside no lights were seen. When they arrived at the liquor store parking lot, they assured Mike he's still in there.

As the clouds danced and darkened shifting precipitously about allowing sunlight to beam momentarily off the target's glistening aluminum skin first from one angle then the next, Mike approached the target passing the side window of the trailer park's office. With each step her mind ran through the bounty of circumstantial evidence. "Did I miss something, anything?" She questioned herself. Within a few short steps the conclusion was reached, "No," she whispered aloud, "Nothing."

The torrent of wind and rain with droplets the size of hail pounding the gravel roadside lessened the sound of her footsteps. As Mike neared - the hooded raincoat nearly negating her gender - she noticed the target's windows. They'd been spray-painted black, inside and out. It was a recent effort, hurried and sloppy. Mike pressed her face to one estimating forty-eight hours tops given the paint's lingering odor. She edged her way through the trailer's surrounding, trash-laden garden to the aluminum structure's solo entry and knocked. No answer. She knocked again. The third time she knocked harder and added: "Professor Shirin, are you home? It's Michaelene?"

The blast from both barrels of a 12 gauge shotgun fired simultaneously into the air complimented the thundering heaven's mounting roar. It was old man, McKinney. He'd slinked his way through the woods off to Michaelene's left to get the drop on his 'trespasser.'

"What the god damn, livin' hell are you doing here, whore?" There was no way of disguising it. He'd caught the pitch in Mike's voice."Get you're fuckin hands in the air," McKinney bellowed.

Mike didn't comply. Instead, she took a few steps towards him. McKinney nervously attempted to reload.

"What the hell do you think you're doing? Back off god damnit, you hear me, bitch?" Mike was attempting to save the old man from a hale of bullets from her colleagues by sharing the line of fire with him. She was hoping too, to get a chance to talk, to find any information possible.

"Sir, I'm..." but there was no way through the howling winds and pounding rain anything even remotely resembling a complete sentence could be conveyed. Mike reached beneath her raincoat to pull out her credentials. With nothing but a fingertip grip, the wind snagged them out of her hand slapping her ID flap down against the aftermarket aluminum 'skirt' wrapping the bottom of Shirin's trailer.

Nervously dropping one shell to the ground McKinney successfully chambered another. Quickly demonstrating his lack of interest in carrying on a civil conversation,

McKinney raised his 'street cannon' pointing it directly at Michaelene's mid section. She didn't flinch.

Accidents happen around loaded firearms. Pointing a double-barreled shotgun at previous trespassers was enough to send them well…skedaddling , hearing in their wake old man McKinney's cackling laughter. He wasn't certain why his little game wasn't working this time. That sent his temper soaring:

"Get the mother fucking Christ away from me you hussy. My pal Bobby Randolph owns that here trailer. He's workin' in secret in der for Uncle Sam, figuring out how to put a stop to dem damn Alien invaders. He wants nothing to do with you and nedder do I. I told 'em I'd be here, standing guard day and night and I ain't no one who breaks his word. Now get down on your knees and let me see you crawl out of here like the gutter trash you are." The old man cocked the hammer back of his vintage firearm. "Move, move before I blow you to fuckin kingdom come."

That was it. The Swat Team Leader had had enough. So too, did the watchful eye of Agent DeMille. Appointed this morning by his boss to act in her stead, he immediately ordered all plainclothes personnel into position. The black-suited, six man forward unit of the Bureau's twelve man Swat Team who'd been crawling in on their bellies for the last eight minutes - now within a yard of the target - slowly rose. Through the torrent of whistling rain and low hanging clouds like spectres of death – without a word - they aimed their weapon at the dithering old fool.

"What, ah hell. You gonna arrest me, for doin what ?"

"Threatening the life of a federal officer."

"How was I to know who that slut was? She said nottin to me."

"Keep it up, pal" said the arresting Swat officer.

"All I'd done is fire ME shotgun in da air? What's the harm in dat? Hey, gimme that back. You can't…"

"Swat Team Leader Tony Bach turns to one of his team members, ordering him to: "Take this man into custody. Secure him in his office. Get him a towel if you can find one. We'll let the local police explain the city ordinances to him. Then we'll see what Special Agent Michaelene Westgate wants to do with this guy."

"Oh, sweet Jesus. That was her?"

7:46 am Sunday, September 10th, 1978.

"Dr. Shirin, if you're home, please come to the door. I'd greatly appreciate a few minutes of your time. I know how busy you are. I had hoped that early Sunday morning might be a good time to catch you." Immediately, Michaelene regretted using the word 'catch.'

Dead silence. No reply.

"It's rather cold out here. Would you be willing to invite me in?" With her left hand, Mike subtlety motions down and back. Seeing that, Agents retreated to their original cover positions while Swat reclaimed the earth below their feet. Still no movement was witnessed inside the trailer. Mike looked at her watch: "Steve must be nearing the airport now. 'Aliens' and 'Bobby Randolph'? She cracked a brief smile."

At the other side of town on the 294 Interstate Highway enroute to O'Hare International Airport:

"Construction delays, damn."

"It would be great if We The People," Steve asserts, "could be advised in advance of scheduled repairs."

"Perhaps someday. Hold on. I'm going to cut across this embankment and drop down onto that suburban street below us, that one right over there. Hang on." Frank's Dodge handled the transition with minor discomfort to itself as well as its passengers.

"Whoa, shit, you really are a Marine!"

"Improvise, adapt and overcome. That's it. That's what we do." While Frank is driving Steve to the airport on his way to London, the two continue their conversation. The subject? What else, Hitler, Hirohito and their respective quests to develop a "Master Race to conquer the world."

Frank offers, "the real difference between the Nazis and the Imperial Japanese is how they perceived women. If a Nazi raped a Jewish girl, he'd be killed for defiling the purity of the Aryan race. The Jap on the other hand, was encouraged to rape and kill all women who were not of their race. After all, room had to be made for their upcoming dynasty. Their victims served no real purpose, just pieces of wood to be used then discarded."

"Like so many soiled napkins. Remarkable. Back at the house yesterday afternoon while you and I were sitting in the Florida Room, you said the United States did nothing in the late 1930's to stop Japanese aggression."

"That's not one hundred percent true. Our State Department wrote letters of protest."

"That's it? Even after the Japs intentionally sank one of our   navy's   ships?"

"The ship was the USS Panay. It was sitting at anchor outside the Chinese port city of Nanking flying the Stars and Stripes. A few days before Christmas in 1937, the Japs under orders, dive-bombed her. For nearly an hour they hurled all that they had at that grand old dame before she sank to the bottom of the Yangtze River."

"And at the time, no declaration of war was offered, right?"

"True. Four years had to pass before that happened."

"What the fuck?"

"I assume you means, why?"

"Yes. Why?"

"Imperial Japanese land forces had overrun Nanking. They wanted total control over the city including its ports."

"But that's just it. I don't get it. why pick a fight with us?

"The Japanese weren't willing to settle just for Nanking. They wanted total control over all of China. The United States in the form of the Panay, was standing in their way."

"So, no one at the Emperor's palace on their way to their war college thought to reach out to our State Department with a quick heads-up, saying Hey, your ship is in our way. Can you move it, like a good neighbor might ask another who parked in front of his driveway?"

"Nor did the Japanese bother when they attacked Pearl Harbor four years later to set forth prior to the act, a declaration of war. Days would pass before that happened."

"The sneak attack on Pearl Harbor, these days, is common knowledge."

"Here's what isn't. Hitler and his henchmen were testing the water, they watched and learned, taking careful note of how the United States reacted to Japanese aggression. It was only then just two years after the Japs sank the Panay, that the Nazis unleashed their war machine across Europe."

"Lesson taught."

"Lesson learned."

BACK AT MCKINNEY'S:

"Aliens...Bobby Randolph, Wow. Colorful?" Mike walks around the trailer attempting to peak through several of its spray painted windows, looking for inconsistencies in application to no avail.

Now standing in the middle of the trailer park driveway some twenty paces from the target, having recovered her credentials, Michaelene is transfixed, glaring at the twenty-five foot aluminum dwelling while again pondering what McKinney said.

"Shirin may be a brilliant physics professor but his creative lying ability is at best, schoolyard level." Still, Michaelene recognized Shirin's need to disguise his intent but the haunting question "Why" remained?

Walking backwards, stepping slowly down the trailer park's gravel driveway, unable to take her eyes off of the target, there was something askew, something she couldn't quite put her finger on. She suddenly stops. Across the way as wind and rain continue to whirl, trailer canopies, boarded-up shutters, lawn chairs and vintage BBQ grills that have failed to be properly attended for years, all yielded to the demands of mother nature; banging, tipping over, with some ripped from their hinges becoming airborne. The downpour with its rushes of wind loosen the aluminum 'skirts' at the base of each travel trailer, those with wheels removed whose owners opted for permanency with its accompanying rental and mortgage payment reductions. Every 'skirt' on every trailer within eye site was wobbling, barely hanging on for dear life except one, the one Mike could not take her eyes off of...Shirin's.

"Shirin had that puppy professionally installed, likely reinforced and bolted into place but why?" She asks herself. "What's the point, preventative maintenance, an example of his advanced way of thinking or something else?" As she watched the runoff rainwater washing away the soil foundation around the skirt, her mind raced.

Still standing in the middle of the trailer park driveway being pounded by incessant rain, the hood of her plastic raincoat whipping across her face, Mike looked up, taking into account for the first time, both rows of mobile home units. On either side they stood, each sharing something in common, something more that skirts and airborne, aluminum folding chairs. Finally, it was clear. She smiled and said to herself, "Puddles."

Agent DeMille is off to her left. She motions to him. Head down against the winds, he steps over to her.

Mike shouts, needing to be heard over Mother Nature, "We need to get back to the office. There are two people central to this investigation with whom I need to have a serious conversation. They'll be more receptive especially on a Sunday, if I initiate the calls from my office. The watchdog formation put into place by Lt. Keating with his people in cars at both ends of the street, I'll ask that to remain. Team Leader Bach..." She turns to the handsome Swat Team Leader now standing off to her right.

"Yes Ma'am."

"You and your men stand down."

"Excuse me, Ma'am. With your permission SAC Westgate, I would like to be posted here. I can delegate Swat One to Mitchell, my second in command. He can..."

"Every State Trooper, especially the detectives who shadowed Shirin last night have done an exceptional job. Foot patrols can redeploy when the weather breaks but you're right. I would prefer someone steeped in Bureau ops as my on-site point of contact. Okay, Agent Bach. Congratulations. The job's yours. You're my POC. If anything inside that trailer or something other than the wind moves it from the outside, I want to be notified immediately.

"Will do, Ma'am."

Agent DeMille offers, "I'll go get the car."

"Wait! I'll go with you."

7:51 am, inside the Dodge pickup making its way to O'Hare International through suburban streets:

"One man is to blame for World War Two and some 60 million deaths throughout Europe and Asia. That man is not Adolph Hitler. That man," Frank sets forth in no uncertain terms, "is Japanese Emperor Hirohito."

"Sure, the guy was a scumbag but…"

"Is a scumbag to use your term."

"I don't understand?"

Dr. Shiro Ishii died a free man in 1959, having never seen the inside of a courtroom. His uncle, the Emperor, is still alive living steeped in luxury in Japan's Imperial Palace. Perhaps you don't recall, President Ford invited Hirohito to the White House four years ago."

8:18am, Chicago's O'Hare airport

Much to the chagrin of airport security, Frank pulls to the sidewalk outside O'Hare's Terminal One and stops. Jumping out, Steve waives his credentials at the on-coming airport officers. Turning on his heels facing the Dodge pickup, Steve shouts, "Sir!" giving the man who has become a mentor, former Marine Corps officer Frank Clifford, a parade-grade, formal salute - one American military officer to another - before bolting through the terminal doors to the ticket counter.

8:58am, Bureau Headquarters, downtown Chicago.

In her office, a glass-enclosed antechamber that looks out onto a far larger expanse of open desks, file cabinets and chairs, Michaelene is on the phone. She is briefing Federal District Judge Bartholomew "Bucky" Harris of her take on the University of Chicago's physics professor, Dr. Randolph Shirin.

"I appreciate your concern. The facts you've provided are disturbing, deeply disturbing. When you've got what we both know you need, I'll be waiting. Keep me apprised."

"Be assured, I will."

"May I ask I ask a personal question before you go?"

"Certainly, your honor."

"My wife Sarah and I saw you on television yesterday afternoon. What was it, twenty years ago, you came to our door selling girl scout cookies? Do you remember that?"

"Sure. Of course. At the time I had never seen a home as big and beautiful as yours. And as I recall, you and your wife bought three boxes of thin mints and two … yes, two boxes of shortbreads."

"You know I knew your father. What a gracious man he was. Watching you on television while you stood on the Parish steps, I caught that same willful gleam in your eyes of honesty and grace under pressure that 'Barnacle Mike' invariably had in his."

"After the war, hearing people in civilian life using his Naval Academy nickname always put a smile on my father's face."

"You are your father's daughter. Smart as all hell and equally determined. The momentum you have already put into play needs to continue unabated if this city is to survive. Rumors have already reached my ear pointing to Chicago's *Gaylords* street gang having their hand in this business."

"That would be highly unlikely, sir."

"No doubt but such misinformation ultimately leads to an escalation in violence. If this professor Shirin is in any way responsible for the Belmont-Cragin explosion and these street murders he needs to be buttoned up and put away quick. You sound convinced that Shirin is your man?"

"I've provided you with the key elements of the circumstantial evidence, your honor. The extent of such is far more reaching. What I'm lacking is the incontrovertible proof."

"The hard stuff?"

"Yes, your honor. The hard stuff. The irrefutable kind."

"I want to work with you as close as the legal framework will allow. Call me anytime, night or day."

"Thank you."

"Good hunting, young lady."

Mike hangs up the phone. "Okay. Ground work laid." Next Mike calls a meeting of everyone in the office. Keeping her team apprised of the data gathered to date while hearing herself, running down all the facts in the case to edit, affirm and boost retention, she takes the floor.

CHAPTER FORTY-NINE

6:19 pm, Greenwich Mean Time, INSIDE LONDON'S INTERPOL LABORATORY ONE:

"He spat on it."

"He what?" Steve asks Juicy Fruit.

"Apparently, minutes before taking the shot the sniper had difficulty affixing the Russian scope to the barrel. So Subject #1 spat on the scope's mounting attempting to lubricate it. We would not have found out how DNA could be applied to criminal identification and ultimately the apprehension of the bad guys had not some fucking psychopath Jap, a microbiologist at the onset of WWII, taught himself how to manipulate it." sayeth the former Green Beret, Princeton grad.

"His notebook outlining years of his experiments weaponizing pathogens and categorizing the results of each has been lost to history but this egotist believing his DNA to be the finest, kept separate notes and samples of his own. What a scientifically beneficial fuck up, right?"

"I'm not certain I understand, Captain."

"It's Robert, numbnuts. The Army has long since moved on leaving us both behind."

Born in the slums of South Tacoma, raised by foster parents outside Rutgers New Jersey now living in a prestigious Central London flat - hating to be called Bob - Robert knowingly enjoys mixing expressions and attitudes inherited across the full spectrum of his experiences. He finds it makes for a far more attentive audience.

"Come over here. Take a gander at this slide." Steve does as asked, placing his eye to a microscope. As he looks down, the lab's side door opens. Walking in is a rather handsome elderly man, dapperly attired.

"Oh Dr. Jeffreys. Good. I'm glad you're here. This is the gentleman I was telling you about. This is my friend, Agent Steve Donaldson of the FBI."

"Yes, quite. It's a pleasure, young man. I must say that this big fellow here has been regaling everyone in London these past several days with tales of you and your first encounter with our brainy, American friend. 'Captain Juicy Fruit,' isn't it? That's the nickname he inherited from you? When put in context, it's quite charming, actually."

"Dr. Jeffrey's, this man saved my life."

"And this man sir," Steve sets forth, "with his brain-teasing jokes and grand tour of the global political landscape saved mine keeping me calm while undergoing battlefield surgery. His persistent chit chat was a welcome distraction calming my heart rate until the medics arrived. I wouldn't be here today if not for this big lug."

"In science we call that a mutualistic, symbiotic relationship."

Steve offers, "I'd heard that term more than once lately."

"Although it generally applies to two different species working together to their mutual benefit," Dr. Jeffreys assures, "I've often felt from a sociological standpoint, the term can be appropriately used to describe a reciprocal bond between two human beings, two men most certainly but most notably between a man and a woman. But Mr. Preston, my apologies sir. I've been rude. We've dragged your friend all the way across the pond to share with him our amazing discovery. Please, go on. Show him the slide."

Steve looks through the laboratory microscope.

"What am I looking for, Dr Jeffreys?"

"Well tell me young man, what do you see?"

"Okay, well, I see two worm-like objects, each having stripes in the same place. They look the same to me, sir. What am I missing?"

"Nothing. What you are seeing are two strands of DNA molecules. The one on the right is from the spittle we recovered from off the scope. The one on the left is from a Japanese microbiologist, Dr. General Shiro Ishii, courtesy of his own hand."

"Meaning no disrespect sir, I recently learned that Ishii died in 1959, some nineteen years ago."

"So he did and good riddance I might add but that fact doesn't matter. His DNA, yours and mine and of all living things has a shelf life of over five hundred years. To be more clear, what you are looking at is the DNA of a father and his son. The spittle on the scope compared one hundred percent to one of the only successfully developed and maintained human DNA sample currently known to exist, that of Dr. Shiro Ishii, a microbiologist and a Lieutenant General of the Imperial Japanese Army."

"What the ...?"

"That's right cowboy."

Robert Preston steps to the table where the microscope rests. Standing by Steve, he offers, "DNA is today, an essentially unknown, forty-one year old discovery that has only now begun to step out of the closet. What Dr. Jeffreys has done Steve, is push beyond its application to the medical sciences and developed a means of using DNA as a crime solving tool. It doesn't smudge or vary its composition given the surface from which it is lifted nor is it's latent identification dependent upon subjective interpretation. What we are saying to you is if the rifle scope the Bureau provided us under your name was used to set in motion that horrific explosion in Illinois, the son of Dr. Shiro Ishii was there. He either pulled the trigger himself or was standing next to the sniper perhaps as his spotter, when the trigger was pulled."

"Holy shit! No way?"

"Take another look in the microscope. You see. Right there. That's Ishii's DNA on the right. And that's his son's Subject #2 on the left. As you'd acknowledged with your own eyes, there is no difference between the two DNA molecular chains. Dr. Shiro Ishii, Subject #1, a deranged microbiologist who murdered millions throughout Asia in the mid twentieth century with his germ warfare experiments, his son Subject#2, name unknown, is alive and well and living right now in Chicago, or perhaps I should say he was seventy-two hours ago."

"Son of a....Robert. I need a phone?"

11:05 am BUREAU HEADQUARTERS, DOWN-TOWN CHICAGO.

When a beautiful woman makes nothing of it, who doesn't flaunt or seek advantage based upon it, who is as smart as she is attractive, respect for her and her word carries inestimable weight. Michaelene is once again, on the phone. This time with University of Chicago President, Robert Marsolan.

"Is this call regarding the Belmont-Cragin explosion?"

"Yes Bobby, it is." Out of admiration for slain Senator Robert F. Kennedy, university President Marsolan encourages all formally and informally, to call him 'Bobby.'

"The rumor is, you're looking at one of my staff?"

"Although I had hoped to tell you myself, yes, I am interested in talking with Professor Randolph Shirin. Do you know where I might find him this morning?"

"I don't keep hour-by-hour track of my workforce's comings and goings, especially on weekends but I will say one thing?"

"What's that?"

"Shirin is a very capricious fellow."

"How so?"

"He's on time for class and shows up on the dot for meetings but you're not the first to question where he is and what he does when he's not on campus."

"Dr. Marsolan, before I ask, let me assure you of one thing."

"And what would that be?"

"I know where the line is. I don't want to air even a hint of impropriety. So help me through this."

"I don't know if…"

"Imagine the voracious public rumor mill that is at this very moment, ripping through this state, picks up even a hint that one of your staff is considered a suspect in the Belmont-Cragin explosion, a man who the FBI expects also has a partner currently engaged in a diversionary tactic brutally killing woman, is being harbored, enabled or in any other way supported by this exceptional institute of higher learning, how long after the horde of reporters and police investigators have trampled your grounds and disrupted classes do you think it will take to remove the stain?"

"I'm confident that you know that I would very much like to avoid what you just described."

"If I can obtain evidence to clear Shirin or arrest him and bring him before a grand jury, once in hand, either way, I can make certain that the Bureau and the press's attention is deflected away from the U of C. As you know, we have a city on the verge of imploding. Time has never been more of the essence. Me and mine must do everything expediently but proceeding legally cannot be overlooked. So, here's my question. Can I rely on you for your help?"

"I'm at your disposal."

IN LONDON:

"Gentlemen, if you'll allow me, I must push on. Oh tosh. I nearly forgot. A private post server approached me in the hallway Agent Donaldson, with this envelope. Your associate, a Miss Westgate, Michaelene Westgate, yes, yes, now I recall, what a lovely name. She has a rather select fan club here in the UK with one woman in particular who is quite taken by her. Be a good chap and pass this envelope onto her the moment you return, will you."

"Sure," Steve replied with a shrug, still a bit dazed, still struggling to process all the information he just learned.

"Good fellow. Thank you. I'm off now." As the door to the hallway closes behind him:

"This cocksucker wouldn't have fit into our clique."

"Dr. Jeffrey's?" Steve asks, puzzled by Preston's comment.

"No, oh hell no. I was referring to Shiro Ishii. He hated women. The application of his experiments before World War Two killed millions of people both men and women, then countless more throughout the war but he didn't stop there."

"Okay Robert, exactly what are you trying to tell me?"

"Ishii was manipulating DNA attempting at first to develop a master race but along the way in the early 1930's, he got approached by someone to weaponize DNA for military application..."

"His uncle, the Emperor perhaps? No one took a dump in Japan in those days without Hirohito's permission"

"...with the expressed purpose," Preston sidesteps Steve's conjecture, "of wiping out the reproductive capability of women living in nations their military intended to conquer."

"Reducing the number of future revenge-seeking, offspring upending the new order, I get it. Calculative and monstrous. Mind-boggling."

"He called it Operation No Pao. Dr. Jeffreys and I had a long conversation about the depth and certain ramifications of Ishii' diabolical scheme when we chanced upon it. With the help of a handful of Japanese nationals with whom we have closely worked in the past - they validated our findings. If successful, it could have radically reduced the population not just of countries but of entire continents. We spoke for days on end and often long into the night. We were fascinated by him."

"How so?"

"The millions of lives Ishii destroyed throughout the mid twentieth century were brought about by dosing rats with various pathogens then using them as the delivery system. Operation No Pao was different. Quite a step up, actually. For what was the first time in known history, Shirin was able to modify the DNA molecular structure of certain pathogens then bind select elements from each, together. The end product was plant-based with its chlorophyll's magnesium atom acting as the gateway. The XX chromosomes in females is highly susceptible to No Pao's toxicity."

"Plant based?" Steve's mind immediately centered on Michaelene and the first time he surprised her with a bouquet of her favorite tulips, watching her breath in their aromatic, honey-like, smell.

11:07 am BUREAU HEADQUARTERS, CHICAGO

"Dr. Marsolan. The Bureau would like to obtain a reliable third party peak at Shirin's office and laboratory?"

"If it was up to me I would say yes and fling the doors wide open but access to either his lab or his office is no longer within my purview."

"Sir, you head one of the most awarded research universities in the world. I don't understand?"

"The front-runner for the University's recently vacated Provost position, Dr. Sedgewick Abelson, a brilliant mathematician and Holocaust survivor was given- as an incentive - autonomy by our board of trustees over the

Fermi National Accelerator Laboratory. In turn, Abelson gave operational control of the lab to Professor Shirin."

"What? Excuse me sir. Are you telling me that Randolph Shirin now occupies Enrico Fermi's...the Enrico Fermi's laboratory?"

"Yes, he has full use of it."

"That sounds like a trophy given to someone for simply showing up."

"I couldn't agree more. I carefully studied Dr. Shirin's twenty-seven page letter requesting use of Fermi's lab. It came across my desk the day before Dr. Abelson arrived. I rejected it on the grounds that like you, I thought that such a prestigious accolade should be earned not simply handed out. A lot of people around here especially those in the government circles, sing Shirin's praises but as far as I can see, he hasn't done anything of even measurable import to earn it as yet."

Michaelene thought to herself. "And that's the way I want to keep it."

President Marsolan further details the position he finds himself in,

"According to the original terms outlined in the contract between the U of C and the National Register of Historic Places, reactivating the Fermi lab as a full-time, functioning facility would result in it being removed from the Register's list. I was quite taken back when Dr. Abelson on the day of his arrival, strolled into my office with a waiver from the National Register allowing the lab to remain as posted, while in use."

"History?" Michaelene thought of her last date at Park Ridge's Pickwick Theater with Terry Winfell, a tenured University of Chicago American history professor, then said: "Mr. President, I have an idea."

11:10 am **BACK AT THE TRAILER PARK**:

Behind the 1949 Spartian Manor, twenty-five foot travel trailer, The Bureau's Swat Team Leader, 36 year old Tony Bach, spots something out of the ordinary. Bending over to investigate, a shot rips past his ear from a high velocity hand-gun. Tony hit the deck hard. State Trooper Lt. Tim Keating on site to check on his detail, drew his weapon and shot the commercial pipe wrench out of the mentally-deranged trailer park owner's hand before it came down on Agent Bach's head. Keating's round grazed McKinney's skull, opening it above his left ear. Still, he would survive.

Keating was furious. He needed to discover how McKinney had gotten loose. Agent Bach wanted a landline to contact Mike. Following the departure of the ambulance, both raced to the trailer park's office. Upon arrival their mutual frustration overflowed. The local police officer called to the scene to haul McKinney into custody, had been met with a desk phone across his face. The sinewy built guardian of Dr. Randolph Shirin's confines who'd been handcuffed to a desk chair by the arresting Swat Team Agent, went completely off the rails when local officer Richard Sweeney showed up, reaching behind the chair to remove the cuffs. Helped to his feet by both Keating and Bach, the dregs from the bottom of an instant coffee jar added to a cup of boiling water from off a portable electric hot plate aided the portly officer's recovery. Keating took the opportunity to debrief Sweeney and draft his report of the shooting incident. Agent Bach, now without a landline, thought to sprint to his car down the block then drive to Bureau headquarters believing that the evidence he observed had to be conveyed clearly and succinctly to Michaelene. That thought was thwarted by a downed utility line across the street celebrating its freedom dancing in the rain with sparks like Fourth of July fireworks, flying. Left with no choice, Agent Bach took to the less clear, often weather-hampered, communication devise provided by the Bureau and placed a call to headquarters.

11:18am BUREAU HEADQUARTERS, CHICAGO

"Stand by. You're breaking up on me. Call back in ten."

With extra agents came extra desks and chairs. Extra telephone lines were installed last year. Now all twelve were lit as a half dozen more were being installed.

Mike is on the phone with Steve. She is anxious to hear Swat Team Leader Tony Bach's report but, if by instinct she took Steve's call first. Special Agent Donaldson is explaining to his boss the result of his extraordinary discovery and by way of Frank, exactly who Shiro Ishii was.

"His name was "Shiro? Is that what you're telling me?"

"I know what you're thinking, Mike"

"Exactly, exchanging the 'o' for an 'i' and..."

"...And add an 'n' along with a truly British surname and you've got Shirin, as in..."

"Dr. Randolph Shirin, Ph.D. So you are telling me that our nuclear physics professor, a guy tied to our nation's national security interests is the son of one of the most diabolical murderers in modern Asian history?"

"Yes Mike, that is exactly what I am telling you."

BACK IN LONDON:

"So how far did Ishii get?"

"Dr. Jeffreys said he got close but well, essentially no cigar. Ishii failed to identify and secure the first term nurturing environment that his bacterium required to enable widespread dissemination."

"What does that mean? In English, please?"

FROM MCKINNEY'S TRAILER PARK:

"Ma'am, you need to get back out here and see this for yourself, insists Swat Team Leader Tony Bach. "It's the way the rain is running down through the trailer park. It's..."

"...Collecting around the skirt of every trailer except one."

"Except Dr. Shirin's. Yes, Ma'am."

"I'll be at McKinney's as soon as I can. I'll call when I'm en route."

"Standing by, Ma'am."

It's Mike, Agent Bach. Remember that."

"Got it. Thanks, Mike. Awaiting your arrival."

Mike pushes the intercom button on her desk. "Mrs. Clayfield."

"Yes."

"Contact Fire Marshal Sullivan. Tell him if possible, I need one of his emergency rescue units at McKinney's in two hours.

"On it."

Oh, and Mrs. Clayfield…ah, Sally. I need a favor."

"Sure Mike, anything."

"Get a hold of Teddy Winfell for me. He has a lower division American history class at 8:00am every Monday. Let him know that …oh, wait one." Michaelene presses the hold button on the intercom as she sees Agent Ron Israel walking into headquarters back for the first time since the accident. Putting aside professional decorum, she stands, reaches for him and the two embrace. "It's great to have you back. How's the head? You look like they put you back together well."

"Thanks Mike. I heard about Agent Sykes and Edwards. Senseless."

"We all share the loss. Sally will be putting together the memorial services for both. So their lives were not lost without reason, we need to capture the perpetrator."

"Do we know who?"

"We have a suspect."

"I need to get back into the game. Who could use my help?"

"Saddle up with Taylor. He'll bring you up to speed. Oh and here. I was jotting down notes when you walked in. Take them. I'll brief you as needed."

"No need. I got it." Agent Israel, chuckled. "This should be fun."

I mean it, it's great to see you up and around again. You're a key asset to this team."

"There's no place I'd rather be."

Back on the phone with Federal District Judge Bucky Harris.

"I'll give you your warrant Michaelene. It's a limited one. That's how we have to start. You'll be allowed access beneath Shirin's trailer but you cannot under any circumstances while acting on this warrant, enter the main body of his domicile. When you come across something more, I'll be right here pen in hand.

6062 Drexel Street, University of Chicago, Faculty Housing:

"Alright, alright. I'm coming." Struggling to get his slippers on Professor Witfell, wearing only a towel around his waist, answers the knock on his apartment door.

"I don't care if this Dr. Abelson is a holocaust survivor, I'll see him in court before I surrender my apartment to..." Teddy looks up. "Oh, so now they got the FBI coming to evict me. Say, I remember you. Oh, no, no no. I get it. Now wait. Your boss got it all wrong. I wasn't trying to get into her pants. I mean, she loves history. That's all we ever talked about. If anything she was using me."

"Listen, Professor Witfell." offers Agent Ron Israel. "You're going to act upon the directive I'm about to give you from SAC Westgate. Am I understood?"

"You can't order me around like I'm a..."

"Man who consorts with under-aged co-eds? You've got ten seconds to acknowledge your full cooperation before I enter your premises to check the ID's of those two young ladies climbing out of your bed right now."

"But ah..."

"And if that's not good enough, I can open up a federal investigation, one I'm certain my boss will be delighted to sign off on, regarding your suspected distribution of marijuana   to..."

"Linda!" Professor Witfell hollers. "Ah.. you and your friend, get dressed and get out of here. I'll see you Thursday in class. Now, Agent Israel is it?" Ron had been holding his credentials in front of him since he arrived, "Please tell me how I can be of assistance to the FBI?"

Agent Israel explained Mike's plan. "Someone will drop a backup pass key in your mailbox later this evening. Whatever you do, don't loose it. If you run into any snags, call President Marsolan. He'll help you though them."

"President Marsolan and I do not get along."

"Imagine that."

The Alcot Inn, Fitzrovia district, **Central London: "late lunch."**

"What kind of a nurturing environment?"

"Dr. Jeffrey's identified it as an environment demanding a naturally occurring, balanced blend of acidic water, phosphorous, calcium, iodine with an enormous dose of sphagnum."

"What?"

"A bog. Specifically, the North American kind. The kind your home city of Chicago rests upon. The kind in which large volumes of stinkweed thrive. Ishii's genetically constructed bacterium works this way. First, it feeds off its host, essentially any form of plant life, to near depletion. Then at a certain point it binds with it re-enriching the host until together they have formed…"

"…a mutualistic, symbiotic relationship."

"I was about to say a devastating toxin that reeks havoc on the female immune system and impedes their reproduction capabilities but yes, you're right."

"Damn! Playing god?"

"Exactly. In the 1930's, Ishii could develop the No Pao bacterium in an incubator but he had no means available to further its development and deliver it en masse to prospective victims."

"He didn't have a Chicago."

"Essentially, yes so he reverted back to his old tried and true means of weaponizing bubonic plague, anthrax and other similar bacterium.."

"But as they say, time marches on. I need to get to the airport. Can you arrange an earlier flight for me?"

"Done but what's your hurry?"

"Stinkweed. I rolled in it."

1:46pm, BACK AT McKINNEY'S:

"Lt. Keating."

"Yes, Mike."

"Now that the rain has subsided, I want a one mile radius search, door to door of this neighborhood. You've got less than four hours till sunset. He's here, our Frog, our Japanese butcherer, he's hiding somewhere nearby. It makes sense that he'd be in the area waiting to rendezvous with Shirin. Let's see if I'm right. Flush him out."

"Will do Mike. If he's here, he's yours."

Michaelene spots a fire hydrant off to the left, half way up the trailer park grade as she and Agent Bach near Shirin's trailer. Lying in the weeds she then notices the large monkey wrench shot out of McKinney's hand. She says to Back "Wait here" as she reaches down and re-covers it. Widening the wrench's mouth to its max, she makes her way up the hill. Like a real pro, Mike wraps it around the hydrant's bonnet. With her second try the city water gushes out, flowing down hill, right beneath Shirin's trailer disappearing as expected, beneath it.

2:07pm(Time is running out fast).

Mike's request for an Emergency Rescue unit arrives. Behind the wheel is none other than the Fire Marshall himself, Stan Sullivan.

"Tell me what you need, Mike?"

"This sheet metal skirt on this trailer, I want it off. Here's my warrant."

"You heard the lady, boys. Get on it. I'll cap the hy-drant."

To expedite the skirt's removal the firemen fired-up two acetylene cutting torches employing one at either end of the unit. Once the skirt was peeled back and an aperture revealed, Mike is first in, crawling beneath Shirin's alu-minum abode with Stan Sullivan and Swat Team Leader Tony Bach taking up either flank.

From beneath, support for the travel-trailer home was laid out in typical fashion with concrete blocks at each of the four corners and a few more randomly placed to hold up a sagging middle. What was considerably atypical was the hand-forged three by five foot steel grate, the one covering a cavernous hole into which the rainwater and that from the hydrant had flowed. The winch at the nose of the Emergency Rescue vehicle once its wire rope was wrapped around the grate, made short order of its padlock and hinges. As Mike lay prone beneath the unit's midsection, flung into the air in what little there was between the ground and the trailer's underbelly, that well-tooled, lattice work, iron screen banged against Shirin's aluminum retreat shaking an unknown number of heavy metal objects onto the floor right above Mike's head. "What was that?"

"Hell no, no flares. Get your heads on straight. We have no idea what's down there.. Lights... drop lights," Shouted Fire Marshall Stan Sullivan to his four man, *Rapid Intervention* crew. "Attached them to a rope line. Hurry. Get 'em over here."

"Nowak, Buckwald, your coats. Toss 'em here!" Mike got EMT Nowak's "turnout" coat, Bach wrapped himself in Lieutenant Buckwald's.

"Whoa. Mike. Watch out! Looking down into the mud filled, darkened abyss, Michaelene nearly fell in.

Nowak slides a ladder under the trailer but it added nothing to the solution. There was no way to angle it into the three by five foot cavity.

"Won't work. Get it out of here and get some web-bing…and get me our climber's rope. Standing by to re-pel." Tossed underneath the trailer, Stan orders Mike and Tony to wrap the bans of heavy duty nylon webbing around the waists of their coats. Then he orders the large double-drum winch with both of its hook clamps, acti-vated. Mike turns to Swat Team Leader Bach laying off to her side and points, "Give me that." From off his field utility vest Tony detaches his personal, shock-proof, mil-itary grade flashlight and hands it to Mike. She immedi-ately drops it into the hole. It hits bottom with a thud not a splash. "Twenty feet should do it." Mike informs Stan.

"So where did the water go? She wondered.

Mike sets forth the order:"I'm going in first. Stan you're our anchor. Agent Bach, once I've completed my as-sessment, I'll call for you if needed."

And that would have worked perfectly had not Tony turned one way attached to his winch line as Mike turned the other. In cramped quarters, that sent Michaelene spread-eagle across the three by five foot aperture cling-ing to the remains of the grate's hinges while Swat Team Leader Tony Bach plunged down the now somewhat less darkened abyss landing half way down on a protruding metal ledge. On impact his eyes closed. A hint of decay-ing flesh opened them. Suddenly, the FBI's 'shatter-proof' Swat Team Leader was nose-to-nose with the tor-tured face of the corpse of a teenage girl. With a fresh, blood-stained shop rag hurriedly left behind, carving on her forearm had apparently been halted just moments before. Instinctually surveying his immediate surroundings, the young Swat Team leader could see no sign of the perpetrator nor any indication of how he could have so quickly gotten away... nor for that matter, where the water could have gone.

The girl had been one of the Frog's last night victims, the unlucky one. Hoisted up a few feet onto the metal ledge, poised with her forearm drooping, easing access to that portion of her on which the Frog was carving his message before being interrupted. Still wearing her boyfriend's high school letterman's sweater the balance of the young woman's body was virtually consumed by the recent runoff of mud and debris. That made it near impossible in such close quarters for Bach to free her. Still, the question preeminent on the young Swat team leaders mind was, "Where did all the water go?"

"Use the skirt, the trailer skirt."

From her prone position, From beneath the aluminum domicile Mike stuck her head out past Stan Sullivan, shouting to his three firemen, "Use your torches. Cut the trailer skirt. Give me a good five and a half feet of it with a hole at one end big enough to fit the winch line's clasp through it. We'll use it like a stretcher to put the girl's body on. And give us all the additional nylon webbing you have. We'll need it to secure her body to it."

"Good call, Mike." Offers Marshal Sullivan who then takes it from there: "Buckwald, hand me our Snagging Tool and Halligan Bar. I'll join Bach when we get the go-ahead. Agent Westgate is right. First things first. We've got to get that girl's body out of there."

"When we free her," Mike continues, "we'll pull her up and out through here."

Cook County's Fire Department's Lt. Buckwald inserts. "Stan, one thing."

"Make it quick."

"The grate. It's marked WPA '5-43.'"

"Okay. May of 1943. The Works Progress Administration, one of President Roosevelt's social incentive acts, putting men back to work building and repairing America's infrastructure following the crash of '29. So what's that got to do with us?"

"That was my question. In what way if any does that impact what we're here to accomplish today?" Buchwald offers, "So, I hiked to the top of this grade to the ledge above it."

"And?"

"There's remnants of railroad tracks there, the same gauge as those across the street in front of the liquor store."

"Okay."

"I think this trailer park sits today where a railroad turnabout or 'balloon' station once sat best guess, circa 1890's. That's when they gained popular use, the "turnabout" that is. A turnabout would have had a dedicated sluice operator. His job would have been to connect that streaming device to the train. Down it, would come all waste material manufactured as well as human, into a bin of what was essentially, a cesspool."

Mike thought to herself: "A cesspool? We're venturing into a cesspool?"

Lt. Buckwald continues, "My concern Stan, Agent Westgate, is that in June of '43, one month after someone constructed that grate, the WPA shut down for good."

"Forty-three?" Mike reflects upon the war in which her father was once immersed. The war she knew better than most due to the love and counsel she and her father, shared. "In '43, in what was known as the Battle of the Bismark Sea, the Allies sank four Jap destroyers and ended the lives of nearly seven thousands of their finest, giving the Jap warlords a clear picture of what lay ahead. U.S. Infrastructure could wait. Manpower and material were needed to push forward hard to end the plague of Japanese imperialism. Shutting down the WPA at this point, yes, good call, Franklin. Made sense."

"Repairs to the sluice" Buckwald continues, "its gate, its operating system and maintenance of the cesspool itself were no doubt cancelled with that grate simply placed over it."

Out of frustration, Stan submits, "Then recently, some asshole parks a travel trailer home over it Why?"

"That's what we're here to find out." Offers Mike.

Buckwald inserts, "My point is this entire quadrant may be unstable especially following today's torrential downpour. You remember, Stan. We have experienced sink holes throughout this area before. Right now we have no idea what if any form of subterranean infrastructure may exist or what condition it may be in."

And just like that, as if orchestrated by some callous celestial entity, the walls of the sluice bin gave way with more than a ton of backed-up, century-old, compressed waste matter exploding down into the cesspool with an untold portion including the body of the girl raining down atop Tony Bach. Weight-triggered as it was designed to covertly operate nearly a century ago, one end of the cesspool opened, flushing the runoff water and debris beneath the grounds of the surrounding community.

Behind the wheel of the Emergency vehicle sat Ed Frank, controlling the winch lines. He heard Agent Bach's holler for help. With Bach's line near full extension, the sudden impact of the dead weight of the girl's body loosened the winch from its mooring. Tony was left in a most precarious position, with an unidentified woman's dead body wrapped around him hanging a few feet above a swirling river of sewage.

"Don't argue with me, Stan. I'm the one responsible for this investigation and I'm not going to allow another one of my people to fall injured or perish on my watch. Now stand aside." Stan acknowledges and does as ordered. "Ed," Michalene shouts, "Take me down slow and give me all the slack you can when I ask for it."

"Got it, Ma'am."

As she's lowered, Mike rocks back and forth. With each sway, she gains momentum. When across from Tony, she flings herself onto him. Pressing up hard against the female's corpse to keep it from slipping away, Mike wraps her legs around the semi-conscious Swat Team leader, unlatches his winch feed and replaces it with her own.

"Ed! Ed, now. Bring us up. And keep it steady." With the dead girl's hair in one hand and Bach's nylon webbing wrapped around her other, the three reach the top of the 3'x5' aperture without further incident. First the body, then Tony and finally Mike arrive at the top. Her adhoc metal sled having performed ideally during the extraction, is now being put to use to transport the corpse from beneath the mobile home, securing any evidence it may hold from being dislodged by the gravel driveway.

"Ed, a body bag. I need one, now." Fire Marshall Sullivan orders.

Immediately, EMT Nowak went to work on Tony Bach's lacerations. Following a tetanus booster, he was up walking around. He was alright. "Wow. Thank you, Mike. Tony says to his boss. You're one hell of a lady. I'm grateful."

4:13 pm, on the ground below Shirin's mobile home at McKinney's trailer park.

State Trooper Lt. Tim Keating returns to the scene and reports in:

"I need to update you, Mike."

"Go."

"We are receiving unprecedented support from the neighborhood and its businesses but we have yet to find even a trace of the guy you call the Frog. My men will continue to search till dark and throughout the night but…"

"Hold one. That may not be necessary. There may be another approach. How many men can you spare?"

"How many do you need?"

"All who are not claustrophobic who can work in shifts."

"What do you have in mind, Mike?"

"Stand firm. You'll have your answer within thirty. Stan, what's Lt. Buckwald's first name?"

"Charlie, why?"

Mike hollers, "Hey Charlie, you got a minute?" Excited, Mike thinks she may have found the key to the mystery of how the Frog has eluded capture and how Shirin moves about unseen.

Charlie Buckwald sticks his head under the trailer. "Yes Ma'am. How can I help?"

"Come on. Crawl in, Charlie and hop aboard. Wrap your legs around me and grab hold of the line. I caught a glimpse of something down there. You know the history of this area better than any of us. I need your help to identifying what I saw."

"Ah Agent Westgate, I don't feel comfortable…"

"Charlie, you're shy? Don't be. Come on, you're wasting daylight. Let's go."

Cook County Fire fighting lieutenant Charlie Buckwald as ordered, crawls underneath Shirin's aluminum habitat, wraps himself around the beautiful federal agent, looks down into the darkened, ever-widening cavity below, snickers and says, "Now why would someone park their mobile home over a giant, hundred year old, make-shift, wooden, toilet?" Before anyone could offer a response Charlie answers his own question, "So the bad guys can get in and out without being seen. Okay. Got it!"

"Ed." Mike hollers,"Take us down about 18 feet and hold." With that the two begin their descent.

CHAPTER FIFTY

Stopping at the prescribed level the two conjoined history buffs ogle what appears to be the uppermost portion of a seven by five foot iron door with an avalanche of dirt and debris in front of it.

"Like something off the battleship Maine, right, Charlie?"

"It's certainly the same vintage. No doubt about that. Good eye but my guess is it's a repurposed boiler room door. If this is the site of a late nineteenth century railroad turnabout, I'd say it's off a steam locomotive."

"You think there's a service entrance behind it?"

"It looks that way but there is only one way to find out."

"We got to get a crew down there to dig."

"Yes Ma'am. Say, I just thought of something. I'm pretty sure I can get a few lead guys from the Illinois Mining Institute down here. The two I'm thinking of love this kind of shit. Excuse me Ma'am. I'm sorry."

"It's Mike. Go ahead, continue."

"What I mean is, a chance to be the first to explore a hundred year old, still functioning underground, waste disposal system while aiding the Feds in solving a crime, hell, they'd pay you for the opportunity!"

"Give me a moment, Charlie. Let's see if we're looking at this issue the same way. The sludge that we recently released is now built-up against our presumed service door, correct?"

"Yes, and there's no way anyone is going to gain access from the other side."

"I want to gain access from this side, Charlie. In order to do that the sludge has to be moved from in front of the door onto the trap flooring to the right, agreed?"

"A mountain of muck? It's awfully tight quarters down there Agent Westgate...ah Mike but yes, you're right. That's what should be done."

"No, Charlie. That's what needs to be done."

From eighteen feet below the earth, with darkness falling and the wind picking up, Mike and Charlie are hauled back to the surface.

"Stan, what's the situation along the Belmont-Cragin corridor?"

"Manpower is stretched. There's been additional disruptions. Volcanologists at the University of Washington reported a 4.5 quake at the Madrid fault. With the size of the Belmont-Cragin explosion and resulting fires above ground, it had originally gone unnoticed. Gas lines were affected along with water and other major utilities. We're on it but the oil company personnel arrived late. They're giving my people a hard time. Some folks are just damn smart for their own good."

"'Smart' isn't the issue, Stan. It's arr⌐ word and I'll call Governor Thom⌐

intervene. If that doesn't get those feds moving forward, President Carter has already offered his full support."

"Let me have one direct face-to-face with them before we call in the big guns."

"Go ahead, take off. If you can, leave me your three men. Get eyes on the problem but don't forget about us."

"Be back as soon as I can."

"Lt. Keating."

"Yes, Mike."

"You asked what I had in mind. First that trailer park's office, that's our new C P. Do you know the guy they call Pig Pen?"

"Sure do, the Illinois Bell phone company Supervisor Thomas Penn, the one always pictured in the news up to his neck in dirt installing buried lines..."

"...And hanging perilously from telephone polls removing wind-swept debris?"

"That's the guy."

"Get a hold of him. His no nonsense approach is now vital to this investigation. I need two, telephone lines, the weather-be-damned type over there at our make-shift command post. That means underground, no exceptions. Secondly, I'm going to need your State Troopers for a special mission."

Mike explains the challenge that lies ahead to State _per Lieutenant Tim Keating and his men.

"Agent Westgate, Mike...please, no further explanation required. If that's what needed, my men will meet the task head-on, whatever it takes. Hell, clearing a path through a mountain of shit that's nothing new to us. There's a Zayre's hardware store down the street. I've had considerable contact with one of the founding Feldberg's grand kids. Let me make a call. I'll requisition all the shovels, hard hats and wheelbarrows the manager can spare."

"Pass on the wheelbarrows. Down there, they'll be more of an obstacle than an asset"

Repurposing Shirin's trailer skirt from a stretcher to a sled now to a far more viable earth moving instrument than a wheelbarrow, it was lowered into the abyss, quickly becoming an integral part of the action taking place, below.

6:12 pm With what equipment the *Rapid Intervention* fire fighters had on hand, Buckwald and Nowak with Mike in the lead are down below doing what they can to breakthrough the mountainous accumulation in front of the iron door.

With a quick burst from his siren Keating, who had been out rounding up his men and making telephone calls, signals his return. Arriving with more than a dozen Troopers walking at the head of two Zayre pick-up trucks loaded with shovels, pick-axes, ten gallon water dispensers, additional lighting and Zayre employees, each wanting to pitch in to do whatever was needed to bring a halt to the bizarre series of violence ravaging their community, was a welcomed sight. Zayre employees quickly disembarked, lining the immediate area with kerosene lamps.

"Don't forget, Lieutenant Keating. Dad said all this is yours. No charge. If you need more just call. He'll have it delivered, pronto." offered the twenty-two year old former delinquent to the man who pleaded the case on the kid's behalf that gained him access to college. "And thanks again. You saved my life. My whole family is grateful to you."

3:46 am Monday morning:

From twenty-feet below, with cops and the citizens they serve working side-by-side, not all but enough of the muck and mire had been cleared from in front of the oddly out of place iron door. As Cook County's Fire Department Lt. Charles Buckwald had predicted, that edifice had once been the face of a steam locomotive's boiler. Like all others of its time, it had a four foot wide metal gateway near its center through which the boiler could be stoked. Or in this case, through which the average five foot eight to six foot tall male could quickly make their way from one side to the other.

5:43 am Monday morning:

The tapping of an Iowa State University graduation ring against the trailer park's office window brought a young man lying on the floor inside springing to his feet, weapon drawn as Special Agent Steve Donaldson pressed his ID to the window. With a finger to his lips, pointing to Michaelene, Steve shakes his head signaling not to wake her. He then motions to the Bureau's Swat Team Leader to join him outside. There, the student and his Quantico small arms teacher reconnect.

"You were the best, sir. Everyone thought so." Tony offers.

"And you were that pesky kid who kept following me around asking so many questions. Of course I remember you. You're smart. Damn smart Listen, I just got back from London. I need to brief SAC Westgate but before I do bring me up to speed."

"Roger that. I'll start by saying Mike well, she's amazing. She's god damn Wonder Woman!"

"Okay, got that but?"

Tony then describes how a fresh application of graphite to the hinges of the iron door allowing its joints to move freely, was the first clue happened upon. That signaled that the Frog and perhaps even Shirin had just minutes before, used it to enter their escape route.

"What iron door?"

Tony stops, realizing he jumped way too far ahead. He restarts by detailing how two state detectives followed Shirin to this trailer park last night. Then, together with their colleagues, they threw a 'No one in/ no one out security blanket' over this entire area."

The Bureau's Swat Team leader goes onto to describe to his former mentor how the rain water runoff and then that from the fire hydrant disappeared under Shirin's mobile home. That led Mike directly below it, to an underground thruway. In that, the iron door was found. Bach then describes how the walls of a century-old, railroad waste disposal sluice collapsed, jettisoning the Frog's last known female victim onto him.

Then noticeably moved, Tony portrayed with considerable detail – using body language - Mike's daring rescue of both himself and the body of the young girl. He then told how he, Fireman Buckwald and two Cook County miners wearing headlamps with Mike in the lead, opened the iron door. On the other side was Chicago's, long-abandoned, sewage canal with enormous cracked and splintered Orangeburg conduit pipes littering the sub-flooring, evidence of why those a century before no doubt, struggled to install that iron door.

"Then the trail ran cold," offers Bach, "and Mike called a halt to the investigation for the night. When all who came to help left, Mike and I took refuge in this old building and fell asleep. Then you arrived. End of briefing. Questions, sir?"

Before Steve could fashion a thought into a query, the door of the trailer park office burst open and out shot Michaelene wide-awake.

"You're dismissed Agent Bach. Go home Get some sleep. That's an order...and thanks for playing body guard. Be back by eleven hundred hours. You'll remain my POC at this location until further ordered. Clear?"

"Yes, Ma'am. Clear."

Tony recovers his gear from the trailer park office then heads down the driveway to his vehicle parked a few blocks away. Mike turns to Steve, grabbing his face with both hands. As the cold, rain-free, *Top of the Morning* Illinois air filled both their lungs, Mike's shoulders relax as she falls into one of her ever-so-rare, school girl giddy states of mind. Steve thought it was a reaction to a lack of sleep. It wasn't.

Steve offers, "You need to hear what I found out in London."

"No, no. Me first, me first."

Given that Mike, Steve's grown-up boss had reverted back to an assemblage of their high school days, he took a shot.

"Damn girl, you look like shit and you smell like it too."

"Shit, yes, shit. That's right. That's exactly it, well almost. No, not quite. Oh, come on. Don't you remember? Galileo and Copernicus? Think, Agent Donaldson you big stud, think?"

"Is this another one of your Aesop's fables?"

"No. Our Junior year high school field trip to the Chicago Art Museum? Come on. You remember! You've got to remember?"

"Oh you're talking about that painting?"

"Yes, yes!"

"The one of a long-haired, greasy looking dude in a robe with his hand resting on a human skull. You were so infatuated with that painting I had to drag you away from it. I mean, I didn't know you then. I just felt sorry for you. The bus was about to leave. Yeah, I remember. It was kinda embarrassing but right now and far more importantly, you need to hear what I need to tell you."

"No, it wasn't a skull. It was a bust of Copernicus, a fellow polymath roughly a century removed from Galileo." With that, Michaelene was now bursting with energy, intellectually rebooted into her adult self.

"A what?"

"A polymath? Okay, well, that's someone whose knowledge spans several of the hard sciences like physics, astronomy, chemistry, how the secular world came to be. That kind of thing. The founding precept of polymaths is widely known. It's simply that nothing exists in a vacuum. Nothing exists without precondition."

"Affirmative. I get that. So?"

"One thing is always built upon another. Don't you see? That's it."

"What's it?"

"When my team and I opened that iron door there was nothing on the other side. No Shirin or the Frog or footprints on the walkway or hand prints against the wall...nothing to provided any indication where these two men individually or collectively, might have gone. There's just this elongated corridor of old, large, broken and discarded, jagged-edged sewage pipes. The fully functioning, updated version ran above our heads. Agent Bach and a miner with a headlamp, headed north through the corridor approximately a quarter mile. There they found that engineers years before, had collapsed that end using boulders excavated assumably from the nearby Chicago River.

"And on the opposite end?"

"Lt. Keating, myself and another member of the Illinois Miner's Association, a man named Joe Wilson, ran into a similar wall on the southern end. It however, was earthen, just clay and sand. As it turned out, Mr. Wilson is also the Assistant Director of Public Works for the city, a close friend and associate of the fire marshall. Wilson reached out to Stan for a briefing before setting out to join us. Joe arrived with maps of the underground infrastructure for this entire area dating as far back as 1898. Neither the railroad's handiwork or its corridors appear on any of the city's official schematics or support documents although the above-ground railroad tracks, does. Wilson concluded that the building of the underground cistern, its mechanisms and corridor was a rogue operation carried out by the railroad to avoid city inspectors. Over time its usage running alongside the designated sewage system of its day stressed it causing irreparable damage. When it was discovered the pipes had ruptured, Public Works shut it down but left the grate over the hole beneath Shirin's trailer to vent the system. Because it was not on the official books, with time its existence was simply forgotten How Shirin's mobile home came to rest over it was obviously by design. When we were down there we were looking up, looking for ways to climb above the modern infrastructure above our heads to street level while trying to determine how…"

"…How breathable air gained access to such an extensive corridor?"

"Yes, exactly. There was nothing. No additional grates or vents. Absolutely nothing."

"That's not possible?"

"You're right. So a few hours ago I suspended that phase of the investigation, came back to this office, fell asleep at one end of the floor as Agent Bach did the same at the other. I awoke seeing two men, he and you through the window. That's when Galileo and Copernicus popped into my head. It's simple, really."

"Perhaps for you."

"What's up is the city of Chicago."

"That's a given."

"To find what Galileo hoped to discover through Copernicus - the answer to whatever riddle of the universe he was seeking - he sought its essence by reconnecting by every available means to its past. The answer to our riddle Steve, how a butchering psychopath and a frenzied scientist continue to appear and then disappear is not above our heads, it's below our feet. There is something else down there, something below that 19th century sewage system."

"Sounds like I returned at just the right time. Now what?"

"I sent DeMille back to the office with one of your on-loan Iowa Agents with orders to let Haskell know that the Frog is still at large. It's nearly six am. We have a car. I have the keys. Let's head for my home. You're right. I do smell like sewage. I need a quick shower and a change of clothes before walking into the office."

"Good god, please. Not a repeat performance?"

"This time we'll be going in together. You can wait in the living room and I'll be grateful knowing you're there. Come on. I'll drive."

As the two make their way across the street to the parking lot behind the corner liquor store, Steve briefs Michaelene on what he learned while in London. Steve reiterates that Dr. Randolph Shirin, a nuclear physicist is indeed the son of the notorious microbiologist Dr. Shiro Ishii. He goes onto explain how Shirin's old man had taught himself how to manipulate DNA, weaponizing certain bacteria to limit the number of female births in human beings. That 'Operation No Pao' needed a first term nurturing environment to grow the virus.

"I remembered the stinkweed I rolled in, its choking scent. And somehow chlorophyll's magnesium atom stitches all the bad shit ingredients together."

"Everything green and growing is chlorophyll based."

"And this entire city area sits on a swamp. The ideal 'nurturing environment' for pathogens."

Suddenly Mike hits the brakes. Turning the car around instead of heading for her home, the two are headed to Bureau headquarters. As they walk in, all eyes are on Mike. An American Army tunnel rat in Vietnam having just crawled out after a day long excursion could not have looked more worn. But as is well known, looks can be deceiving. Mike was one hundred percent on point.

"Sally, Get me Chief Willard on the phone. Agent Donaldson, in my office." As the two enter the headquarter's anteroom, Sally's voice on the intercom, penetrates its deafening silence.

"Line three Mike. It's Professor Winfell."

"Tell him to hold, Sally. I'll be with him as soon as I can."

The phone rings in Chief Willard' office. "Yes, Agent Westgate, I know exactly who you mean. She's sitting across from me this very moment."

Still badly shaken, the twenty-two year old African-American woman seen by Steve wearing a blue, polka dot dress is in the local police headquarters filing a formal report. The Frog was staring into her apartment window late last night. Nearly an hour ago, Teresa Williamson, a single mother, had walked into the police station, laying her purse in front of its desk sergeant, asking him as she stepped back, to extract her 38 caliber revolver from it."

"It's illegal. I know that." she said to the desk sergeant. "I bought it off the street. I wasn't willing to be the Chicago area's next female victim. I went out after him. When I got there he was gone but I knew it was him."

"Really? How?" asked the desk sergeant wanting not to appear gullible.

"I recalled his scent."

As Teresa was escorted down the hall, the next police officer she encountered interrogated her. "Are you certain you weren't hallucinating?" Miss Williamson's answer was "ripe with pluck and persistence," the officer reported. That got her in front of Chief Willard. As she agreed to take a seat, the phone rang.

"No, Agent Westgate, it wasn't an offensive odor. The Japanese man I stood next to in the crowd you addressed had an earthy scent about him like the Peat Moss my father before he passed, would add to our lawn each year."

The two women spoke for another moment before Mike offered, "Thank you, Teresa. I mean it. You've been a big help. Congratulations. A perfect score on your SATs. You bested mine."

Mike picks up the other line. "Yes, Teddy, What do you have for me?" Michaelene quickly changed her tone of voice.

"I just returned the key to Shirin's lab as ordered. I'm certain no one saw me at any point."

"Good. Go ahead. You're on speaker phone. Tell me, Once inside, what did you observe in Shirin's lab?"

"There were mathematical equations filling each of four large blackboards, hieroglyphics to me save for one group that looked like the astrological sign for 'female' followed by the infinity symbol, a minus sign then a whole lot of numbers that looked like comparative calculations. I have no idea what they mean but apparently Shirin was hard at work."

"Why do you say that?" Michaelene asks.

"Well, in the middle of the lab there's an elongated metal table. One end faces the blackboards. There, on that one end, was a nine to ten inch wide binder made out of what appeared to be bamboo. In it were two, tightly rolled scrolls with a third unrolled stretching out a good foot and a half along the top of the table. The writing on it was delicate, Asian of some sort. The only thing I could make out were an assortment of diagrams and timelines. The diagrams were cross sections of human anatomy. Weird huh?"

"Go on."

"Aside the wooden binder was a more modern, eight by eleven inch college workbook, the kind a student would have. The information in it was handwritten in German. I could make out bits and pieces of that. It looked like Professor Shirin was deciphering information from both sources then compiling what he learned onto the black-board. You know what was really odd?"

"Tell me?"

"While there it struck me. I had met this guy."

"In what context?"

"He showed up after class a few months back with of all things, a Swiss, grammar school textbook titled ' History of the Development of the United States.' Inside it, was a foldout map of Ft. Dearborn, you know, the last one, the one built in 1816? You went to high school around here, right?"

"I told you that I had."

"Right, on our first date. I remember. So, back in high school you must have learned something about Ft. Dear-born?"

"Please. Get to the point, Teddy."

"Well, professor Shirin was fascinated by the size of the fort but especially its outbuildings, asking what they were used for. I told him that they functioned primarily as sentry posts, part of an early-warning system. They were connected to the fort and each other by an under-ground tunnel system. Each tunnel was built tall and wide, allowing its sentry to run upright as fast as possible to the main fort to provide advance warning of an emi-nent attack or for additional riflemen to quickly move unencumbered from one position to another. Shirin was fascinated by one outbuilding in particular."

"Which one?"

"The one that sat nearest the southern bank of the Chicago River. I had to confess as a historian, that outbuilding held a certain allure for me as well. I told him that it was doubtful that even its remnants were still there. The whole structure was most likely destroyed when the river was dredged in the 1850's. I told him I once went looking for where the tunnel's exit might have been. I wound up in some trailer park. I mean heck, around the turn of the century, the railroad built one of their turnaround stops atop of where the tunnel might have been long before that trailer park was laid out in the 1940's. Like all modern developments, this area and Chicago itself, is like one of my grandmother's Southern Lane cakes."

"Meaning what?"

"It's a hodgepodge of cream-filled leftovers layered one on top the other. So, is all forgiven? Are we good?"

"Yes, we're good."

"Oh heck, I almost forgot? Maybe you can help me understand one thing."

"I'll try?"

"Why would a nuclear physicist need an incubator in his lab?"

"I'm not certain I understood?"

"It was an incubator. Isn't that the damnest thing? I wouldn't have known it was there if I hadn't tripped over the edge of a blanket covering the thing."

"Not only are we even, I owe you one. Good job. Thank you."

"Well, you know I'm free this Saturday night if…"

"Good bye, Teddy."

Michaelene then dialed Federal Judge Bartholomew Harris. As his phone rang, her head filled with the sound of heavy metal objects and broken glass hitting the floor above her head while lying beneath Shirin's mobile estate.

"Could that have been the sound of numerous incubators," Mike pondered, "falling onto a hollow wooden floor?"

Bucky listened to Mike's explanation without question for a good thirty seconds before authorizing a warrant for a complete search of Shirin's trailer park home, lab, office, lecture hall and classroom. Wasting no time, Director Kelly was next. To her boss, Michaelene strongly suggested that he alert the headquarters of the Center for Disease Control in Atlanta then brief President Carter. She'd coordinate with the local CDC mobile center at O'Hare. Michaelene made it clear that the Belmont-Cragin explosion, the resulting devastation to the oil refinery, an elusive savage killer and even the recently discovered breach in the Madrid fault line were each part of a well-researched, well-laid out and exceptionally well executed plan to divert attention while the weaponization of the principal instrument, a recently learned hybrid contagion enters its final phase of development and distribution. A threat to the people of the United States and potentially to all throughout the North American continent is imminent with Chicago to be the first hit. An odorless, colorless contaminant bearing the Imperial Japanese code name, "No Pao" has the potential to literally spread through every blade of grass and blossoming flower ultimately reducing the number of females born throughout each exposed region for generations. "No Pao" also has serious ramifications to the living, eating away the immune system of the physically weak and aged. To thwart the contagion's spread the first step was the eradication of nature's 'aerosol can,' Stinkweed. Throughout the Chicago river basin and into the uplands action had to be taken immediately. For that Big Jim Thompson was the man to call.

Still, through all this, save for Teresa Williamson's eye witness account of the night before, no sighting of either Shirin or the Frog, had been reported. Too, no new bodies of mutilated women had turned up on any police blotter throughout the greater Chicago area and that was very good news! But it also raised suspicions.

Shortly before nine am, the CDC unit from O'Hare arrived on the University of Chicago campus as Michaelene promised, without fanfare. Wheeling-in a large wooden crate marked 'toilet' pass an onslaught of students rushing to various classes, the CDC team was comprised of two female bio-tech pros and one burly African-American Bureau Agent named Israel assigned to make certain that all went smoothly. Using Dr. Marsolan's passkey they entered Shirin's lab. Once the door was closed, the three broke open the crate, dawned hazmat suits stashed inside and extracted rebreathing units. With attire secured, the two women carefully set the incubator into the crate, sealed it then rolled it off campus into the back of a panel truck with Agent Israel providing the heavy lifting. All the while none about were the wiser.

Across town, the dual air brakes of a very long, non-descript, mobile lab pulled by a Freightliner turbo diesel, gave off a final gasp as it settled in for the duration at McKinney's trailer park. Before the door to Shirin's mobile home was opened the CDC team on board, distributed four, Level A, encapsulated chem suits, hairnet and boot covers to Mike, Steve, Tony Bach and Tim Keating. With none willing to leave, none were allowed a step further without them. When the phone rang inside the trailer park office, Mike was dawning hers. A CDC official answered it.

"Agent Westgate, it's for you, Ma'am. It's Washington."

The CDC official did her best to fain a suitable level of disappointment as she saw in the distance, Agent Westgate shake her head side-to-side. "Sir I'm sorry. Agent Westgate is inside her chem gear. There's no way I can get her attention right now."

"This is Director Kelly of the FBI. Let her know she is to halt her investigation immediately. Until the CDC provides me with an all clear notice, she is not to risk her life any further. Fighting a microscopic enemy falls well outside her training. She is to report back to her office immediately. Let her know that's a direct order."

Not being one to disobey such an order but rather to interpret it as she saw fit, Mike stepped out of her hazmat gear. Steve, Tony and Tim, following suit did the same. The four instead, led by Agent Westgate, crawled under the trailer and were already twenty feet underground probing the earthen corridor below as a crowbar pried open the mobile home's door. Michaelene would later learn she was right. Inside there were perhaps a dozen incubators stacked in a corner with several more with splintered glass spewed out across the floor. And there was something else. Four, corked test tubes once elevated by a metal hanging devise, were lying in the sink.

The man most likely to be the University of Chicago's newest Provost, Dr. Sedgewick Abelson, a brilliant mathematician who's convinced that the only way to save the planet was to radically reduce the number of its human inhabitants- thus during the war having collaborated with his Nazi captors - was now young Professor Shirin's enabler, providing the physics prodigy and Sonny, his pet Troglodyte whom he labeled a necessary evil, with jacks and timbers to secure the historic tunnel the two had adopted. As the need to prolong the distraction arose, a series of safe houses throughout the greater Chicago area were also made available to the deceptive duo, frequented especially by Sonny, the "Frog."

After the war, pointing to where the Nazis had hidden his fellow descendants of Jacob's treasures for a cool fifteen percent per item brokerage fee made Abelson a very wealthy man. But the university's vetting process had not reached a final conclusion nor had this investigation.

Shirin and Abelson had rendezvoused at a specific location they both knew well, a ditch on the southern shore of the Chicago River. There they scheduled to meet with Sonny. He was late. Through a mishmash of previously conveyed hand gestures, it had been told to the son of Kempeitai Sgt. Hiroki Yoshida - the conductor in July of 1944 of the deaths of thousands of sexually abused women and children by way of the jungle's hidden refractory ovens - that he needed to kill again. To keep investigating authorities distracted and tethered to their emotions, this time the scene had to surpass all that had come before. For the task, the Frog envisioned Teresa Williamson and her ten year old daughter Maya but Sonny was soon to confront the harsh reality that he'd never lay eyes on Teresa, Maya or on any other living being, again.

From 1850 through 1914 the industrial age in America, went balls-to-the-wall, ballistic. Among its most heralded achievements was the brilliantly engineered reversal of the Chicago River. Completed in 1900, it is the only river in the world that runs backwards.

Seventy-eight years later, prior to the firing of that single shot from the eighth floor of an abandoned Belmont-Cragin apartment complex, the one that set in motion a devastating chain of events ultimately reaching the ear of the President of the United States, Abelson had hired two workmen to build a reverse throughflow with a control gate off the river's boggy southern shore. The throughflow would allow water from the river to rapidly rush downward filing the earthen cavities below - including the Ft. Dearborn's sentry tunnel - with silt and soil while unleashing unimaginable horror on anyone trapped beneath. The throughflow's width, depth and mandated running time had been calculated by Abelson. The 1816, reconstituted Fort Dearborn tunnel in which Sonny the "Frog" remained in hiding would fill to capacity in exactly three point eight minutes. The tunnel above filled with jagged-edged broken sewage pipe in which Mike, Steve, Tim and Tony were continuing their explorations, would be completely sealed off in under nine. That gives the quartet of law enforcement's finest plus or minus twelve minutes to live or die.

"Wait. What are you doing? He's still needed."

"Get your hands off of me. No! He is not. You should have eliminated him days ago. What if he's captured. What then?"

"He wouldn't talk."

Oh, thank you for reminding me. I neglected to mention that I happened upon Sonny at one of the safe houses. I hadn't filled its refrigerator with his demands. He lost his temper telling me to…oh what is America's favorite colloquialism? Ah yes, to go fuck myself. His English is better than yours and less burden by accent." With that, Abelson says, "time to settle accounts" and lifts the control gate.

Tony Bach when first settling in at the twenty foot mark, recovered his military grade, transistor radio-sized, flashlight. Checking it, its built-in, three colored lens and emergency signaling strobe were still in tact.

534

"Look out! Move. Get out of the way!" Tim hollered as he dropped a packaged, thirty foot, climber's rope and pick-axe down the narrow aperture beneath Shirin's mobile fortress landing inches away from Tony's feet. Both rope and axe were acquired by way of a last minute 'snatch and grab' acknowledged by the store's security guard as the State Trooper walked out of Zayre's hardware store.

Upon Tim's descent, he and Bach elected to retrace the tunnel's quarter mile long northern heading hoping to find yet another up or down passageway while Mike and Steve headed in the opposite direction towards the earthen, southern wall. Both men were less than a hundred yards in when a sinkhole crashed to the bottom of the man-made tunnel right behind them. Believing at first that the water at the soles of their feet had gained access by way of that natural phenomenon, they're minds quickly changed when the water rushing in began splashing above their ankles.

At the other end, Michaelene watched as the water released by the control gate began percolating through the aged mud and sand barricade. At an ever-increasing pace, tension rose as its composition deteriorated. Then suddenly as if shot from a pellet gun, bits of earthen wall spat out loosening large chunks falling to the feet of the two agents.

"Here. Steve. Over here. Quick. Help me. Come on, push."

"No wait. You want to punch a whole through the wall? That will only make it come down faster."

"You're right. So get over here and help me push this thing." Moments away from either drowning or being buried alive, Steve looked at Michaelene and saw in her eyes the love for him to which she had clinged so tightly for so many years. And then he recognized her game plan.

"Oh yeah. Good call. Just try and stop me now." He said as he gave her an affirmative nod, setting aside his oft-repeated f-word, in deference to her.

With the backs of the two former high school sweethearts to that of a near-century old broken piece of serrated sewage pipe, they pushed, giving it all they had until the heavily saturated earthen wall began to fatally crumble.

"Go, go. Duck inside. The pipe will protect ..." Michaelene ordered, gasping for air... "It will protect you. I'll give a final push then jump in behind you."

"No way, you go first. I'll push."

Mike shook her head at Steve's stubborn, albeit calm and kind of sweet, cavalier gesture but it ended there. Grabbing him by his shirt collar, Mike pulled Steve into her, kissing him hard on the lips, then kicked him in his right knee.

"What the..." admonished Steve. As he bent in agony.

Michaelene gave it an all-out, last minute, *hell's a'comin,* push. Still, it was the weight and momentum provided by Steve's body as she heaved him into the over-sized sewage pipe before diving in herself, that propelled the two federal agent's makeshift berth forward, collapsing the earthen wall emptying like a sludge-filled aqueduct onto the southern shore of the Chicago River. A few yards away stood two men, the enabler a quisling Jew and the executioner, a mad Japanese scientist each hell bent on achieving their version of a better world by way of the mass destruction of human life. Both were busily pounding the last breath out of the washed up body of Sonny Yashida. Startled, they looked up.

Recognizing both agents from the Parish steps, Shirin shouts, "FBI". Then like a frustrated little boy who never played catch with his dad - or anyone else for that matter - throws the rock in his hand in limp-wrist fashion at Michaelene. Pathetically it falls short, landing at the river's edge, a good two feet from its intended target. Seeing that, nuclear physics professor Dr. Randolph Shirin, Ph.D., begins to weep. First at being caught, recognizing that his grandiose plan to be the hero of his nation would never come to light. Then, it dawned on him. He was just like his father Shiro Ishii. He too, was a failure. The only difference was, dad lived out his days a free man. No such luck would befall his bastard son.

Abelson, the treasonous Jew - a 'Kapo' to his people - a trained gunman only to the extent his ego provided such an illusion, pulled a German Luger from behind his back, aiming it at the first Agent he saw, the Bureau's lead small arms and explosives expert. Failing to steady himself before pulling the trigger, he missed. Big mistake.

With its three beep, emergency call signal unable to transmit from such a depth, Tim's walkie-talkie, was useless. Unshaken by the reality of their pending demise - as the water rose nearing their knees - FBI Swat Team Leader Tony Bach and State Trooper Lieutenant Tim Keating had only one option. They improvised.

Banished from McKinney's trailer park by the on-site, Center for Disease Control Commander who told them to, "Get as far away as possible but don't leave the area. We may need you," Cook County Fire officials Lt. Charlie Buckwald, EMT Nowak and machinist Ed Frank chose the parking lot behind the corner liquor store across the street. There they sat on a curb waiting the return of their boss, Fire Marshall Sullivan.

"What the hell?"

Dawning his eye glasses to read nearby signage, Charlie Buckwald noticed something odd bouncing off its lens. It was a signal from tiny red strobe light behind where the three men were sitting. It seem to appear out of nowhere then slowly fade.

Swat Team Leader Tony Bach, thinking laterally, replaced the clear lens on his flashlight with its red counterpart. He then set it on strobe. State Trooper Keating fashioned Tony's flashlight to the pick-axe. It took several attempts but on the fifth the two men were able to toss the pick-axe with Tim's thirty foot rope attached, up and through the gaping sinkhole to catch hold to the ground, above. Buckwald and Nowak having hurried to the scene, pulled on either end of the pick-axe while machinist Ed Frank the only one with gloves, steadied the rope as all pulled. Tim was first out. Seconds before the water from the Chicago River gushed upward through the sinkhole, Agent Bach popped out. His smile was infectious. His laughter even more so. "really god? Twice in one day?" he shouted.

Tim nudged him with a boot to his shoulder saying, "Hey Febe, what do you say? I'll buy the first round."

"You got it pal but only if I can buy the second and the fourth and these firemen come along."

Steve the former Army Ranger, seeing a German Luger raised in his direction, dove into the icy cold water of the Chicago River, returning fire.

Like so many who dream, who count and speculate dismissing their fellow human beings as nothing but statistical anomalies, Abelson's blood-soaked brain matter slapping the face of the 'hoity-toity," wanna-be, mass murderer standing but a few inches behind the turncoat Jew, brought Dr. Randolph Shirin, Ph.D nose to nose with the fragility of human life and on his knees awash in a pool of his own vomit, urine and meaningless tears.

Michaelene arrested the son of the most hated Japanese physician in modern times as she read him his Miranda Rights. In a free society where the rule of law presides, even the most debased and depraved of douchebags, those who facilitate others like Sonny 'The Frog' in the commission of a series of horrific crimes, have rights. Of course, that didn't stop Michaelene from dragging the good professor's sorry ass into the Chicago River 'to wash him off' before again, bringing him to his knees on shore to cuff him.

The CDC carefully removed the incubators and glass test tubes from Shirin's 1949 Spartian Manor, travel-trailer. Each were judiciously examined then all but two were placed onto the rotary kiln in the portable lab's hazardous waste incinerator. Joining them was that brought from Enrico Fermi's lab under the watchful eye of Agent Israel. Before reaching its 1,800 degrees Fahrenheit operating standard, the modern incinerator inside the CDC mobile lab upon ignition, went immediately to 850 degrees, the exact temperature that the jungle's refractory ovens reached as *five thousand sons and daughters of white clad souls in the month of July, 1944* - stripped of their rights at the hand of the Imperial Japanese - were forced to leave this earth with but one thing… a cry for mercy.

THE FINAL CHAPTER

"The way Frank explained it, the US was concerned after the war, that Japan would fall into chaos with militant groups struggling to cease power to again invade mainland China to cease its resources. China itself was deeply torn, in the throes of a civil war with Nationalist leader Chiang Kai-Shek vying for power against Mao Tze-Tung and his Communist party. It had been our guy, General Douglas McArthur's plan from the get-go to retool the Japanese economy, given that it was the most advanced throughout Asia, and refocus it with the hope of providing stability throughout the region. Many of Japan's war crimes were simply swept under the table by his orders, to accomplish that goal. The US occupied Japan for eight years with McArthur as 'Emperor,' He and Truman got them to enact a Constitution based upon our own with a "never go to war" clause in it. The treaty between us and them, the Treaty of San Francisco, was signed in 1951 but in Frank's view that wasn't even close to being enough. The Japanese require constant vigil and that treaty needed to be reviewed and revised every decade or so but Frank was not optimistic."

"In what way?" asks Mike.

"He felt DC would fail to keep tabs on them. That's how he summed the post war era while on our rather harrowing drive to the airport."

"Do you know if they agreed to ban Shinto?"

"Shinto is still practiced today by the vast majority of the Japanese people. Did you lock the front door?" asked Steve as he fluffs the pillow on his side of the bed.

"Yes, go to sleep."

"Are you sure?" Steve sarcastically persists, subtly reminding Michaelene of the time that he flushed Sonny from this very same house, likely saving her life.

For that, Steve got an elbow to his ribs followed by a quick kiss on the forehead and a deeply sincere "Thank you. Now go to sleep."

What's this? You've been crying."

Agent Sykes," Michaelene stops in mid-sentence. "No her name was Susan, Susan Ann Sykes. I was thinking of her and how she died helping that little boy. And it's sad too, I use to think Agent Edwards... Tommy was gay. As it turned out, his fiancée was a waitress at Chicago's Oriole Restaurant on West Walnut. Her name is Donna, Donna Fitzpatrick. She came by the office. I set aside a few minutes for her. She was hoping to find...well, a little piece of his soul. She loved him like I…"

"His loyalty to you demonstrated to me that he was one of the good guys."

"Thank you for that." Michaelene mused, wondering if the time was right to…

"Earlier this evening on my way over here," Steve speaks up, "I flashed on the Passport photo we pulled from our data base of Burt Tomlinson, Jeannie's husband. His resemblance to a younger Frank Clifford is uncanny. Same height and build. Ironic isn't it?"

"That our Frog was one pond removed from his target?"

Steve notices a book on Michaelene's nightstand. He picks it up and reads the inscription on the cover, aloud: "*The Sketch Book of Geoffrey Crayon, Gent.*" Wanting to change the subject he joked, "What, did you pose nude for this guy?"

"It's not that kind of sketch book. You would have liked him." She said as she brushes back a linger tear. "He too was a soldier."

"Should I be jealous?"

"It's a collection of short stories. Go ahead. Peel back the plastic cover. You'll see. It's a first edition signed by the author. Dad had it sealed when he bought it years ago to…"

"…protect it from your cream-soaked teenage hands?"

"No doubt. Dad was a huge fan of the author. Unfortunately, the much beloved *Barnacle Mike* passed away before he had the chance to break the seal and read the book, himself. Now that I'm on administrative leave, I pulled it out of dad's storage boxes. I had set it aside to read until you invited yourself over."

"Umm, Ma'am…you asked me, remember?"

"Is that what you're going to tell our kids?"

"Irving? This guy's handwriting is as bad as mine maybe worse. What does it say?" Steve rolls to Michaelene's side of the bed. "Hey, hey! Don't fall asleep yet. Wait. insists Steve. "I need your help. Can you read this inscription?"

"I don't have to read it. I know what it says."

"So?"

"Washington. The hen scratch to which you so dismissively referred reads, 'Washington.'"

"As in George?"

"No, as in Irving...Washington Irving."

"As in Sleepy Hollow fame?"

"Yes."

"But you said he was a soldier? What kind of a soldier or for that matter, what kind of a man goes around calling himself *Geoffrey Crayon Gent*? I don't get why your dad was so taken by this guy. Admiral Mike was a giant, a true historic figure of a man. I mean, this guy Irving had to be what, some kind of a wuss, right?"

"Look. If I walk you through this will you allow me to get some sleep tonight?"

"Sounds fair."

"You once said that if you had a chance to go back in time to any point in history, you'd choose..? Do you remember what you told me?"

"1814."

"And why?"

The Battle of New Orleans."

"And why?"

"To savor that one true, idyllic moment in American history... to stand alongside some four thousand, genuine patriots who came together from vastly different backgrounds..."

"...Free slaves, the town's women?"

"...Sharpshooters from Kentucky and Tennessee, Choctaw Indians, Jean LaFitte and his pirate crew all manning long rifles and cannon under the command of Colonel Andrew Jackson fighting selflessly against nearly eight thousand British regulars for a cause greater than themselves."

"America's freedom from foreign rule."

"And that was the ideal. There was something very grand about being a soldier then, chasing the British out of the colonies once and for all. What you were fighting for and what you were willing to die for was unmistakably clear not like my war, not like Vietnam."

Michaelene smiles knowingly and says, "Read the back cover, Hop-along!"

"What? How did you…? Okay. Oh wow, it says, "To Washington Irving, with gratitude, Andrew Jackson, General.""

"And beneath that?"

"To my most gracious friend Monsieur Irving, I would proudly stand by your side again, any time, anywhere. humbly yours, Jean LaFitte.""

"Like many of his fellow Frenchmen of his day, he was fluent in English.""

Are the signatures, real?""

"Dad thought so.""

"So the man who wrote *Sleepy Hollow* fought alongside Andrew Jackson and Jean Lafitte against the British at the battle of New Orleans? Really? No shit?""

"Washington Irving once stood right where you once dreamed of standing. Dad was fascinated by the duality of Irving's character.""

"In what way?""

"Dad, like Irving, was a warrior and, there can be no doubt about, my father was a romantic. I believe he hoped to discover more about himself through Irving's writings.""

"And the headless horseman?""

"A metaphor for facing one's fears…as did Irving the soldier.""

"As did you."

The phone rings.

"What time is it," Michaelene asks?

Steve reaches for his pants on the bedroom floor aside the bed. In one of its pockets, is his wrist watch. As he reaches for the instrument needed to answer Mike's question, his hand brushes the now bent and crinkled envelope given to him by Dr. Jeffreys. "It's 0:406... a little after four am?"

Mike answers the phone: "I see. Okay. No, I understand. That's fine. Thank you. I'll be there. What? No, but if I see him I'll give him the good news and tell him to call in."

"It looks like I've been reinstated."

"What about me?"

"Oh yeah, you too."

"Cute."

"However, you need to know one thing. My Temporary Duty assignment was revoked and I was passed over for permanent SAC status. It doesn't feel good but it's the decision I would have made if I was in Director Kelly's shoes."

"Well what about the CDC report? He got it last week. It proved that you saved the lives of countless millions in the nick of time."

"And I lost two exceptionally talented agents – two people with deeply meaningful lives - in the process."

"So, was that, Director Kelly?"

"Yes."

Michaelene turns to Steve and offers, "The Director gave us two options. He'll authorize a thirty day paid vacation for us both but when we return, we'll be brought before a review board..."

"For what?"

"Or, he said, he can make that go away if..."

"Tell me?"

"If we forego the vacation and accept an assignment to aid our Canadian allies with a recently discovered series of murders."

"We?"

"Yes, apparently some think we work well together."

"What's the issue?"

"The Vancouver police have discovered a series of mass graves throughout Stanley Park, a place for centuries, a center of Pagan rituals. A series of recently uncovered graves however, range from fresh to no more than ten years old. The RCMP sees us as two people experienced in dealing with ritualistic cult murders"

"Oh joy."

"The Director promised the Canadians our answer in twenty-four hours."

Remembering the folded envelope, Steve decided they'd both had enough for the night. He'd give it to her tomorrow.

Spooning, holding Michaelene tight, Steve stroked her hair then whispered gently in her ear, "I love you. See you in the morning." But Mike was already fast asleep.

There is in every true woman's heart a spark of heavenly fire, which lies dormant in the broad daylight of prosperity; but which kindles up, and beams and blazes in the dark hour of adversity.

Washington Irving, (1783-1859).

- WARNING: -

Be advised. The following addendum contains graphic photographs and quotes of a deeply disturbing nature.

It is the hard evidence invaluable to understanding the actions and motivations described throughout this novel.

Here lie five tho... ...els... souls, belov...
and daughters of white clad folks. These are of...
a homeless race suffered b... ...ins of ru...less Imperial
Japanese army, by whom ... were deprived of their rights
and were taken to the islands here and there like
innocent sheep, and th... were fallen to t... gr...
leaving behind them an eternal grudge.
Remember! A month of July 1944.

(What the facades of two of the Shinagawa Refractory Ovens on Tinian Island looked like in 1998 after Emet Saures, Glen Palacios and I spent the day with machetes, clearing jungles vines off these edifices)

http://www.shinagawa.com.au/   Their motto: *GLOBAL PROVIDER OF THERMAL SOLUTIONS.*

The Shinagawa Refractory Company began in 1875. On 12-12-01, its on-line history conveniently skips from 1938 to 1950, wiping clean nearly all reference to the war years save for a vague 1943 reference to its Manila branch. There is no mention of any construction activity at any time in the Mariana archipelago although this re-fractory oven, one of two still standing in 1998 amidst a field of bricks on Tinian Island, clearly bears the manu-facturer's signature trademark at its entry (It appeared next to my left shoulder as I crawled onto the first heavy steel grate. I had no knowledge of the Shinagawa com-pany at that time. What caught my attention was the "SS" above the manufacturer's name).

FOR FOURTEEN YEARS ACROSS HALF THE KNOWN WORLD, AN ESTIMATED *TWO MILLION* FEMALES WERE ABDUCTED FROM THEIR HOMES AND USED AS SEX SLAVES.

LABELED BY THEIR CAPTORS AS, "PIECES OF WOOD," OFTEN THESE WOMEN RANGING IN AGE

FROM PUBERTY TO SEVENTY-FIVE, UPON BEING DEEMED OF NO FURTHER USE, WERE BOUND TO-GETHER WITH BARBED WIRE, MARCHED AT THE TIP OF BAYONETS DEEP INTO THE NEAREST HIDDEN JUNGLE ENCLAVE, THEN FORCED TO STAND IN FRONT OF ONE OF ITS MANY HUMAN INCINCERA-TORS STARING DEEP INTO ITS APOPLECTIC FLAMES, THE WIRE AROUND THEIR NECKS MAKING IT IM-POSSIBLE TO LOOK AWAY. AS THEY STOOD SOOT-LACED, THE SICKENING ODOR OF BURNING FLESH WASHING OVER THEM , EACH KNEW THAT WITH THE NEXT *SNIP-SNIP* OF WIRECUTTERS THAT THEIR FATE WOULD FOLLOW THAT OF THEIR PREDECES-SORS; BEING STUFFED ALIVE THROUGH THAT RE-FRACTORY OVEN'S FRONT DOOR. OVER THE COURSE OF THREE NIGHTS, FIVE THOUSAND FE-MALES AND YOUNG BOYS MET SUCH A FATE WHERE THESE TWO OVENS STAND TODAY. WHAT ALIEN LIFE FORCE PERPETRATED SUCH UNCON-SCIONABLE ACTS OF EVIL…A VERY TERRESTRIAL ONE, THE IMPERIAL ARMED FORCES OF THE JAPA-NESE EMPIRE.

WORLD WAR TWO IN THE PACIFIC, ENDED ON AU-GUST 14TH, 1945. THE GOVERNMENT OF JAPAN

"SURRENDERED UNCONDITIONALLY." VIEWED BY SOME AS MERELY A "CESSATION OF HOSTILITIES," IN

A XENOPHOBIC CULTURE IN WHICH YOUNG BOYS LIKE THE CHARACTER IN THIS NOVEL "SONNY" ARE

RAISED, THE DEPRAVITIES OF THE FATHER GO UN-SPOKEN WHILE HIS IDEALS ARE PASSED DOWN THROUGH GENERATIONS, FROM FATHER TO SON. THE SUMMER OF '45 BROUGHT AN END TO WAR BUT NOT SO FOR *SHINTO*, THE PSEUDO-RELIGION THAT PROMOTED IT.

Someone once asked, "Why am I the one person in the world best suited to tell this story? The answer is easy. Simply because in June of 1998, I was perhaps, the only living being to unwittingly crawl into the human incinerators featured in this novel since they were last in use on July 3rd, 1945." Author, *Kenneth James Moore*.

THE RAPE OF NANKING

On December 13th, 1937, nearly two years before World War Two began in Europe, Imperial Japanese soldiers invaded Nanking, the capital city of China. Over the course of the following six weeks, 300,000 Chinese lost their lives to the genocide that ensued. Of the 300,000, most were women and children.

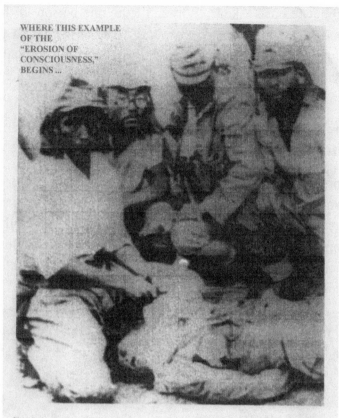

These Japanese soldiers are carving out the heart of a Chinese woman "to be an appetizer that goes with wine." The victim was Wang Jia-rang, a worker at the Nanking Yogilya Factory. The photo was taken on December 14ᵗʰ, 1938 as a souvenir of the occasion by one of its participants(Archives: Tokyo War Crimes Tribunal). By the time this photograph was taken, Japan had occupied China for 7 years.

FACTS OF THE MATTER:

Preface: For more than 62 years, from 1931 until 1993, The Japanese government categorically denied any knowledge of the use of "Comfort Women throughout the 20th Century." Faced with mounting pressure resulting from the1992, United Nations, *Commission on Human Rights* (Doc ECN 4SRR34), the Japanese government interviewed dozens of its citizenry, each a former member of Imperial Japan's wartime military. On February 24th, 1992, Japan's Economic News, reported a story that inspired this novel. The report contained the testimony of the real life Seijji Yoshida. The following year in 1993, the Diet, the Japanese Parliament, made public some of the less damaging, testimonies they had gathered. Here is a sample:

1992: The testimony of Seijji Yoshida, **Japan Economic News, February 24th, 1992, reporting on official testimonies before the Diet. Available on Lexus, Asiape Library, Jen file)** "When we arrived at a village, we dragged all women out into the streets. If anyone tried to flee, she would be beaten with a baton and loaded onto a truck. We beat down screaming young mothers and if two or three year old babies followed us, crying, they would be thrown away."

1992. **University of Melborne, Political Science Professor Toshiyuki Tanaka** "Officers ordered troops to eat human flesh to give them a feeling of victory." AP News 8/11/1992 published under the heading, "Japan Hears of WWII cannibalism a half century later."

<u>1994</u>: **Hastings International Law Review** *"Compensation for Japan's War-Rape victims,"* **1994. Page 505:** "Twenty Korean women from Seoul, were forced into becoming sex slaves in Burma. The women provided sex daily for up to 90 noncommissioned officers and soldiers and fifteen officers."

<u>1995</u>: **UN Commission on Human Rights UN DOC e/Cn.4/1993/Sr.27, as reported in the Harvard International Law Journal #36, 1995. Page 528** "High-ranking government officials knew of and authorized the systematic recruitment and deployment of 'comfort women.'"

<u>1995</u>: **Hastings Law Review, Spring Edition Volume 17, Page 499**Seijuro Arahune, a member of Japan's Liberal Democratic Party and parliamentary (Diet)) statesman, offered: "I know of 142,000-145,000 Korean comfort women alone who died. We killed them.".

<u>1995</u>: ." **Hastings Law Review, Spring Edition Volume 17, Page 499**Testimony before the Diet of Kiyoharu Yoshida, former Imperial Japanese police official operating in 'North Korea' during World War Two: "Police along with military officials took Korean mothers who were still nursing their babies to satisfy the army's demand for at least fifty 'special,' new, comfort women per week.

<u>1995</u>: **"'Comfort Women' in the Philippines," as reported in** *War Victimization and Japan:* **U.N. International Public Hearing Report Page. 148 (Available at Lexus, World Library)** "Some sex slaves were killed

shortly before Japanese soldiers surrendered. The women were lined up and beheaded."

<u>1996</u>: **Hastings International Law Review, Vol. 17, 1996. Page 506** "Women, including mothers and girls as young as twelve, were physically seized, torn from the arms of their families."

In his 1978 memoir, *Commander of 3,000 Men at Age 23*, Imperial Japanese Lieutenant

Yasuhiro Nakasone writes that he set up a 'Comfort Station" on the island of Borneo after "'procuring' *three* Indonesian women." From 1982 to 1987, Mr. Nakasone was the prime minister of Japan. (3 women to service 3,000 men? Prime Minister Nakasone's recollections as well as his mathematical skills may be drawn into question.)

<u>**Beginning in 1934, the Imperial Japanese military developed no fewer than six biowarfare experimental centers across occupied China with one in Beijing(Unit 1855) and additionally, one in Singapore(Unit 9420, the *Oku Unit*). The Kempeitai, Japan's army of secret police, operated their own facility, Unit 100. Unit 731, located in the Chinese province of Harbin, was under the command of Lieutenant General Shirō Ishii, "the Prince." At the largest of the six units, employed more than 3,600 physicians and support staff.**</u>

-Watts, J. (2002). Tokyo: Victims of Japan's notorious Unit 731 The

Lancet,360(9333), 628 (The Lancet is a weekly peer-reviewed general medical journal. It is among the world's oldest and most prestigious general medical journals).

- Yoshio Shinozuka, a Unit 731 veteran who was 16 years old at the time, recounted how the unit cultivated, bottled, and infected fleas with plague. He admitted taking part in five dissections of live Chinese prisoners, saying the Japanese soldiers at Unit 731 dismissed their victims as "logs".

- Shoichi Matsumoto, a former Unit 731 pilot, offered that he dropped fleas in 1940 and 1941. A Chinese bacteriologist explained that the plague that struck in 1940 was unusual because it came in winter rather than summer, killed human beings but few rats, and was carried by a flea that was not native to the region."

Japan's Emperor Hirohito was 'prevented from voicing remorse' over war

- According to newly disclosed documents, the wartime emperor had wanted to publicly express his regret after World War II

- But the prime minister stopped him, over fears the emperor would be perceived as having started the war

Agence France-Presse

Published: 12:18am, 21 Aug, 2019

Brief Author Bio

Kenneth James Moore

Ken received a Bachelor's of Science in political science from Arizona State University then continued his studies in international relations as a graduate student at Georgetown University. Following an internship with the National Security Agency, he was hired at Beverly Hills Securities in Beverly Hills, California, leading to a post as an international investment banker. Thereafter, and over the course of the next decade and a half, Ken owned and operated his own firm, THE MOORE FINANCIAL GROUP. He successfully sold it at age 45. With that Ken now sought to fulfill his life-long passion of bringing closure to the families of America's MIA's, the brave men and women who fought and died to preserve our nation whose remains still linger on yesterday's battlefields. To accomplish the objective, he designed and headed a 501C-3 non-profit organization known affectionately as Moore's Marauders. From all around the world volunteers stepped forward setting forth on a global mission to locate the remains of America's fallen. Married to the love of his life now for 40 years, at age 71, Ken and Patti live in Scottsdale Arizona, where he as the "First Marauder," continues to write, seeking to tell the tales of the unparalleled bravery and determination of his teams of volunteers and the heroes they sought."

Made in the USA
Las Vegas, NV
11 March 2021

19372576R00329